The Wind at Oak Hollow

Book One of Realm of Light

MELISSA WIDMAIER

Cartography by Fred Kroner at whiskeynink.com
Cover illustration by Tanja Demchenkova

This is a work of fiction. Names, characters, places, and incidents are products of the author's imagination or are used fictitiously. Any resemblance to actual events, locales, or persons, living or dead, is entirely coincidental.

DEDICATION

For my children. Always for my children. May they find a world of light even in their darkest days.

To my sweet husband: Thanks for the pizza.

ACKNOWLEDGEMENTS

Thanks to the Central Phoenix Writer's Workshop for helping me to find the confidence to put my thoughts on to paper.

To Tamber Kroh, thank you for your careful eye and insight.

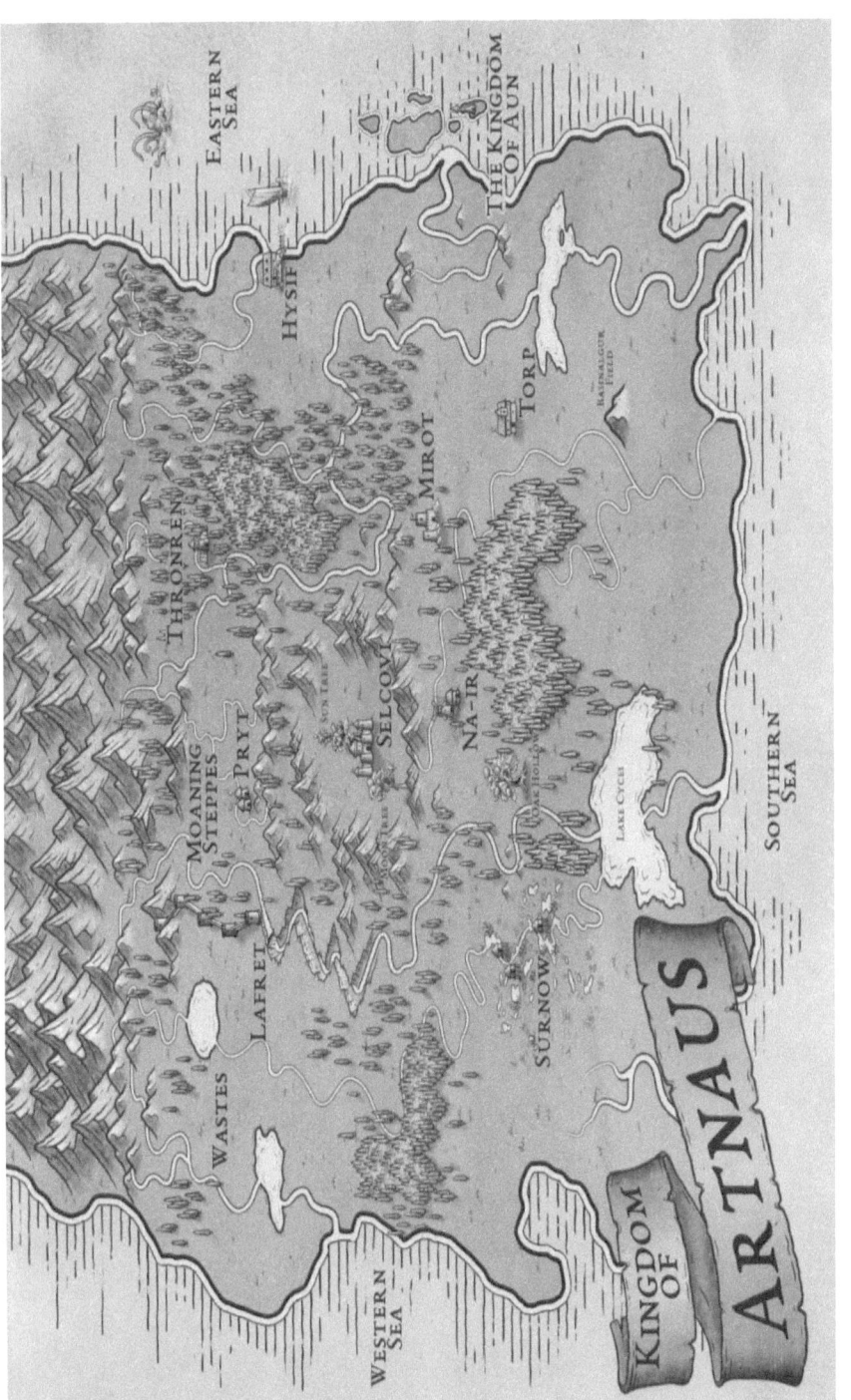

ONE

Wind fluttered over his body and dove into his ears. Her voice the buzzing of bees, the tinkling of bells on a street dancer's skirt.

Marl. Wake up. You're in trouble, little man.

He swayed with her caress. Nothing she could say would upset him, not here in the blessed forests of Na-ir.

On his bare chest was a slow rumble, warm and soft. Dark Pilgrim stretched a ragged claw across his chin. A lean, silken tail slashed across his loins.

Marl opened his eyes. Mother Sun shone down through the canopy, setting leaf-shaped tattoos on his skin. Unashamed, he contemplated the parts of his body not hidden by the black cat.

Too skinny. At least he had a beard now, scraggly as it was.

"Marl! Marl!" This masculine cry wasn't beast or spirit.

Wind's favorite child stretched his lithe back against the tree. Pilgrim jumped to a neighboring branch. They were several feet up, but they were more comfortable in the boughs. Where else could one find peace? Well, by the river, but Marl was easier to find there. Here, among great, gnarled things, Marl was a benevolent monarch. He owned this land, and it him.

"Where in the darkened forest are you?" The voice carried across the waving branches and into the sky, increasing in intensity and aggravation. "Marl! I know

1

you're out here!" A great, golden man came stomping through the litter. The parts of his face not flanked by an ample beard were flushed. "I need to beat some sense into that boy."

Marl shrugged. He didn't care what schemes the old giant concocted. Father wasn't the first person to be angry with him today. "I'm up here."

"There you are! Where are your clothes?"

Marl pointed to a black oak with a cave-like hollow burned into its base. The wound hadn't hurt the tree; it was as wide as it was tall, towering over the antediluvian forest like Father towered over the people of their village. On a low branch hung his grey shirt, black breeches, and ragged shoes.

"I jumped into the river to clean up," he admitted, shivering with the memory of Water's tickle.

"Why under the stars did you jump in with *all* of your clothes on?"

Marl swallowed and tried to think of a delicate way to tell Father the truth. He'd been up to mischief, but not the permitted type. "I was covered in dirt and blood and I didn't want Mother to worry."

"Well, that was smart. Your mother scares easily. Come on. We've been worried sick…"

Marl jumped from the venerable oak.

Father scowled. "Wait! Did you say blood? Why were you covered in blood?"

Damn!

Meaty hands examined him. His lips were more pronounced and there was a tint of purple around his eyes. "Fighting again, eh? Get dressed, boy. You may have wasted your time. Nothing is going to hide this from your mother."

Marl pulled his shirt over his head and sighed. The guilt was bad enough but he hated breaking her heart more. She was so perfect. Father could just whip him. Mother didn't need to know it had no effect.

"Aren't you going to ask who I was fighting?" His black mop of hair popped out of the top of the shirt. Two intense blue eyes surfaced next.

Father suppressed a grin, colossal arms crossed. "I don't need to. You and Lufnis have been spitting like cats for suns!"

This was truth, but there were other opponents in the village he had left more than a few marks on as well. No one was going to mess with him or those he loved.

"He threw the first punch." Marl pulled on his left boot. The sole made a disgusting squish and bled brown water. The cold tickled and traveled up his leg. He liked it. The shock and the tingle made him feel invincible.

"Doesn't matter."

"I threw the last," Marl added, savoring the crack of Lufnis's cheek on his knuckles.

Father shook his head and rammed a fist into the side of the oak; neither man nor tree was affected by the blow. "Father Moon, save me from myself!"

He threw his hands into the air and began the long march back to the cottage. Marl watched his powerful, long legs make the distance.

"You coming, crow?" The name-calling had already started.

I'm coming, old man. Marl smiled and raced after.

***

Marl threw open the door and danced in squishy shoes past the beds by the hearth. His eyes met Mother's bright with unshed tears. He should've stayed in the forest.

Father stormed inside and doubled over. His back heaved and his face twisted. "Stars, Messa! When did I get so old?"

Marl snickered. He'd bested the beast today.

Mother turned a chair from their carved oak table and slammed it into the floorboards. The sound echoed off the four cottage walls. "Sit, love." Her movements betrayed her temper, though her tone was honey sweet. "There's no shame in aging. It's the way of nature."

Father hobbled over to the chair and eyed Marl with frustration.

"You two are so vain. Just because the boy runs home doesn't mean you must match his pace. You'll both get here eventually, no worse for wear." She reached for a pitcher of water and produced two pinewood cups from her apron pockets. "Here, drink. You've been under the gaze of Mother Sun all day."

Marl hid his face behind his cup as she sat next to him. Nothing could protect him from the storm in her stares. He concentrated and breathed. Water had a smell, like pure air, with earthy tones. *If I could sit by a forest stream all day. I'd bother no one and no one would bother me.*

Mother folded her hands together and sighed. "Look at me, son. I shouldn't have to repeat this. Verbal slights can't be met with fists. Why do you let Lufnis get to you so?"

Marl slammed his cup on the table, splashing a drop of water on Father's hand. "How do you do that? I haven't said anything and you already know what happened!" He narrowed his black eyebrows and tried to read her the same way she read him. His mind met silence, but his eyes saw a matching resolve.

Father choked into his cup, put it down, and wiped his scruffy beard. "She's your mother. She can do anything."

He acted as if this was a satisfactory explanation. It wasn't. Marl was determined to discover her secret. He'd already ruled out his older brother. Natsir wasn't a tattletale.

"Maybe she's magic," Father teased.

Mother ignored the nonsense. "Marl there's no magic needed to tell you've been fighting. Lufnis is full of vinegar and hate, but you've had some hand in that. Stop provoking him, *please*."

She stretched her arm out to take his hand. A strange pulsing sensation ran through him, like nature itself was trying to comfort him. Nature knew better. He could not be stilled.

"Please, child. There's no reason to start wars with our neighbors. G'Nirac has been good to us. For his sake and Para's, please stop this ridiculous conflict. You may be younger, but you can still be the better man."

The words *child* and *man* made him flinch. Mother was a peace seeker and her idea of a good man was one who used his strength in patience more than protection.

In his nineteen suns in this world, Marl had heard every plea, every prayer. It wasn't that he didn't believe her. Mother was always right. Every time he showed force, more unpleasant things happened. Yet, standing by and watching Lufnis insult him—or worse Natsir and Para—was as far from his purpose of being as holding his breath forever. There was a satisfaction in strength, being able to change situations with the flick of his wrist.

"I know, Mother. You're right. I'll avoid Lufnis."

She sighed. "I suppose that's all I'm going to get from you. Thank you for trying. There's more to you than your youth, Marl. One day you'll see."

She was always trying to tell him what he could be, but she was never happy with what he was. He liked his youth. He wanted to spend it, not sit back and watch as the world moved without him.

Father coughed and tapped the table like a drum. "Where is Nat?"

"He's with Para. I left them there after Lufnis... insulted them."

The old man chuckled. "Ah, Luf is just being protective of his sister."

So am I. Marl had seen the marks left on Para's arms, the tears in her light blue eyes. Those things should never be on a woman. Her perfect smile and gentle hugs of gratitude were payment enough for punishment later.

Father slapped his hands against the table. "Well. Let's get to work. You promised to help me bring the beans to town. Remember?"

Marl groaned. He made many promises, but he hardly kept them. Natsir was always willing to pick up the slack. Subsistence wasn't for Marl. He was considering other pursuits—far-off adventures, or at least a vocation where he could ramble through the forest without being dragged back against his will.

"You're going back into town?" Mother stood and crimpled her apron.

Father kissed her cheek. "Don't worry, love. I'll keep an eye on him."

Marl tried not to laugh. He was very good at making Father a liar.

***

They found Natsir in the shed with the sacks of beans and squash. He held a dreamy countenance, covered in dust and sitting next to a small hole in the floorboards. He smiled when he saw Marl. "Hello, baby brother! I'm warning the mice Pilgrim might find them when he returns."

"Stop calling me a baby," Marl snapped.

Natsir turned his bushy face to the dirt. He looked so much like Father, it was hard to see him behave timidly. Tall, strong men weren't supposed to be gentle; it was unnatural. "I forgot. Sorry."

Guilt stayed Marl's temper. *He's always been this way.* "Sorry, Nat. I know. I didn't mean it. Wanna help us?"

He nodded.

"Good!" Father snapped. "We need to hurry. It's almost midday." They were already starting to look like beets. A smart man was lazy on warm afternoons.

They made short work of fifteen heavy burlap sacks. As usual everything was a game, a test of agility and ability. Marl was proud of the seven bags he'd placed in the wheel barrow, but the winner of this contest was the more experienced and heftier Natsir.

Father stayed by the wall as they worked. He enjoyed watching them compete, though he refused to ever judge a contest outright; it was also another way for him to avoid doing the work himself. Marl's laziness had to come from somewhere; he already had the temper.

"Happy is the man with sons to help him! Let's get these things out of here."

Natsir took the wheel barrow and sped down the path. Marl let out a fantastic whoop and ran after. For once, Nojhi Ganwin listened to his sage wife's advice. He followed along at a generous, but more reserved pace.

Mother Sun was high when they reached Na-ir. As they passed through the pine and oak marking the beginning of the town center, Natsir walked slower and slouched. His back arched and his hazel eyes stayed parallel to the ground. His hands twitched against the wheel barrow. After nineteen suns in Na-ir, he had never been able to condition himself against the monotony of village life.

Marl gave his sensitive brother a gentle pat on the back. It pained him to see the big guy so agitated. "Hey! It's my turn to push."

The moment his hands left the barrow, Natsir went into a trance of crushing sensations. He stayed so close, Marl could feel his warm breath on his neck. He smelled of horses, sweat, and hay.

"Uh, Nat. Could you step back?"

The request was a mistake. As soon as Natsir moved, his focus on Marl shifted to the square again. Head to the sky, he twirled around the square, a dancing giant, coming within inches of unsuspecting villagers. Marl hissed as his feet nearly clomped down on a small child playing with a stick and ball.

"Careful!"

Two sacks of beans slammed down next to him. Marl jumped. Father grunted. "Well, are you going to help me or watch your brother dance?"

Marl took a sack and placed it to the ground. "It doesn't bother you when he does that?" He hissed again as a cart of vegetables missed his brother's ankle. *Why did I ask him to come?*

Natsir stopped in the middle of the square, holding his arms close to his chest, mumbling. It was like watching a man counting a thousand grains of sand in a matter of minutes.

Father shook his head. "Used to worry me, but he's not as bad as he used to be. He's trying. The man can plow a field on his own and ride a horse like a king. He'll be all right. People here are forgiving as long as you pull your weight." He gave Marl's arm a smack. "You don't, but your brother does."

Marl loved his brother too much to pretend this behavior was harmless. "One day it's going to get him killed. He'd walk over a cliff if we let him."

Father tossed the last bag to the ground and stretched out his back. "It's a good thing we don't live anywhere near the cliffs then. Shut up." He preceded to bellow like a war horn. "Beans! Beans for sale!"

They took turns shouting.

Natsir settled down in the grass next to the stone pillar and stared into the trees. Marl wished Para was around; the glazed expression on his brother's face would disappear. She had a good effect on him.

Only one merchant wanted beans today. They loaded twelve bags into his wagon. He dropped several copper pieces into Father's hands and drove away.

"You'd think he valued beans more than jewels," Marl laughed.

Father left a few tan smears on his britches. "He would've bought the whole lot if he'd the money. Selcovi's having a difficult harvest." He leaned against the barrow. "Too much building, not enough planting."

"Building? What?"

"Not sure. Some say fortifications, digging wells."

They reloaded the remaining bags.

"Come. We did well. Let's find something to nibble before dinner."

Marl was disappointed. He wanted to learn more about the great Mlaerian kings, but his stomach lurched at the mention of food. He'd pry later.

They woke Natsir against the stone pillar and headed for some of the local merchants. Father purchased two strips of dried meat and one roll of seed bread.

Marl enjoyed his brother's look of disgust as he tore at the bitter animal flesh. It was over-spiced, possibly veal.

"Don't tell Mother," Father reminded.

Natsir nodded but the smell of the meat made him flinch.

"I have to visit the elders today. Why don't you boys take the barrow home; I shouldn't be long. Watch your little brother."

Marl winced.

Once Father's massive form had faded from sight, the oldest frowned and asked an incredulous question. "Do you think I'm useless?" It was one of the least offensive words Lufnis had used to describe him earlier.

Marl shrugged and pushed the barrow. "No. You're odd, that's all. Different."

"Oh!" Natsir coughed into his arm.

"Nothing wrong with that. I'm odd too. We're alive and we're strong and healthy. There's nothing we can't do." He waved a hand as if *nothing* was air. It was better to lie than reinforce Natsir's fears.

A gentle noise like the lapping of a stream echoed from a stall in the square. Radiant Para was giggling with some girls Marl had never seen before. They stopped to stare.

"At least you've a sweetheart."

Natsir's complexion matched Para's hair. "She's my friend, that's all."

Marl doubted Para felt the same. Her entire body danced whenever Nat was near. "What were you two up to all morning then?"

He meant it as an accusation of something naughty, but Natsir was too respectable. Para was a lady and he had the foresight to treat her like one. "We were cleaning the stables and exercising the horses."

Marl sighed. There was no denying Para loved those horses. "All right. Explains why Lufnis was at your throat when I found you."

Natsir grimaced. He didn't like the chieftain's son either, but he maintained a polite pretense whenever he was around. "What were *you* doing in town then? You were supposed to be helping Father."

"I was listening to Wind." She'd said there was fun to be had in Na-ir, but she hadn't said what kind.

Para waved them over to a stall filled with fine cloth. "Hello! Boys, meet my new friends!"

The girl on the left had eyes brown as oak and mousy auburn hair as soft as lamb's wool. Marl would've given anything to touch those curls. He pretended to be a well-behaved Telmah boy instead. "Hello," he began. "I'm Marl."

She blushed. "Hereu." Her voice was fluid as river song. "We're from Selcovi."

Having nothing witty to say, Marl pounced on this topic. "We saw a merchant from there a few minutes ago. He liked our harvest."

The girl to Para's right nodded. She was a different shade of brown, and her countenance didn't radiate the same autumnal warmth. "Yes. It's too hard to eke out a living there anymore."

"Yes, but Para's father is so nice," Hereu explained. "He's going to let our families stay here." She bristled and her eyes darted to the many shops and passersby. "Eurgi and I were friends in the city too," she added, placing an arm over her grumpy counterpart's shoulder.

Eurgi sulked further. "None of the other villages were welcoming."

Things had taken a sour turn. Para knew what to do. "Cheer up, sweethearts. We're happy to have you both in Na-ir."

Eurgi forced a ridiculous smirk akin to a scared rabbit, but Hereu returned Para's welcome with a bright smile that made Mother Sun and all of her starry children jealous.

Marl wanted to get a closer look at the pink lips guarding those teeth. He surprised himself with the sudden weight of his desires. This girl would kick him if he dared to be so forward.

"I'm sorry I won't be here for the harvest dance," Para continued, giving Marl a wink. "But I'm sure you'll have a *splendid time* without me."

Natsir stiffened. "Where are you going? You didn't say anything this morning."

"It was decided today." She lowered her pretty lashes. "Papa says they want to discuss business in Lafret. Probably trade again."

"I'll miss you."

Hereu giggled behind her hands.

Marl's entire being stirred. The other girls he had ever dared to snuggle into and kiss had turned out to be stuffy and cross. This was a rare opportunity. He needed to take her by the hand now, or flee to the comfort of some tree.

"I won't be gone long." Para's clear-water eyes sparkled and she rocked on her heels. Natsir twitched. She waited for his response. She'd wait forever.

Eurgi stared, but not at the lovers. "What happened to your face?"

"Oh," Marl laughed, running his hands through his hair. "I fell out of a tree."

"And you landed on your eyes?"

Jealous little bitch isn't she! He paused, not sure how to react. A village girl would've smiled and changed the subject.

Hereu cringed. "I'm sorry. We're still tired from our trip."

Eurgi crossed her arms and huffed, looking back on his brother and the red star. Para held out two scarves: one blue, one green.

Natsir scratched his head and stuttered. "I like whichever one you like."

Marl tried not to groan. It wasn't his brother's fault she made him lock-jawed and feebleminded.

Para sighed. "I can't decide. Perhaps the green. Dasha women wear such pretty wraps. Are you sure you don't have a favorite?"

She pushed the scarves closer. He twitched and shook his head. She frowned, but said nothing as she placed the blue one back on the table and laid a silver coin next to the merchant.

"I guess green would be best."

"Your brother's an idiot," Eurgi mumbled. "Not much of a man if he can't speak his mind."

Marl stepped forward and the unpleasant woman recoiled. "I suppose you'd make a better man?"

Hereu plucked his raised hand from the air and squeezed it. "Ignore her."

There was no pride in fighting with sour fruit, especially when a much sweeter individual was nearby. Marl concentrated on the little tree holding on to his limb.

"You've beautiful eyes. They're blue like Para's, but deeper."

Marl's cheeks warmed. Were the bruises too ugly? These city girls were more forward than he'd realized; he liked it, but it was a struggle to think of a compliment to give in return. "Thanks. I think you've the nicest brown hair. It looks so soft."

Laced within Hereu's giggle was a contemptuous snort from Eurgi's direction. They ignored her.

"Not really. It's a pain. But *you've* the most interesting hair. It's purple."

Marl was eager to feel her caress, but a shadow, short and bulky, moved in between them, knocking him down with the force of a small rock slide. The man grabbed Hereu by the arm and slapped her across the face. Marl would've gone to her rescue in an instant had Natsir not held him back. It was as if his brother had seen the danger coming.

"Get home! Now," shouted the man. "Haven't I told you about Erutani?"

The citizens of Na-ir gasped.

Hereu's father turned to Marl still on the ground and spat. "No-good heathens. Trouble, all of them!"

Marl watched his new heart's desire leave the square. Eurgi lifted her skirts to step over his legs and hurried off after them.

I should've tripped her. Bitch.

"Oh my!" Para was now modeling the green scarf. It was pretty, but not her color. "I'm sorry. There was no call for that!" She helped Natsir pull Marl up and tried to dust off his shirt and britches. "Are you well?"

He nodded, though he wanted to pummel the man.

"I should go." She patted his shoulder and made her way through the square. She'd have to give a detailed report to her father later.

Natsir looked as sad to see her leave as Marl had been to see Hereu's tears. "Are you well, brother?"

"I'm fine. We weren't doing anything wrong. What's his problem?" Marl sighed and wiped more dust from the backside of his britches. "Mangy cur's worse than Lufnis. I can't believe what he did to her! Let's go."

They walked back to the cottage feeling dejected. Marl fumed—a spirited girl who didn't find him odd and her father turned out to be a monster.

"What'd he mean by Eru... Erutani? Yes, I think that's what he said."

Natsir stopped and stared out into the trees. "You should talk to Mother."

They entered the cottage, looking sullen and weary. She was sitting at the table, cat in lap, next to a stone mort, its pestle, and a pile of grain. If it weren't for the tidy house and steady supply of food stuffs, a causal visitor might think she spent all day in that wooden chair, a queen on a throne.

Her voice rose over the birds and rustling trees. "It's time you know more."

The air around them was charged with importance. Wind floated through the doorway and whispered in his ear. *The Wanderer comes.*

Mother sighed.

The cottage door slammed shut with the spirit's passing. The noise and vibration rushed through Marl's spine. He felt rebellion from his heels to the ends of his hair. Wind always had that effect on him.

"All right then. Tell me."

***

"Don't misunderstand me boys," Mother resumed.

They sat on the floor by the empty hearth.

Natsir was nestled into her shoulder. He looked ridiculous. Marl refused to be so familiar. Men didn't rely on their mother's for support. The best his pride would allow her was a kiss on the cheek.

"When I say we practice a lifestyle beneficial for the world. I don't mean we do no harm whatsoever. That's impossible. We're all capable of great harm."

Marl shook his head and scoffed. *"That's* impossible! Look at Nat. He's a great monster of a man, but he'd never hurt a fly. No one could say he was harmful to anything except himself."

Natsir stuck out his tongue and shifted off of Mother.

She smiled. "Some people are gentler than others. We're all flawed, though. When Natsir walked in to the cottage, he stepped on an ant near the door. It was unintentional, the whim of happenstance. It was still harmful to the ant." She clasped her hands in her lap. "It's the way of things. All life under Mother Sun and Father Moon must find their own way to the Star's Passageway. We mustn't seek to cause this journey for others."

Marl kicked the hearth stones. Mother meant peace seeking. "Is this why you hate me? Why you're always telling me to be different?"

She took him in her arms. He refused to accept the embrace or look into her piercing eyes. "Sweetheart, I don't hate you. You're one of the kindest young men in Na-ir. You're protective and intelligent. I remind you not to use your strength because there are better ways to make a point. Doing the least harm isn't just beneficial to the world, it makes us better too, provides us with many opportunities for happiness and growth. You know this is true. If that man hadn't attacked you, would you be upset now?"

Marl raised an eyebrow. She matched the gesture.

"He's a fool because he hasn't learned by adulthood what I'm trying to teach you now in your youth."

"I'm angry because I couldn't punch him back. If I had, he wouldn't say such things anymore." Marl balled a fist and shoved it into the floorboards to satisfy his lust for vengeance.

Mother shook her head. "And then the girl you're enamored with would've seen your temper and never wanted to speak with you again. There are always consequences."

He wrenched out of her arms. It was such a burden to have a mother who was consistently right. "The Erutani sound like a bunch of nonsensical idiots. I'm glad the other half of me is Mlaerian."

Her delicate jaw dropped to her chest. There were tears in her eyes.

Natsir pulled on the half of him that was also Mlaerian. "Apologize!"

Briefly, Marl thought he was looking into their father's unforgiving face, and he curled into a ball, knees to chest with memories of deserved punishments.

Mother wiped a tear from her cheek. "It's all right, my boys."

Natsir leaned back.

"I won't tell you how to think. I can only offer advice. You're my son as well as your father's." She shifted toward the hearth. "You think ill of your own people because you don't know them. You're relying on what little I've told you and the Selcovian's opinion. But we're not weak people, Marl. We've a power a strong man can't match."

Mother placed a hand over the coals and whispered. An orange spark rose from the ashes. He had never seen such a satisfied smirk on her face.

"Whoa!" Marl ran to the other side of the cottage, tripping over a chair. "How'd you do that?"

Natsir chuckled from his place on the floor. Marl wanted to smack him.

Mother floated over to his hiding spot. Two delicate, warm hands cradled his head and forced him to look down. It was an awkward feeling, being afraid of this tiny woman. He closed his eyes and tried not to panic, but she found him in the darkness.

"The Lights have blessed us." *It's a gift that must be opened, Marl.*

He tore apart his eyes; the invasion of his mind had been a painful one.

"That's why you've never known it until now. It's been tucked away in a box inside your mind. Every now and then, you've jostled it as you've made your way through life." *Sometimes it opens and shuts.*

Marl struggled to break free, but her grasp was surprisingly strong.

She radiated youth. "Those are the times when your gift was shining. It's limitless and it grows with you. Like learning to sing. When you discover you've a talent, you can produce beauty." *That beauty is a gift to others.* "This is the purpose of gifts, to use them, to preserve goodness in all of its forms." She dropped her hands from his face, standing before him more like a divinity than his mother. "Do you understand?"

Marl had always wanted to uncover her secrets, to understand her mental prowess, but this was more than he'd ever expected. "I guess I shouldn't be surprised. We've always been treated like curiosities." He crossed his arms and shuddered. "Is this why Wind talks to me?"

The youthfulness left her. "Let me tell you a story. That might explain things."

Marl didn't want to listen to parables, but he allowed her to lead him back to the fire. It was engorging the hearth. Natsir had fed it another log, taking care of things like nothing strange had ever happened. Was it courage or familiarity?

Mother pulled Marl to the floor to cradle him. He allowed this to avoid another display of her powers.

"Now, don't interrupt. I'm going to do the best I can to explain. There once was a king." She closed her eyes.

Marl felt another terrible sensation under his skull. He closed his eyes too, but the vision intensified. He could see a man, tall and powerful in his raiment, astride a chestnut warhorse.

This king was a great warrior, a mighty man with a quick temper and little patience. He detested insubordination of any kind, and he felt entitled to all known territories. He used an aspect of tribal law to justify his wars. A bloody and unforgiving man. Many bowed rather than fight and lose everything to his wrath. Some did not.

Marl watched as the king and his army hacked at innocent villagers and tossed their bodies into fire. This violence was unprovoked. It made him sick.

There was nothing this king could not possess. He was invincible, but there were a people he feared. A crowd of happy, petite, and gentle people marched passed his mind,

16

performing mundane and innocent tasks in a glade. *The king knew of a prophecy but he ignored the warning of the spirits. If we would not be subjugated, we had to be eradicated. So, he sent his largest army to confront our chieftain.*

The warriors, led by a different man in glinting armor looked like a tapestry across a wall, colorful and deceptive in its history. Mother shivered.

The army had been warned of terrible consequences if they hesitated. Their orders were to slaughter everyone. But we didn't fight back. We tried to reason with the army. Many were slashed down like wheat in a field.

The army faltered under the weight of the crime they'd committed. The king's plan failed, but we scattered, searching for a place where we could rebuild our heart. By this time, the king was too old and foolish to realize his mistake. He allowed our survivors to live and he forgot the prophecy.

Mother stripped all pictures from him. Marl longed for more, though he was starting to get a headache.

This prophecy spoke of someone called the Wanderer. He'd be born on a stormy night, away from his homeland and his history. The shattered Erutani hoped his birth would signal a rebuilding of their homeland. The king's scholars warned he might be something more sinister.

Mother stopped her tale.

Marl opened his eyes. "That's terrible. But I don't understand what it has to do with me and Wind." He fiddled with a black river stone from under his cot.

"Because *you're* the Wanderer, and Wind has taken it upon herself to prepare you for your destiny, whatever that may be."

The stone sailed across the room and hit the wall with a loud crack. Their cottage rattled with the blow and a small key with one blue gemstone fell to the floor, clattering like the weight in his heart.

"Natsir, love." Honey returned to Mother's voice. "Why don't you make us some tea?"

TWO

All who rested near Para's hearth were well-fed and comfortable, even if she herself wasn't in attendance. Eight men gathered around her kitchen table strewn with basil and carved fowl.

Nojhi smiled. It was an omen, their finding this place, hopefully a direct result of spiritual forgiveness. He sat back and thought about the future while the rest of the men chatted.

Natsir and the girl would make adorable babies: strong, beautiful, and stubborn—like their mother—but also kind and sweet.

Marl still had a few suns, but he would undoubtedly produce striking, black-haired rapscallions for Nojhi to spoil.

"I hear he's been at his tricks again."

"Hum." Nojhi shook himself awake. The butcher had addressed him. "What tricks are these, Retat?"

The village healer, Etutsa, ran into the room, a collection of strange things in his arms. He tossed them on the table and pulled parchment from his bag, silent.

Retat turned back to Nojhi and laughed. He was a stout man with beefy limbs and a jolly expression, the sort who liked gossip with his ribs. "I hear everything from my shop. Today alone he was spotted naked in the forest by a pheasant hunter, and this morning in a fight with Lufnis. He doesn't care for convention."

Nojhi's good humor waned. "No, I suppose *he* doesn't."

The head of the table coughed. "Yes, well, it's only youth. Lufnis is often headstrong. Marl's no different. Given time, they'll settle down."

Nojhi didn't agree, but a father needed to believe the best in his son.

"I tell you one thing," said the blacksmith, waving a tanned finger covered in duck grease. "If one of my daughters ever spies him walking naked through the forest, I'll give him trouble."

Laughable. Namnor had the tendency to be too permissive with his headstrong girls. "If your daughters wander the forest alone, *they're* looking for trouble."

All but the blacksmith guffawed.

Nojhi could no sooner direct Marl than tell the oceans to still. He didn't want to, though he did his best to maintain discipline. Maybe Chieftain G'Nirac *was* right. Youth were meant to make mistakes, discoveries. He'd certainly made his share of them.

"What if they were given more responsibility?" Etutsa looked up from his herbal scrolls. "Lufnis will be chieftain someday. He should be here, in fact." He scratched a line and gave G'Nirac a flippant smile. Nojhi loved him for that blatant gumption.

"I agree, brother. I've been remiss. Lufnis and Para will be joining me on another visit to Lafret. I believe he'll be able to practice diplomacy among friends."

"And I'm sure Rippan will be thrilled to see your ginger sprite again." Retat winked.

G'Nirac hummed. It was uncertain if he approved of the nobleman, but the Dasha man wasn't a catch one threw back into the river.

Nojhi felt bad for Natsir. *Poor lad's got competition.* But Para was obviously smitten. The chieftain wasn't the type to deny his precious daughter anything.

"What do the Dasha want?" Lortews asked. The warriors of the impenetrable canyon had a prominent reputation for cold, decisive action.

"Onaryc's messenger told me they wish to discuss an alliance. The details will be revealed upon my visit." G'Nirac smiled at his trusted villagers. "Don't worry, my friends. Onaryc and I have an understanding."

Nojhi knew the man too—many suns ago and in a life no longer lived. The chieftain of the Dasha wasn't one to be crossed, but neither was he dishonorable... to his friends.

"He could be worried about the capital. It *is* suffering now." The tailor leaned forward in his seat and knocked over Etutsa's tonics. Several bottles lost their corks, releasing a potent, bread-dough vapor.

G'Nirac sputtered. "Yes, um, I thought about that too, Daerth. Ah, Etutsa, what're you curing now? Surely it can wait."

"If you must know, a certain gentleman in town has developed an unsavory and persistent rash. I'm trying to find a way to relieve him of it."

"An unsavory what?" piped Lortews.

"Don't ask!" Nojhi's stomach lurched. Etutsa's profession was disgusting.

Retat snickered. "Hope it didn't come from one of those Selcovian girls."

Etutsa gave a general look of distain. "Of course not! They've only been in town for two days. However, I do need to check my supplies for more bruise poultice. Lufnis may have used all of my stores."

Nojhi didn't appreciate Marl taking matters into his own hands, capable though they were, but he couldn't find fault with anyone who wanted to give the chieftain's son a good thrashing. It was good for boys to be a little rough. "Wait! Why would a *girl* from Selcovi be so bruised she'd need a poultice?"

A foreboding fell over the table.

Etutsa sighed. "Her father approached me before the start of the meeting. An Erutani boy was making advances and the daughter refused him, only to find herself injured for her virtuousness."

Nojhi hissed. His son was a scamp, not a womanizer. *I've only been away a moment!*

The healer waved his hand. "I don't believe him one bit. He's a drunken, bitter sort. And Marl would never hit or proposition a woman. I'll confront him tomorrow. We'll not suffer violent behavior from those who should know better."

"Thank you, brother." G'Nirac rubbed his neck. "I can't say no to those down on their luck, but our people aren't safe with men like that."

Several of the men agreed, tossing out their own violent but suitable punishments.

"Perhaps the woes of Selcovi *have* found us here in Na-ir." Nojhi cracked his knuckles.

"Don't worry, my friend. I promise no harm will come to you and your family as long as I'm here."

The rest of the company spoke to the same effect. They'd all been entrusted with the Ganwins' secrets and the Ganwins had learned to appreciate that trust.

"One bitter man won't persuade the town of anything, and none but us knows. Na-ir will always welcome you."

A deep, unforgiving cold settled over Nojhi's spine. "Thank you, gentlemen, but I can't help worrying. We've been here for nearly twenty suns without one mention of the Erutani."

Etutsa nodded and placed his quill on the table. "Encourage Marl and Messa to lay low until we can figure out what'll be done with this new resident and his over-exuberant opinions. Natsir won't be a problem. He's gifted with your dashing good looks." He winked.

G'Nirac nodded. "Yes. Let's be cautious. While I'm with the Dasha, I'll do my best to learn more on the situation in Selcovi. If there's a way we can help, there may be no reason for us to fear."

Fear? If Nojhi was caught, it could have frightful consequences for the whole community. The village elders knew what to say—that they knew nothing of his past, they were innocent tradesmen who welcomed all. But gossip and panic would divide the village. Discontent was a powerful thing.

"Do you think Rayr will institute the tax again?" Daerth wondered.

G'Nirac smiled at the tailor. "He would be smart to reinstate the produce and grain tax, though at a modest rate. There's no use in people starving when there's much to be shared between villages."

"It's unfortunate Rayr didn't inherit Ril's abilities for diplomacy and economy," Retat mused, staring at his chapped hands.

Etutsa slammed his quill into the table, marring the edge of his scroll with a dark blot. "It was Ril's *abilities* that got them into this mess. Selcovi! The sun city! A new prosperity." His hands fell to the table with a thud. "Absolute bull. Ril built a city in a barren valley with limited water. Pure pride and selfishness. Gullibility drove people there to consume and multiply."

Retat shook his head. "It was a dream, Etutsa. Ril made mistakes, but his children squander what's left of his legacy."

Nojhi hissed and leaned toward the butcher. "Some legacies are written in blood my friend. Rayr doesn't have his father's eloquence, or his sister's strength of will. But he's an intelligent man. I'm sure if a delegation was sent, he'd listen to reason."

"Ah!" Namnor raised a finger. "But there's the problem. Let's not fool ourselves, gentlemen. We all know Rayr doesn't make the decisions."

Lortews nodded. "True. Enisnus has a tight grip on Rayr's reign. She has her father's warrior sensibilities."

"But none of his sense," Etutsa interrupted, pretending to read his scrolls.

G'Nirac wrung his hands and coughed. "All right, all right, brother. Things are what they are. We can't repair the past, only build the present. As I've stated, I'll glean as much as I can from Onaryc. When I return better informed, we can discuss sending a delegation to Selcovi."

The men grumbled.

"I must prepare for my journey and you should attend to your families. Good evening, gentlemen." Everyone filed out after their leader.

Etutsa fumbled with his supplies. "Need a hand, friend?" Nojhi asked.

They exited the chieftain's house with arms full of parchment and bottles, the contents of which reeked at close range. It was fortunate the healer didn't live far, or they might've gagged to death on the fumes.

The healer's shack consisted of a bed and a table. Both were strewn with plants, bottles, and bits of parchment. Several cuttings were drying on nooses from the ceiling. Odd how the torturous death of plants could ease human aliments.

For a tall man, this vine-infested hovel was a wretched confining space, but for the little man, who spent much of his days in and out of the shack, this tiny abode was more than sufficient.

"Place the bottles on the bed."

Nojhi frowned and examined the cot for a bit of unclaimed property. He decided to let Etutsa handle the mess and plopped them on a pillow. He spent a few moments pretending to look around. "Well, I should head home."

"Yes. Yes. Remember what I said, will you, my friend?"

"I will. It'll be easy for Messa. But Marl… I don't know."

"Especially since he was insulted today. Keep him preoccupied. Surely there's something he might do. Such an intelligent lad shouldn't be idle."

There was plenty for Marl to do, but nothing he liked. The boy was a tall mass of emotion and ridiculous, youthful notions. *He's too much of me, always looking for a challenge.* An idea crossed Nojhi's mind. "I believe I might have it. Thank you, Etutsa."

"My pleasure. Thank you for your help tonight." He meant the counsel not the tonics. Etutsa and G'Nirac often disagreed. "Send my regards to your lovely wife."

Nojhi waved and rushed outside. It felt good to be back in the cooling air of dusk. He took his time meandering to the cottage, wanting to mull over Marl's new venture before he met with Messa. She'd the ability to see through him and he needed to have things decided and finalized before meeting her gaze. Only then could he shut the ideas behind the doorway of his mind and lock them.

Twenty seven suns as the lover of an Erutani had strengthened his mental abilities and he could now meet her mental powers, match for match. Whether she knew he was hiding anything, she never said—or *thought*. All he knew now was that their safety was of the utmost importance. Anything that made Marl complacent and satisfied would be something Messa wouldn't approve of out of principle.

He'd broken a promise to her suns ago and now he'd have to break it again. He couldn't bear to see her heart shattered. This information would have to stay hidden, but the particulars would be difficult given Marl's inexperience.

The over-excited young man would give away their secret. Some mental coaching would be necessary. What if they used a code? *Tracking! That's it! I'll call it tracking.*

Surely Messa couldn't object to Nojhi teaching Marl hunting skills without the hunting. It was always good to know your surroundings. What he wanted to teach was more useful, but a real lesson or two in tracking wouldn't hurt either.

Having settled his mind on the term and cleared out all thoughts of his other plans, Nojhi strode inside and assumed a self-satisfied pose. "I'm home, sweet wife!"

The stillness in the cottage made him nervous. His family was gathered around a meager fire. Natsir with his head in Messa's lap and Marl by the flames. Three cups sat on the stones.

"Asleep?" Nojhi scratched his head. "It's not late!"

"I gave them sleepwart. They've had a big day." She ran her hands through Natsir's delicate golden hair.

Nojhi was jealous. He would've rather been the head in that lap. "I've heard." He frowned and pulled up a chair. "Etutsa…"

"Sends his regards. I know."

"I know you know." The boys were right to sleep. This day had been exhausting. He ran his hands through his hair. "What've you told them? Nothing about me?"

No, love. I told them how we Erutani have a way of communicating with the world.

How'd Marl take it?

Her frown said it all. *I told him how some of us can hear Wind or understand animals. I don't think I should tell them more. I'm afraid Marl wouldn't be able to handle the power.* She looked at him sprawled out on the stones. *He's angry with us. He's far angrier with the world. I think it hurt him; Natsir knew more than he did.*

Nojhi shook his head. *He'll find out, won't he?* The boy was too smart to leave things alone.

Messa shrugged and pursed her lips. Her defiance blazed brighter than their youngest child. *Wind cried out "The Wanderer comes" when he entered the cottage today. She can keep her prophesies, but she* cannot *have my son.*

The sharp sting of a claw fixed into his leg. Nojhi looked down to see Pilgrim pawing. He patted his thigh and allowed the old cat to settle into his stomach.

"Where've you been, old fellow?" He caressed the nape of the creature's neck. It purred.

Messa watched Pilgrim. *Our friend the cat says the bitter man from Selcovi might be dangerous.*

Nojhi nodded. *Etutsa and the rest of the elders agree with him. It would be better if Marl knew what it was to be a seer. At least he'd be able to protect himself.*

She lifted Natsir off of her lap and stood. *That's not what the gifts are for.*

He stopped stroking the cat. The Erutani still confounded him. Their superior understanding of nature made all other beings seem ignorant.

Messa placed her hands around his face, resting her head against his brow. *There's danger in these gifts. They must be cultivated early or we risk using them for ill. I can't give my children this burden.*

Nojhi kissed her forehead. *But you didn't give them these gifts. The Father and Mother did. They'll have the burden whether you show them or not. One day they'll have to accept it.*

Her sapphire eyes pooled. She slumped into the floor again. The forces of the world were her support in times of trouble, but, in Marl's fate, they were her greatest enemies.

Nojhi held on to her trembling hand. He saw the terrible images in her mind as she tried to still her troubled heart.

Pilgrim was persuaded to leave. The cat settled on Natsir's cot.

Nojhi took his wife into a strong embrace. *This is my fault. If it weren't for me, you wouldn't have to make these decisions. I'm sorry I've put you through this, that we must live under the threat of our secrets.*

Messa wrapped her arms around his neck. *NO! I chose this more than you did. I've wasted so much time trying to protect them. I relent. Marl and Natsir should know more. I'll teach them, but not now, not while there's danger looming from Selcovi.*

Danger may never leave.

The cat curled into a ball on Natsir's pillow and opened one penetrating golden eye. Messa watched him, gleaning the wisdom Nojhi could never possess himself.

Pilgrim thinks the man will leave. He'll take his family to some other village. I'll wait until then. Marl is too attached to the girl now to be objective.

Nojhi laughed. *Pilgrim is a wise cat. Hope he's right. Very well, my love. Let's give it a moon. If the danger still exists, we'll have to come up with a plan.*

Yes. We'll give it a moon. I promise.

They sat by the fire, minds on nothing more than their love, trying to avoid the fearful rush of blood against their nerves. Messa's small form rose and fell against his chest and he cherished every curve in her face. She'd sacrificed much to be his. How could such a small thing have such strength? No other woman on this earth was like his.

Calloused fingers ran through purple-tinted locks. Messa gave him a gentle kiss. Her eyes were still moist, but they sparkled with brilliance unmatched by the stars.

There was no need to read her mind. He knew what she was thinking.

THREE

The weeds in the garden didn't deserve his wrath. Mother had taught him how to discourage this, but he'd been lazy. Now, innocent dandelions and an odd collection of roots would have to be culled so his patch of earth could provide the family stews with onions, leeks, and parsley.

Why would they lie to me? Tears welled. *I'm not a child.* The weed in his fist gave a little, but refused to budge. *I'm NOT a Wanderer.* "I'm Marl and I can best anything in my way!"

He'd produced a deep hole. It wasn't a weed, but a rotted root, left behind by some long-dead tree.

Be still, boy. Be still. We're not your enemy. Wind floated over the parsley and danced into his face, a cool reminder of who he denied to be.

He was used to these casual whispers in his ears, but this time they made him ill. Wind had once been a captivating woman, guiding him through life in a fanciful dance. He'd longed for her. Now he knew she was nothing but a temptress. Her motives were clear. Lead the Wanderer to his destiny.

The time is coming. There will be no more play in the forest.

"No!" Marl threw the root across the garden and hit the side of the shed.

Wind floated past, stirring up wet dirt and the green blood of plants. *I can't stop this. It wasn't my decision. Sorry.*

"No! Shut up!" He swung a fist at the breeze. Soil scattered onto his shirt.

Sorry. We must make the best of this.

Footsteps crackled in the gravel behind him. Wind dissipated into the clouds overhead.

"Are you yelling at plants?" Father leaned on his axe handle, amused.

Marl sneered as he dusted dirt from his britches. "What do you want, old liar?"

"Here now! Is that how you treat your papa? I need no reminders I'm aged, and liar takes things too far." Father twirled the axe.

Marl crossed his arms and squared his sights. "That's what you are, isn't it? You've lied to me for suns. Supposedly, I'm a savior, or some bringer of destruction—depends on the interpretation of ancient and ridiculous scrolls." He balled his mud-caked hands into fists. "Right?"

Father shrugged.

"Well, then. Isn't that something I should've known?"

"Nope. You've an ego larger than the sky, cur. Your head would be massive if you'd known about your grand destiny." He pretended his head was heavy. "Oh, woe is me," he squealed. "I'm perfect. It's such a burden." Father collapsed. "Oh no! Oh no! So much pressure from this massive head of mine!"

Marl wasn't amused, but his anger abated. "Oh grow UP!"

Father stopped rolling and sat up. "And here I thought I was old!" He stood and shook like a horse out of the river. "Feeling better?"

This was a stupid question. "No."

"Thought as much. You should put that anger to good use. We need firewood."

"Fine. Whatever." Marl threw up his hands. There was always work.

Father gave him the axe. "Hold on one second, my liege." He tiptoed to the shed and disappeared, returning with a long object wrapped in a fine but weathered, black velvet cloth.

Marl forgot his misgivings. "Is that…"

"This is mine. I've been hiding it for a few suns now. For protection." He emphasized the last word as if it absolved him of all wrong.

"More secrets?"

"Yep. And this one your mother doesn't know. I think."

"Where'd you get it from?" Marl stroked the velvet, ashamed of the mess on his hands.

"I was a soldier. Once. Long ago. Wanna learn how to use it?"

"Why now?" If he took this offer, where would it lead him?

Father shrugged again and placed the bundle under his arm. "I'm not getting any younger. And I think you're ready to wield it. If anything ever happened to me, I want you to protect them."

"What about Nat?"

"Natsir's a good man, but he's not a warrior." Father's green eyes pleaded. "What do you say?"

Marl nodded.

Father slapped him hard on the back. "Let's get some work done and we'll get started."

When they reached the end of the clearing, Father looked around.

"If your mother ever asks what we're doing, tell her I'm teaching you to track." This was a stupid lie, but Marl didn't argue. "Tell her we spotted a red fox. Rehearse it in your mind. Got it?"

Marl watched him march, feeling the weight of the axe in his hands. *Father had been a soldier.* He'd always admired the man's strong, swift gait, but it had never occurred to him it might be a learned feature. *I've always tried to match that stride.*

***

They found an appropriate corpse, a storm-fallen oak and set to work carving the remains.

"Where did everyone go this morning?" Marl asked, trying to be casual.

Father tossed a log into the pile. "Natsir went to see Para off. Pilgrim went out hunting I suppose."

The axe landed with a satisfying crack and the wood took on a Lufnis countenance.

"And you and Mother?"

Father didn't answer.

"What were you and Mother up to then?"

"Hmmm... oh, we were... working... in the shed." Father placed a hand to his neck and blushed. "She's picking wild strawberries now." This was a peace offering. Marl favored wild strawberries.

"That's nice." He slammed the axe and the tree split again, another gaping wound.

"Yep. Nothing better than your mother's summer tarts."

Marl had no response to that strange and useless remark.

Father was still blushing. He coughed and looked around. "Shatter the stars! We forgot the wheel barrow. Keep cutting. I'll get it."

Marl balanced the axe, moving its weight from center to head. The oak smelled fabulous. He thought on Hereu's woody eyes and had to smile. Did her hair smell as earthy and fragrant as this tree?

A slight movement in the distance drove her to the back of his mind, though his face still burned with her spiritual presence. The creature stopped and started, a spark jumping out of a candle.

"Para?"

A tender breeze rushed under his chin. *You think of many girls.*

"I told you to leave me alone."

The red flame flashed across the forest. Marl caught its brown-gold eyes and prominent nose before it disappeared.

Wind laughed again, swept against the leaves of the canopy, and took off. Marl set back to chopping sections out of the tree, slashing them down to more manageable sizes.

Father returned, grunting and moaning as he pushed the wheel barrow over several roots.

"You missed it. There was a red fox."

"Perfect! Imagine that little critter next time your mother asks what we were doing. Concentrate hard on him." He grabbed the axe and started on the remaining oak. "Let's hurry. We're running out of time."

Marl nodded and thought. *Did Wind bring that fox to help me? Was she trying to apologize?* While they loaded the wedges, he felt his intestines tangle. He wanted nothing more than to sit down and cry. "Father?"

"Yes." He wiped some sweat from his nose and stopped, giving his full attention to his son. He never allowed anything to get in the way of their discussions.

"I'm sorry I lost my temper." Marl trembled.

Father slapped his shoulder. It was the surest way of knowing you weren't in trouble anymore. "It's all right, lad. Sorry we had to lie to you." He pointed to the barrow. "Ready? Let's head toward the bend. There's less chance we'll be spotted there."

A quick race to the outer banks of the river left them both winded. They laughed as they crashed into the moist soil.

"We should learn to listen to your mother. But don't ever tell her I said that."

Marl snickered, doubled over with his hands against his knees. "Don't worry. I won't. But she probably already knows."

The river flowed deep and gentle. Several bushes and shade trees lined her shores and cattails waved hello to passing avifauna. One could see a great distance around the banks and hear for miles.

"Yes. This place will do." Father retrieved the bundle from the top of the wood pile. He marched forward and thrust it into his son's chest. "Open it. Go on."

Marl peeled back the cloth. The blade was dull, but it gleamed in the rays of Mother Sun. The hilt had once been exquisite. Greens, reds, and blues shimmered and danced over lacy carvings in gold. They could purchase all of Na-ir with this.

"She's beautiful, isn't she? She was a gift. Once my most precious possession. Not now, though."

"What happened?" It was missing a gem and the blade was rusted. "Was this from battle?"

"Yeah. Battle." Father shivered and frowned. "Come on. Let's see what you can do. How should you hold it?"

Marl was transfixed on the craftsmanship and the power. "With respect."

Father's demeanor brightened. "Well now! That's my boy! Show me."

He placed the hilt in his left hand and balanced it with the blade pointing toward the trees.

"Good start. You've a good grip." Father scratched his head. "I forget you're left-handed; that can make things harder for you. Spread your legs more. You're tall; you need a wider stance."

Marl complied.

"Good! Good. Now stay there a while."

"Like this?"

"Yes, sir. You need to develop the right muscles to handle her."

Marl was aware of the combined weight of his arm with the sword. "How long is a while?" He was hoping it didn't translate to hours. *Is he teasing me?*

"I'll let you know when," Father snickered. "Concentrate. Stare a bit."

Marl nodded and tried to still his shaking hand. The sharp stings in his wrist, elbow, shoulder, and thighs were distracting. He singled out a slight chip on the blade. What devious perpetrator had fallen by Nojhi Ganwin's great hand?

"All right. You can rest. You're a natural. Good concentration. Not enough though. You need to be aware of your surroundings as well as the sword. Everything works together." Father motioned for Marl to give him the weapon. "Now, close your eyes. What do you see?"

"Nothing."

"Wrong! It's possible to see without eyes or to hear without ears."

Father was behaving like Etutsa teaching Mlaerian writing, more engrossed in the subject than the pupil. *Can we get on with it?*

"Try again. Close your eyes and tell me what you see. Any man can do this, but it shouldn't be hard for you. You have your Mother's gifts."

Marl frowned. He was still sensitive about the possession of those gifts.

"Listen. Listen to the world and then you'll see."

He focused on the sound of his breathing. Marl could hear nothing else but the shuffling of feet in the gravel. Then the scraping disappeared. *He's testing me.*

A new sound. Happy exclamations resounded through the trees. Marl loved warblers. They floated with Wind, jewels hanging from her neck.

A sharp smack knocked him down. "What was that for?"

Father loomed with a stick the size of the sword. "Sorry, lad. I got carried away." He helped Marl up. "You were in such a trance I thought you'd fallen asleep. What'd you see?"

"Yellow warblers."

"Ah, how'd you know they were yellow?" Father patted dust off his back.

Marl shook dirt from his shoes. "By their song. Yellow warblers sing differently."

"Good! You're making progress."

What're you talking about? I haven't done a darkened thing yet!

"Let's do this again tomorrow." Father wrapped the sword in the velvet and place it in the barrow. He manipulated the logs so it wasn't visible.

"That's it then? I was hoping for more. I'm not sure I learned anything."

"Don't worry. We'll come out here every day possible." Father placed the infernal stick in a groove between two branches of the warbler's tree. "It takes time to learn good swordsmanship."

Marl doubted this. It was a sharp tool that you smashed against your enemy.

"Let's get back. Your mother is probably worried."

They walked along for a while rehearsing.

"We saw a red fox. You learned to track his prints."

Marl nodded and repeated everything, sometimes adding a new detail to the story to make it sound believable. The exercise was pointless, but he trusted Father.

I tried emptying my mind. Filling it might be a better strategy. Before they reached the fallen tree, he decided to pose a difficult question. "Can Mother *read* minds?"

"Well, sort of. Information comes to her from the thoughts of others."

Marl screwed his face. Father laughed.

"It's not hard. She asks the spirits for help and they show her things. She's like a healer, asking for protection and guidance when needed." His hands shook.

"So, she can *see* what I'm thinking."

"Yep, and interpret it." This time there was no mirth in his tone.

Marl didn't have to contemplate long to realize what this meant. "Sun's tits!"

Father boxed his ears. "Watch it! We're talking about your mother. Show respect."

"This morning you called me a cur. Speak for yourself!"

Father turned red trying not to laugh. "You have your mother's beauty, but there's no doubt you're mine. Stars bless you, you've inherited my ridiculous pride!"

They walked on.

When the cottage was in sight, Father turned. "So, what've you been thinking on that you don't want her to see?"

The color drained from Marl's face.

"I love making you speechless! Don't worry. She doesn't monitor your thoughts every moment. Using her powers too often makes her weak. There's a price to this gift. At any rate, there are many things mothers would rather not know about their sons. Trust me."

He removed the sword from the wood pile when they reached the shed, and concealed it in its spot between the rock and the loose boards.

Mother met them as they rounded the corner. Father gave her a kiss.

"I thought you two were back. Nojhi, could you help me fetch the honey? I don't know how it's possible, but I swear I've gotten shorter."

"Of course, love, but it's the chair you're standing on that's lost an inch or two." He placed a gentle hand around her waist.

Marl groaned. If there was anything that man was good at, it was flattery. Why did women prefer teasing to honesty? Mother had always been of small stature. Did it matter?

"You saw a fox and some yellow warblers today!" She grabbed Marl's hand and sighed. "I should go into the forest more. I miss those beautiful creatures."

Father shook his head and twisted his mouth in a warning.

She took them both by the hand, and walked with them to the house. For all they knew, she was pretending. That was what she was good at.

***

Dinner was noisy. Mother and Father chatted about fair weather and strawberries. Natsir sulked and picked at dinner. When Para was near, he was a bumbling idiot. When she was gone, he was a stumbling idiot.

Marry her already! Bring her here. Then we'll never have a reason to see Lufnis again.

"Natsir, love," Mother cooed. "When does Para return from Lafret?"

He sighed. "In a few weeks."

There was a low meow from under the table. Pilgrim dropped a very dead brown mouse into Natsir's uneaten dinner and sat down to lick his paws. *I told you I could still catch a thief!*

Marl squirmed. The cat stared. His golden eyes said there was no longer any need for secrets.

"Yes, thank you, Pilgrim." Mother wrapped her hands in her apron. "Take your prey by the fire."

The black cat stretched out into a long strip of fur and retrieved the mouse from Natsir's platter. The unfortunate creature was now covered in olive oil, parsley, and spices.

Did he do that on purpose, to make the mouse taste better? Marl clutched his stomach. Mother passed him another platter of squash and onion.

Very good meal, remarked Pilgrim as he crunched on bones by the gentle fire. Natsir pushed his platters away and slammed his head into the table.

Father patted him on the back. "Don't worry, son. Weeks fly by. There will be other dances."

"It's for the best," Mother remarked. "I met Posgi while picking strawberries. She says that man has been grumbling about the quality of a village harboring Erutani. He's questioning G'Nirac's sanity."

His name is Vill. Pilgrim turned his gaze back on Marl with a slight hint of amusement.

Father tapped the table. "Nice of him to start a stink while G'Nirac's away. A perfect coward. The village will ignore him."

Mother folded her hands. "Even so, stay home for the dance. I'd rather not give him a reason to be angry with us while he's gone."

Marl had been contemplating ways to attract Hereu, to convince her that her father was a moron. She should follow him into the secluded boughs of the forest. They would never leave. Mother's declaration took some time to sink in. Hereu vanished down into the fertile soils of his mind, leaving him heartbroken.

"Wait! So we're going to hide?"

"It's not hiding; it's laying low. People like this man tend to throw tantrums and then cool down when they're ignored. He'll find something else to complain about."

Not likely! Pilgrim jumped into Marl's lap and purred. Marl was half tempted to knock the cocky cat off his legs. He wasn't that cruel, though.

"Be careful for now." Mother cleared the platters. She dumped all but Natsir's in a bucket of water by the fire. "It does us no good to annoy a bear. In the end, he'll always be a bear."

Natsir looked up from his massive pout. His forehead was red and his hair was stringy with sweat. "I'm going to bed." He slumped off to his cot.

"You don't want to help me give the remainders to the creatures?"

Natsir groaned.

Mother pushed the uneaten strawberry tart in front of Marl. "Here. Several rabbits followed me home today. I'm sure they would appreciate this offering."

He took the platter and followed her outside. The sky was a dull yellow. Mother got down on her knees and scraped a spot in the dust. She poured the vegetables onto the ground. "Please accept this with our thanks."

She created another area for the tart, took the platter from Marl, and repeated her actions.

A collection of red lights gathered near the piles of food. A warren stood as high as their little, fat bodies would allow. They were all a beautiful shade of honey brown and cream white.

Good evening, Arnab. Mother bowed to the rabbits.

Their noses moved rapidly and their ears bent. *Thank you, priestess. We accept this extra bounty from your garden. As promised, we'll leave your garden in peace.*

Their forepaws returned to the dirt and then they gobbled the strawberries.

Mother hummed and gathered the platters before heading back to the house.

Marl was stunned. It had never occurred to him this ritual had a purpose other than appeasing her spiritual beliefs and satiating the stomachs of adorable critters. "Why have I never heard the creatures talk before now?"

Because they were told not to frighten you, and it was for your own safety.

"But Wind always speaks to me."

"I'm afraid Wind does whatever she wants." Mother's demeanor darkened. *Much like you. Don't go into Na-ir without us. Remember, the spirit and I aren't the only beings watching.*

Turning on her heels with the agility of a rabbit in flight, she marched back into the cottage. Marl sighed and reluctantly followed her in.

FOUR

Nojhi watched his dark horse of a son move with the grace of a breeze and attack with the shocking force of a storm. Marl was a lethal opponent. In Nojhi's magnificent youth, he would've been no match for this skinny, determined man. Once he set his mind to something, he was invincible.

Their current battle was reaching a climax and Nojhi could feel his old body slackening with the strain. *Damn! Lad's made of something other than flesh!*

He took an ill-advised step to the side, fumbling for stability. Marl's stick landed hard on Nojhi's head with a loud thwack. The pain was red-hot and debilitating.

"Ice in summer! Sorry! Sorry, Father. I'm so sorry!"

Nojhi's eyes spun. "Don't apologize. You bested me." *Ril would've taken this boy in a heartbeat.* He tried not to think on it. Never would his son be a madman's tool.

Marl's blue eyes lost their lightning fierceness; the simple love of a boy shone through. "I wasn't trying to kill you though." There was a shift of gravel. Then, a moist, soft thing pressed against Nojhi's tender head. "This will help."

It did, but it shouldn't have. Marl was still unable to understand or control the healing gift he'd inherited from Messa. Nojhi sighed and sat back, letting the forest breeze amplify the medicinal properties of his son's love.

Marl sat down cross-legged and waited, shirtless, handsome, and solemn.

He's not a child. I was the captain of a battalion at his age. Nojhi staggered up. "I'm well. My head's as hard as yours."

"What'll we tell Mother?" Marl took his shirt back and beat it against the air.

Nojhi chuckled as his son shivered with the river's chill on his skin. He knew the irreverent joy of that feeling too. "Tell her we were horsing around and I stumbled into a tree." It was an embarrassing thing for an old man to do, or admit to, but Nojhi felt it was a better substitute to the reality of an aged warrior.

Marl nodded, yet the worry remained. "That knot on your head is bad."

There *was* a distinct lump. "You think we should stop?" Nojhi barked. He was counting on Marl's stubbornness. He wanted no more reminders he'd lost his edge. Messa was the only good thing weakness had ever given him.

"We should come back tomorrow. I don't want you to kill yourself."

"Nah, I'm fine." Nojhi retrieved the sticks, tossing one back to Marl. "Let's spend another half hour. If we go home, your mother will notice the swelling." He gave his head a pat. "I can already feel the bruise settling in."

Marl shrugged. "If you say so." He took a stance, ready to practice the same maneuver again. A few thwacks later and the boy was flat on the ground. "Ah! I missed."

Bull crap! Little man's trying to make me feel better. He let me have that.

Marl came down on Nojhi again with fierce agility.

But he doesn't want me to think he's too soft. Give a little, push a little. Right, lad?

Through the rest of the practice, Marl avoided Nojhi's head. This meant he lost a few matches, but Nojhi was grateful for this humble sacrifice.

He could feel hot blood rushing again in his skull when the stick came down on his shoulder. It was a gentle blow for the boy, but it would have been a slow, painful way to die had they been using a sharpened sword.

"All right, I think we're done."

Marl bowed and took the wooden weapons over to the warbler's tree. He was eager to be the best and wanted to do everything by the book: all customs, all rituals. These bruises were worth it.

"What animal should we say we tracked today? An owl?" They hadn't seen any creatures save for fish, which had been tasty.

Marl laughed and threw an arm around his shoulders. Nojhi recoiled; he was still dizzy. "Track an owl in the day? How about a fawn?"

"I haven't seen deer in this forest in ages."

"But I saw one yesterday, a ruddy fawn was watching us. I never saw its mother." He pointed. The spot was several yards away. "By that willow."

Nojhi looked his son square in the eye, but the boy's visage split in two. "You were able to concentrate on our lessons yesterday and notice a fawn from that distance?"

"Yeah. She was such a sweet little thing." He talked to animals like they were babies. Nojhi didn't mind. Marl needed something to temper his aggressiveness. "We made her nervous. I forgot to tell you. We'd also seen that badger."

These past few weeks, this stubborn youth had resisted the urge to best his father in *everything*. Now, only the warrior practice presented that thrilling challenge. Messa had noticed the change. It was good Nojhi was spending more time with the boy. To see Marl standing straight, proud, and carefree next to him, he had to agree.

Nojhi's head was purple by the time they returned home. Messa demanded they postpone everything for the next day. She wouldn't permit him to move another muscle and she spent the rest of the night and the next day scolding and pampering Nojhi in kind.

What a horrible bruise! I'll get you something to ease the pain. She returned with a salve, sharp and sweet. *I can't believe your nonsense. Running into a tree! You're too smart and too old for these shenanigans, love.*

He didn't mind her bitter words. He hummed while the salve and her chants soothed his aches. It was all right to show weakness around Messa. She preferred to have a fat, lazy husband who sat by the fire. As long as he came home each day with the boys in tow, to her unharmed, she was happy.

But he'd never been that sort of man. He knew his own restlessness.

When Messa wasn't soothing or scolding, she was working. Nojhi watched her chop vegetables and knead dough. The boys popped in by midday to shovel down a meager lunch. He tried to query their activities, but she spooned stew into him instead. They were gone before he could swallow.

After lunch, Messa cleaned the table, the hearth, and various pots. When something was out of reach she would place her hands on her hips, slide over a chair, and tiptoe to reach it.

Nojhi had forgotten how much she did to look after their family. She made it look like an elegant dance, even with her apron covered in flour. She reached for a pot of honey, her backside elevated.

You're beautiful.

Messa gave him a coy smile and leapt off of the wooden chair. It made an infernal roar as she pushed it back against the table. *You did hit your head hard.* She put down the pot.

You don't believe me?

Messa planted a small kiss on his head and took him in her arms. The ache subsided as she placed a hand to his cheek. *Sleep, love.*

"You're still beautiful," he mumbled. Within seconds he found himself traveling through the Blessed Unknowing in unusual bliss.

***

He woke to scratching and hooting on top of the cottage.

With the warmth of his wife pressed against his back, Nojhi surveyed everything he possessed. The boys were asleep, long legs spilling out of their cots across from the blackened, empty hearth.

Pilgrim was awake, listening to a bird even he wouldn't challenge. The old cat's eyes collected moonlight.

Nojhi touched his head. The bruise was healing and he felt vigorous again.

But night was unbearable awake and alone. He hated this stillness, this void creatures with talons and huge eyes navigated. He shut his eyes tight and concentrated on more jovial things—his wife's kiss, swimming in the sunshine with old friends, a pot of mutton stew—but darker images from the past wouldn't cease their torment.

Messa groaned and rolled over.

Pilgrim settled in between them. The old cat's purr drowned out the sudden yelps from Nojhi's stomach.

He tiptoed to the hearth. There was usually something in a basket on the mantle. Nojhi pulled out a heel of rosemary bread. It was new, not hard, though the crust gave a satisfying crackle against the inside of his cheek.

This would've been excellent with mutton.

Nojhi understood Messa's need to forgo meats. Still, some of the happiest moments of his life had been with others gathered around a table of bounty. He did and did not miss those days.

He was too awake now to return to bed. Nojhi wiped saliva on his shirt and looked around for his britches and shoes. Messa had patched the hole in the right back leg, a casualty of the sessions with Marl. He marveled she hadn't yet discovered their deceit. They were winning, cleverer than her, but Nojhi was starting to wonder if she was humoring them.

No. If she knew, she'd kill me. Such a transgression would break her heart.

Messa was getting old too, not as sharp with her powers. This worried him. He'd grown reliant on her abilities to keep them abreast of any dangers. Could she tell now if some threat was headed to Na-ir?

Nojhi had come to love this place. It was home and it was a stable freedom. This he didn't take for granted. But secrets couldn't be held forever.

The bread pushed back into his throat. He never wanted to use that sword again for anything other than practice, but precautions had to be taken.

What was that proverb? Man's pride often ruins his lofty plans. He looked on his favorite son, his greatest source of pride, before marching out of the cottage. *If Vill ever touches him again, I'll ram my sword through his head!*

The air outside was pure and cool. The first glint of a red, cloudy morning peeped over the trees. The brown owl hooted and dove from the thatch, a small bird clutched in its powerful talons. Nojhi ducked and watched it disappear into the trees.

The boys had been busy. The garden fence had been repaired.

Nojhi inspected the barrow. *Good job, lad!* Natsir had a knack for fixing and mending.

He surveyed the other repairs: patches to the thatch, grain bagged and ready for market, scythe and tools sharpened.

Stars! My boys do know how to work. I should forbid them to go into Na-ir forever!

It occurred to him Marl and Natsir should've already planted the melons. He licked his pointer finger and placed it into the air. A cool breeze was starting to form; light from Mother Sun was intermittent. A storm was brewing. Rainwater was best for growing. Any later and the summer sun would scorch the tender seedlings before they matured.

Nojhi marched to the small field behind the house. His good mood was squashed. Crows and sparrows were breakfasting, digging with sharp talons and powerful beaks. Those seeds had been saved from last sun's harvest. They didn't have anything else worth planting in this season.

"Darken my light!! Shoo, you damned beasts! Shoo! Pilgrim! Do your job, you old scoundrel." He cursed at animals seen and unseen.

The tilled ground was scared by a full night and morning of the birds' efforts. Most, if not all of the melon seeds had been devoured. Nojhi tried not to seethe. It was an accident, an oversight.

A damn bloody mess! Well, if the boys can fix everything else, they can fix this too.

He marched back to the house, this time ignoring the sounds of his massive feet on the floorboards or the banging of the door against the wall.

"Up boys. We've a problem!" He sat backwards in a chair to stare his sons down. If Nojhi was going to have to knock some heads together, he'd do it. "You boys did some great work yesterday, and I'm grateful you took the initiative to lend a hand. But I *know* I've taught you how to seed a garden."

"Sun's tits!" The youngest shouted.

Natsir moaned. "We forgot to net the area! The seeds."

They scrambled out of bed and tried to pull on their britches and shoes.

"Too late," Nojhi snapped. "It's all gone." They sat back on their cots half-dressed and defeated. "Now, something needs to be planted."

Messa approached the hearth. "Do we have any coin? I could go to town."

The tone of her voice was steady and kind. She was trying to temper his temper and, with the guilt it induced in him, it usually worked. Not this time. They knew better, and Nojhi was having none of this game. When they had their own families, this could be a deadly mistake to make.

He could feel the veins in his neck bulging; his hands were restless. He took a deep breath and shook his head. "Not enough to even buy one bag." He tapped against the back of the chair and growled. "To make matters worse, a storm's coming."

Marl rummaged under his bed, pushing a pile of colorful stones away. Nojhi watched his backside and managed not to kick it.

"Here! This should do it." He dropped a bag into Messa's hands. "Every coin I've ever earned."

She opened it and gasped. "Marl! I thought Etutsa and G'Nirac were only giving you coppers."

She pulled out two silver coins and played with them in her hand. Once again, another interesting fact had avoided her detection. Nojhi stared. Marl had been running errands for suns.

"I thought you spent it on sweet buns!"

"Nope. Never had a need to." Boyish charm gave him many things for free. "Let's go! We don't have all day."

Beaming, he snatched the bag from his mother and raced for the door.

"Hold it!" Nojhi shouted. "G'Nirac's not back. You're staying here."

Marl pouted, but he didn't show disobedience.

"*I'll* go to town. You two idiots will rework the ground and start building the nets to keep out those ridiculous birds." He ignored the slight harrumph from his wife. "Got it!"

"Yes, sir!" Marl tossed the bag over to Nojhi and raced out the door. The sweetness of this gesture made him regretful. Mistakes were mistakes, but sometimes learning had to be difficult.

Natsir nodded and raced after, still bouncing to get into his britches.

Nojhi sifted through the coins. "I can't believe he had this!"

It's not bad, love. Messa settled in beside him. *We won't starve. If you're worried about the rent, G'Nirac has never demanded us to pay what we don't have.*

He grunted. *It's the principle, sweetheart. They wasted time, food, and coin.*

She turned away. *Your sons wore themselves out yesterday thinking of everything possible to make you happy. Marl was keen on it. He said it was his fault you were injured. I find that unlikely.*

Nojhi refused to acknowledge she was right. His reckless streak was undeterred with age.

The planting was the last thing they did. The lesson has been learned and Marl handled it well. You're criticisms aren't easy to swallow.

Nojhi grunted again. Everything her boys felt, she shared tenfold.

You called your sons idiots for a simple mistake. I suppose I'm an idiot too for not controlling those birds! She rounded her sapphire eyes back on him. *What more do you want?*

He took three silver coins from the pouch and looked up. *No, you're not an idiot, love.* He didn't mention the boys. He always called them names. Messa was being too sensitive. *What do I want? I want this family to do well, to be happy.*

He was dumbfounded by her question and her scolding. A father had the right to be angry when his children were remiss.

It's not this; there's something else troubling you. This anger inside of you, this resentment you have, let it go. She took the bag and placed it on Marl's cot. *Remember your youth and be glad in theirs.*

A chill crept over his neck. His youth wasn't one to be proud of, but Natsir and Marl had made better use of the time. "You know what he wanted to use the money for, don't you?"

She sniffled into her hair. *He was saving it for Natsir... so he could marry Para.*

Nojhi sighed. "I guess my son does have more common sense than me." He jumped from the chair and pushed it back into the table. "You're right. I overreacted."

He approached her, hoping for a forgiving kiss, but she turned away with crossed arms. It was no use fighting. He'd offended her sensibilities as a mother and that made it hard for her to be a wife. All he could do now was let her indignation cool.

"I'll be back soon."

She didn't answer as he left the cottage.

***

What anger? I'm not holding on to anything.

By the time he'd stomped to the village, he was breathing heavily. The coins branded his hand with the great seal of Artnaus: two warriors locked in mortal combat.

No. She's right. Why am I on edge?

An hour ago, he'd been a benevolent king; all had been right and good. The mangled garden changed that. Why?

Because it's the only thing I do now. It's the only thing I'm in charge of.

The boys no longer needed to be carried or guided. If he were to die, they would survive. Messa humored him in his masculinity, but she no more needed his help than he wanted her sympathy.

I used to lead armies. He stared at the coin with the last warriors under his command. *Don't dwell on what can't be changed, idiot.*

Several shops were dealing in grains, herbs, and vegetables, but there were no melons or fruits of any kind to be found. He was sick of vegetables. Nojhi lingered by Retat's shop to smell roasted mutton and beef on the spit. A dirty, stocky man, not much younger than himself, rounded the corner.

"Smells good, don't it? Must be a damn fine thing to be a butcher." The man wiped his hands on his britches and offered one up. "Name's Vill Misyl."

"Ah, one of the new residents. Name's Nojhi."

"Yes, I've heard your name too. Pleasure to meet you." They stared. Vill jumped. "Dropping off a ewe for Retat. Must get back to the ladies!" He nodded and hobbled off.

"Ho, friend," cried Retat from the stall. "Has your wife relented her delicate eating habits? I've acquired some nice mutton. She'll cook up very tender. This one here." He pointed to the turning spit operated by pulleys and strong apprentices. "She's for the festival tomorrow. You coming?"

Nojhi laughed nervously. Many suns with Messa had helped him to find the visible results of Retat's profession obscene.

"No, afraid not." He was avoiding the subject of the harvest celebration. Marl was still whining. "I'm in town to buy seed."

Retat wiped his hands on his apron. It did nothing to remove the stains; if anything, he was reapplying the blood like an ointment. "Storm's coming. Shouldn't that have already been planted?" The butcher knew little of farming, but he'd a good ear for information from those who did.

Nojhi scratched his head. "Um, yes, well, we met with a mishap."

"What'd you think of that fellow? The dirty man you spoke with?"

"Vill? Seems decent, I suppose. Not what I expected." Nojhi shifted his stance. "Honestly, a breeze could kill him. I'm surprised he was able to knock Marl over."

Retat chuckled. "Women are often distracting things. They can make the weakest of men warriors." The butcher pointed a finger. "Vill's on real hard times. Wife's ill; he has to rely on his daughter."

A sour lump formed in Nojhi's throat, it tasted of rosemary. *Here I am worrying about being useless. This poor guy would love strong sons to help him with the sheep.*

"Etutsa gave him a talking to after what he did to the children, and he's been really careful since. Can't blame him. I wouldn't want to go back to the mines if I were him."

"Such a shame." Nojhi feigned empathy. "Well, now they're in Na-ir, they can feel more secure. G'day to you, friend."

"G'day, Nojhi." Retat retreated to the back of his smoky shop.

Mother Sun disappeared behind another deep-grey cloud.

I'm as easily distracted as my sons. Nojhi laughed.

There was no danger. Vill was a tiny, broken man and Na-ir was still peaceful and welcoming.

I let my past get the better of me. He approached a vegetable stall. "Hey-o!"

Toren was snoozing in the corner, his white whiskers pressed between his chest and his face, giving him the impression of a furry ermine.

"I'm in need of seed. Whatcha got?"

Toren snorted awake. "I've still got cabbages, carrots, and cucumbers." He emphasized each *C* and tossed three bags on his counter. It was slim pickings, but it'd have to do.

Cucumbers would be nice though. Nojhi scratched his beard. "All right, I'll take them." He plopped the silver coins in the outstretched palm.

The old man grunted. "Better get with it. My bones are aching. Big storm." He settled back into his shop chair and snuggled his head to his shoulder.

Nojhi snickered. The strange characters in this village never ceased to amuse him. He spent the rest of the walk home feeling in much better spirits than when he'd started.

The boys had made quick progress on the mangled field. They looked hopeful as he rounded the corner of the cottage.

"This looks wonderful! I knew my sons would make it right." He breezed over his praise, not yet willing to admit he lost his temper. He tossed the bags. "Ready to get started?"

Marl shrugged. "Sure. It's good we have some variety. Too bad it's all vegetables."

The boys mapped things out. The carrots and cabbages would do well in the center, but the cucumbers needed support. They should be planted near the edges of the netting, to use as a trellis. They dropped seeds into the upturned soil rows and used their feet to cover them.

They know what they're doing. He didn't. Messa was still seething inside the cottage. "Keep at it, boys. I'll be back."

Natsir cocked his head and smiled. "Going to talk to Mother?"

"Yeah." Nojhi winked. "Something like."

A gentle breeze carried out a haze when he opened the door. Messa was stirring some warm-water concoction, a witch at her cauldron.

"So, you're back." It was a declaration of war.

"Uh huh."

"I still think you owe them…"

Nojhi stopped her snarling pink mouth. The wooden spoon flailed, dripping bits of boiled beans. She gasped as her feet rose off the floor, but she didn't fight him. A brief moment later, he deposited her into a chair, her sapphire eyes wide with surprise.

He gave her one more kiss and tossed the spoon back into the pot. "Come on, woman. There's work to do!"

The priestess jumped from her chair and balled her hands. "Nojhi Ganwin! You infuriating, ridiculous man!"

She growled as he slipped off the porch. Nojhi could hear her clack the wooden spoon against the metal pot as she returned to their meal.

The boys were stalled with shock, steadying a small pole draped in netting. "What happened?"

"Nothing. We were settling an argument."

Marl glared. "Doesn't sound settled."

Nojhi examined the pole. "Trust me. We're good. Where are the nails?"

They pulled nails and a hammer from their pockets and handed them over to the master of this fertile plot of land.

"I need to teach you boys a few things about women." Nojhi winked. "But let's get this done."

His command was muffled by the nail in his mouth. He placed it near the top of the netting and gave a decisive thwack with the hammer.

"Today seems a fine day to go swimming."

His unusual offspring looked to the ominous sky. They didn't dare disagree.

FIVE

Mother was still fuming when they reentered the cottage. Red-faced, she slammed bowls of spiced beans in front of them and puckered her lips. She didn't eat, but sat there watching. Father had a special capacity to make her mad at everyone.

The boys slurped. The silence, save for the smacking of their lips, was excruciating.

Father sat back in his chair and tapped. "Finished?"

They placed their bowls on the table and nodded.

"Let's go then."

"Tracking again?" Mother hissed.

Father jumped. "Nah, not today. I figured the boys and I would go swimming, have a talk."

"I see." This meant more than the literal *see*. She was accusing him of something.

"We'll be back before the rain, love. Don't worry." He approached cautiously. Mother was a whirling storm. He leaned into it, kissed her head, and rubbed her shoulders. It had no effect.

Mother got out of her chair, took a step back, straightened her apron, and sighed. "Fine. Don't expect me to clean the mess you'll drag into this house."

Father laughed. "Of course, love. You won't have to lift a finger. We can take care of ourselves."

Mother snorted. She spent most of her days *lifting a finger*, sometimes her whole hand. Her sons would've never dared to presume otherwise.

Natsir knew how to soothe her. "Is there anything we can help you with before we go?"

Father and Marl frowned; this was a dangerous offer.

The creases in her face disappeared. "No, sweetheart. Thank you. Go with your father. I'll be fine." She walked to the front of the cottage, picked up a ragged broom, and opened the door. "Enjoy yourselves."

"Are you sure?"

"Quite! The sooner you're out of my hair, the better."

The slam of the door echoed. Natsir wouldn't have been surprised if all of Nair thought they were under threat of an earthquake.

Father scratched his head and stared before waving them to the trees. They were all eager to get to the river and away from the epicenter of the tremor.

"What did you do?"

"Stars if I know! Guess I'm not the only one holding on to rage. She wanted me to apologize; I am. I'm taking you swimming."

Natsir would've preferred a true apology, but this wasn't something a son could command. He was no fool; he did as he was told. Being right didn't win any battles.

"She's going to kill you! I'm sure of it." Marl cautioned.

Father scoffed and stepped into a rotten patch of mushrooms. He caught himself mid-slip. "Nah, don't exaggerate. She's a peace seeker."

"She can identify poisons, you know!" Marl reminded.

"Nah. She would've done that suns ago." Father pushed back on a small twig in his way. It broke from its mother tree with a loud crack.

Natsir struggled to catch up. He'd never been able to match the old man's stride. It came easier for Marl. *At least I'm not insufferable.* No woman would ever say that about him.

By the time they reached the gentle bend in the river, the sky was more overcast and ominous. "We should do this tomorrow, Father. The storm is very close."

There was an oppressive heat in the air, though the sun was masked by the clouds.

"Nonsense." Father removed his shirt to reveal a hairy chest with a myriad of scars. "Those clouds are too high to do any damage. All they can do is spit."

Natsir shrugged. Father was wrong.

Several willows leaned into the river bank, their tentacled branches playing in Water. One great pine sheltered them all, with two warblers chattering on it like yellow fruits. "Hello, my pretty friends."

They flew down and landed on a strange limb where the trunk split into two sections. Natsir examined it. The strange branch was evidently two well-worn ash sticks.

The male warbler accepted his polite invitation and jumped onto his forefinger. *I'm Veem. This is my tree.* The bird chirped and bowed. *You're the Gifted One.* Creatures always called him gifted. He supposed it was a gift to speak with them.

Marl and Father had already jumped into the river and were whooping and hollering from the cold.

Veem ruffled his wings. *I must give a warning. Tell them they'll face…*

Wind shook through the trees and slammed against the yellow-feathered jewel. *Silence Veem!*

The warbler gripped Natsir's finger, but didn't puncture skin. Feathers still puffed out, the bird jumped back onto his tree. His mate pushed a tiny head into his chin. *We must fly.*

Natsir shivered as they shot for the top of the pine. He was glad the birds had been obedient. He didn't want any reason for that horrible spirit to stay.

"What're you doing, Nat? Come on already!" Marl bounced in the current and waved. If Wind had spoken to him, he wasn't allowing it to show.

"I'm coming," He threw off his shirt and tiptoed over to the bank.

A bowled, sandy bottom allowed for a lush splattering of vegetation. Large, gangly-legged birds and prickle-furred rodents kept a respectful distance. He offered mumbled words of apology, kicked off his shoes, and placed them near the other two pairs. It was a ragged sight.

We look like peddlers.

Natsir slid into the chilled current and hissed.

"Cold, isn't it?" Father laughed. "Just the thing to wake us up."

This wasn't snowmelt from the distant mountains, it was a rush of rainwater from upstream. Natsir listened as the drops told of the endless fall from great heights, melting from their cloud.

Marl cupped his hands together and sloshed a wave. It crashed over Natsir's frozen chest and into his hair, diamonds on gold. The jewels raked tortuously down his back.

"Hey!"

"What're you complaining for? You needed a bath anyway."

Natsir's teeth chattered. Swimming wasn't enjoyable for him. Water talked an awful lot, in many voices, and his overtaxed mind was never stilled. He swam because the other men did.

Marl climbed the opposite bank. His gangly, black-haired legs flailed in the air and sliced through Water. Father grabbed him and tossed him into another part of the current.

They're reckless. Natsir swam to the spot where his brother had vanished.

Marl popped up, grinning. "Hello. Who were you talking to in the tree?"

"Oh, the warblers. They were worried about you and Father."

He snorted. "Yeah, we're idiots."

This made Natsir angry. It wasn't right to brag about less-than-acceptable traits. These were things they needed to moderate, not encourage. "Not that. They said danger is coming."

"Birds are excitable creatures. They're worried about the storm. Did they say anything else?" Marl looked at Father, now sprawled on the bank with his feet dipped into the rushing water.

"Nope, Wind wouldn't let them finish."

Marl sighed and patted Water. He always tapped on things when he was thinking critically. He usually thought critically when there was a reason to lie. "She always has my back."

"Why? You aren't tracking are you? That's why Mother's mad."

Marl jumped and swam over to the bank beside Father. He left a wet and muddy trail in his wake. "Hey! Brother's asked about our tracking lessons. Can he join us some time?"

"Sure. I don't see why not."

Natsir felt like an annoying noise in a small room. "No, thank you. I already know how."

"You do?"

"Yes, sir. When I find one, I get down." He settled next to one of the footprints and grinned. "And ask it which way the creature went. After that, I know where to go. I've done it before when G'Nirac's chickens wandered off." He scraped mud from his hands.

Marl plopped onto the sand and pulled his legs to his chest. His mouth fell open in childish wonder. "We can do that? That's amazing, Nat!"

"I don't know if *you* can do it, but *I* can. At any rate, I want to know what you two do every afternoon. Those rods would be an excellent way to get a lump."

Father shot up. "I should've known better! All right. We'll tell you."

Marl released his knees and pushed his feet deep into sand. "We will?"

"Sure." He went to the warbler's tree and tossed each boy a stick. "Let's go. It's time you sparred with someone more your age."

Baby brother looked surprised, but he stood, covered in gravel and sand, and moved to the clear area near the tree. He bowed and took a strange wide stance.

"Now, Nat, match everything he does," Father commanded.

Marl swung his stick in elegant slices, approaching with force and grace. His left-handedness made mimicry hard. Also, their hands were moist. After wiping them on their dry shirts, they tried again.

Natsir was enjoying Father's praises when Marl brought his stick down with a thunderous clack on his arm. He could feel the vibration burn as it raced through him. It wasn't a sensation he wanted to repeat. Natsir lowered his weapon and stared at his brother's satisfied smirk.

"So, this is what you do? You dance around with sticks, hitting them together."

Marl frowned. "It's more complicated than that, brother."

Natsir handed his weapon back. He didn't wish to beat against his little brother, no matter how capable the boy was. "Too reckless for my taste."

"I figured. You're a more reasonable man." Father slapped his back. "You aren't mad?"

Natsir shrugged, although the apprehension painted on his brother made him think he should've been insulted. "No, I'm fine. You two can hit each other to your hearts' content."

Marl gave him an awkward bow and put the sticks into the groove of the tree.

"I won't tell Mother." Natsir reassured, sorry for upsetting them.

Father gave him another painful slap on his back. "Good. We know how worried she gets."

There was a reason for this.

A splash echoed in the canopy. Marl was back in the river. "What's the matter? You don't think swimming is reckless too, do you?"

Natsir resisted the urge to say yes.

Father snorted. "Your poor baby brother. He seeks your approval more than mine sometimes."

Baby brothers were always baby brothers. Was that why Natsir couldn't stop calling him that? There was very little maturity shown to convince his subconscious otherwise.

"Don't be offended. It's just not for me."

Marl bobbed in the current, arms across his chest. "Ah, you're a better lover than a fighter."

Blood rushed as Natsir slipped into the river. "You mean farmer." He'd never been anyone's lover. He'd never expected to be.

Father laughed. "You do make an excellent farmer, son." Boys teased about carnal desires; men kept their thoughts to themselves.

Marl's black hair fluffed out like a crow airing its feathers. "Nah. I'm pretty sure that's not what the Star of Na-ir would say!" He gulped air and vanished, then yanked on his brother's arm.

Natsir turned redder still but he didn't give chase. *Always the combative one.* He missed the days when he and Father could catch that crow in a cloth and tie him on their backs until he fell asleep. Nat had fond memories of that baby hold.

"Admit it," Marl shouted as he surfaced several yards downstream. "If you have to choose between farming and Para, you'd choose the maiden." It was a fair assessment, but life wasn't always about the choices they *would* make, more the choices they *could* make.

Natsir stuck his head under. The rush of the stream pounded his eardrums, men roaring in battle. Water giggled and caressed his hot cheeks. He couldn't bear the excess, so he surfaced.

Marl was inches from his face when his green eyes opened. "What's the matter with you? She's not going to wait forever."

Natsir frowned. There was a lot the matter with him. He was a strange farm boy who'd no business being her friend; he was grateful she gave him that. Natsir couldn't read or write. Lufnis's appraisal was accurate. He was *useless*. If he'd any redeemable quality, it was patience, but even he had moments where he wanted to smack foolishness out of his little brother.

"It's none of your business. Shut up!"

"What if someone else gets to her? You think she's going to ask you to help with the horses then?"

Father growled. "Marl! Enough!"

Natsir was tired of this. He walked over to his shirt by the warbler's tree. Father followed. They pulled their tattered rags over their heads and leaned against the truck of the pine.

"Look. Your brother's being stupid. Gets it from me."

Natsir crossed his arms and stared at the wet dirt.

"He does it because he loves you. We all do, Nat." Father placed a hand around his shoulders and squeezed. "He's not wrong though. G'Nirac says Rippan is vying for Para's affections."

Natsir stiffened. *Rippan of the Dasha!* Para had mentioned him before, in offhanded ways. She mostly talked about the future chieftain's sister. He shivered. Para would move to the canyon lands readily.

"You know, your mother told me Marl was saving that money for you both," Father offered.

Natsir watched his brother splashing in the river and sighed. He felt stupid for being mad.

"I'm sure he still means it for you, a wedding gift. Ask him."

The temperature of the forest dropped to the consistency of Earth's breath from a cave. The trees lost their outlines against the sky. Gusts rattled through the canopy in terrifying hisses.

"Sun's tits! Storm's here."

Thunder crashed in rolling laughter. They were pelted with icy, unforgivable rain, the same sort that had accompanied Marl in his birth. Now the boy was wailing again, but not so baby-like, as he jumped out of the river. His skin was white as a corpse and every visible black hair stood on end.

"Let's get out of here!" He gathered his clothes into a muddy ball and broke into a run. Wind whipped as they followed him back to the house.

They dove into the shed and tumbled into their food stores, bagged and heavy against the wall. Father slammed the door. "Heck if Toren wasn't right. This is a wild storm!" He sat beside his sons. "We might be here a while."

The interior of the shed was eerie, with intermittent light floating in from loose boards and peepholes in the wood. Some of the rain had flooded a small corner of the building. Thankfully, none of their food stores were anywhere near that corner—a task to be tackled tomorrow.

Natsir groaned. "Should've stayed at the house."

Marl laughed. "There's a worse storm in there. I'd rather stand outside and get pelted. Are all women crazy?"

A fuzzy frown appeared on Father's face. "Your mother isn't crazy."

"Why is she mad then?" He wrapped his arms around his chest and rocked forward.

"Oh, I don't know. I guess it's because I kissed her." Nojhi stroked his beard. "And then I might have told her to get back to work."

Natsir was certain of it now; Father was a cur.

Marl hissed. "Are *you* crazy?"

"Yep." He grabbed the boy's neck and rustled his feathers. "Don't worry. She'll be fine. She's probably wringing her hands wishing we were home."

Natsir didn't agree. "She knows we're safe in the shed. She always knows where we are."

Father shrugged. He was used to playing dumb, lying to keep her secrets.

They heard a faint sneeze. The old man laughed. "We aren't alone. How are you, Pilgrim?"

I was sleeping before you came running in here like wet, cawing ravens!

Marl and Nasir smiled.

Father hadn't heard the answer. He turned to the shed door.

The priestess shouldn't have so many to care for, Pilgrim declared. *None of my kittens ever troubled their dames for so long! Find mates to relieve her of this burden. That's how humans live, is it not?*

Marl fell into a sack of beans and guffawed. He clutched his sides and kicked his legs, a skinny black-and-white turtle on its back.

Father jumped. "What's funny?"

"Now *Pilgrim* is teasing me about Para," Natsir grumbled, feeling more an adolescent than the one in front of him.

"Huh?"

Marl sat up, his white chest still heaving and his mouth quivering. "Pilgrim told us to find mates and leave Mother alone."

I wasn't that rude.

Father reached out to stroke the protruding bones. He laughed as the hind end bounced to meet his touch. "Smart old thing, aren't you? He's right." He gestured to the door with his thumb. "Get out of my house! Both of you."

Natsir didn't find the joke funny. "Where would we go?"

Marl wiped tears from his eyes and welcomed Pilgrim into his lap. His answer came quickly. "I'd apprentice myself to Etutsa. He could teach me all he knows. It wouldn't be so bad."

Father snorted. "Good thing you're a skinny runt. That man has no room to stand." He picked a piece of wheat grass off the floor and twirled it around with his teeth. "What about you, Nat?"

Outside the rain was falling in hard smacks on the mud.

Marl's plan was practical and reasonable from all ends, but Natsir wouldn't have wanted the same life. A healer had to be focused, to take on any emergency. *I'd rather stay here.* It wasn't a stretch to say he could. After all, the eldest inherited everything, farm and all. But something in Father's demeanor told him he needed a second plan. "I don't know. I guess I'd work in someone's stables or be a woodsman."

"Fine professions for strong and able men." Father took the grass from his teeth and waved it. "It's settled then. I won't be seeing you much now you've found your callings."

Natsir choked. "You're not serious, are you?"

Marl placed a hand on his shoulder. "Don't worry. He's trying to get a rise out of us."

Yes, he is. Mother boomed like the roll of thunder. *It's time to come in.*

They peeked from the shed door. By some magic, all colors were intensified after storms, and the scene outside glowed green and brown. The ground was a muddy vat of muck. Mother stood on the porch, her arms crossed but her demeanor softened.

Light poured from a crack in the clouds. A small beam fell on the shadow cat as he stretched to his full length against the floor boards. *Go without me. I detest falling water and there will be mice later.*

Natsir cringed for the impending death of friends and followed his brother and father outside. Wind pushed against their moist bodies.

Mother frowned as they approached. Marl's naked chest and legs were spotted with dirt and grass. Father and Natsir were gleaming all over, soaked to the skin. She gestured them inside.

Marl declared he'd mop the floors for her, taking a cue from Natsir's earlier politeness. It was a relief to know someone was showing him a good example.

"Thank you, sweetheart. Natsir, love, we'll need to wash your clothes."

He nodded and proceeded to drag the cauldron out into the porch. Within seconds, the rain intensified again. Water was happy to oblige.

Inside he heard Mother screech and giggle. Father was trying to give her a massive embrace. "We're not that wet, love. See!"

They laughed as he caught her around the waist and squished her into his chest. Her apron was missing. She'd changed into her favorite dress, a green one from G'Nirac. It still fit well. Father gave her several compliments.

Good. He owes her a few.

They worked quickly to remove any trace of the muck. Clothes and rags boiled on the fire and the floor was scrubbed. True to his word, Father didn't let Mother move a finger. He did, however, allow her to give them small directions and warnings. A woman's wisdom was always welcome.

The cauldron full of laundry sat precariously near a baking stone topped with the night's meal, pastries stuffed with vegetables, herbs, and cheese. Marl, who was in charge of the nasty mess on the fire, was reminded several times not to slosh anything on their dinner.

His father's son, he pinched his nose and made a rude sound. "Sheesh, Mother, this is the worst stew you've ever made." It wasn't a stretch of the imagination. The pot smelled like old fish.

She laughed. "I'm not taking any credit for that monstrosity. You're the cook responsible."

The ebb and flow of their merriment was like the current of the river, but more relaxing. Father removed the pastries and laid them out on the table while Natsir hung the contents of the laundry stew on the mantle.

Marl brought him odd knickknacks to keep the clothes from falling as they dried. He gave him a wooden cup and the stink eye when the discussion turned to the warblers. Natsir stuck his tongue out, but didn't reveal anything the birds might've witnessed.

With britches, shirts, and clothes hissing into steam, the Ganwin family sat down to dinner. The mouthiest of them gobbled his pastry. A lanky string of cheese slid down his chin. Marl frowned, picked it off, ate it, wiped his mouth on his shirt, and then gulped water from his cup.

Natsir shook his head. *Heavens help me if I ever have children as crazy as my brother.*

The thought transformed into a tiny person with green-brown eyes and red, wavy hair. His heart quicken and his lungs pushed his breath out in massive spurts. It was everything he'd ever wanted. Water had told him that a vision would let him know if and when it was time to act. Did this count as a vision?

"Are you well, love," Mother placed a hand on his forehead. "You look pale."

Natsir shook himself out of the dream. "I'm fine."

Marl smirked, blue eyes penetrating. "I know why. He's been dreaming about pretty Para."

Mother scowled but had sense enough to let him fight his own battles, if indeed they needed to be fought.

Natsir smiled. There was no need to consult the spirits. It was better to pursue what he wanted. "Marl's right. Do you think she'd marry me?"

Father dropped his pastry on the table and stared. Marl opened his mouth.

Mother slapped her hand across it. She turned to Natsir in a frenzy. "Of course! Is that what you want?"

He didn't hesitate with an answer. He wanted this more than Marl wanted to be a healer. "Yes."

Mother removed her hand. Marl gasped as if she'd been suffocating him. "Finally!" It wasn't clear if he was referring to her or the announcement.

"I hope you don't mind if I use some of the coins, brother. Father told me you intended them for me." Now the decision had been made, his mind was flooding, and he wanted to act on every idea.

"Take it all!"

"I won't need all of it, but thank you." Natsir turned to Father. "Would you mind if I go into town tomorrow to buy parchment and pigments? I've an idea for a gift." He may not be able to write, but he'd another talent for communicating. *I want Para to see herself as I see her.*

Father laughed and slumped into the table. "You're going to ask her to marry you with a drawing? Son, I'm not sure…"

"What's wrong with that?" Mother interrupted.

Marl frowned. "Yeah, Nat, you're supposed to find her a treasure."

Mother crossed her arms and glared. "I think it's a sweet idea. Para's always encouraged his talent."

Natsir appreciated her support, but he didn't need it. No amount of teasing and prodding was going to make him change his mind now.

"What about that shawl?" Marl added.

"That's a wonderful idea. I'll do both." Natsir mused on the blue. He'd need some cerulean.

"A shawl!" Father slammed a hand onto the table. He looked like a man who'd been told a joke he didn't understand. "I'm not sure you appreciate…"

"All right then. What did you give Mother?"

The table fell silent.

Mother pursed her lips. "Your father and I weren't fortunate enough to woo in a traditional manner."

"Ha! And you were making fun of our ideas." Marl bounced in his chair, kicking his legs. "Let's go to town, Nat. I'll help if you want."

Father placed his head in his hands and sighed, trying to hide his temper. "You're not going anywhere, boy! Remember, G'Nirac isn't…"

"Back," Marl snapped and sulked. "Yes, I know."

"I can go with you tomorrow, Nat. Make a day of it," Father offered.

"I'm afraid that can't happen either." Mother smirked.

Father put his pastry down again and tapped the table. "Oh, why?"

"Well." She snorted. "I'm the only one with shoes."

The three men looked under the table. Their toes were unconfined. *We left them on the bank*. They were probably already floating along the goose-pimpled river down to Lake Cycei.

Marl fell out of his chair, laughing.

SIX

She couldn't sleep in this noisy cave. Her legs, for one, were groaning and shouting. Her spine whispered mutiny. And her heart tried to throb out of her chest.

The beast next to her reeked of dirt and fish, snoring with untamed abandon in her right ear. In her left ear were the rumbles of a skinnier creature, its claws lying in delicate repose on her arm.

Two cubs snored across the room while the fire crackled. Yet, all around this strange wilderness of the night, everything was still.

Messa tried not to scream. Her husband's powerful body had rolled against her, a boulder falling onto a blade of grass. "Nojhi, love. Please move."

He snorted and buried his head, thigh, and arm into her body.

She hissed. "You're hurting me."

Marl stirred. Pilgrim meowed and shuffled away.

Messa rolled over, grunting and straining, using her limbs to push against her man. He wouldn't budge. He continued to snore, a stupid smile painted on his face.

Damn it, Nojhi Ganwin. Get off of me!

That proved effective. He rolled and ceased snoring.

A cool caress of air enveloped her skin and filled her compressed lungs.

Hesitant to permit her husband another chance to smother her, she rolled out of their marriage bed and stood, bare feet against the chilled floor boards. Her knees creaked as she hobbled over to the chair by the hearth and threw another log onto the fire.

The rain had ceased outside, but the night air was colder than a stone below a lake. She sat and stoked the flame.

Marl muttered. He was dreaming of the girl from Selcovi again.

It pained her to deny him the simple joys of courtship and affection. Noise from Na-ir was strangely calm. No echoes of discontent rang through the trees, and she could no longer find a reason to be worried. Still, G'Nirac's return couldn't come sooner.

Marl tossed, knocking his fortune to the floor. Messa placed the coins under his cot. He was so much like his Father, but his gentle kindness far outweighed her husband's. It was easier for Nojhi to be cynical. Innocent Marl had yet to experience heartache.

Messa couldn't resist running her fingers through his feathered hair and putting a hand against his cheek. Twenty suns since she'd first held this boy in her arms and heard Wind's breath awaken in his lungs. Could they really have survived this long in the loving embrace of the people of Na-ir, undetected and free?

The prophecies were wrong.

The signs had all been vague: an Erutani with dominion over great forces, born on a journey, Father Moon in a black cloak, and the three sisters all present. These were simple, stupid descriptions. All of her people had been on a journey that fateful night. Father Moon put on his black cloak regularly. There could be several *Wanderers* born in the exact conditions.

Still, Wind is sure. She won't let go.

Marl was as wild as starlight and deeper than the expanse of sky that held them. It was easy to think of him as some great force of nature and man, joined into some fearsome thing. Yet, nothing about him screamed savior or destroyer. He'd been an impetuous boy; now, a temperamental young man. And he wanted what all men wanted: to live a happy life.

But he was still so young. She'd no doubt her son would do wonderful things. He'd also make some horrible oversights. She was guilty of this. Nojhi was guilty of this. Marl was, after all, their son. Yes, the blunders would come, but he'd learn from them as they had done.

Marl's hand hung off his cot and his fingers thrashed, eager to find something to tap on.

Messa sat down beside him. She wanted to see more of this girl who'd captivated her boy. A small, young woman with chestnut hair and tree-bark eyes floated to the surface. The maiden reached out to touch Marl's hair and then vanished with a trilling giggle. That was it. The image repeated, a spell meant to entice and exasperate. Their brief encounter had left its mark. Messa released his hand and tucked it over his chest.

Natsir snored as loudly as his father. *I may be losing both of my children soon.* It was for the best. What had joined her and Nojhi hadn't been courtship. *By all rights, I should hate my husband.*

There'd been so much red on the day they'd met: flames, blood, eyes stained with tears. Nojhi had painted this color on their past, yet she could no more despise him than a person who'd bumped into her in a crowded market.

When she'd first taken his hand and stepped into the Mlaerian world, she'd questioned her sanity. But she followed him anyway, through fields, meadows, forests, and streams. After twenty seven suns as the bride of this rowdy and impetuous man, Messa knew she'd made the right decision.

Nojhi had long since passed the days where he could satisfy some of her wants, and he had a tendency toward patronizing when he didn't get his way. But it didn't matter when Messa contemplated their life together. It had started off uneasy. Now they were resting in a cabin on the outskirts of a welcoming village with their chief concern being their sons, not their sins.

She kissed Marl's forehead. *You've a choice to make, my son, and I shouldn't be making it for you.*

A roar akin to a bear erupted from her bed. Nojhi yawned and stretched out of hibernation, rubbing his eyes. "Where's my wife?"

Messa tiptoed to him. *Hush. I was only putting on another log.*

He grabbed her by the edge of her night shirt. Messa stifled a squeak as she fell into his embrace. He kissed her temple and buried his head into her neck. *I'm glad you haven't left.*

She wiggled as his breath tickled her ears. *Leave! Why would I leave?*

Because I'm a patronizing oaf. He pulled her in tighter and sucked her jugular.

Messa snickered. "Yes, you are. What brought on this realization?"

"A dream. I thought you were gone forever. I owe you an apology. You're far too patient with me." He ran a hand through her black hair and then slid over her back. She wanted to ask him to rub the lower section of her spine, but he stole a kiss from her lips instead.

I know. I feel sorry for our sons' future brides.

Nojhi scowled. *There's not a thing wrong with our boys.*

Of course not. But they're going to have a hard time keeping them happy if they resort to your tactics. She flicked her hair. *Not all women are as forgiving and strong willed as me.*

Point taken. But it's amusing setting a bad example. He dove into her, growling.

Messa slapped him upside the head and tried not to shriek for the sake of her sleeping brood. Even when he was being a cad, he could still make her laugh.

Light filtered in from the window above their bed. The clear skies foretold a pleasant morning. It'd be nice to wonder out into the clean air and take in the trace smells of rain, but the temptation to stay abed in this quixotic moment made her slothful.

They spent some minutes in affectionate embrace trying to be silent. She was enjoying the rare bit of attention until Nojhi stopped tickling her back. Messa opened her eyes to see their bed was now draped in a long, skinny shadow.

"Hello. I thought it best to warn you I'm awake and I can see and hear every creepy thing you're doing." Marl flashed Nojhi a blue-lightning look of disapproval.

"If you don't mind, I think I'll wait outside." He turned on his barefooted heels and ran out to the porch.

Messa blushed behind her hands and shook with laughter. Living in this one-room cottage had made privacy difficult. Too bad the shed was soggy.

"Creepy? He's no idea." Nojhi bit her skin again.

Messa squealed and Natsir gave a loud snort. Tears of mirth streamed down her cheeks. "To him it is creepy. We can't leave him out there."

Nojhi restrained her in his embrace and tried to kiss away her protests.

"It's...cold...and...he...has..." *no shoes.*

Nojhi rolled back and flung his hands into the air. "Gah! Let not the wee man freeze."

Messa found her dress and apron draped on a chair, but she needed her stockings first. Her backside erupted in a sharp sting. The smack reverberated against the cottage walls.

Nojhi!

Messa glanced out the window and then turned to see if Natsir was sleeping before pulling her gown over her head.

Her lover was still grinning when she emerged from the folds of green cloth. She took her pillow and slammed it into his face.

What? It's not a bad example if no one's looking.

Messa tapped on her shoes, careful not to bend over anywhere near her aggressive lover, and marched outside to retrieve their son.

He was sitting on the edge of the porch, his toes dangling a mere breath from the surface of a small puddle.

Marl careened his head around her skirts. "That didn't take long."

From inside the cottage, Nojhi gave a mocking howl. "Ha ha! Cheeky, crow."

***

It troubled her to leave the men alone. Tempers were running high, although they were respectful over their porridge. She couldn't put it past Marl to escape the cottage and run barefoot to his favorite oak in the forest. The act itself didn't bother her, but the mess he'd bring back made her cringe. If Nojhi went after him, there'd be double the work and several hurt feelings to quell. Life was never tidy living with wild men.

Natsir will keep them preoccupied. She thanked the stars for his gentleness. *Without him, I'd be insane.*

As she neared the village, her spirits lifted; she hadn't set foot in the square for many moons. Her reasons for not entering Na-ir had more to do with her own strangeness than theirs. These delightful, wide-eyed people exhibited a kindness and resilience she admired. It was a perfect place to raise children and to settle into a quiet life.

But… the noises and smells stabbed her temples. The more she tried to block everyone out, the louder they thought. It was easier to focus on the flow of the village from the safety of the cottage, though it did drain her energy.

Natsir didn't have this lack of vigor; having Para and Marl to look after gave him something to keep his mind focused.

Messa adjusted her white scarf and corrected the pins. Blue eyes were rare, but not unique to the Erutani—as the chieftain's daughter proved—but black hair was obvious. She didn't want to incite worry in the new residents of the village. Those who already knew her wouldn't care or they would be too polite to point out her deception. It was a cool morning and many women would be protecting their delicate features.

Her first purchase would be the blue shawl. It was a sweet gesture, but she was unsure what the significance was. It didn't matter. This was what Natsir wanted and it was Marl's money. She'd find the sacred bit of cloth.

Gerna was sitting behind her counter with a sweet, dreamy expression on her wrinkled face. The seamstress understood Messa, having had five rebellious boys and three marriages of her own. "Could that be our Mistress Ganwin? I haven't seen you in many dances of the Father."

"Hello, Gerna. Blessings of the Mother upon you." The ritual rolled off her tongue, but induced a slight twinge of nausea. "I'm sorry I've been remiss in my visits."

The pudgy seamstress bolted from her chair and reached across the stall to administer a vigorous embrace. Messa had to rearrange her shawl over a stray lock.

"What can I do for you, precious?"

The stall brimmed with textiles and delicate metal chains. Gerna was an industrious woman. "I'm looking for a blue shawl. My boys told me it was here."

The seamstress bustled over to a trunk and rummaged. She produced two shawls. One was embroidered with golden thread, but the other was a sheer fabric that matched Para's eyes.

Gerna sighed. "You would look stunning in this, but I was saving it for someone it'd look better on."

Messa cringed. "Oh, too bad. I believe that's the one my son wants me to buy."

"I've never known a man to care like your Natsir! He's an eye for beauty."

"That's why he wants to buy it. It's a gift for... a young lady."

She might as well have been secretive with a frog. Gerna shrieked and clapped her hands over her mouth. Every inch of the woman bounced. "Oh mercy! I knew it! It's for Miss K'Parre, isn't it?"

Messa placed a finger to her lips. "Please, Gerna. Don't tell anyone. I don't want the entire town to get to her before he does."

The seamstress danced around her stall, half listening. "You're in luck then. I was saving it for Para. Our lovely girl almost bought it, but that horrible man came by and ruined everything." She waved a hand. Gerna had an unforgiving streak to those who'd harm her babies, even if those babies weren't of her womb. "If this is a gift for Para, you may have it."

"Oh, no. I can pay you." Messa hated charity. A priestess was meant to bestow it only.

The seamstress brought out some brown paper and a few sprigs of rare patchouli to preserve the cloth from insects. Messa was mesmerized. She loved patchouli. When preserved fresh it smelled like the soil after rain—almost, nothing could ever match that scent.

Gerna clicked her tongue. "If I recall, Miss Para isn't fond. It reminds her of dirt and sweat. Let me see if I've any mint." She returned with some lavender. Her arthritic hands folded the flowers into the shawl and wrapped the bundle into the brown paper. She tied off the package with twine, making a pretty bow. "There you are, love."

Messa took the bundle and passed a silver coin into Gerna's hands.

"Now, sweetheart. I told you this was no charge."

"I know, but you work very hard, and your cloth is the finest in the town. I'd be remiss not to pay."

The seamstress's not-too-stern features softened a bit.

"Spend it on your grandchildren."

Gerna smiled and pocketed the coin. This was how things were done in the Telmah village of Na-ir.

"I'll see you at the wedding," Gerna shouted.

Messa stiffened, but waved back before dashing out of the way of a group of curious villagers.

She didn't know the man who ran the stall with pigments and papers. He was an unobtuse person with squinted eyes and a pointed nose. Messa tried to ignore his acerbic expression as she purchased a cut of parchment, bleached to a slight cream yellow. The pigments were very expensive.

He might as well rob me! She bought the crushed sapphire, but the other colors would have to be prepared by hand. *I know the roots and berries to make them. They won't be as brilliant, but they'll do.*

Struggling with her packages as she made her way to the cobbler's shop, Messa stopped at Telm's pillar to rearrange everything. She looked up to see a young woman, auburn-haired and tanned-skinned, pushing a cart laden with wool. The cart had a loose wheel. Several townsfolk, many of them strong men, passed the girl by and cast mocking glances normally reserved for street dancers.

That's not nice. Poor child! Messa marched over to the girl. "Can I help you?"

Those oak-brown eyes! She was speaking to the object of her son's obsessions. Hereu was dirty and barefoot in a tattered green dress, but her smile was white and genuine.

Yes, she is pretty. Messa wasn't sure why that mattered to her.

"Thank you, mistress, but I don't want to trouble you."

"It's no trouble. Here." Messa took the front of the cart with her free hand and pulled. The young woman pushed. The wheel rose out of its entrapment. "My name is Messa."

"I'm Hereu, mistress." The shepherdess didn't look up from her cart. "Thank you."

It was nice to hear respect. The girl could teach Marl a few things. "My pleasure. Where are we headed?"

Hereu stopped. "I, um… I'm sorry. I already forgot her name." She frowned and fiddled with an auburn curl, biting her lower lip. "The seamstress: Gertie? Gunna?"

"Gerna." Messa remembered the day she was introduced to Na-ir, standing in front of Telm's column, wide-eyed and reluctant. "I can show you the way."

"Back again? Did you forget something?" Gerna gasped when she saw the cart. "Ah, I see you've met Miss Hereu who's brought me my wool. That black looks fine. Place everything in these baskets here, sweetie. These old hands will be busy spinning tonight."

Gerna remarked on the softness and beauty of the wool as Hereu worked. Messa felt guilty not helping, but she didn't want the parchment and shawl anywhere near those pungent shorn coats. When she was finished, the girl put her hands behind her back and rocked on her muddy heels.

The seamstress furnished two silver coins. "Here you are, sweetie." She either didn't remember this girl was the offspring of the *horrible man,* or her generous nature wouldn't allow her to be cross with any young person. Messa figured it was the latter reason.

Hereu took the payment and curtsied. Her cart didn't get very far. The infernal wheel popped off, rolling through the mud to a startled man and his horse.

"Oh no! Not again!" She retrieved the wheel and tried to reattach it.

"Ah, here's a fortunate encounter!" Gerna waved to a man in the square. "Fane!"

Her oldest son was a stocky man with a mustache fluffier than a lap dog. He smiled as he approached, casting a sidelong glance at Hereu.

"My boy, this young lady needs help. Could you fetch your tools and fix that old cart?"

"Please don't trouble yourself," Hereu protested. "I'll be fine." She dropped the wheel and then dropped the cart, just missing her vulnerable feet.

Fane grunted and shrugged. "Of course, Mother. I'll see what I can do." He tipped his hat. "Morning, Mistress Ganwin. Pleasure to see you again."

They waited for him to retrieve his tools. He grumbled as he heaved the cart onto its side and hammered the offending piece back into place. Hereu's cheerful eyes watched him work.

Messa tried to think of something else to discuss while her friend performed his manly obligations. She couldn't mention Marl; that would make the girl suspicious. Messa wasn't interested in the mundane life of a shepherdess. What did the young people in town talk about?

"Are you going to the harvest celebration?"

"I think so, mistress." She blushed.

Messa tried not to blush herself as the image of her own child made a prompt and gallant display in the girl's mind. It was too bad Hereu knew nothing of Marl's stubbornness. She could have a calming effect on the troublemaker, though.

"Papa said I could if all of the sheep are sheered. Never been to one before."

A devious plan was starting to form. Were Nojhi's antics rubbing off on Messa? Gerna winked. "Ah, you'll enjoy it, sweetie. All the young folk do."

Fane returned, dragging the cart with one strong arm, and tipped his hat. "That should do it, Mother. It shouldn't give her any more trouble." He excused himself in the gruff manner of a tradesman.

"Thank you," Hereu called. Her fragile limbs danced over a few sharp stones.

"Wait." Messa placed a comforting hand to her back. The girl flinched but forced a smile. "Do you have shoes?"

Hereu frowned and turned away. "Well, I did, but I forgot them by the stream near the meadow when the rains hit. I was so intent on bringing the sheep back home, I left them. Mama says otters steal shoes from girls who go swimming alone and wear them when no one's looking. You think that's true?"

A family of otters stomping around in four pairs of empty shoes was indeed amusing. Hereu's cheeks turned into cherries as Messa laughed. "A silly coincidence, my sons and my husband did the same thing yesterday. Lucky otters!"

"Oh! I don't feel so stupid now."

They stopped in front of the cobbler's shop. Hereu tried to slink off again. Messa stalled her. "So! How are you going to dance tonight without shoes? Or take out the sheep?"

"I suppose I'll have to go barefoot. It could be worse." She scratched her left foot with her right toes.

The days were warm and pleasant now, but ants with fire bites lived in the meadow. There were many ways a girl could slip and sprain an ankle on rocky hills and dew-soaked grass.

"I wouldn't advise that. Come into the shop. I'm certain we can find you something practical."

Tears welled in Hereu's oak eyes. "You're very charitable, mistress, but I couldn't. I mean…" Terror choked her response. *Father would kill me!*

"Nonsense!" Messa guided her into the shop.

Chaun was delighted to be selling four pairs today. Hereu allowed him to clean her feet and fit them, mumbling thanks and gracious protestations with a dirty, tearstained face.

He shook a finger at Messa. "Where are your men? I could ensure a better fit if they were here."

"I apologize, Chaun. Their current footwear met with an unfortunate accident." She winked. "With some otters."

The girl gave her a grateful smile.

"Let me see. If I remember, these should do for Natsir and Nojhi." He tossed two pairs on the table. "But what of Marl? Surely he's grown by now!"

Hereu gasped. "I should be going, mistress! Thank you." She dashed out of the shop, surer of foot in her new shoes.

Messa laughed, the girl's obvious affections were too comical.

"My goodness," cried Chaun. "What came over her?"

"Not sure. My men have big, destructive feet. If they don't fit, I'll return."

Chaun laughed and tallied the bill. She exited the shop, her arms full of pretty new things.

Hereu was still in the square, staring at the ground with her new shoes tucked into her arm. The girl had sense enough not to ruin them before the dance. A white-haired man was speaking to her. He gave her a tilt of his head before walking away.

"Good morning, Etutsa," Messa called.

His waving hand brushed his head and foliage floated to his shoulders.

"Goodness, what've you been up to, my friend?"

He scowled. "I'm at my wits' end! I know it was my idea for you to lay low, but when can Marl return to my services? I've been traipsing all over the darkened forest looking for my remedies. I feel like a wild boar, rutting through the muck!"

"You've stores of remedies."

"Not anymore. Those idiots from Selcovi don't know how to do anything. Constant injuries. Half are ill. I've never seen a sorrier lot!"

Messa tried to remember Etutsa was speaking from a place of inexperience. One couldn't fault people used to mining, metal work, and baking for not understanding the full ramifications of life in a farming and ranching community.

"Hereu is healthy enough."

"Yes." Etutsa frowned and lowered his voice. "Poor girl. Her mother is the worst. Her lungs. I'd be surprised if she lived the rest of the sun."

Messa stiffened and shifted the packages in her arms. "Is she that far gone? Can you not help her?"

"No, but you could, I think. If only darkened Vill had a better head on his shoulders, you'd be able to see the poor woman, but I'm not holding my breath."

She nodded, knowing of the unreasonable stubbornness of men. "Perhaps he'll relent in his desperation. I hope he doesn't wait too long; I've my limits."

Etutsa wagged a grubby finger in her face. "Ha! Don't pretend modesty, lady. If you'd take over my practice, I could retire and settle down, not a care in the world."

"I suppose so." Messa laughed. "You should train an apprentice."

He cracked his face into a wide smile and his brown eyes sparkled. "I'm glad you said that. What do you think of asking Marl to come help me?"

It wasn't unusual for parents in Na-ir to place their children into employment without their consent, but Messa wasn't authoritative. Gifts were to be cultivated, not forced. "I, uh… well, that's Marl's decision." She remembered the overheard conversation from the shed. He wouldn't say no to such an offer. "I'll let him know you inquired."

Etutsa jumped and clapped his hands again, spraying her arm with dried mud. "Splendid! Please don't leave me without an answer for too long, my girl. I don't know how much more nonsense I can take."

"G'Nirac will be back next week. Marl can start under your tutelage then."

Etutsa leaned in. He smelled of mushrooms and fresh cut grass. "If he starts sooner, I'll double his pay!"

***

Marl dashed from the porch and snatched the packages. She was grateful for the relief, but not keen to discover why he was agitated. He took the shoes from the paper and shoved a pair on his feet.

Messa bit her lip as he stood and knocked them against the porch boards. They were tight. *Rivers and mountains! He's grown.*

He tapped his fingers on his leg. "These will be fine, Mother. Thank you." She handed him the money bag. "Sheesh! Everything was more expensive than we thought." This didn't seem to bother him much. He placed it into his pocket, waved, and ran.

"Where are you going?"

"Nowhere. I'll be back soon. I promise." *I'm suffocating.* He bounded like a hunted rabbit.

My poor son. Etutsa's profession would provide him with thrilling challenges.

Natsir took her burden at the door.

Inside, Nojhi was standing next to the bubbling pot, barefoot and wearing her apron; it was too tight around his middle and bunched ridiculously from his chest.

"Hello." He pretended to stir. "We made lunch for you. Marl didn't want any." He frowned.

"That's because you're burning it, love." Messa removed the spoon from his hand and swiveled the pot away from the fire. Inside floated several bits of onion, beans, dried peppers, and spinach. It was an odd mass of vegetables, but she supposed it wouldn't taste too bad. *I might add some parsnips.*

A mass of beans on the bottom was the source of the smell.

Nojhi ran his fingers through his hair. "Sorry. I thought I was helping."

I know. It's dangerous to leave you men in my house alone, Messa teased as she searched through a basket of vegetables on the floor. She took a knife from the wall.

"Father wouldn't let me help because he wanted to surprise you." Natsir was already sketching with a small bit of charcoal from the hearth. "But Marl was distracting him."

Messa sat down next to her son to chop the parsnips. "Oh, I don't doubt it. What were they fighting about this time?"

Nojhi threw off the apron and crossed his arms. "We weren't fighting. We were having a discussion on privacy and respect."

"You said no less than fifty curses." Natsir smirked under his beard. "Marl said about seventy."

Messa tried not to laugh. "What was the outcome of this *conversation?*"

Her husband gave a tremendous sigh and slammed his arms into his sides. He sat down on their bed. "Apparently, *he* wants more of it. Can you believe that little monster?"

Too bad. She winked. *I've decided to teach the boys more about their gifts. He'll know less privacy with me in his mind.*

Is the danger still there? Did something happen while you were out?

No. Everything's safe. She picked the apron off the floor. *It would be better for the boys to know more. If they can learn to control their powers, we can avoid any future problems.*

All right then. As long as we're careful. He kissed her on the ear.

Messa giggled.

Natsir shuffled awkwardly. "Would this be a time where privacy *is* needed?"

SEVEN

He was king of this land. He knew every hollow of every tree, every whisper Wind told the flowers shivering against the hillsides as she passed. Hunger and thirst were satiated by berries, nuts, and cool stream waters.

His feet burned, but he didn't mind the uncomfortableness of his new shoes. They would be broken in soon enough.

Marl hadn't expected to return at dusk. Time had slipped away from him.

Mother was on the porch mending clothing. *Glad you're here. Your father and Natsir are splitting wood. They'll be back before dark.*

"Whew! Thanks, Mother." He sat down next to her and kicked his feet against the side of the porch. He was regretting ever returning; his wanderlust hadn't been satiated.

She was reattaching a copper button to a bit of blue fabric. "Is that my good coat?"

It is. Mother appraised her work and then tossed it into his lap. *Try it on.*

Marl obeyed, but with some difficulty. The coat didn't want to be buttoned. He smiled. The practices with Father had given him some muscle.

Mother frowned. *I'll have to let it out.* She cut along some of the seams. This time, the fit was better.

"Why do I need it?"

Mother dusted him off.

"Sorry. I should've washed."

Yes. Well. It'll hide your mangled shirt. I don't have time for the rest. She straightened his collar. *I suppose it won't matter. You're still very handsome.*

"I'm confused."

I need to discuss something with you before your Father returns.

Mother gathered her thread, wooden needle, and knife and marched back into the lavender-scented house. She placed the coat on a peg behind the door, positioning Father's rain coat over it, and then took a basin from the mantle and filled it with water. With the hem of her apron, Mother washed Marl's face.

I want to make a deal with you.

"What sort of deal?"

Speak to me with your mind. She grabbed his chin. Her fingers squished his cheeks. *I know you've been feeling trapped; it torments you. I want you to go to the celebration tonight.*

"What!" Marl jumped, nearly upending the basin. *Is this a trick?*

No trick, love. She crumpled her wet apron. *I want you to learn who you are and what you can do. I should've taught you long ago, and this will be a more enjoyable exercise than sitting with me all day.*

What's Father say?

He doesn't know. Don't tell him. Mother's eyes flashed a warning.

Marl sat down again and gulped. *How will he not know? If he catches me, he'll kill me.*

Mother lifted one eyebrow. *You're going to obey your father?*

He folded his knees to his chest. *I thought you wanted me to be safe.*

That hasn't changed. However, I think the problem has sorted itself out. She gave him a coy smile. *Your father will never know.*

Marl stiffened. *All right. What's the catch?*

I've some rules. First, you'll behave yourself at dinner. Nojhi requested a second chance. She nodded toward the table—something wrapped in lettuce. *Don't be rude. Once your father is asleep, you'll leave here quietly. These dances last several hours. You'll have plenty of time. I've made some more rosemary bread for you to bring.* She pointed to the basket on the mantle.

All right. I can do that. It was too bad he couldn't leave now.

Mother stood. *Lastly, you must stay in contact. Communicate with your mind.*

You're coming with me? Marl's elation faded.

No, of course not. It's harder to channel that far, but it'll be worthwhile for you to learn. If you're ever in trouble, you can contact us with this skill.

There were so many ways this plan could fail. *What if I forget to check in? Or what if I can't manage?*

Impossible! I'll come down there and drag you back by the ear! Her eyes pierced his. *No wondering off alone… or with anyone. Got it!*

Father and Natsir returned, chatting loudly about building a house in the forest as they headed toward the shed.

Mother grabbed Marl's face again. *Listen! Hereu will be there, but I think not her father. If he is, you'll avoid them at all costs.*

If he's not? He wasn't one to leave chances untaken.

She cocked her head and sighed. *Remember to be respectful. I'll be listening and watching.* She waved a stern finger in his face. *In other words, don't do anything your father would do.*

Right! No groping, shouting, chasing, or teasing.

Mother blushed. *You're too observant, my son. Remember to behave.*

The other men came storming through the door.

Father pulled out his chair and sat with tremendous force. It was a wonder it didn't break. "About time you showed. Thanks for leaving us to do everything."

"You said I could go out."

"For an hour! I said you could get out of my hair for an hour!"

"I'm sorry, Father. I was distracted. I won't do it again."

Father sat back and stared. "Well, it's your birthday. Try not to be such a cur next time."

"Yes, sir." Marl turned to his mother. *It's my birthday?*

Yes, love.

We don't count birthdays. He'd attended parties as a boy, Para's among them, but his family never had much to celebrate with as it was.

I think two decades on this earth is something to commemorate. She passed him a wrap.

"What do you think? Made it myself!" Father sat motionless and waited for them to eat.

Marl took a large bite. It was like chewing on a muddy blade of grass. The aftertaste resembled mashed carrots. *It tastes like dung!* He swallowed. "Not bad." *I wonder if I could toss this to the rabbits.*

Mother took a small bite. *It does taste bad. Natsir, you don't have to try it.*

This was unfair.

Natsir shoved the entire thing in his mouth. He chewed on the morsel for some time before swallowing. "It could use some spice, but not bad." He smirked. *It's just food.*

Marl glared. *Yes, we won't keel over. Show off.*

Nat stuck his tongue out, a few bits of carrots still in his mouth.

Father took a timid bite for a man of his size before coughing and sputtering. He threw the wrap down on the table and reached for a cup of water. Seeing their cue, everyone else did too.

"That was awful! I created a pile of green manure."

Marl and Natsir laughed, but Mother cast them a reproachful eye. "It's not that bad, love. Natsir ate the whole thing. Why don't I make something else for us? I'll start with tea." She looked over her shoulder and raised a delicate black eyebrow.

While she placed a kettle on the coals, Natsir showed them his drawing. Mother took a small packet from her pocket.

Marl knew it instantly. The delicate leaves were mixed with mallow and honey for sweetness and given to fussy children. *You're making sleepwart tea! That's a cruel trick.* It'd take a lot of it to knock Father out, and the after effects could make a person feel dizzy if too much was given. He knew from experience.

Don't worry. He's an old man and he needs to rest.

Marl turned back to the drawing. Natsir *had* captured Para's grace. Her lithe form was suspended on bare feet. Hair fell in ringlets, enshrining her faceless head like sun rays. This was her true nature: radiant and free.

"It'll take me a bit to make the other colors, but Mother says she'll help."

She placed four cups of tea on the table. "This looks like the temple."

"What temple?" Marl pretended to drink, happy to enjoy the smell.

"You're right." Father already swayed with the tell-tale signs of drowsiness. "Para looks like Mother Sun here."

"Before you were born," Mother explained. "We lived in a meadow by an old temple. It was deserted, but the tapestries and paintings were intact."

Marl gasped. He had never seen a temple. That sort of reverence had become something of a fairytale.

Father hiccupped and put his tea down, only a few dregs left. "Natsir was a little man then, but he'd draw those icons in the sand, line by line. You've always had a gift." He blinked a few times and winced.

Mother placed a hand on his arm and pressed her face closer. Her forehead creased with false worry. "Are you well, love?"

You're devious! Marl commented, but he tried not to smile.

Father placed his elbows on the table and cradled his head. "Ah! It's like someone pushed a boulder on me. All of the sudden…" He trailed off, moaning.

Now he knows what it feels like. "You need to lie down." Mother tried to coax him from the chair.

Father's head slipped down his arms and onto the table. Natsir slid his drawing closer to himself and moved his cup of tea.

"Come, love. You've had a rough day. All will be well tomorrow."

Mother led Father to the edge of their cot and removed his shoes for him. He mumbled something about hay in the shed before drifting off to sleep. She placed a finger to her lips.

Marl lifted her off the floor, set her down, and danced in place. *The two of you are horrible, mischievous, and wonderful. I love you!*

Natsir handed him the loaf of bread and his coat. He accepted them graciously. *Coming, brother?*

Nah. I've got too much left to do. He gestured to the parchment on the table. There was no reason for him to go into a raucous, crowded area unless Para was there.

Marl wanted nothing more than a chance to talk to the brunette beauty from Selcovi.

Mother took his head in her hands. *Your father should be out all night, but be back before morning.* The lightning returned to her eyes. *Remember our agreements.*

The moment her touch on him was gone, he flew outside into the chill. Hidden colors in his midnight hair shimmered in the light of Father Moon. Follicles flashed past in brilliant purples and blues.

There was a definite rhythm to the noise in the square, a barrel of rocks rolling down a set of stairs.

He took in the aroma of the bonfire crackling into thick grey smoke. On this unusual alter, large spits turned. The juices dripped into the flames, hissing like rain on the river. Retat was at the helm of this crazed fire boat, leaning against a braided ribbon pole.

Marl threw the bread on one of the tables. Several young men passed by and gave him hearty slaps on the back.

"Good to see you, Marl."

"Where've you been, man?"

"Wonderful. The Mouth's here."

They wore traditional dun-colored doublets and britches with starched shirts. One of them dragged a fair-haired, hazel-eyed girl by the hand. She smiled before disappearing behind the large mass known locally as Fane.

Nerid's always had her eye on you. She's a bit old though.

Marl jumped. *Forgot you were there. Not my type.* He concentrated on exotic eyes.

Mother knew him too well. *If you're looking for Hereu, she's by the linden tree, alone.* "Excellent!"

He side-stepped several people, returned a wave from Mister Fane and his identical, bush-faced son, and walked past the tables full of meat pies and mulled wines. The elderberry wine caught his eye.

I should eat something first. His heart was pounding. The vibrations rattled his empty stomach. *If I vomit on her, I'll die of embarrassment.*

Grab some pheasant and two cups of wine. You need to eat and Hereu is actually starving.

Marl nodded. He knew little of women. It was a bad idea to be snippy with one who had his best interests in mind. *Wait! I can eat meat?*

Don't be daft. I know you and your father buy it in the market. I can't stop you.

Marl shrugged. His childhood must've been full of secrets.

Two skewered, roasted pheasants were procured and two wooden cups of wine were poured. Dashingly appearing with provisions while Hereu waited by the tree was romantic, although it was difficult for him to carry. *Mother Sun don't let me drop all of this on her.*

Mother Sun has bigger things to worry about than your clumsiness.

Sorry. He looked around the celebration. The twirl of dancers made him dizzy, and the pounding of the little lap drums seemed to target his ears. *I don't feel well.*

Nervous? This time Marl could tell her mood; she was laughing.

No. Yes. A little. He stumbled. *My head hurts.*

Sorry, love. Channeling can be exhausting. I'll give you breaks.

Marl took a drink of wine and swallowed hard, enjoying the tingle as it slid down his throat. He cursed the dizziness and braved the crowds. Hereu might not wait forever.

He was halfway around the square when he felt a sharp poke in his shoulder. Mother responded to this in a panic. *Don't turn around! Don't turn around!*

Marl had already stopped to survey the sensation. To his great relief and displeasure, the figure before him wasn't Hereu's ragged father, or his own. *Shatter the moon, it's Yimette!*

He ignored his mother's contempt. That curse was adequate for anyone in the vicinity of this rambunctious woman. He loathed her. She'd a laugh louder than any blackbird, and not nearly as pleasant. She was always giddy.

Yimette poked him again. "Well, if it isn't baby Marl. Where've you been?"

"Hello."

She knocked him forward with a hug. A cup landed on the ground staining the dirt and the edge of his shoes a light red. He bent over and the second cup made a disgusting sound, trickling into the mud.

Yimette pulled him to his feet. "Oh my. Sorry, sweetheart. Looks like you might've had too many of those already. Your face is so red." She pinched his cheeks.

Can I hit her and run?

Marl Ganwin! Don't you dare! I told you not to turn around. This is your fault. Behave.

Behave, behave, behave. He set the cups against a tree. "You as well. You're *very* chipper."

"Oh, you're funny. No, I'm not allowed wine." She leaned into his ear. Marl brandished the pheasants in self-defense. "I'm with child. Etutsa says I should be careful."

He backed into the tree, tripping over the cups. Mother laughed.

I don't need to know this. "How nice," he stammered, still brandishing the naked birds in her face.

Yimette pulled a cord with a thin ring of gold from under her blouse. She winked and pointed to Fane's son. Gan was a no-nonsense person, the opposite of Yimette.

Marl tried to hide his look of shock. "How pretty. He must be thrilled."

"Don't tell. We've been married for five moons. Gan wants to join in Mirot. Father's against the idea of me marrying a soldier, and I don't know how to break it to him that I'm leaving."

Mother interrupted. *Ask her more. This is the first I've heard of this.*

"There are soldiers in Mirot? Since when?" Marl knew about the Mlaerian village two days' march, but he'd never seen it. It couldn't be much different from Na-ir.

Yimette laughed and pushed him hard in the shoulder. "Didn't you hear about the poor merchant attacked on the road?"

Mother gasped. *No!*

"No," Marl repeated. He hoped it wasn't the merchant who'd bought their beans.

"Bandits. That's why Gan wants to join. No one will be accosted on his watch."

"I don't doubt it. Gan's a good guy."

"I knew you'd understand. We're leaving in two weeks. You won't tell a soul, will you?"

"Of course not. Well, congratulations, Yimette. I wish you both happiness. Sorry to cut this conversation short, but there's someone I'm supposed to meet."

She squeezed his arm. "Of course, of course. Go enjoy yourself!"

He sighed when she was no longer visible, or audible.

Very diplomatic of you. Yimette's as dense as Gerna's puddings, but I suppose she has her virtues. They're stupid for going to Mirot. The life of a soldier is hard.

Marl didn't want to talk anymore. He was frustrated and hungry. *Is Hereu still by the linden?*

No, love. She's moved. Still alone. Concentrate. You might be able to find her.

He took a deep breath and focused on Hereu, her brown hair waving with the night breeze. It wasn't long before the pleasant image changed to something more unsettling. She was standing in the middle of the square, people shoving her closer to the flames. *She's crying! Why?*

It's not easy being invisible.

Marl kept on, muttering apologies to indignant strangers and tucking in his meal so he wouldn't skewer anyone. A brief opening in the crowd allowed him to catch sight of her. She was in a pretty, if a bit short, peach-colored gown, sitting on the ground near the fire. Her head was resting on her knees.

There she is! She looks pitiful. He wasn't thrilled to see the object of his affection looking dejected, but he was happy he could be her rescuer. He'd a talent for it. His pace quickened as he rounded a corner of dancers and musicians. This night wouldn't be a waste after all.

Manly confidence shattered the moment Mother intruded. *I'm sorry. I forgot!*

A hand grasped him by the shoulders and forced him to stop. The voice came as a shock. "Marl! My boy!" Etutsa's cheeks were flushed. "Have you spoken to your mother?"

He was about to shake his head no, but Mother caught him. *He wants you to be his apprentice. I've already spoken with your father; it's your decision.*

Marl nodded.

"Excellent! What's your answer, boy? It's time you honed those talents of yours. You're much too old to be without a profession."

"Of course, sir. I'd like nothing better." *Except to be talking to Hereu.*

Etutsa bounced. "You've no idea how happy this makes me. Can you start tomorrow?"

Yes, Mother said helpfully.

"Yes." Marl hiccupped.

The healer slapped him on the back with a bottle. "Good! I'll see you at sunrise." Etutsa shoved the wine into Marl's chest and stole one of the pheasants.

"Compliments of my brother. My goodness, boy. This bird is cold." He wandered off, nibbling.

Marl chose not to dwell on the unfairness of it all or the fact that tomorrow morning he'd have to have his wits. Instead, he stomped toward the fire.

Her face was buried in her skirts, her body heaving. "Hello, Hereu!"

The shepherdess stood, wiped water from her eyes, and backed away from him in one fluid gesture. Her heels caught on a rock and she fumbled.

"Whoa! Be careful." Marl found himself holding her by the waist with his right arm, the wine against her back. The skewered meat was brandished like a sword in the other.

Hereu shrieked.

Retat laughed, waving a mug of something stronger than mulled wine. "Good catch, lad!"

This broke the spell. She pushed his chest and stumbled, away from the fire.

"I didn't mean to startle you." Marl took a few steps forward to escape the pocket of heat.

Hereu's tearstained eyes glowed. He followed them to the remaining pheasant. It had caught fire in his heroics. He beat it out in the air and laughed.

"It was cold anyway. Want some?"

She shook her head no.

She hates me.

No, she doesn't. She's nervous. Trust me. She has her eye on you more than Nerid does.

Hereu was so unsure of herself, standing there, waiting for something good to happen. It was like trying to tame a frightened field mouse. Marl inched closer. "Look, there's a nice area near the trees. We could get away from this crowd."

The girl's thoughts rammed into him. *Where's he get off being so forward!*

That was a slap in the face.

Son, you don't ask girls to go off into the forest with you, Mother scolded.

That's not what I meant! She looked overwhelmed. I was trying to be thoughtful.

Mother snickered. *To her it sounded different.*

"Or," Marl continued, trying to rescue his pride. "We could go sit by the little, old ladies near the tables. I'm sure they won't mind company."

Hereu winced.

"At least we'll be out of the way of these drunken, noisy slobs." He gestured to the crowd with, of all things, the wine bottle, aware he might as well have been one of the inebriated in her eyes.

She gave him a wide smile. The firelight pulled the red out of her auburn hair and glistened on her white teeth. "You don't take no for an answer do you?"

Marl choked on his desire and frowned. "Is your answer no?"

"No, I mean. It's not *no*." She fumbled. "I'm not supposed to talk to you."

"Oh, you're the only person I want to talk to."

Mother snorted; it reverberated in his head.

That's not funny. I'm serious!

I know. You're adorable!

"All right. We can sit by the trees if you wish."

The echo of the square was less pronounced near the entrance to the village; the leaves and branches created a wall. From here, Marl could hear the beat of his heart. He sat down with a thud against an oak and patted the acorn-covered ground next to him. Hereu sat, but several inches from where his hand had been.

"Do I make you nervous? Why?"

She bit her lip. *Because you do magic; you're dangerous.* She shrugged.

Marl groaned. *This is frustrating. When we first met, all she wanted to do was talk to me.* He handed her the pheasant and sighed. "Here, eat something."

She obeyed while he uncorked the wine. He was tempted to drink the whole thing, but he only managed one swig.

Hereu took it from him with a curious smile. *Those stories are wrong. He doesn't look dangerous.* She passed the roasted bird. "Sorry about Papa."

Marl leaned against the tree and took a large bite of the meat. He felt sick, but shoving something in his mouth would keep him from blurting out the wrong thing. "Don't worry." *He's not the only idiot in my life.* "You're all right, aren't you?"

She took her pretty lips from the bottle and pressed them together. "I'm fine."

They watched people dance and stumble around the square. Hereu was mesmerized, stopping every now and then to suck the juices from her fingers.

Marl didn't know why, but the delicate way she nibbled made him giddy. He slid in closer and smiled. She stiffened, but didn't move.

"So, why was a pretty thing like you crying?"

Mother felt the need to make her presence known. *Too much, Marl!*

Hereu agreed. *He wasn't this cock-sure when we met. Maybe it's the wine.*

He ignored this and Mother's laughter. "Is there anything I can do to lift your spirits?" He was tired of waiting and wondering.

"I don't know anyone here, even the people from Selcovi. It's difficult to get used to another town. There've been so many."

That's the largest string of words she's said all night! Marl swallowed his pride. "What about Eurgi?"

Hereu screwed her face and stuck out her tongue. "Yuck! She can jump off a cliff for all I care. She spends all her time nattering about Para's brother. Thinks she's something special now."

"Lufnis is nothing to gush over. He can jump off a cliff with her."

The shepherdess giggled and leaned into Marl's shoulder. He tried not to move in case she thought better of her actions.

"You don't need her anyway. I can introduce you to all of the important people here." Her skeptical smile encouraged him. He pointed over to the side of the square. "Look, that mustached man over there is Fane, with his son, Gan."

She frowned and put a hand against his chest. "We've met."

Marl placed an arm around her shoulders. She shivered and this gave him a little satisfaction. "That girl over there pretending not to look at Gan is Yimette.

She's a lunatic, but she doesn't mean any harm." He looked for more people he knew. It was like telling a bedtime story. "Over there's Lyrig, her little sister. She's not too bad."

He thought it prudent not to mention his previous attachment to this girl. She felt nothing for him now anyway.

"The man at the spit is Retat; he's a good guy." Marl scratched at his beard. The elders were always easy to spot. "Hmmm… I don't see Namnor, Yimette and Lyrig's father; he's the blacksmith. I do see Lortews with his wife Posgi. He's the baker, to the left is the tailor, Daerth. That white-haired man over there is G'Nirac's brother, the healer named…"

"Etutsa." Hereu paused. "He scares me. He told Papa off after he pushed you."
And hit you!

"I'm afraid he'll make us leave." She shifted closer. *I like it here. Right here.*

"Don't worry. Etutsa won't bite. He's got a temper because he handles everyone's problems."

Hereu traced one of his copper buttons with a slender finger.

Marl felt a burst of pride. "Starting tomorrow, I'm going to be his apprentice."

She jumped. "You're going to be a healer then?"

Mother mumbled in his mind. *She's thinking you're too good for her, in case you were wondering. She hasn't seen your temper though.*

Ha. Funny.

Marl forced himself not to sneer, although he was grateful Mother hadn't interfered in their discussion thus far. He passed Hereu the bottle of wine and squeezed her shoulder. She took several careful sips, smiling with every pause. All of the craziness in trying to reach her had turned out to be worth it after all.

"You're a cad aren't you?"

What's she mean? I'm being a gentleman. Marl snorted. "You don't like it when men smile at you?"

Hereu jumped and blushed again. Her tan skin was far prettier with hints of pink. *You're killing me.*

Stars in heaven, you're just like your father!

Marl ignored this, seeing a possible chance to steal a kiss. He snatched the bottle from Hereu and leaned into her face. Her oaky eyes met his.

Such a pretty blue... but we shouldn't.

Because the protest had been unspoken, Marl planted a small kiss on her lips, tasting the recent coating of sweet–sour elderberries. Hereu didn't resist.

Sweetheart. Mother's voice contained a hint of worry. *Marl, you're being watched.*

They heard a shuffle over gravel and opened their eyes. Three individuals had stopped to stare. One was snickering. Hereu trembled and grabbed Marl's hand.

Rej Corraidhin, a large mud-colored individual in a yellow doublet, was grinning broadly. He came from a family of hunters and they'd learned long ago the wonderful thrill of taking down another living thing. Rej made a show of it, dragging the fair Nerid along.

"Hello, Mouth."

Marl decided to be the better man; Mother was watching. Pulling Hereu up with him, he started with introductions. "Rej, Nerid, Cyan." He gestured to the blond boy next to them. "Have y'all met Hereu?"

She looked to the ground and offered Rej her other hand. He refused it, crossing his arms over his chest. "I know who she is. She's filth from Selcovi!"

Nerid ruffled her white skirts and whined. "You're mean. Leave the little thing alone."

Marl could feel the hatred rising within Hereu. He leaned into her soft cheek and pressed his lips against it. The fire remained, smoldering.

"Looks like Mouth will kiss anything."

"I think he prefers to be called The Fist." Cyan crossed his arms and stared. Marl laughed, but felt apprehensive about that being his most common reputation among his peers.

"What's funny, Mouth?" Rej took a step forward.

Marl released Hereu's hand and came to meet him. There was no way this cur was touching another woman tonight.

Sweetheart! Don't do anything rash! Mother cautioned.

"My name is *Marl*. I don't appreciate how you're insulting the lady. Stop."

Nerid's eyes flashed. She'd witnessed these scuffles many times before. She placed her hands on her tiny hips and gave Hereu a distinct look of jealous hatred. Cyan put a hand to his mouth and snorted.

Rej turned red, angered by the many times Marl had bested him before. "Listen, I call rubbish like I see it! Why don't you fondle the sun?" He inched closer, smelling of ale.

"She has a right to be here. The elders make decisions, not you."

"Ah, but not forever."

Cyan jumped and stepped in between them. "What's that supposed to mean?"

Mother gasped. *He knows something we don't, but I can't seem to sort it out. Come home.*

No, he has it out for Hereu. I can't leave her alone. He's a coward and I can take him. Marl took a warrior's stance, steady and sure. Father had been right to teach him, and he was determined to use every skill he had.

Rej pushed Cyan out of the way and then pushed on Marl's chest. "Things change, my friend. I guess I shouldn't be shocked. You're used to rubbish since you live with useless Natsir."

Oh no! Mother cried. *Marl, no!* She knew as well as anyone he couldn't let this slight go.

I'm not going to throw the first punch. But punches will have to be thrown. We're trapped against these trees and he's not leaving without a fight.

"Didn't you hear me, Mouth?" Rej goaded. "I said your brother is more useless than bird droppings. He's nothing. Dances all day, not a thought in his head. Always in everyone's way."

Cyan placed a hand on Marl's shoulder and glared at Rej. "Enough! What's the point of this? Let's go!"

Rej pulled back his fist and slingshot it into Marl's face with the strength of a skilled archer. Marl caught the punch a breath from his eyes and twisted Rej's arm so his entire body moved in a half circle. Then, he pushed him to the ground.

Nerid showed her man no remorse.

Marl picked a nearby stick, took another stance, and released a steadying breath. *Don't go for the head,* he reminded himself; it could still count as murder if he wasn't careful.

Hereu screamed as Rej rushed them.

Marl went for the legs and Rej fell forward. A broad chest was next. The huntsman was on his back again, with the stick against his jugular.

"I told you to leave, idiot."

Cyan let out a whoop of satisfaction and laughed. He kicked dirt on Rej and clapped with the rest of the village youth. "That was brilliant! You'll have to show me your technique someday."

Yes, Mother snapped. *We'd all like to know where you learned that move.*

Rej stood and stumbled away, mumbling about how Marl would pay.

Nerid swayed over. "Thanks. I knew I could count on you to kick some sense into him." She kissed his cheek.

Hereu's hand closed around Marl's.

He dropped the stick. "I didn't do it for you."

Nerid frowned and strode off after Rej.

"See you later, Fist." Cyan threw his own fist into the air and ran to the crowd, straight for Gan. "Did you guys see?"

A rewarding smile flashed under a bushy mustache.

Hereu gave a nervous laugh. "You can take care of yourself!"

Marl slipped an arm around her waist and guided her toward the crowd, eager to share in the spoils of his victory. She resisted. He couldn't blame her after what had happened.

They turned to their tree. The wine had toppled, watering the oak; the remainder of the roast pheasant was coated in mud. Marl briefly wondered if trees could be intoxicated.

"Are you still hungry? I'm famished!" They walked around the crowd.

Hereu helped herself to the heel of Mother's bread. He grabbed several sweet buns and another bottle of wine. G'Nirac had been very generous in his absence.

Mother interrupted again. *Son, I think you shouldn't...*

Stay? Marl's heart ached. He'd promised to behave himself and here he was celebrating another fight. A better man kept his promises. *All right. I know. I'll tell Hereu goodbye.*

He released her arm and she stood there, pink, lovely, and shocked.

No! Mother gasped. *I wasn't going to say that. You can stay. I hate to admit it, but you did the right thing. You fought for the right reasons, and no one was hurt.* She sounded faint and weary. *I don't think you should have any more wine. Etutsa won't be happy with you.*

He laughed. Hereu wiped a crumb from her mouth and blushed. "What?"

"Nothing," he lied. "I was thinking I'd be a ham-fisted healer if I had any more of this stuff."

They slopped cool water from an open barrel into two clean cups and walked toward the linden tree. The crowds were starting to dissipate, and Retat was gone; the fire was dying.

"You don't need to go home do you?"

Hereu winked and bit her lip. "No. I told my parents I was with Eurgi."

They snuggled into the shadows and ate in pleasant silence as they stared out into the adjacent forest. Marl offered Hereu his last sweet bun. She waved it away, so he shoved it in his mouth and grinned. She made a face and pushed him in the chest. He tried not to choke.

"You're strange," Hereu laughed. "In an hour, you've scared me, rescued me, fed me, let me tell you my troubles, kissed me, rescued me again, and made me laugh. What sort of person are you?"

She ran her fingers through her auburn hair. Marl wanted to touch it too, but his fingers were sticky.

"Are you trying to flatter or scold me?"

She kissed his cheek. "I'm trying to thank you."

Marl thought about his next move. His head was starting to ache and his eyes were clouded from exhaustion. He couldn't read the girl, but he understood her smile.

Mother, are you there? There was no answer. Had she fallen asleep?

Father Moon hung high, full and bright, directing light through the canopy. Marl scooped Hereu into his arms and kissed her again. This time, she reached a hand across his neck and held onto his hair.

They spent the rest of the night wrapped in each other, breaking away from kisses to breathe or talk. The shepherdess was interested in every aspect of his life, and Marl was eager to know more—every inch of her. The only thing not discussed was the apparent lack of support for their togetherness. He wondered why Mother had let him go this far.

"I still can't believe how you walloped Rej," Hereu giggled. She was spread across his lap. He could feel the warm pressure of her back as it fit in the groove of his legs. "I guess you *are* dangerous." She stroked the tiny hairs on his chin that pretended to be a beard. "I'm sorry I got you into that mess."

"It's not your fault."

Hereu played with his buttons again. "But it is. Rej was angry with me because I turned him down. The creep was watching the girls at the ribbon pole. He tried to force himself on me. But I told him I didn't like barking dogs. I hope his leg hurts forever where I kicked him."

Marl laughed loudly. She placed her little fingers to his lips. He kissed each tip. "I thought he was picking on you because he hates me. Seeing us kiss must've killed him." He took another swipe at her lips. "You insulted him twice."

***

They parted before the moon settled behind the trees. The shepherdess's house was on the north edge of the village, very near Etutsa's shack. A ragged-coat dog waited by the front door. It didn't bark, but it did run to Hereu and give her hand several licks.

"Hello, Broom. This is Marl. We like him." She gave her escort a last kiss before muttering goodnight. *Let's see where this goes.*

He let Wind laugh with his heart and carry him back home.

Mother was nestled into the chair by their cold hearth. Marl kissed her cheek. "Thank you."

Pilgrim was sleeping on top of Natsir's back. The cat looked comical rising and falling with his brother's varied breathing. The rhythm of their Blessed Unknowing made him realize his own fatigue.

Marl ripped off the blue coat before falling into his cot. Sleep never came, but he might as well have been dreaming, staring into the oak eyes of *his girl.*

A few hours later, a giant bear yawned and stretched, jumping out of his bed dressed. Marl closed his eyes, hoping to hold on to the night longer. Father stretched to his full height and strode over to Mother in the chair. "Good morning! That was the best sleep I've ever had." He leaned in to kiss his wife. "How are you, my lady?"

Mother struggled to pull herself out of the chair. *This is our punishment for mischievousness.* "I'm fine, love. I'm glad your headache has passed."

Father didn't notice her grimace. He bounded like Hereu's dog and slapped Marl on the shoulder. "Hey, son. I feel like I could take on the world today! Ready to get started?" He threw a pillow at Natsir. "Let's go, boys! Up and at 'em!"

Pilgrim hissed.

Mother lifted a wheel of cheese from a clay pot on the table and broke off two pieces. She handed them each a morsel. "You'd better hurry, Marl, if you're going to be at Etutsa's by sunrise."

Father stopped short before putting the cheese in his mouth and frowned. "Oh. I forgot. I take it you accepted the offer?"

"Yeah. I'd be stupid not to."

The old man stared, his lips quivering. "Right. Well, I'll walk you over."

Mother placed a hand on his shoulder. "Don't fuss, love. The boy can handle things himself. We'll see you tonight, sweetheart."

"Are you sure?"

Marl grinned and reached for his ill-fitting shoes. "Of course, Father. I'm a big boy. See you tonight!"

He ate the cheese as he ran. Light from Mother Sun gave him chase, following him across the pathways and tickling the tree tops.

A patch of charred ash and a few bottles were all that remained in the square. A gentle but resounding voice entered his thoughts as he past the oak, still lapping elderberry wine. *No, we don't get intoxicated. But we do enjoy watching you.*

Marl laughed. Trees must know everything.

When he reached Etutsa's shack, he knocked and tried to catch his breath.

The healer opened the door holding a wet cloth against his head. "Good heavens boy! Are you here for a remedy or are you here to learn?"

"Huh?"

"Well, look at you! Your eyes are blackened; your clothing's in tatters. What did you do last night, drink a bottle of wine?"

Marl laughed.

"I don't see anything funny, young man. I expect decorum of my apprentice."

"Of course, sir, but you *did* give me that bottle."

"Did I?" The healer slammed the door and recoiled. "I don't remember."

EIGHT

They met at the river. The warmth of summer days had long passed, and the air was crisp. There were few noises but for the occasional goose honk, rush of water, and waving canopy.

Nojhi loathed silence. It forced him to listen to his mortal body: stomach rumblings, lip smacks, and the beat of his temperamental heart. His thoughts were louder. Nothing was more tortuous than the space behind his eyes.

"Sorry, I'm late." Marl waved as he passed the warblers' tree. "Etutsa's shop's a mess. It'll take me suns to go through everything."

He hung his clean, brown doublet and white shirt on a branch. Etutsa had forced him to buy them. Marl had protested about the waste of coin, but Nojhi had to admit his son looked a respectable man now.

"That's better!" Marl clapped his hands, a habit picked up from the healer.

"Ready?"

The young healer accepted his weapon. "Of course! Let's go, old man."

Nojhi envied his son's energy. "Are you sure? Etutsa might've worn you out. What does he have you doing all day?"

"Awful stuff!" Marl's stick took on the force of a windmill. "Have you smelled his shack? I've thrown out half of it. I can't tell if it's all spoiled or nasty by principle."

Nojhi laughed and poked his ribs. The boy didn't flinch. "Yeah, he brings that stuff with him wherever he goes. Meetings at G'Nirac's are always…um…pungent."

Marl snickered. "I'm labeling things too." He took a stance and waited for Nojhi to copy. "Some of the remedies don't look familiar. *I* didn't find them in the forest when I was his errand boy."

He pounced, a fox on a vole. His blue eyes were wild with repression, eager to move, to exert his presence on the world.

"Does he ever let you out of that rabbit hole he calls a house?"

"Sometimes." Marl flashed a wicked smile. "I make deliveries."

I miss you, lad. An ache formed in Nojhi's chest. "Must be lonely. Etutsa's not talkative."

"It's not bad. People come by. He snaps when he's grumpy, but usually he's encouraging."

"Oh, good. So, you're happy?"

Marl stood at ease and stared. "I'm happy, Father. You're not worried, are you?"

"No. No. Just curious." He coughed and took another stance, eager to get back to something more manly than thoughts of his baby boy alone in the village every day. "You *are* staying out of trouble?"

"Um…yes!" *You would've heard. She's annoying. I can't concentrate with her yapping.*

Nojhi winced. He'd forgotten about Messa's lessons. She kept a constant connection to both boys. He gave Marl a smack on the backside. "Be nice to your poor mother. I know the lessons aren't fun, but they're necessary. You've the gift. Think how hard it was for me."

Marl uncrossed his arms and stared. *Hey! How did you learn to do this?*

Practice. Nojhi wagged his stick. "Like sword play. Anyone can do it. Some are better than others."

"I'm surprised you didn't run screaming." Marl scratched his head and kicked dirt. "Hope the girl I marry doesn't care, but I wouldn't blame her if she found it terrifying."

Marriage! Where'd that come from? "Well, you don't have to tell her, I suppose. You're mother and I were different." Nojhi rubbed his beard. "You got a girl in mind?"

Marl jumped and stammered. "Um, no! I've been thinking on Nat and Para." He tapped the rod against his leg and ruffled his hair with his free hand. "How's his picture coming?"

Nojhi took the bait. He'd get the information later. "It's great! He's adding a horse to it!"

"Bet he's stalling. Knew he'd get nervous." Marl beamed.

"Nah, you know your brother. He's declared his decision. It's done. He just takes forever to get going! I guess he's a better man than us. He takes his time to make it right."

"Speak for yourself! Para's going to fade into dust waiting. At least I don't hesitate."

"That can be a dangerous talent to have, son."

"You think I'm *dangerous*?" Marl's eyes widened. His exposed skin took on a greenish hue.

The question and the strange reaction threw Nojhi off-guard. *Nothing fazes him! Shatter the stars!* He embraced his boy. "I don't think *you're* dangerous. Not thinking before you act is."

Forget it.

I wish I could read him like Messa. Nojhi gave his son's shoulders an affectionate shake. "Why don't we go into town? There's an elders meeting. We could mull around until then."

"Fine by me." Marl made off for Na-ir.

"Hey wait up. You can't go half naked."

The boy mumbled. He retrieved his shirt and struggled to pull it on.

Nojhi wanted to goad him. "But… if your lady prefers you that way, then…"

"Shut up!" Marl's crow-feathered head surfaced before his blue look of death. He didn't bother to fasten the doublet's buttons.

Nojhi laughed. *There's my son!*

The hike to the village was pleasant. Na-ir's new healer was a wealth of information. Yarrow and golden seal were excellent ways to combat colds and fevers. Willow bark was a tremendous help with pain, also good for the heart. Something called burdock was popular for treating youthful blemishes, among other things. The most popular remedy among the girls was wild carrot seeds.

"What's it do?"

Marl blushed and pursed his lips. "Well… their fathers wouldn't be happy with them."

"Oh. Oh!" Nojhi's stomach jumped. "Don't marry one of those girls. I'm surprised Etutsa doesn't tattle on the lot of them."

"He says idiots will be idiots no matter what. I think he doesn't want to be caught in a fight."

"Etutsa, a peace seeker! That snippy fellow!" Nojhi guffawed as they entered the village.

Marl's pace quickened when they neared a small cottage. A hairy, cream-colored dog sitting in the yard waved its tail. Nojhi gave it a pat, but the boy didn't slow until they were well past Etutsa's shack.

"Hold up, lad! What's wrong? Afraid he'll pull you back into his shop?"

Marl ran a hand through his hair. "Sorry. I've got a lot on my mind."

"Let's have a treat."

Despite his instance to pay, his son placed two copper coins on the counter. Sucking on charred flesh, they leaned against the side of the butcher's shop and watched villagers pass by doing villager-like things. Scruffy children rolled around in the dust chasing after bladder balls.

"So, what've you been thinking about?"

"Nothing!" Marl startled and wiped his hands on his britches.

A small, tanned girl in a tattered, green dress sauntered by. She was carrying a bleating, black lamb. She stopped to look at the black-haired boy before scurrying away.

"You told me you've a lot on your mind. *Nothing* doesn't weigh that much."

Marl groaned. He slid to the ground and rested his face in his open palms, his elbows propped on his legs.

Nojhi sat down too. There were few things that could make his son this nervous. "You sound like Nat tormented about Para," he teased, wrapping an arm over the boney shoulders.

"Why do you have to be obnoxious? You could ask Mother. She knows everything!"

He removed his arm and threw it around his own neck, embarrassed. "I already did. She told me I was being obnoxious and to shut up."

The ends of Marl's mouth twitched. "Serves you right."

Nojhi made a silly face.

The boy erupted in snickers. "All right! It's a girl!"

"I was right. How'd that happen?" He sat back and contemplated every young lady his son might fancy. A certain blond woman stood out, if only because Messa had mentioned her before. "Don't tell me it's Nerid."

Marl grimaced. *Um, no. She's one of those girls.*

Nojhi stared.

THOSE girls, Marl emphasized, moving his head mockingly. *Carrot seeds.*

The recollection caught Nojhi square in the throat and he coughed. He was half tempted to ask who Nerid shared this transgression with.

Don't tell Bolar. She might think I'm getting revenge.

Nojhi thought of Nerid's forester father. He'd stick to Etutsa's plan of action for such issues. *Revenge for what?*

Marl didn't answer. He nodded to two ladies in the alleyway. They giggled as he dusted his britches.

Anyone you know?

"Nope."

"Well, you're going to have to tell me sometime."

"Not likely."

"Oh come on! You're driving me mad. You know I don't like secrets."

A black eyebrow rose.

"I'm going to pester you until Father Moon falls from the sky. You might as well talk now."

"Go pester Nat, please." Marl marched into the square, fists clenched.

Nojhi chased after. "But Natsir doesn't need me," he whined.

Marl opened his mouth and shut it again.

They looked down on their shadows, long and definite, but not as powerful as the pillar's shadow between them. The sky shifted to orange. It was time for Nojhi to take his obligations elsewhere.

"Suppose this falls under the privacy issue. I'll leave you alone."

They bumped fists. "I'm holding you to that, old man. See you tonight." Marl ran, black hair bobbing like a bird bathing in a puddle.

"Wait! Where are you going now?"

Marl smiled. His open doublet pulsed, great brown wings, and he flew away.

My little crow. Is he flying to the woods or the meadow? Why did I concede to Messa's stupid privacy request? It's rubbish. A man has a right to know what his son is doing.

He took a deep breath and resigned himself to try and forget it. A handsome and mischievous young man might have many admirers—slim chance he'd fall for them all. But every maiden Nojhi passed looked like a potential daughter-in-law.

I'm getting old if this is the biggest thing to bother me now. He rounded the corner to G'Nirac's. *But this will be my daughter someday.* "Hello, Para, love."

Her pale blue eyes met his and radiated happiness. "Good afternoon, Mister Ganwin. You're early, but my father is waiting for you inside."

She was wearing her green riding gloves and her boots were muddy. Red hair fanned out, unkempt, but as beautiful as the visage in the drawing. Her dappled cheeks were flushed.

Para pulled off her gloves and sat down to remove her boots. "Do you know where Nat might be?"

Nojhi scratched his beard. The answer should've been obvious. After twenty suns, Para knew all of Natsir's haunts. "If he's not with you, he's at the cottage."

"Oh. I think he's hiding." She kicked her feet against the porch and sighed.

"Unlikely. He'd follow you anywhere." Nojhi wanted to tell her the truth, but Marl had already shown him that meddling in these affairs was pointless. "I'll let him know you're looking for him. He's probably distracted." *Or waiting for her birthday.*

Para gave him a tender hug and motioned for him to follow her into the house.

Men cackled at G'Nirac's table, but stood to attention when they entered. *Must've been a rude conversation.*

Para embraced her uncle and said pleasant hellos to the rest of the men before leaving to change out of her windswept clothes. As soon as the room was without a female, Lortews coughed into his sleeve and pointed to a chair. Nojhi squeezed in next to the baker near the wall.

"I'm not the only one early today." He looked around the room. G'Nirac wasn't present, but there were two empty chairs waiting. "Is there any news?"

"Oh yes." Etutsa waved his quill. "You're going to love it." He scribbled something on the parchment.

Retat fumbled with meaty hands and smiled at Nojhi. "Your boy looks well."

The healer shifted into the butcher. Retat cried out and rubbed his hand on one broad thigh.

Nojhi leaned into the table and fixed his eyes on his friend. "What's Marl done now?"

Everyone stared at the healer.

"Not a damn thing. Hiring him was the best decision I ever made. He eats little, talks less, and takes direction well. Makes me wish I'd had a son."

"You're teasing. My son wouldn't take direction if you told him his path would lead to certain death with a hot poker."

Everyone chuckled.

"Why would I tease?" Etutsa clutched his chest and pouted.

"Marl says you snap."

"He snaps at everyone, friend." Lortews snickered. The others grumbled in agreement.

"Forgive me, friends. I've been out of sorts of late." Etutsa threw down his quill and sighed. "I spend my days subject to village problems, all the gossip I can stomach, and my brother's demands. It leaves a sour pit in me. I can't help it if some vitriol spews your way. It's a symptom of the disease known as healer."

Nojhi had a vision of Etutsa's bile, bottled and smelling of spoiled bread dough. He felt sorry for Marl having to label it. *Or catching this disease!* That was a horrible thought. "Understood. We appreciate you, but consider how your *disease* might spread if you're not careful."

Tears welled in Etutsa's eyes.

"Also, I don't see why your temper should mean Retat can't compliment my handsome son." Nojhi pulled the whiskers of his blond beard and winked. The company, save for Namnor and Etutsa, burst into raucous laughter. "Besides, I already know about his girl if that's what you're trying to hide."

Every man in the room jumped. Nojhi jumped last, startled by their reaction.

"You do?"

Retat stared at Lortews. Lortews at Etutsa. Namnor stared at the floor. Daerth twiddled his thumbs.

"Stars and mountains! You'd think I'd declared a moratorium on love! I'm happy for him. I just wish I knew who she was."

"Oh," Etutsa stammered. "Yes. We all do too."

Unable to take the uncomfortable situation, Lortews made the situation more unbearable. "Namnor! How's your daughter?"

Nojhi gave the man a less-than-gentle pat on the back of the head. The fat baker let out yelp and shrank into his seat.

For once, the blacksmith answered. "Yimette's fine. She wrote to me last week. They've moved out of Mirot though." He pulled his grey beard. Losing his eldest daughter had been a terrible blow. "My grandchild will be born soon. It's been quiet at home."

"We're sorry, Nam," Daerth consoled and placed a hand against the blacksmith's back.

"Don't be. It's my own fault. I protested against the idea of her marrying a soldier. She took me seriously. I was just trying to keep her from danger."

"As any father would," shouted Retat. "Don't blame yourself friend."

"I was a soldier," Nojhi noted.

"Ah, yes. But the one you love now doesn't pace the floor worrying if you'll come home."

He understood. Yimette's willingness to take this risk was breaking her father's heart. It made sense the one man in the town who had the ability to manufacture weapons would fear the use of them most.

"At least we're not at war. That stupidity is long past us," the baker remarked.

Footsteps tapped in the doorway. "I'm sorry to say, but war may be upon us again if we're not careful."

G'Nirac entered the room with his son. The grey and white of his hair and beard were duller than usual. They took their seats and surveyed the attendants.

"I apologize for keeping you waiting."

"You're too late. Everyone's already depressed," Etutsa remarked.

G'Nirac ignored his brother and folded his hands. "I've received word from Onaryc. He's made up his mind to attack Selcovi."

"What?" Every man stood to attention.

"Is he out of his mind?" Namnor shouted, wringing his hands for the sake of his daughter.

"He's resolved. I tried to persuade him to forgo this ridiculous scheme, but he thinks he must act or Enisnus will. She's given him an ultimatum—release the rights to his water and his army, or his chiefdom will fall."

Nojhi sat back down and sighed. Enisnus had a way of forcing people's hands. She was tall, formidable, and more stubborn than any man on earth. "She must be playing with him, hoping he'll give her what she wants without much effort on her part." The company looked to him, their faces wan with fear. "She's underestimating him, I think."

"I think you're right, friend." G'Nirac frowned. "She's too much faith in her father's legacy and not enough of it to go around. Onaryc's army is as well-trained as he is stubborn." He shook his head. "The delegation to Selcovi didn't go well, I'm afraid. The city might collapse. The summer was dreadful. There are no protections in Selcovi; no fortifications as we'd supposed. They'll all be slaughtered."

"I've never been so shocked by a place before," said Lufnis.

"Rayr wasn't receptive?" Nojhi was shocked. His old friend had never been unreasonable.

"King Rayr is a reasonable man. He knows the suffering of his people. He welcomed our offer to help with provisions. He didn't believe other chiefdoms would make the same offers. We're one of the few villages not scorched by drought or disease."

Etutsa grumbled. "So, what you're telling us is that Na-ir may continue to grow, until we too succumb to the excess."

"No, little brother. I don't think so. I'm content as we are now. If others come knocking at my door, I'll turn them away. I won't hurt *my* people. We can't save them all."

"What about Onaryc's war? Surely we'll not take sides. What does Rayr intend to do?"

G'Nirac sighed. "It's difficult to tell. Some say Rayr leaves those matters to his sister. Others say he's no military strategy at all. He feels his time is better spent building wells. I agree, but I don't think appointing Enisnus as his general is wise. She's broken." He cast Nojhi a meaningful glance.

I know. It's all my doing.

Etutsa pounded the table. "There isn't a copper's worth of sense between them. Supplies must be had for war. Protection must be had for the people to cultivate land and resources. Why do the two of them sit on such different thrones?"

"For the same reason you and I disagree on many things, brother. They're siblings. What they lack is cohesion." G'Nirac placed his hands on the table and shuddered. "I can't promise this ridiculous skirmish won't reach us, but I've told both Onaryc and Rayr I don't intend for our people to fight. We're farmers and ranchers. The Telmah don't have it in us."

Nojhi remembered another tribe who'd refused to fight for and against the Mlaerians. "We can't sit by and watch while they approach our borders. You know they will if this escalates. Our men may be forced to fight to defend this village."

"We can't fight," squeaked Daerth. "None of us knows how."

"Wrong! I can train any able man willing to learn." Nojhi turned back to the chieftain. "You know this is true. My son could fight circles around anyone if he had to. Namnor can manufacture weapons. Let's prepare for the inevitable."

G'Nirac contemplated this offer and nodded. "I understand your worry, my friend, but I don't think it's wise. If we start a small militia of our own, it'll look suspicious and may invite an attack. I think it would incite fear as well. Your offer to teach them is admirable. You of all men would see to it this village was safe, but I believe you would do this without an army."

"G'Nirac... I..."

The chieftain held up his hand. "What would it look like to Rayr? I tell him we're peaceful; I swear we'll not get involved. Yet, one day his soldiers come down here from Mirot on their patrols to find our villagers wielding swords, led by a man named Ganwin! Enisnus would be suspicious."

I'm not a child. I know the risks.

Etutsa threw down his quill. "I'll stand with you. I'm not a coward. If Onaryc comes for vengeance, he'll be the first to feel my fist."

G'Nirac wiped a withered hand across his face. "Brother, Onaryc's men would have your stubborn head on a pike before he rode his horse through Na-ir. But I think he won't stray far from his holdings, especially with Enisnus salivating over his water."

The men sat in silence. Some tapped or kicked on the table.

Nojhi didn't agree. *He can't even see the offences of his own son! What if he's wrong?*

Onaryc was capable of anything and demanded everything from his subjects and his loved ones. G'Nirac's refusal to take sides might be seen as a great act of betrayal, worthy of punishment. Water flowing into Na-ir did so by the grace of the Dasha. The dam was Lafret's greatest pride.

"I want to reason with him, as warriors. There has to be a way to resolve this."

"Are you mad?" Lortews shouted. "He'll hang you by your heels and beat you! He'll deliver you to Enisnus in a heartbeat. He'll..." The baker stopped short before saying what they all knew was inevitable: Onaryc would kill Nojhi.

G'Nirac stood and straightened out his back. His face remained still and resigned, but his tree-bark eyes blazed. "I forbid this!"

He slammed his fist on the table as the old warrior stood to challenge his authority. The company jumped.

"No! There will never be a time in which I tolerate such a meeting. Ever! He doesn't know you're alive. If you set foot in that canyon, everything about this place will cease to exist!" G'Nirac took deep, rasping breaths and fell, clutching his heart.

"Father!" Lufnis jumped to catch him.

"Radiant Mother!" Etutsa pulled a small bag from his pocket and measured some white shavings onto his brother's tongue. He forced G'Nirac's mouth shut until the remedy had dissolved into his saliva.

Willow bark. Nojhi choked. *Have I killed the old man? Has his heart had all it could stand?*

After some minutes, G'Nirac regained his composure. Lufnis helped him to his seat.

Etutsa placed a hand on his forehead and sighed. "You need rest, brother."

"I won't rest until every man here understands my position." His face contorted. "I need your solemn oath, old warrior—no armies, no Dasha."

Was this what it was like to watch your father near the Gates of the Passageway? Nojhi choked back tears. "All right. I promise, old friend. Please don't be troubled."

"All of you," G'Nirac snapped. "All of you swear."

Every man save for Etutsa mumbled their allegiance. The healer held on to his brother's wrist, pretending to count heart beats. "Are you finished?"

"Yes, brother. I'm ready to accept your advice. I'll rest."

Lufnis tried to carry his father out of the kitchen, but G'Nirac waved him away. "Stay. Finish the meeting without me. You still have news to share."

They called for Para. When she entered the room, her speckled face turned whiter than Marl's new shirt. She sobbed, her hands clasped to her mouth.

"Don't fret, my girl," G'Nirac groaned as he tried to stand. "I need some rest. Take me to my room."

As soon as they were gone, they sat as one, creating a reverberating tremor in the table. G'Nirac wasn't well and they weren't ready to let go.

"I'm worried about him," Lufnis shivered.

His uncle gave him an affectionate pat. "I know, boy. All things must pass." He shuffled his papers. A tear fell to the parchment, mingling with the ink. Etutsa needed his brother more than any man in that room. G'Nirac was his remedy. "Let's cheer up. Rac will be fine after some rest." He forced a smile. "Tell them your news."

"It hardly feels the time…" Lufnis twiddled his fingers. "I'm getting married."

"Well, at least it's good news!" Retat barked and pulled a cloth from his pocket to wipe his brow. "Blessings on your union, boy."

Lortews stumbled over felicitations. "We're happy for you. Who's the girl?"

Etutsa took pity on his nephew. "Her name is Eurgi, the daughter of a carpenter from Selcovi. To be clear, this was the news I declared you would all love."

No one chuckled. They all stared at the table. Namnor tapped it. "When's the wedding?"

"Forgive me. In two weeks. We want to marry before the frost comes."

Nojhi tried to hide his disappointment. "That's Para's birthday, isn't it?"

"Ah, yes." Lufnis shuffled in his seat. "My sister has been most gracious."

Etutsa let a bitter mumble slip from his lips. "She's probably glad she doesn't have to wash your clothes anymore! Oh! I'm sorry boy. I didn't mean… Oh."

"Don't trouble yourself, uncle. Para has been a constant source of comfort. I understand all she does for us. I hope my Eurgi will be of some help to her."

Retat ran a finger along the grain. "You know, your friend Rej will be married. I overheard his mother discussing the matter with Toren. Nerid's quiet a girl too."

"Good!" Nojhi shouted before he could stop himself.

The company looked confused.

"I mean… it's good they're settling down."

The healer gave him a knowing smirk.

"I'm startled by how many of our children are courting and marrying of late. They're so young!" Lortews exclaimed.

"I'm not," barked Etutsa. "Some two decades ago, you were all young and stupid. You got married, produced several little runts for me to take care of, and now they're repeating the cycle. The creature called man won't be eradicated any time soon."

The mood changed. The healer's vitriol was sometimes necessary medicine.

Daerth made a face. "What a horrible thought, Etutsa. Eradicated!"

The healer shrugged. "We'll I suppose we should all trudge out of here. I've too much work to chat with you layabouts."

Everyone fled, slapping the engaged man on the back or shaking his hand. Etutsa patted him on the head and strolled out.

Nojhi was the last to leave. "I wish you much happiness."

"Thank you, Mister Ganwin. I appreciate your kind words. It's a pity your sons haven't found it." Something like hate suddenly smoldered behind Lufnis's eyes.

"They're young yet."

"Ah, yes. Still young. They would make poor husbands now."

Nojhi clenched his fists. "There's nothing wrong with my sons!"

A glimpse of red brought him out of the rage. Para strolled past the door, carrying a small basin.

"You should pay a visit to Selcovi, Mister Ganwin. You'll find the Moon Tree interesting."

"What's that supposed to mean?"

Lufnis smiled his badger smile. "Most of your friends are there. It might do you good to relive old times. Good night." He went after the girl. "An answer must be given," he hissed behind the door.

Para glowered. "Leave me alone. It's not your decision to make."

Nojhi had seen enough. A horrible thought reverberated through him as he slammed the front door. *If G'Nirac dies, that manipulative cur will be chieftain.*

NINE

It was difficult to leave Oak Hollow. Holding Hereu under its boughs was Marl's most cherished part of each day. The world was theirs in those dusky moments—calm and pure.

Things changed when he left her side.

Mother cried out as he took his first step onto the porch. Marl rushed to her aid, but there was nothing he could do. She was tucked into Father's lap on their bed. Her tears covered the old man's shirt.

"What's happened?"

"Hey, son." Father looked wretched.

Marl took a seat and waited, balancing on two wooden legs.

Mother moaned. "Promise me. Promise me."

"I've already promised. G'Nirac made me." *He practically killed himself to get me to swear! Don't break my heart too. Hush, love. It's all right.*

It was strange hearing Father's thoughts. Marl didn't have permission. *I need to learn to block other minds.* He decided to speak lest Father think something private again. "What did you promise?"

"Onaryc's going to declare war on Selcovi. I've promised not to get involved."

Marl's chair landed with a smack. "That's the most dishonorable thing I've ever heard. What a darkened cur!"

Mother leapt into his arms. "My sweet son. Always a protector of the weak."

Father shook his head. "He's within his rights to attack. The princess has singled the Dasha out and declared they must bear the brunt of Artnaus's problems. No other tribe has been treated in this way. Enisnus is bringing this on Selcovi, and Rayr is doing nothing to stop it."

Marl felt sick. "Stars and mountains! Still doesn't make it right. A starving dog is placated with kindness more than aggression."

"Yes, son, but Enisnus will bite you after you've thrown her the cut of beef."

"Surely some agreement can be made?" Mother dabbed her apron on her eyes.

"I'd love the chance to reason with Onaryc, but G'Nirac is right." Father ran his hand through his hair and lay back on the bed. "I'd cause more trouble for this village than a war."

"Why?"

Marl's parents stiffened.

"Well, there are a lot of people who hate me. I wasn't always the sort of person I am now."

"You're a darkened cur! What were you like before?" Marl eyed his father.

"A lot like you, little crow. Thought I could do anything. Careful who you cross, boy."

Mother sat down. "So what happens now?"

"It'll take moons for Onaryc to prepare. G'Nirac wants us to sit here, but I'm worried things might escalate. If other tribes side with the Dasha, we may be forced to decide."

"What do you think we should do?" Marl was feeling vigorous, eager to defend his village.

"Depends on who forces our hand. The Telmah have ties to the Mlaerians and the Dasha. There's no clear allegiance accept that Rayr is our king." Father shrugged. "We'll have to obey G'Nirac and ignore it. The threat alone may force Enisnus to give up."

"I'll never watch this town fall." There were too many people Marl wanted to protect.

"Good man! We'll do what we can. Even if it's just you, me, and Natsir."

Mother grimaced. "My people believe in doing the least amount of harm possible. Some think that means letting whatever happens happen. But you and I both know that doesn't always work."

Father looked to the floor.

"You would fight, Mother? How?"

She smiled wickedly, dark secrets concealed in her white teeth. "There are many things I can do that would boggle your mind. I'll boggle a few Dasha soldiers too."

***

Natsir returned home well after Father Moon had risen. Marl poked his arm as he passed. *What've you been up to?*

The eldest glanced to the rising and falling forms of their parents and sat on the bed. *I was with Para, baby brother. Mother knew. Father told me she was looking for me.*

I know, but you're the last person I'd think to sneak home in the middle of the night. Marl leaned in close, flashing a mischievous grin. *Moonlit strolls are romantic. What was her answer?*

I was comforting her. Natsir frowned. *Lufnis is being disagreeable again.*

Seriously? Marl ran his hand through his hair. *Lufnis is always disagreeable.*

He's marrying Eurgi.

Marl stuck his finger down his throat and pretended to vomit. That union was the product of everything nasty and evil. The noise made Father stir.

Natsir grabbed his hand. *Don't be childish.*

I'll be whatever I want to be.

Little brother, please.

Pilgrim stole past a patch of light. The great glowing eyes regarded them with interest.

Natsir grimaced and turned away. *Rippan's also asked for Para's hand. Lufnis is trying to force her decision.*

And you told her not to choose him? Marl tussled his hair.

Natsir kicked the floorboards. *Why should I tell her how to think?*

"Gah!" Marl clasped his hand to his mouth. This time Mother stirred. *Because you love her, idiot! Rescue her. Sweep her off her feet! Be a darkened man for once!*

I am a man. And that plan sounds too aggressive. Para can make her own decisions. She doesn't need a rescuer. She needs a companion. It's her choice who that is.

Pilgrim elicited a painful meow and took a shaky leap onto the bed. He rubbed his greying cheeks against Natsir's calloused hands. *Might I interject here?*

No, Marl snickered, still slightly grumpy. *We're not ready to have kittens.*

Two small moons shone against ash-dark fur. An arthritic tail smacked him in the nose. *I know more than you realize. No one ever thinks to ask the cat.*

Natsir stroked the bony backside. *Tell us, wise one. Who's right?*

Pilgrim's fur bristled. He leaned into the massage, giving a raspy purr. *I find the Gifted One's sentiments to be sound and noble, but I regret I must side with the loud, crude one.*

"Ha!" Marl shout-whispered. *Wait! That was rude.*

The cat hummed.

You think my baby brother is right? Why?

Pilgrim yawned and pawed the sheets, tearing threads into little nooses. *Did it ever occur to you she's already made her decision, but she isn't certain you have? Sometimes it pays to be obvious. Why do you think cats yowl? Announce your intentions.*

Natsir's jaw dropped. He turned away, bowed his head, and put his hands together.

Marl fought the urge to giggle. Hereu would probably punch him if he yowled.

The black beast licked his nose with one bright tongue. *See, cats can be wise. Ask me anything?*

All right, Pilgrim. I was going to ask Nat, but maybe you'll have better advice. I want to declare my intentions. What should I give Hereu?

Easy. He slumped from the bed, flicking his tail. *Give her something that smells nice.*

Marl spent the rest of the night trying not to chortle while Natsir moaned in his bed. He knew his brother would figure out what to do eventually. He resolved to stay out of it. He had his own love to please.

What could he get Hereu that smelled nice? Pilgrim had made some suggestions: grass, a fish, or a dead mouse. He imagined the look on her face as he handed over packages of these feline delicacies.

She'd definitely punch me.

His favorite smell was apple blossom. He had no way of capturing such things, though. Grass did have an invigorating smell, especially after the rain. Last storm, Hereu had been a barefoot fairytale sprite.

It has to be like her: sweet and free.

***

Marl's existence reached an exhilarating climax. Mother and Father spent more time worrying about Onaryc and G'Nirac to bother him. All lessons had halted, although Mother checked in on him occasionally and Father mused over the idea of creating the family army.

Etutsa was less strict, often sharing jokes and little portions of his colorful history for their amusement.

The best development was that Hereu was growing more accustomed to his antics. She didn't put up with much, but what she did left small marks on the back of her neck, concealed behind her mass of curly, brown hair.

Two days after his discussion with Natsir and Pilgrim, he was fortunate to find a perfect treasure.

The end of Etutsa's clutter had been reached. The floor was visible. The bed was usable. He'd even built more shelving, now nailed into the walls. There was only one place he hadn't scoured.

Marl moved the bed. A tiny, blue vial rested along the dusty wall. He took a rag to the dirt and then to the bottle. It shimmered and radiated, ripples in a pond.

Accustomed to smelling anything now, he removed the stopper and wafted the vapors. *Apple blossom!* He couldn't believe his luck. There was something else too. He placed the bottle under his nose. It was earthy and wet. *Like rain!*

The healer was bent over a collection of plant materials, working hard to pulverize them into something easier to ingest.

"Where did this come from?"

The old man squinted and raised a grey eyebrow. "I thought I'd lost that. Where'd you find it?"

Marl gestured to the bed.

"Ah! My old bones can barely open the door. I don't bother the bed." Etutsa held the bottle between two fingers. "This was payment for services to a traveling dancer some suns ago."

"Services?" Marl tried to imagine Etutsa, with darker hair and an easier disposition, being dapper with a woman in many colorful skirts covered in tiny bells. The dancers were stars walking out of a dream.

The healer smiled. "Nothing like that. Her mother was sick. But she had nothing to pay me, so she gave me this. A silly thing for an old man to keep, don't you think?" He bounced the bottle and laughed. "I'd meant to give it to Para."

"Oh," Marl couldn't hide his disappointment. It had been so perfect, he'd assumed it was fate. "I'm sure she'll love it."

Etutsa placed it on the table and folded his hands into a ball. "It's worth eight coppers. I'll let you have it for four. Para hates patchouli anyway."

The apprentice produced the required payment and stowed his treasure in his pocket.

"No more chitchat. We have much to do!"

Marl's wolfish teeth gleamed. "But I've finished!"

The healer whirled on his chair. "Stars on high, boy! My house is clean!" He walked around, running his fingers on surfaces. "It hasn't looked like this in suns. I'm very impressed."

He gathered a couple of amber jars and plopped them on the table. Marl fidgeted. If the bottles crashed, he would spend the rest of the day cleaning.

"Right! Now! Let's get started on the real work. Take this aloe and press out the juice for me. It's good for burns. Well… you know." Etutsa handed him several green fronds. He produced a mort and pestle to demonstrate. "Push out as much as you can and place it in this jar."

"Where'd you get aloe this season?" Marl was eager to start on the real tasks of a healer, although he'd been eavesdropping for moons.

"I've been growing it in a clay pot out back. I've moved it under the desk now that it's cold. My fat backside in this chair hides it."

Marl resisted the urge to laugh and pressed out the pungent goop.

"It's nice to have something for little ones who burn themselves on the winter fires. There are other measures, but for minor burns, this stuff is helpful." Etutsa returned to his powdered substance and pushed aside the moss.

Marl looked around the cabin. Something essential was missing. The healer would never run the risk of burning himself on a hearth here. "How do you stay warm?"

"When I was younger, I weathered it under blankets, but now I sleep at Rac's."

"Why don't you live there always? This shack isn't very sturdy." Marl wiped a drop of aloe from his hands on the rim of his bottle.

"Ah, Rac and I can't bear each other's company. It's better if we keep our distance."

Marl grinned. The subject of older brothers united them. "Nat doesn't always understand me either."

Etutsa tapped the powder into a wooden box on his desk. He was pulverizing willow bark. Marl had never seen him do this before. Was this some new method to control dosage?

"Yes," the old man continued. "But you and Natsir don't have the problems Rac and I have. Siblings always disagree, but most often, they forgive. I'm unable to... completely."

Marl tried to lighten the mood. "But you're such a magnanimous person."

Etutsa's laughter turned into a raspy cough. "Oh, shut up! I know I'm a cur." He pounded his chest. "No, the blame's on me. I wanted something I couldn't have."

Marl pushed too hard on an aloe frond and jumped as some of the juice splattered. "What?"

"What else? Love." Etutsa dropped his pestle on the table and turned, oblivious to the mess for the shimmer in his eyes.

"You were in love?" Marl wiggled in his seat. "Was it the street dancer?"

The old man blushed. "I was too decrepit by then. No, I've loved two women, but they were already taken." He stared into the pulverized willow bark and sighed. "The first was Para's mother."

A stone pestle hit the table and rolled onto the bridge of Marl's foot. He winced and hissed to drive away the sting before bending over to retrieve it. "Seriously?"

Etutsa nodded and sighed, ready to tell his tale.

Blessed to be the irresponsible, younger son, Etutsa was free to spend most days chasing after the red-haired Laedi. They were inseparable, always on the cusp of loving. But something caused a rift in their friendship. Etutsa refused to say what it was.

Marl was afraid to ask. He sat there, mouth agape, and marveled at their similar circumstances.

Etutsa left Na-ir—with no money and no skills. "I ran away. It was foolish. I went to Selcovi, and then to other outlying towns. I was miserable. But a healer in

Thronren took me in and taught me everything. He convinced me to return home. I trusted his advice, so I did." His return wasn't met with jubilation. The family had disowned him. "I paid for my pride. The worst part was that Laedi had married G'Nirac. She thought I was dead! I put her heart through something vile. By then, Lufnis had already come."

Marl shivered and tried to concentrate on their tasks. It was hard to imagine someone beautiful and sweet, the same visage of Para, being the mother of something as despicable as Lufnis. *I already know she dies! Where's the end of this terrible story?*

Etutsa didn't seem to notice Marl's discomfort. He continued with the misty look of one who was no longer on earth but somewhere more complicated.

"G'Nirac forgave me and gave me this shack and the means to begin my practice. At first, villagers avoided me and my strange medicines. I put my heart into this practice, trying to avoid the hole in my soul. But I was forced to confront everything the night Para came into the world.

She was early, like the winter, and it was cold and merciless outside. G'Nirac was traveling so Laedi begged me to stay. She was weak and Lufnis was too young to be of any help. I was of little used to her too."

A tear rolled down the healer's cheek and into the willow powder.

"Her heart gave out. Like someone snuffing a candle. I'll never forget the look on Lufnis's face as I held his bloody sister. When G'Nirac returned, he found one life traded for another. I don't think either of them can forgive me."

Marl swallowed and placed his hand into his pocket. The little bottle full of joy felt reassuring in his palm. "You didn't do anything wrong. You were there for her. Para wouldn't be here without you."

Etutsa pulled him into a gentle embrace. "I know I told you too much, but you'll have to see things, boy. It's not all burns and sniffles. There can be more blood, more sorrow than imaginable. A healer must face the ridicule for failure as much as the praise for success." He was old and wise again.

"I understand." They were warriors of another fashion, fighting invisible battles.

They finished their preparations in silence. It was hard to concentrate on the present when the past had been so intense. Marl pitied the man, but surged with pride. He hadn't given up on life. He'd learned from his mistakes. There must've been some forgiveness between the brothers. They were both still here.

Light from Mother Sun crept in from the west. Etutsa gathered their work and placed the bottles back on the shelves. "This whole place is new again. Tell you what. Why don't you take tomorrow off? I think we both could use a break from all of this." He coaxed Marl outside.

"Thank you, Et..." The door shut before he could wave goodbye. *Good night.*

Marl was supposed to meet Hereu at Oak Hollow, but the sad tale of a man in pain made him feel less than romantic. Halfway through his stride to the forest, Marl turned around and headed for home. He'd visit Hereu tomorrow in the meadow.

I hope Nat doesn't make the same mistake Etutsa did.

On second thought, he didn't want to return to the cottage either; Father would notice his silence and prod him for an explanation. He turned west into the brambles and made his way to the river.

Marl pulled out the little blue bottle and unstopped it. The aroma meshed with his thoughts and carried him to warmth and light.

Secrets and unspoken intentions—pride—those had been the downfall of the Sinbels. It wasn't the tragedy of Laedi's death; unvoiced anger and regret had made them falter. *I hate secrets. I hate lies. What good do they do?*

He tucked the bottle back into his pocket. The smell of the cold river, wet soil with a hint of fish, slapped his mind awake.

Etutsa had mentioned two women. The previous owner of the bottle wasn't one of them. Laedi's story was heartbreaking. *What happened to the other girl? Was she from Thronren?* His curiosity got the better of him. *Mother? Are you there?*

Hello, sweetheart.

He found the gentle response reassuring. Marl had told Father that she was annoying, but that was for the old man's benefit. In truth, he was enjoying the shared connection. She was a constant source of information and comfort. After all, she'd seen the good in him and allowed him to venture out to the town. If it weren't for her, he'd have no one to give the little bottle to.

You know everything about the villagers don't you?

No, love. Etutsa told you something personal. I'm sorry it upset you.

Marl tossed a pebble. It made a satisfying plop. *I'm glad he did. But I'm curious.*

About the other woman? I'm afraid that was me.

"What!" Marl hit his head on the bottom branch of a willow. *What!* Rage flush his cheeks. He clutched his stomach, fighting the urge to vomit. *How could you?*

Excuse me. Mother's tone was as accusatory as his. *I turned him down, obviously.*

The charge of infidelity tore a rift between them. Marl could feel the scar form as the mental knife severed their already fragile bond. He'd no right to be angry with her; she'd told the truth. But he *was* angry. All pity for Etutsa pushed to the back of his heart. *Why hasn't Father torn out his spine?*

They're friends. It doesn't matter. Etutsa told me the truth. I respect him.

You should tell Father. These secrets were a violent storm. He wished Wind would blow them away.

His real mother was in no mood to pamper tonight. *No. I don't think so.*

This wasn't a disagreement, but a mandate. Marl had overreached. But he couldn't put aside the foreboding. *We should tell Father a lot of things. There are things I should tell you too. Did you hear me?*

Yes. I'd rather not discuss anything now. Please be home before dark.

The familiar connection that had always been a part of his soul was missing; he could feel the loss like a gash in his neck. Her loving watch on him was gone. The hole made him bitter.

I'm tired of running away from problems!

He climbed into the willow tree and fondled the vines, trying not to cry. *Father Moon*, he called into the canopy. The ancient god of night hadn't yet risen, but he needed someone to offer him some reassurance. *Please guide me.*

***

Marl. Wake!

The healer's apprentice opened his eyes from a tormented rest to see a woman-like thing smiling from a branch overhead. She was draped in chains of yellow leaves swaying across a convincing body of red earth. Her iridescent hair moved and shimmered with a pleasant dampness as her slender fingers fluttered in a caress around his cheek. Never had he seen something lovelier and more terrifying.

Greetings, child.

Marl recognized the buzzing, fluid sound of his old playmate, but this countenance left him speechless. She wasn't an innocent, invisible fairytale, a figment of his adolescent mind, but something mature and dangerous: both alluring and horrible. He stammered, unable to look into those hollow, night-black eyes.

She cooed like a human woman patting a kitten. *Don't be frightened. I'm here because your heart begged for someone to ease the pain, to show you the way.*

Marl propped against the willow and took a deep breath, clutching a vine for strength. Wind hovered, waiting for his response. He met her intense, onyx eyes and shivered. "Why have I never seen you like this before?"

She pushed her false, clay lips into a pout. *I've always wanted to show you this. It causes amusing reactions. I withheld this vision because you were young... and your mother's presence was strong.* Pure-white energy streaked in her stone eyes. *She's constantly in the way. But now you're stronger than her. She's lost that hold on you, and you can decide for yourself what's truth.*

The spirit pushed him into the bark. The leaves made a deafening crunch in his lap as she vibrated against his skin. He was used to her constant touch, but the sight of the monster behind the force gave each sensation new meaning.

It's time you see with those blue eyes what it means to be the chosen son of Erutan.

Marl stammered, holding on to the vision of a flawed, but sensual shepherdess. He closed his eyes and tried to focus on things that didn't constitute disobedience or infidelity. His curiosity and the spirit's body were tempting, but he knew they were tangible realities. The little bottle his hand closed over was real.

"I'm not sure I want to. I promised I'd be careful, and I'm happy with my life now. I don't want things to change." He fiddled with the vine and the stopper, pretending they were something else, something made of flesh. "And honestly, every time I listen to you, I get into trouble."

Marl remembered many times being snatched from a tree and whipped for things the ancient spirit had encouraged him to do. She was confused by the human propensity to punish, and it never bothered her when his backside was sore.

Wind took hold of his chin and pulled him into her gaze. She giggled as he gasped and let go the vine of mangled leaves. *My boy, we've made much trouble, and I'm glad for that, but now we've work to do.*

Marl released the bottle in his pocket and squirmed.

This won't be play. Our task is serious. You're a man now; make your own decisions. Do you think you can trust me as my Father's messenger?

He nodded. In things concerning powerful fathers, he'd learned to trust obedience.

Don't worry, love; we'll start slow. The Wanderer should know everything he's capable of. Wind brushed through his hair and swept her lips against his forehead. It felt cold as stone. *There's still a box to open. Let's get started shall we.*

TEN

A stone flew into his arm. Another whirred over his head. Hereu was sitting on the hill next to a massive pine, ready to throw the next projectile.

Marl sidestepped. "Hello, sweetheart."

"Don't you dare!" She brushed grass from her skirt and folded her bare arms.

Marl blushed. Her tanned body would look alluring draped in golden leaves. But her countenance told him she was in no mood to fulfill any of his fantasies. "What did I do?"

The shepherdess sobbed and whistled for her dog. Broom came to her ankles. *We waited a long time for you.*

Stars and mountains! I never told her we weren't meeting. The guilt of his near unfaithfulness consumed him. *I should teach her to channel.*

Seems reasonable, remarked the dog.

"Are you talking to Broom again?" Hereu snapped.

Marl put a hand through his hair and tried to look apologetic. "Yes. I'm sorry. It was a difficult day yesterday. I forgot to tell you."

Her face softened. "It *was* a difficult day yesterday."

An autumn breeze wafted over them. Marl ripped off his doublet and placed it around her shoulders. The cold was often a playful, tickling friend to him, but it was murder on Hereu. He'd buy her a cloak later; it'd be worth the expense.

"Why aren't you at Etutsa's? You never come to the meadow."

"He gave me the day off." Marl led her back to the pine and sat, giving her space. Her small fists were powerful when she didn't want to be touched. His stomach knew from experience.

"I'm sorry I threw rocks." Her apology was unconvincing. She didn't forgive easily. "You still should've found a way to tell me you weren't coming."

Marl's muscles relaxed as he placed an arm around his love. The touch of real flesh and cloth was refreshing, but it worried him to see her so wretched. "So, what happened? Tell me now."

"Eurgi came to visit, to invite us to her wedding. She told Papa how she missed seeing me." She stuck her finger on her tongue and pretended to gag. "Papa realized I must've been lying all this time and caught me headed to Oak Hollow to meet you."

Marl asked the question he hated to ask. "So?"

"So, he whipped me and sent me back home." She pulled his doublet tighter and coughed into her shoulder. "He doesn't know it's you though; I don't think. I snuck out later to come find you, but you weren't there. You're always there."

Standing to attention, Marl looked for something to abate his anger and guilt. He selected a stick of pine.

Hereu gasped and furrowed her eyebrows. "What're you doing?"

Marl brandished the weapon, delighting in its hiss, and performed a comical warrior's dance for her. "Let's see how he likes it." He winked.

Hereu laughed, rubbing her swollen eyes. "Don't do that, idiot. I'm fine. I'm a shepherdess, not a glass window." She reached out, arms wide with longing.

Unable to resist such a sweet request, he threw the stick back to the ground and snuggled in to her. She hummed with the touch of his warm hands.

"I can't stand it when he's upset with me. We may never meet at the hollow again."

Marl leaned into her curls. A few blades of bleached grass poked him in the cheek, but they didn't bother him as much as the thoughts pressing into his mind. The certainty of his plan was beginning to form. He reached into his pocket and produced his treasure.

"I've brought you something."

Hereu eyed the blue bottle. Her face twisted and she pushed it back into his chest. "I'm not falling for that trick."

Marl's jaw dropped with his stomach. "Trick! Why do you think it's a trick?"

She scowled. "You go on about how nasty his shack is. You've described some of the strangest smells. Yet here you are trying to hand me a glass bottle. I can only guess where you got it from."

"I did buy this from Etutsa, but it's not what you think. See." He waved the treasure like trying to tempt a squirrel with an apple core. "Etutsa's medicines are in amber bottles. This is blue. Trust me."

Hereu snatched the bottle and glowered. "Last week, you threw a dead lizard into my hair."

Marl blushed. He'd forgotten. They'd climbed high into the giant oak to evade passing soldiers. Not seeing any reason to climb down, they'd enjoyed a few hours staring over the forest from its boughs.

"Well, I never intended… You can't call it a trick."

He'd been twirling the lizard to tease some crows. The tail had detached and the corpse had gone down her dress. It was a shock the village hadn't come to rescue her. It was more of a shock Marl had been able to catch her before she fell.

"You weren't mad after I rescued you." He winked, remembering how she had slapped him before lapsing into kisses. He took the bottle out of her ice-cold hands and opened it, taking a strong whiff of the contents before smiling and passing it under her nose.

She reclaimed her gift. "What is it?"

"It's apple blossom and patchouli."

"You're right. They are pleasant. Rain in spring time." She replaced the stopper. "Too bad I can't wear it. Papa will be suspicious."

"Oh, well." Marl tried to snatch the bottle. "I suppose I'll take your present back."

She gasped and hid it behind her skirts.

"Now I *am* teasing you." If things worked out, she'd be wearing it soon enough.

Hereu turned it in the yellow autumn light and giggled. Her lips trembled, as grey as the glass.

Marl pulled her into his lap. "Your father should be ashamed. You're going to freeze."

Hereu threw her arms around his neck and groaned. "Please don't blame Papa. He gave me a blanket, but I left it for Mama. She's colder than I am."

"I doubt it." Marl took her face in his hands and forced her to look him in the eye, mimicking his mother's tendency to condescend. "Next time, take the blanket."

"Are you ordering me around, Marl Ganwin? You know better!"

Yes. I am, Hereu Misyl. I love you. He wasn't sure why he chose to channel his thoughts to her now, but it did give his words more weight. *No more childish behavior.*

Hereu gasped. "Is that how you speak with Broom?"

He gave her a stern illustration of his blue-lightning eyes. *Yes. Are you going to answer me?*

She nodded, biting her tongue.

Good girl. Do you want to learn?

"Can I?"

I'll teach you. It's easy. He'd forgo teaching her Wind's lessons; they'd no practical application. Marl moved her into the base of the pine. *I'm going to gather wood for a fire. Talk to me while I'm away.*

Hereu watched him stroll into a nearby copse. *Please come back.*

I'm here. Don't worry, he reassured her as he gathered kindling. *Keep thinking.*

Can we do this from anywhere?

We sure can! They now had the perfect means of communication. Marl was giddy. There was potential for mischief here. *This might solve our message delivery problem. Don't you think?*

Hereu giggled. *Yes, but if you'd tried this last night I might've thought you were a ghost and screamed. It's unnerving.*

He was fortunate. She was nervous, but not terrified. Marl was certain no other woman in the village possessed the same curious courage—save for Natsir's Para. He marched up the hill and threw the wood scraps into a pile.

Several black sheep settled near him. *What're you doing?*

Making warmth.

Energy was easy for him to control. The fire crackled and sparked. Marl concentrated on it, willing it not to get out of hand. Sometimes the things he did took on a life of their own. These things made Wind laugh last night. But there was much the spirit had yet to show him.

Thank you, Wanderer, chorused the flock.

"I wish I could talk to them," Hereu mused. "They must have such sweet thoughts. All they do is eat grass and bleat."

And poo everywhere! Marl laughed to himself and settled in next to her.

The black lamb climbed into her lap and gave a comfortable grunt. Soon all of the sheep had gathered around the fire, a strange particolored wreath. They weren't stupid creatures.

You're better off not knowing what animals think. The first time I heard our cat speak, it was creepy. He tossed bits of grass into his fire and willed them not to burn. A few complied. He recalled Pilgrim sitting by the hearth with his fresh-killed, seasoned mouse and shivered. *Also, he's kind of a cur.*

Hereu giggled. *Cats can be. The ones in Selcovi are mean.*

See that ewe? Marl pointed to a white sheep on the far edge of the fire. *She's mad. She says her name isn't Fluffer. She finds it insulting and prefers to be called Kerna.*

Hereu's eyes widened. Marl enjoyed her innocent pout.

The black ram over there thinks you're bossy too.

Hereu threw another clump into the fire. It burst into erratic flames and died in a pile of ash. *That explains things. Those two never listen; I always have to send Broom after them.* She leaned into his shoulder and sighed, stroking the black lamb in her lap. *Do they all hate me?*

No, Trouble loves you.

Hereu snorted. "I call her Trouble for a reason." *She's as naughty as you are.* "And just as black!" She swiped at his warm lips, leaving a sensation sweet as strawberries and as cold as snow.

Marl was grateful her anger with him had abated. It would've been a miserable day without her. *You're good at this. You can already switch back and forth.* "I think it took my father suns to master."

My head hurts, but it's exciting. You know I'm going to bother you while you're working. She batted her long lashes. *It's lonely out here.*

Marl didn't need another invitation. He pushed Trouble from her lap and dove into her neck, hungry for more of her sweetness.

Several grumpy members of the flock uttered curses. *Who knew sheep were so foul mouthed? They could teach Father a thing or two.*

***

He was a tall, a capable creature—strong enough to load great sacks of grain and beans into a wheel barrow and push the mass into town. He was agile and attentive enough to find the smallest bit of moss on a rock in the woods and smart enough to turn it into a remedy for open wounds. He was handsome, and though he could never be as charismatic as his father, he still had ways of getting what he wanted. But now, this perfect specimen of strength and intelligence found himself unable to knock on a door.

Marl had spent several hours with Hereu, fondling her and playing tunes on her fife. He told her that he had to help Father shuck the wheat. She let him leave once he'd made another promise to meet her tonight, very late to avoid detection.

He ran his fingers through his hair and took a deep breath. There was no use mimicking a dark scarecrow. He rapped twice.

The door opened to reveal a skinny, wane woman with brown curls patched in grey. Her pale skin hung loose around her cheeks and neck. He seemed to be staring at the skeleton of a woman and not the woman herself.

"Hello. May I help you?"

"Hello," he stuttered. "I'm here to speak with Vill. Is he here?"

"You must be Marl." Her voice was airy, dreamlike. "Hereu's told me about you. You *are* handsome."

He blushed.

Boney fingers wrapped around his hand, enveloping him in ice. She made him sit in a rocking chair and stooped over to stoke what was left of the fire.

Marl grabbed the iron poker from her. "Please, allow me." He took a deep breath and jabbed the rod once into the fire. It burst into a steady and attractive blaze.

"Such talent. Thank you. My name is Dalis. Vill is out fetching Hereu and the sheep."

He coaxed her to the rocking chair and pulled a chair from the table. "Should I come back?"

Dalis sat up, her rib bones poking from her thin, ragged gown. "Of course not. They'll return soon. We can get to know each other before Vill tries to kill you."

"You're not afraid of me."

"Not in the slightest."

A whistle emanated from the hearth and Marl flinched. He hadn't noticed the cracked, leaking kettle in the coals.

"Lovely. Let's have some tea."

Marl took it before she could. It should have scorched his fingers. "Let me. I want to help."

Dalis shook her head. "I'm perfectly capable, sweetheart, but I'll humor you." The chair gave a small creak as she shifted back down into it. She pointed to the cupboard nearest the table. "You look whiter than snow child. Nervous?"

He found two dusty, wooden cups and blew into them. Several beetle exoskeletons floated out. The tea smelled like salty vegetable matter stuck to the bottom of a metal pot.

Dalis mumbled thanks as he handed her a cup. "Much better." Her gaze penetrated. She was like a spirit haunting this house. "You do have pretty eyes. You don't have to be afraid, boy. I know why you're here. I've been telling Hereu for weeks to talk to her father. They're too much alike, I'm afraid."

He nodded, grateful again for the perfect honesty. "You understand I love your daughter?"

"I see nothing wrong with it. From what I gather, you're a nice young man. Very protective. I also know you're an adept apprentice. Etutsa speaks well of you." She grabbed his whiskered chin. "A bit of a temper though, too bold. I don't care for the marks you leave on Hereu's neck either, but I'm sure my daughter would disagree with me."

Marl started and placed his tea on the table with a clack. "I… you seem to know a lot."

Dalis laughed. It was a perfect, ethereal sound, but it turned into an abrading cough. Red splotches formed on the handkerchief she held to her mouth. She folded the cloth and placed it on her lap. "People think that because I'm trapped in this house, I don't know anything. But my daughter has always confided in me. I'm observant enough to determine the rest."

"Well, if you find me acceptable, why doesn't Vill?" He'd been prepared for a fight, but her gentle honesty was sleepwart to his temper.

She patted his leg. "Sweetheart, it's not you. First, he's her father. Nothing is going to convince him you're worthy. You don't have sisters, so you may not realize how protective men can be of their daughters. Mine certainly was." She beamed with remembered youth. "Second, my husband witnessed something in the mines that's convinced him your people are dangerous."

Why would Vill have any reason to fear people who worshiped Light and swore to do no harm? *I'm more troublesome because I am my Father's son.*

But Mother's people had given him something powerful too. What he was meant to use these gifts for, he couldn't say.

"I can do things. Some weird things, but I'm not evil. Everyone's dangerous. We're all capable of something; most of us chose not to because… well because." He pointed to the hearth and sighed. "You could knock me into the fire if you wanted to."

"Wise words! I'm afraid Vill doesn't see it that way." She reached out to take Marl's hands with one of her own, stroking them with a terrible but loving chill. "My husband used to be a miner. Many men are… until things fail. When the mine collapsed, only he and two Erutani men remained. Vill believes like the others—that they made it crumble with their magic." She dropped his hands and wiped a tear from her cheek. "It still upsets me. They were tortured and killed."

"That's horrible! My mother's people are stewards of the world. I'm surprised they were miners. Doesn't that leave permanent scars in the earth?"

"Yes, it does." Dalis shook her head. She placed her tea on the table next to his. "Ril decimated your people, son. You were scattered like leaves. Lately though, all problems have been attributed to your kind. They call you black-hairs and spit. There's still talk of a Wanderer, and that frightens the idiots more. Vill believes; it breaks my heart. He wasn't always this way."

"What do you believe?"

"Life is too short. It's more enjoyable when we put aside such ridiculousness."

The back door clamored open and the rest of the Misyl family stormed inside.

"Hereu get back here right now!"

"Go away! I'm fine!"

The door slammed behind them.

"You're going to freeze to death, li'l mouse! Why didn't you tell me your cloak was damaged? What happened to the blanket I gave you?"

This declaration gave Marl some confidence. Vill agreed with his sentiments. There was some footing for creating familiar ground; they shared little else in common.

Hereu's voice was shrill. "Stop calling me mouse! I left it for Mother. I was fine."

Dalis placed a hand to the side of her mouth and giggled. "Her name means field mouse. She hates it with a passion!"

Two sets of determined footsteps echoed down the hall and into the front room.

Vill continued the screaming match. "Ah, you had sense enough to build a fire. But I'm confused as to how you found the time to do it while still watching the flock."

As they neared, Marl prepared to make his stand. "I'm afraid that was me."

Two ragged, wooden dolls stood in the back entryway with their mouths agape. Broom at their side.

The lady of the house clapped gaily. "You two look like fish!"

"What's that boy doing in our house, Dalis!"

A one-sided fight between the couple ensued. The youths blushed and tried to stay out of the way.

Hereu flashed her pretty eyes. Her fists balled. *Sweetheart. I'm going to kill you!*

Marl snorted, pleased with this game. *How am I to die?*

I'm going to choke you with a dead lizard. Her frown turned into a wicked smirk. She folded her arms across her chest, daring him to think of anything better.

Creative!

Vill placed a hand on his shoulder and broke the spell. "Get out. Now!"

"I understand your shock," Marl began, trying to remember how Etutsa calmed those reluctant to try his cures. "But I'm not leaving yet. I'm here to speak with you about Hereu."

"I don't care. Get out!"

A white hand crept up the old man's shoulder, a ghost from a winter fog. The shepherd stiffened and his eyes took on a softer shade of brown.

"Let's all gather at the fire. It's getting cold." Dalis placed her daughter in front of the hearth with Broom. The girl only looked at the dog. "That's nice."

Vill hobbled to a chair and sat. "Wife, what do you think you're doing?"

"Making us comfortable. If you're going to have a breakdown, I want an excellent view."

"Mama!" Hereu clutched Broom and gasped, kicking Marl in the ankles as he snickered.

The shepherd tapped the table. "Is it your intent to emasculate me in my own home?"

Dalis grinned.

Vill turned back to Marl. "Well! Talk!"

Marl fumbled. Now the fight had come, he felt ill-prepared. Dalis had broken down his defensive nature. *She intended to do that—to both of us!*

"Spit it out, idiot!" Vill slammed his fist; tea sloshed out of Dalis's cup.

Hereu stroked Marl's britches and pushed out her chin when her father turned red. *I'm still mad, but don't let him win. If you're willing to fight, I am too.*

"I want to marry your daughter!"

There was no shouting, but a giggle came from Dalis's chair.

Vill grabbed his daughter's hand and yanked, then gestured toward the door. "No. Goodbye."

"No!" Marl took her back. She squeaked and he sent some healing power into her arm. It had a comforting effect on him too. "No. I'm not leaving!"

"You're too young. You don't know her. We've only lived in Na-ir for a few moons."

It was a valid point. Waiting twenty suns to declare your love like Natsir and Para was ridiculous, but a few moons could seem reckless as well.

"It feels longer." Marl gave Hereu a kiss on the cheek. She stiffened, but only because her father looked ready to tear them to pieces.

Vill groaned. Broom stepped in between the lovers and his master. The shepherd looked down to his dog and groaned again. "Let me explain something to you. I've seen a lot in my life, much of it absolute misery. The best thing I've ever known is sitting right there." He pointed to Dalis who beamed with genuine affection. "And that stubborn girl you have your arm wrapped around. I'm protective, mind you, but there's more to this than losing my baby girl."

"What then?"

"I've done some spying. The people of this village talk freely about you. Did you know?"

Marl shrugged. The Telmah talked about *everything*.

"I've heard things, boy. Someone saw you run through the woods naked. What sort of idiot does that?"

Marl looked into Hereu's shocked face and smiled. *I'll explain later.*

"You're also a hot head—breaking people's noses and bruising other young men. Everyone laughs. I don't find it funny. What if my daughter ran into that side of your temper?"

I'd never hurt you.

I know. She had heard of the times he'd rescued Para and she was proud of his resolve. "My temper is worse than his, Papa. So is yours!"

"He's bigger than you, more dangerous." Vill crossed his arms and hummed. *Brute's had his big hands all over my daughter. I'm going to kill her.*

Marl took a step forward.

Don't give him the satisfaction, Hereu chirped, placing a hand against his chest. *He's not as dangerous as Rej. He's all talk.*

This time he refused to believe her lies.

"You must be talking to different people than I am, love," Dalis remarked. "I agree with my husband, however. Marriage is a reckless endeavor after only six moons."

Vill relaxed. Marl was disappointed. He'd hoped Dalis would support them; there'd been every indication she would.

"After all, we waited a whole eight moons before I scurried off to be your bride. I thought you were dashing standing up to my grumpy, old father."

Vill sputtered like a dying fire. "This has nothing to do with us."

"You ran away, Mama?"

Dalis took her daughter's hand and scrunched her nose, a mouse herself. "When your father asked for my hand, my father chased him out of the barn with a pitchfork. He thought he was too old for me. I was seventeen. Can you imagine?"

Hereu shook her head no.

Marl laughed. *Dalis, you're crazy and I love you!*

She gave him a rambunctious smile. *You're welcome, young man.*

Vill slammed a boney backside into his seat and threw his calloused hands into the air. "Is anyone in this damn household going to listen to me?"

"We're listening, Papa, but we don't agree with you. I love Marl. I know he can be an idiot. So can you. You're both stubborn, but he's a good man and *he'll* do what's right."

Vill rolled his eyes and slammed his head into his hands. "Mother Sun, why? Two headstrong, smart-mouthed women! Can I ever win?"

Dalis ignored her husband and batted her eyelashes. "So, tell us your plans."

"The meadow. I'm going to buy some land from G'Nirac on the meadow for us. I'll take over Etutsa's practice when he retires. It'll be a good living, I think. She could have a flock. We wouldn't need much."

"Such a reasonable idea." Dalis took Hereu's hand. "Sounds similar. Doesn't it, love?"

Her husband looked like he'd been pummeled by a mad horse. "It failed, Dalis."

"No it didn't. We were fortunate to live it for a while. Other opportunities came and we went." She was still smiling, but a few tears sparkled in her eyes. "Don't tell me you're dissatisfied."

"No! Dalis, please stop. You're dying... and that was never our plan."

With much effort, she moved to Vill, taking his head in her shaking hands and kissing his brow. "Husband, we all die. I'm happy." She pointed to Hereu. "I can never regret this."

The old man's voice cracked. "Love, you're torturing me."

They embraced, an ash tree towering over a stone of granite.

"Why don't we leave you both alone?" Dalis winked and motioned to Hereu. "If there's going to be a fight, please try not to break anything."

The men watched them go.

She's an interesting woman, Marl thought.

"Yes, she is."

Marl started; he'd never intended for Vill to hear that.

Vill forced him into a chair. "Those women are going to do what they're going to do. They've always been like that." He shook his head, defeated. "Doesn't change how I feel. There's something not right with you: Erutani or no." *I know what you're capable of, boy.* He cocked his head like a curious dog. *You heard me didn't you?*

Marl scowled. *Yes.*

Good. I'm going to tell you something Dalis don't know. I was a soldier under the greatest general in centuries. His name was Hama and he wasn't much older than me. We were marched out to a place called Surnow. Have you heard of it?

Marl shook his head. It wasn't a word he'd ever heard spoken before.

Vill grinned. *I'm surprised. It was the Erutani capital. Under orders from King Ril, we marched on it. I saw unspeakable things. Your people say they believe in doing no harm, but I didn't get this limp from the mines.* He pointed to his crooked leg. *I killed several of you bastards before escaping with my life.*

Marl raised a hand to slap him, but found the wherewithal to hit the table instead. *You're proud of this slaughter!*

I'm proud of my service to the kingdom. With your people decimated, there was no longer the threat of the evil Wanderer looming o'er our heads. He's dead. Nothing stood in Ril's way after that.

We weren't decimated, Marl retorted. *I'm still here.*

Vill sat back in his chair, startled.

Look. I don't know about that stuff. The two halves of me are Mlaerian and Erutani, but I was raised a Telmah farmer. I'm apprenticed to a healer. The prospect of playing any magical tricks on anyone is the furthest thing from me. You're a damned fool if you believe otherwise.

A smile crept across the old man's face. "Spoken like a man." Vill shrugged and slapped his hands on his legs. "I'm a fool either way. You've got my daughter's heart; I suppose I can't keep it from you now."

Marl raised an eyebrow. Vill laughed.

She'll grow tired of you anyway. She's a flighty girl. He balled his hand into a fist and placed it between Marl's legs. *You ever hurt her, or use any magics, and I'll rip you apart.*

Like you could touch me. I can say the same to you. Touch Hereu again and I'll make sure every bone in your body breaks before you hit the bottom of the northern cliffs.

Vill chortled. *You've got a spine, boy!* "All right, we're in agreement."

Marl shook the outstretched hand. *Does this idiot only understand force? Or is it because I'm protective of her too?*

Footsteps tapped in the hallway. The fair damsel was still waiting to be rescued.

"I have your blessing then?"

"Yes, and you also have my curse." Vill nodded to the women in the hall.

Hereu was dressed in a blue gown, old-fashioned but much warmer than her previous garment. Her eyes were wide.

"Your curse?" Marl repeated.

"Yes." Vill placed his wooly-scented hands on his head. "If you can stand my daughter and she can stand you back, then I curse you both with a daughter of your own. May she be pretty, feisty, and smart, and may she be an absolute *thorn* in your side!"

Dalis cackled.

Vill grabbed the youths and shoved them outside. "Good luck with that!" He slammed the door.

They stood on the porch, hands clasped as they stared at the north edge of Na-ir. Mother Sun was beginning to slip down behind the wooded area surrounding the village.

Marl scooped Hereu into his arms. She shrieked and slapped him. "Don't ever do that again, idiot."

"I'll never *have* to." He rubbed her nose with his. "You're *mine*. Besides, I was right."

She scowled. He was never going to live this down, but, for now, only her kiss mattered.

"Come on. The village needs to know the latest gossip. Wanna take a turn?"

Hereu didn't mind the stares from the gawkers as he paraded her through the square.

ELEVEN

"Hello, Mother. Look who I've brought to dinner."

Messa couldn't help it. She squeaked and slammed the door.

From the other end of the wooden panels, she heard a small curse word. It hadn't come from her son.

She'd been feeling unwell for days; a strange movement from within her body left her weak and disjointed. Marl's sudden appearance with Hereu had thrown her into a dizzy state of shock.

Messa hadn't been monitoring him. She hadn't been thinking of him at all. He never came home before nightfall.

"Mother? Is everything well?" He tapped on the cottage wall.

Messa tried to steady her nerves before reopening the door. They were standing, hand in hand, on the porch, worried and indignant in the shadow of dusk. "I'm sorry. You scared me."

Marl laughed and raked a hand through his dark hair. "Scared you! You could terrify a dragon with one look—if they existed. What's wrong, Mother?"

Why did boys have to mimic their fathers? She'd a hard time saying no when he acted like Nojhi. She pulled them inside, locking the door. "You shouldn't be here. What if Vill saw you?" *What if Nojhi had?*

Marl pulled Hereu closer and narrowed his eyes. "It's not a problem now. I spoke to Vill."

It was hard to see him acting like a man. He was too young to be this determined, or to pretend to be this wise. Messa wrung her apron. A sweet, sweaty smell made her retch. "You've Vill's blessing?"

"Yep. We've his curse too." He laughed as Hereu punched him in the chest.

"Curse?" Messa's stomach moved into her ribs. She believed in curses. Spirits listened.

"Papa told him we'd have a stubborn daughter like me. He was being a cur."

Marl kissed her, happy as if he'd discovered all the secrets of the Lights. "I don't mind having daughters. Even if they're thorns in my side. I've heard boys are worse any way."

Messa forced a smile. "You are. You're impossible!" She took Hereu by the hand. The girl *was* wearing a perfume. Patchouli, and… something else. She tried to concentrate through the aromatic fog. "I'm happy for you, sweethearts."

Marl kissed her cheek. He smelled of moss and dust. "Good! Where's Father?"

"I… I… that's not such a good idea, love. Not now."

Nojhi had stormed out of the house earlier, aggravated with her changed state of consciousness. Things were becoming hard to see, hard to find in the darkness of her mind, and she'd no strength to deal with his eccentricities. They weren't used to being alone day in and out. He had a need to control things, and she wasn't one to be directed.

Marl slumped onto his bed and pulled Hereu down into his lap. "Not this again. I'm going to tell him. What're you going to do when we move to the meadow? I think he'll notice."

Messa wound the apron in her hands. She hadn't planned this far ahead. She'd miscalculated allowing her son freedom. He'd gobbled it like wild strawberries.

"I think you two are perfect for each other," she admitted. "I don't know how to break it to your father. He's sensitive, and we've told several lies so you could court. I'm not ready to admit I betrayed him." This was only part of it. The foreboding was consuming.

"We're not afraid. I'm sure Marl's father will understand once we tell him what happened. He can't be worse than my father... or Marl!"

He goosed her waist and she gave a squeak.

"My son's had the benefit of a mother," Messa answered, unamused by his inappropriate antics. "I've seen the worst of your father's temper. You haven't."

"Mother, I think he's learned to control it. He hasn't done anything terrifying in twenty suns."

Marl repositioned Hereu on his bed, stood, and took his mother into his arms. She melted into the unfamiliar touch. There was a boy behind the strong embrace, she was sure of it.

"Please. This is silly. Please don't be difficult." He sighed. *Father can be intimidating, but you know as well as I do it's an act.*

He was wrong. Nojhi's patience was an act, a good one too. "Me? Difficult? Why do you always push forward blindly? Don't you trust my judgment? I'm trying to protect you!"

Her knees faltered. Hereu caught her as she tottered.

Marl set his jaw. "I'm not falling for this. You're never sick. I'm telling Father! That's the end of it!" *And you think Wind is a manipulative bitch!*

She is! Don't tell me she's got her hold on you again!

The girl snuggled into her and dragged her to the table. "Marl, I know you're upset, but please don't yell. She looks sick to me."

For some moments, Marl looked at Messa as if she were a wayward child in need of whipping. He placed a cool hand against her forehead and his temper dissipated. *What's this?*

Hereu's perfume mixed with pumpkin stew and bile rose. Marl was quick. A pot was placed under her before Messa vomited. When she had finished, he set it down on the floor.

"You *are* sick!" He took her in his arms and carried her to bed. Messa burned with embarrassment and guilt. She wasn't trying to be a nuisance.

Hereu gave her a pillow. "Should we get someone?"

Marl shook his head. "I'm sorry I yelled. But there's no need to lie. Father's a massive *baby*." He put an emphasis on the last word and paused.

Messa recoiled. *Could it be?* Hot tears trickled, counteracting the healing touch. "My life's never been simple, love. I've seen things that haunt me."

Is it Surnow? He took her hand with the empathy of a healer. *Vill was there.*

I don't remember Vill. Did he say anything about us?

He said the Erutani were using magic to hurt the Mlaerians. Nonsense. He said he was under General Nam…no, Hama. Not much else. Was Father there too?

Marl, this is dangerous knowledge. Tell no one, and keep a shrewd eye on Vill. I'm surprised this information has escaped me.

You've been too busy lying about everything else.

Messa's cheeks warmed with fresh tears.

"Is everything well?" Hereu sat on the floor beside them, her arms folded in her lap.

"Forgive us. Marl's anger with me is justified. However, my fear of your father may be justified as well."

The girl startled.

"Also, I'm afraid the smell of your perfume makes me dizzy. Can we discuss your engagement later?" *I prefer to handle one problem at a time.*

Marl pointed to her abdomen and sneered. *You've a few moons before that problem is obvious. If you tell Father now, he may not care about us.* He turned to his love. "Let's go. I'll walk you home." Marl guided Hereu out, casting a defeated and reproachful glance at his mother before shutting the door. *My love has never been your problem. Neither have I.*

Messa lay on her bed and sobbed. *My wayward son's making more sense than I am!* This was troubling.

***

He entered the cottage again moments later, slamming the door. The flurry of motion woke her. "Father and Nat are coming with Etutsa. I've told them you're sick, nothing else. For everyone's sake, don't be stubborn. Father's worried crazy."

Nojhi burst through the door shortly thereafter followed by Natsir and a gasping Etutsa. All three men looked wretched and forlorn.

"Messa, love. Marl said you were ill. How can you be ill? Is it my fault?" He raced to her side and gathered her into his arms.

Etutsa set his sack down. "I didn't think it possible for the priestess to be in such a state."

"It's not. Erutani are blessed. Something's wrong."

The healer placed a hand on her forehead and stared into her eyes. Marl stood by the fire with wide-eyed Natsir. He made a fist and glared.

Who called for Etutsa?

Father. He sneered. *It's not his, is it?*

Anger welled inside of her, hot and reckless and hard to temper. She was guilty of many things, but never that. Never! *If I had strength, I'd slap you!*

Etutsa was startled by her aggravated look. "So. You're moody, clearly. Tired. Feverish. You can't eat, according to Nojhi." He looked at the pot. "Yes, you can't stomach much."

Marl apologized and removed it. He tossed their damaged dinner into the grass.

"When was the last time you bled, Messa?"

She didn't answer. It had been two moons.

Etutsa hummed. "Well, if I didn't know any better, I'd say you were…"

"I was what?" she snapped.

"I suppose you're a bit… old for it, but stranger things have happened. Tell me, apprentice. What do you think troubles your mother?"

Marl chewed on his tongue and glared. *She's insane.*

Messa was grateful Nojhi hadn't heard him; her husband didn't suffer rebuke of women easily.

Taking advantage of the pause, Natsir crept behind his little brother to get a better look. "She's with child."

"Oh come on!" Nojhi laughed and slapped the side of their bed. "Have you two lost your minds? It's been twenty suns!" He scoffed and gestured to his body. "I'm an old man, and that's impossible."

Natsir took her hand, smiling. "Amazing! I can see her quite clearly."

Nojhi's face went white. "Her?"

Etutsa ignored the magics. "It's possible. Look at Gerna's sons. What else did you think it was? Women since the beginning of time have endured this. It should've been obvious. No talents needed!" He chuckled. "Surely you paid attention the first two times!"

"Messa never acted this way." Nojhi ran his fingers through his hair. "Remember? When we came here, you marveled how fit she was after giving birth to Marl in that wagon."

Messa winced. There was still a pain from that wet and miserable night she could never share.

"Both of her birthings were benign."

She flinched; she had a hard time concealing her secrets when confronted with the inevitable. "There were seven. I lost five after Natsir."

Nojhi shook his golden head and creased his brow. "What? How?"

"It shouldn't be possible. Erutani aren't supposed to suffer, to be barren. But I left the village; I renounced the ways. What else but I'm being punished again?" She avoided her husband's glare. The last time she'd declared her self marked for punishment, they'd been roaming the Wastes.

Natsir looked at her with pity. If the others were her curse, he'd been a mark of forgiveness. What Marl was, she wasn't sure.

Nojhi shifted her onto the bed. "Five? Why didn't you tell me?"

It was hard to see him in such pain. "I hid them because I knew you'd be heartbroken. I'm sorry. After Marl, I thought I was barren, so I never mentioned the matter again." There had to be a reason for such losses. *We were on the run. It was easy to pretend they never existed.*

Marl slammed a chair away from the table and sat.

Etutsa jumped. "This isn't favorable, Messa. But I doubt you're being punished. You should rest until the sickness passes. It lasts a couple of moons." He patted their legs. "Come, no sulking. You're two adults and you love each other. It's not worth the fight."

Nojhi sighed. "You *will* do whatever Etutsa says!" *I won't allow there to be a sixth.* Messa nodded.

"Until you're out of danger, the boys and I will do everything. Rest. We'll talk later." He and Marl marched out, determined and hot with suppressed rage. Etutsa and Natsir shuffled after, smiling affectionately as they left.

Things were strange, but bearable. Messa contemplated the new soul within her and managed to smile. This one would last. She was sure. The punishment of the three sisters hadn't completely broken her.

***

Nojhi's anger was redirected. In the walk to the cottage, he'd learned of Marl's day off, but not how he'd spent it. Messa watched them bite and scratch. Marl kept his promise. He never wavered, but he did send her disrespectful thoughts.

"I know what you were doing. You better watch it, boy. Show respect."

Marl pulled his hair. "Worry about your own problems instead of creating more for me." The boy left, slamming the door again.

Nojhi growled and threw his hands into the air. "What're we going to do with him? I thought he had more sense."

Messa yawned in spite of herself. It felt like several stones had been heaved upon her, yet her husband wasn't in bed. "He has a lot of sense, as much as you do. You both forget to use it."

Natsir brought her a cup of raspberry tea. She took several careful sips and felt a little relief.

"Perhaps the answer is to leave him alone," Natsir noted, placing the pot on the table.

"Do you know what your brother's been doing?"

He nodded and Messa's stomach tensed again. She prayed he would have sense enough not to contribute to his baby brother's inevitable strangulation.

"He's working diligently for Etutsa. He's also helping out here the moment he gets home. I'm indebted to him for his help with the firewood a few nights ago while you were in town. Many in this village will be better for his skills. I'm proud of him." Natsir cocked his head. "Aren't you proud of Marl, Father?"

Nojhi didn't like being confronted with his own petty nature. He slammed his arms into the table. "Of course I'm proud! But that's no excuse for lying and slinking off with some girl. His duty is to us first."

"Is it?" Natsir barely made a ripple in the air with the gentleness of his words, but the force of them hit his father square in the chest, a sword through armor. "I'm going to the shed. We still have some beans. You need to eat, Mother."

He left Nojhi groaning with his head in his arms, thinking on what he should expect of his sons. The brief peace was enough to lull Messa to sleep again. Several moments later, her lover woke her from the tea-induced bliss to talk.

"Do you think Nat's right?"

She rolled into his arm. "Yes, love. Let's give him time to calm down."

"All right. We're letting our tempers get to us again, I suppose." Nojhi rested his chin on his knees and frowned. They were so much alike, the man and his son. "You don't think the girl is Vill's daughter, do you?"

Messa swallowed her beating heart.

"I recognize him. I swear I do, but I can't place from where."

"Don't worry, love. He was all smoke. If he was going to do something, he would have done it by now."

Nojhi looked at her, fire in his earthy eyes; the same fire she'd seen on their first meeting. "Don't lie to save my feelings again, woman. If you're losing your gifts, there may be things you haven't seen."

This logic was irrefutable. She wiped a few tears from her eyes. "I'm sorry, Nojhi."

He wrapped his arms around her and gave her a stern look. "This is happening to you because of *me*. Don't apologize. And don't hide anything anymore. I couldn't take another blow." He gave her a shake. "I'll talk to him tomorrow. I promise, no shouting."

Marl didn't return.

Nojhi went wild, pacing the floor of their cottage. He refused to let her channel for fear she'd make herself weaker. Messa felt helpless.

In the afternoons, he trudged down to Etutsa's shack to catch Marl leaving, but the boy was always one step ahead of him. Gone. The healer swore Marl was in his shack daily; where he went after was his business.

"He's like you, love. Think," Messa advised. "Where would you go?"

Nojhi tore his hair and paced again. "If he was as stupid as me, he'd be in Mirot enlisting to fight against Onaryc's darkened war, but I know he's not there. I've asked everyone. They've *seen* him."

She pretended to sip her raspberry tea.

"Honestly! He's a ghost. He flits around the village like he owns it."

"Please let me channel him. I think I've strength enough." Messa hated spending her days in a nightshirt on their uncomfortable cot. The nausea was starting to wane, and it felt good to stretch her legs.

Nojhi shook his head and took her into his arms. He didn't return her to the bed, but carried her over to the chair by the fire. As he set her down, his jaw dropped.

"The little crow is in the trees! Why didn't I think of it before? He's hiding in the woods." He slammed a fist into the back of the chair. "He's made a palace out of those branches and leaves since he was three."

Nojhi kissed her and ran out the door.

Please let him be in the trees! Messa prayed. She sat by the fire, anticipating the moment she could hug her son again and beg his forgiveness.

It wasn't meant to be. When Nojhi returned, he looked like he'd been pummeled with logs. He sat beside her.

"Marl was at the old oak. He wouldn't talk to me. He bounded off like a black rabbit. I *lost* him." He stared into the fire. "I shouldn't have yelled. What did it matter?"

Messa felt a deep remorse for her husband and her son. She tried to see Marl as he climbed higher into the trees. Such a strange child, a stranger man.

Please come home. Your father is broken without you. I'm worried you'll freeze.

Deep from the chilled night air, one word came to her in answer: *No!*

Messa sighed and placed a trembling hand on her husband's back. "Nojhi, don't blame yourself. You need to know…"

"No, love. I don't think you can solve this problem for us. I'll let him be." This was a lie; Nojhi was incapable of standing by while the world moved on without him. "He'll come to his senses soon."

"But…" Messa tried to keep him from standing. It was useless. His still muscular frame broke free of her as he kissed her on the forehead.

"Rest."

She stood there stuttering as he left the cottage. There was no tea strong enough to ease her conscience or her anguish.

TWELVE

Messa sat in the middle of the forest. *Sisters three, I beg you. Converse with me.*

Father Moon was wearing his cloak again this night, a wise thing to do. She could see her white breaths in the glow of the stars.

The stillness of the trees unnerved her. It wasn't like Wind to avoid confrontation. *Spirits, please, I implore you. By all of the stars in the heavens and by the Father and the Mother, don't desert your flawed servant.*

The ground shifted and warmth spread, starting with her backside and legs and soaking through to her nose. It was a comforting sensation she hadn't felt in over twenty suns.

Greetings daughter of Erutan, gifted Priestess of Light. What troubles you? Dirt shape-shifted into a hand that clasped her own. *We've missed you.*

A sturdy woman rose from the soil. Clothed in yellow-brown leaves, Earth's supple body was formed of mud, brown and glistening. Her eyes glowed with emeralds. Her hair was as grey as granite. If a villager of Na-ir had happened to walk by, he'd have been driven mad with the sight.

Messa smiled.

The other sisters apparated before the priestess. Water was translucent and silver, hair of billowed clouds. Her gown and eyes were of the most marvelous iridescent ice.

Wind was dressed in dirt and twigs, hair falling like blue water over a cliffside and eyes black as coal. Her form never ceased to move.

Messa bowed in supplication. *I'm grateful for your presence.*

I was certain you renounced us, priestess. Water's tone was sharp and cold, but her jeweled eyes were kind. *Why have you called us now?*

Forgive me. I've made many mistakes of late. I need your wisdom—for I'm lacking in it.

Wind pressed vibrating fingers to her neck. *What do you think you deserve to know?*

Messa refused to flinch. She'd known these tactics since childhood. *Tell me what's happening to me and what you intend to do with my son.*

He's no longer your son, Wind hissed, twirling around her in a violent but contained flurry. *You gave him to me. Don't you remember? It was I who filled his lungs. It was I who named him. He's the Wanderer.*

Yes, I know. But I'm not quite certain what that means.

Earth placed a comforting, mud-cooled arm around her waist. *You know the prophesy, priestess. What more can we tell you?*

They chanted, recalling ancient promises and future worries.

> *A Wanderer comes, child of Erutan, born of air,*
> *moving far from the devoured heart and her children there,*
> *drenched in the tears of water, and a force upon this earth,*
> *the rocks will moan as in the hour of his birth.*
> *He will wear the Father's black cloak of destruction*
> *And from the air take instruction.*

Why did prophesies have to rhyme?

Messa reminisced on the heart of her people, Surnow, and tingled with remorse for its passing. She leaned into Earth's shoulder, heedless of the dirt smudging her night-black hair.

Those verses tell me more about how and when he was born than what he will do. I was there. I know the particulars of his birth. For what purpose was he granted this life?

For that, you must look to the covenant, child. Two globes refracted in the light, shooting stars, and slammed into the dust.

Messa understood. Prophecies were warnings, not instructions. *Erutan's people will never suffer as long as they remember the old ways.*

Wind hissed and sent a flurry up Messa's nostrils. *Wrong, wrong. Erutan's people were given great gifts and knowledge. An element of my sister Earth flows in your blood, seared into your very bones. But you're all still human. Torment is as essential to life as your breaths.* She backed away with a brief heartbroken frown. *The covenant was that Erutan and his people would be fruitful, happy, and protected from total eradication.*

The priestess wiped debris from her face. "That covenant wasn't kept!"

The leaves of Earth's gown crunched against her. *No, my girl, you're not eradicated. This torment was caused by humans and only humans can solve it. We oversee the results because we care. You're our children.* She displayed chalk-white rows meant to be teeth. *Our little Marl is here to restore balance, to make right what was wrong. It's a noble task before him.*

So, noble he must give his life? Messa stared into eyes like grass peeking through snow.

It was Wind who answered. She cast a respectful glance to the cloaked moon overhead. *My sisters and I aren't told everything by Father. We do as we're bid. But I do know your sons will be happy.*

Her lightning smile was unnerving. What constituted happiness for an immortal?

They'll have so much love it'll radiate through all who know them.

Why do you include Natsir? He's not the Wanderer.

Wind pressed her erratic form against Messa's cheeks; it stung, drawing blood. The spirit opened her mouth and the sound of a small child emanated from the black hollow there. "He's Marl... and I'll look after him."

Messa gasped. She hadn't heard that tiny, frightened voice for many suns. Now it had taken on the form of a deep, resonating gentleness—the voice of a man.

Natsir will keep his promise from his youth. Father has chosen me to carry out his wishes. I've chosen them, and I'll ensure they fulfill their destinies.

We'll ensure they survive our sister, Earth interjected, casting Wind a disgruntled, mossy glance.

Messa placed her head in her hands. If Marl would need Natsir to protect him, this was dangerous business. Would it come on Onaryc's wings?

What about their women? Brackish tears slid into the corners of her mouth. *What about this child?* Messa placed a hand to her abdomen, a useless attempt to protect the girl inside. *Will you make use of all of my family in this dangerous plan?*

I've no use for troublesome Ganwin women, especially you. You're always in my way.

A hand of pure energy touched Messa's throat, harmless but petrifying. Splatters of dirt landed on her skirt, like blood. The priestess gasped in terror, but not for herself.

Of all Erutan's children, you vex me most. The spirit whirl-winded hysterically.

Enough! Water's comforting hands were extravagantly cold. *The daughter within you is a gift, to help you cope with the things to come, though the price of bearing her will make you weaker.*

Messa remembered Marl's birth and how strenuous it had been. She'd been too weak to reach out to her husband in the thick of a massive storm. This child might make things very difficult for her.

Don't lie! Wind hissed at her sister. *You gave her the girl so I couldn't find a way to kill her. I don't need you Messa of Surnow.* White lightning sparked out of her mouth, jagged fangs. *Your purpose was to bear two strong boys! I'm forbidden to touch you now because of the girl, but don't think I won't try!*

Water held back her sister with a reproachful glare. *Don't forget; you wouldn't exist without us. You're the space between and we surround you. Whatever you do, we know.* She turned back to Messa with a gentler tone. *Natsir and his love will grow old together and have many children. This I do know; I've been advising him of these things of late.*

Leave it to Natsir to discover reverence for the spirits on his own.

Marl and Hereu will know love as great as Erutan and Esimor.

Earth giggled. *Hereu is like Esimor, isn't she? A sweet, headstrong thing. Perfect for our rambunctious Marl.* She mimicked Gerna, rejoicing over the simple follies of the village youth. *It gives me great joy to see them together.*

Wind disagreed. *It matters little. Say no more. We're finished here.* She cast Messa another hate-filled glance before releasing the bonds of her form. The leaves, water, and dirt fell in a great pile where she'd once gyrated, leaving a strange, misshapen crater. *We haven't much time left. Stay out of my way.*

Earth caressed Messa's cheek. *Worry not. All will be made right.*

They sank into the ground beneath her, leaving her alone with her thoughts.

She was more troubled now than before she came. Messa dwelled on Water's insistence that Marl and Hereu would be like Erutan and Esimor. What she knew of those ancient ones was nothing like her rebellious son and the mischievous girl from Selcovi. They'd been honorable and self-sacrificing, gentle. But, it was possible tales had a way of masking the truth. Only the best or worst traits survived the ages.

She shivered and pulled her cloak closer as she trudged back to the cottage. Her mind kept forcing its way through the histories. There was something there she couldn't grasp. As she placed a foot on the porch, it came to her like a flash of red fire in her soul. Esimor had been Erutan's first wife. No Erutani, living or dead, had ever descended from her womb.

***

Nojhi spent his nights pacing the floor mumbling and his days wandering Na-ir. He couldn't rest until Marl had returned. His eyes had grown sunken and hollow, black with bitter tears and sleeplessness—a blond phantom: some strange mating of darkness and light.

Messa knew the boy was trying to punish her. She ignored the warnings about harm to the baby. The sisters had given her no indication the girl was in any danger.

Their daughter was safe within the warm confines of her womb, not yet escaped—but Marl, on the other hand, could be anywhere.

She stayed on the edge of his mind, watching. Sometimes she could hear his thoughts and the voices of others around him. The silent images were crudely drawn into her senses. His abilities were strengthening. She saw what he wanted her to.

Today, he was running errands, taking long detours to steal kisses. Messa tried several times to alert her husband, but he was too engrossed in his obsession to allow her much room into his mind.

I'm half tempted to go down there and drag them both back by the ears. Why were the two of them so damned stubborn? They defied all logic.

There were pleasurable moments though. Marl danced with Hereu in the golden forests. He would snatch a fife from her skirt pockets and produce a cheerful song. They would climb the trees and snuggle in the branches. Messa recalled the days when she and Nojhi were younger. In the thick of terror, there could be peace.

Etutsa's interactions with her son gave her much joy as well; though she was certain the healer was also helping Marl to avoid his father. At least when Marl was working, he was in the company of someone level-headed and kind. He was calmer around Hereu and Etutsa. Wind could not stir his soul in their presence.

No wonder he'd rather be with them than with us. He wasn't a child anymore. Could they really continue trying to shape him to their wills?

Messa stared into the hearth and concentrated on her sewing. Natsir was the only one tending to farming matters now, though there wasn't much to harvest in this cold. His clothing had taken on much of the added stress of tending to thatch roofs and creaking doors. A large torn, grey shirt rested in her hands as she watched Marl skip back to Etutsa's shop after delivering his tonic to Gerna.

Marl opened the door and waved before settling into a chair. The healer's chatted. Through Marl's clear, blue eyes Messa looked deep into Etutsa's brown.

They had settled in for a long task. Messa tried again to reach out through the village. *Nojhi, love. He's with Etutsa. Nojhi?*

There was no reply.

Nojhi, love. Are you there?

Marl answered, sounding torn and dejected through the void. *Father's asleep by the door. He's been there for hours.*

Oh, my poor husband! Why didn't you wake him?

Etutsa tried. I don't want to talk to him, or you. He's too heavy, so we left him.

You've been cruel, my son. She couldn't contain her fury. How could they leave Nojhi out on the cold ground, open and easy for ridicule? *Don't you see how sorry he is? He needs to know you forgive him.*

I'm done with you both. You're always in the way. The words of a spirit echoed.

Messa clutched her chest and tried not to faint. She focused. The noise of the shop crept into the space behind her eyes and the pictures became more solid.

"I see your eyes, boy. Are you talking to Hereu again?" Etutsa winked. "She can have you later. I need you now."

Marl shook his head and sighed. "No... Mother."

"It's always good to hear from her. Is she well?"

"I don't care. All she does is lie."

Etutsa slammed down his bottle and stared. "Such horrible things to say. What's gotten into you?"

"Nothing!"

The whine stabbed Messa's ears. He was so spoiled, and she was tired of being permissive.

Messa slammed the cottage door and raced to the village, intent on ending this ridiculousness now. As she went, the child inside her bobbed and weaved, causing her gait to rock unevenly. She groaned, feeling strain on her hips and feet. *Sweetheart, please let your mother move freely. I need to go beat some sense into your big brother.*

"Don't you think this behavior is childish," Etutsa continued. "What good does it do you to break their hearts? There are far worse offenses than lying, believe me. I thought you'd more heart. The young man I know is a protector, not a tormenter."

"It's none of your business. Drop it!" Marl pushed the chair back violently. Messa was certain his hand had never touched the wood.

The healer cracked his back trying to look up. "Did you learn anything from my experience? Running from your problems is stupid. Don't tell me you're as much of an idiot."

Messa approached the entrance to Na-ir and stopped to catch her breath, listening to Marl's ridiculous excuse.

"I'm not running. I'm choosing not to be involved in someone else's problems."

Etutsa's jaw fell as he stammered.

Messa forced her aching legs past Nojhi and turned the handle of the door.

"Marl, you've been our problem from the moment you were born," she snapped as she entered, scaring the wits out of the healer.

She nodded to her friend, trying to keep the rage from boiling into poisonous vapors. Messa pointed a trembling finger and slammed the door shut. For a few moments, she'd scared herself, worried she'd awakened the sleeping giant outside.

"Sit down, Marl! I've had it with you!"

Etutsa sat down instead.

"Now, Marl!"

He rolled his eyes, but found the chair behind him.

She clutched her stomach. It wasn't usually within her to yell. "Have you been talking to Wind again?"

"Yes."

Messa sighed. It was easier to forgive him knowing the manipulations of Wind could be absolute, but she couldn't stop her heart from pulsating. "Whatever she's said, she doesn't care about you. Her own sisters find her deplorable!"

Marl's eyes gleamed with a terrible and magnificent power. He licked his lips. "She's teaching me things. Why should it matter to you?"

"Because I'm your mother, Marl. Everything you do is a part of me."

She placed a hand on his feathered head. He flinched but didn't attempt to strike her. She saw images flash by, glimpses inside a cramped room with a sour-faced Vill and his family. He was refusing to show her what she wanted to see.

"You've been sleeping at Hereu's this whole time?"

Etutsa leaned in closer.

Marl's features relaxed and he frowned. "No, that wasn't my plan. I've only been sleeping by their hearth since yesterday. Dalis forced me to."

Messa took a step back. She was curious to know more about this woman who could pull the Wanderer away from Wind. *I don't even have that power over him.* She raised a black eyebrow. "Forced you?"

He pulled a leg to his chest and blinked tears. The youth returned in his eyes. *There's my son.* "Marl, please tell me what's going on."

His voice was hollow as a well. "Hereu told her I was sleeping in the trees. Dalis marched out to the old oak and screamed like I was a stupid child. I was worried she was going to hurt herself, so I conceded."

Etutsa offered Messa his seat. He glided over to his bed and watched the drama unfold with too much glee, clapping his hands as if he was watching a wrestling match. The priestess tried not to laugh, though his simple response was refreshing.

"Marl enough is enough. You can't keep doing this. I know you love Hereu, but this is no way for a man to behave."

"I am a man! And this isn't about Hereu. You always think I do everything to hurt you. Did you ever consider everything you do hurts me?"

Messa felt a weight of a thousand stones on her shoulders. "What do you mean?"

"I'm not a doll. You can't decide what I will or won't do and expect me not to try and reason why. How dare you and Father force me to choose between you! I can't. How can I honor one without harming the other? At least Wind allows me to be."

"You're more a plaything to Wind than you know, my son. You're a hunting dog on a short leash! Her very intention is to put you in harm's way."

Marl placed his chin on his knee, still much like the child he said he was not. "I can't solve this. You're tearing me into pieces, expecting me to be obedient. The two of you are on opposite ends of things, like you've separated your souls."

What's he talking about? Messa narrowed her eyes. "That's rubbish, Marl. Your father and I have our differences, but we're united in everything."

"No, you're not!"

What's Wind told you? "We both love you. That's all that matters."

He turned away and trembled. "Please, go. I can't solve your problems."

How dare he? The strength of their love was none of his business… Messa stopped short of slamming a fist into his head. Isn't that what he'd told her in the cottage? His love wasn't her problem. But why would he think there was a problem?

There were shouts outside. The door reverberated.

Etutsa ran to open it. Gerna's youngest son was slumped against another man, blood seeping from his arm. "My stars, Pas!" He ushered them into the shack, slammed the door, and helped the stranger to lay the boy on the bed.

"What's happened?" Marl pushed his mother out of the way and retrieved a jar from one of the shelves. It contained blood moss.

They had to pry the man off of Pas's arm.

"Hurry!" Etutsa took the moss and motioned for a knife hanging from the wall as he examined the wound, holding it high over Pas's chest.

The bleeding slowed, but the arm was nearly severed.

"The axe slipped! I never meant to…"

It must've been a newly sharpened axe to have caused such damage. Messa shushed him and placed a comforting arm around his shoulders. To help him cope, she asked his name.

"Mercen."

"A tourniquet! The knife! We're going to have to finish the job. Quickly!"

Marl clutched the knife, now clean and ready for surgery, and stared. There was a wild look in his eyes; a fire from the depths of the world had erupted. "You can't cut off his arm!"

"It's already cut off, boy. This man will bleed to death if we panic now." Etutsa tried to snatch the knife.

"Mother, do something."

The priestess took the knife. "This wound is beyond me, Marl. Listen to Etutsa." She handed it to her friend, aware doing so was nothing short of betrayal of her son's faith. She couldn't let this young man die. It was better to be armless than lifeless.

Mercen trembled on the floor, choking on retched sobs. "I'm sorry, Pas. I'm sorry."

"No!" Marl shrieked as Etutsa began slicing through his friend's arm. "Don't do this to him. I can fix this!"

A great explosion of air pushed under the door. The shack rattled as the whirlwind hissed and sputtered.

Marl dove behind the white tornado and grasped the patient. He whispered something into the whirlwind. Papers and jars tumbled. It all happened in moments. Then, the mating of energy and air slipped under the door.

Everyone stared. The arm was now whole.

"I did it! I helped him! She told me I could."

Mercen prodded the perfect flesh. "I don't believe it! There's not a scratch on him! How did you... Magic, this is. You used your magic! I knew you black-hairs were..."

Messa didn't let Mercen finish. She retrieved a bottle from the floor labeled Sleep Juice, a crude name for the liquid of a potent-smelling plant. It wasn't as effective as sleepwart, but there was no time for tea. She poured some of the liquid on her apron, held the contents to the Selcovian's face, and waited until he slumped to the bed, passed out.

"You have your mother's gift," Etutsa stammered.

Messa's heart couldn't decide if it wanted to stop or beat in a frenzy. "No. He surpasses me. He surpasses all Erutani." She slowly crawled to Etutsa and stared down at the miracle. "We can mend only what's already mendable, just better than the remedies of a normal healer. Pas may be grateful and forgiving, but Mercen isn't from Na-ir. He may cause trouble."

"I don't understand." Marl sat with his knees in the air, back against the wall and mouth agape. "I thought you wanted me to learn. What's unwise about helping someone with a grave injury if you've the power to do so?"

The priestess wrapped her arms around her child. "There's nothing wrong with it, baby. But if the Selcovians find out you've such gifts, it'll only prompt fear. You've heard how Vill thinks of our kind. Mercen called your powers magic. It's not the same thing, but, in their eyes, magic is evil."

He furrowed his brow. "But, if I hadn't done this, Pas's life would've been ruined."

"Not necessarily," Etutsa chimed in, scooting over to sit next to them. "I've seen many grave injuries over the suns. Mankind is resilient, young one. People always find ways to live within their means, even if their means is minus a limb." He patted Marl's leg and sighed. "That doesn't make what you did any less noble; but it's still…well, it's terrifying."

Messa sat back and ran her fingers through her hair. "You were confident you could heal him. Have you done this before?" She cupped her hands across her son's tear-stained cheeks, wiping Water away with her thumbs.

He nodded.

"Did anyone see you?"

He blinked and nodded again.

"Show me."

Marl closed his eyes and showed her the meadow. Specter-like screams came from the bottom of the hill, near the little stream to the north. Hereu was backed against a tree clutching a black lamb. She pointed a small dagger at a grey wolf. It was Gyr, the head of a pack that often roamed near the village. Under him laid a mass of cream-colored fur and blood.

Marl tossed rocks and screamed. They came within inches of each other, blue eyes to yellow. After much shouting and gnashing of teeth, the wolf left.

This surprised Messa. She had an agreement with this pack, but they weren't easy to persuade, especially when they were starving. She rested her head on her son's brow. "Why did Gyr leave?"

"I told him where to find the herd of deer downwind of us. He felt it was a better meal for his pack than treacherous dog and boney youths. I feel bad for the deer." His broad cheek twitched in discontent.

"So, you healed the dog?"

Marl nodded. "Hereu was sure Broom was dead. But I begged for his life. Wind told me I could."

Pride mixed with terror. She glanced at Pas and Mercen. "You're lucky only Hereu saw."

Marl swallowed. "What're you going to do?"

Messa took the knife. "We can't let the rest of the village know."

Etutsa closed his eyes and nodded. "Let me."

He sliced around the limb, stopping short of severing bone and tendon. Blood poured, fresh and pure: red. Messa turned away.

Marl jumped. "What're you doing? Why would you do that?"

"Boy, we have to convince them that what happened here was normal. People need to see a wound." Etutsa wrapped cloth around the arm to keep Pas from bleeding out and stood up to retrieve a needle and thread. "We can convince them they overreacted, that the damage wasn't great, but we can't say there was no damage at all."

Marl slammed his fists into the wall. "There's no reasoning with either of you! This is on your heads! I don't care if people hate me. I had to do it. You're both idiots." He stormed out of the cottage with one thought on his mind. *Lies, lies, always lies.*

Messa followed him out but she wasn't intent on a chase. Etutsa would need her comfort after this day, and there was no comforting the Wanderer.

Nojhi was no longer there. She closed the door and turned. Mercen was stirring near the cot but not yet conscious.

Etutsa's hands were trembling as he sutured the wound. "Messa, might I ask you to finish this? I can't anymore."

She took the needle.

"Ah," he sighed, placing an affectionate hand to her shoulder. "I've always been told that old age means wisdom and great strength of character. Why do I feel more foolish now than I was in my youth?"

Messa relaxed into his unassuming touch. "I know what you mean."

Etutsa kicked a shattered jar. "Look what Wind has done to my shack! Darkened bitch."

THIRTEEN

Natsir entered the empty cottage with a heavy heart and placed three ripe pumpkins on the table. His shirt hung over the side of Mother's chair, the stitching unfinished. No matter. He was more than capable of sewing his own garments. He'd allowed her to take it on because it gave her something to still her mind.

He removed his work shirt and washed his soil-splattered hands in the unused dish pot. Then, he stoked the fire and settled into the chair.

Mother's hand was usually sure, but the stitches in his sleeve were chaotic today. He ripped them out.

What makes them difficult? He did not mean the stitches.

Water had told him some people were born to be loud and emotional, unstill because of the passions within them. Shouting wasn't a will to harm, but a way to release the tension. His family was full of that.

It pained him, but Natsir had confidence the tremors would pass. Until they did, he'd ebb and flow with it, always standing behind them, ready to extinguish fires.

Two yellow jewels set in darkness apparated in front of him, breaking his concentration on the thread. Natsir peered into his cot. *I didn't realize you were here, Pilgrim.*

The black cat stretched and yawned. His fur had lost its sheen. *It's quieter here without the youngling causing havoc.* He spent several minutes judging his hop down to the floor boards and landed with a great harrumph. *I enjoy the simple warmth of fire in these bones.*

Are you well, old friend?

Old friend is right. I'm ancient among my kind. It's been an honor to have hunted this long. However, I feel it's time to give myself back to the comforting arms of Earth.

Natsir dropped the sleeve into his lap and stared. *I grieve to hear this. I've always enjoyed your company and wisdom.* He stroked Pilgrim near the nape of the neck.

And I you, Gifted One. I would've liked to have seen your kittens. Will you do something for me, friend? Please be there with me when it's my time. I want to see you before I go.

Tears fell on the cat's bristled fur. *It would be my honor.*

Thank you. Pilgrim twitched as the salt water sunk into his skin.

Natsir stroked the drops away.

Might I sleep by the hearth now?

Of course. He placed the cat on the warm stones and finished mending.

Pilgrim wheezed and groaned, drifting into sleep, his stomach heaving.

Natsir shuddered. He wanted to speak with Mother, to talk about the loss of things familiar. He wanted to speak with Father, to have a hearty slap on the back that said all things work themselves out.

He didn't want to speak to Marl.

I need my heart strengthened, not pounded to mush. He put the needle on the mantle. *I need Para.*

Natsir threw on his shirt. The stitching wasn't perfect, but it didn't matter. He was clean and the fabric was whole. She would know he'd tried. He tiptoed over to his cot and retrieved the blue shawl and painting, catching himself mid-sniffle as he noticed grey-black hair flecking the image. He wiped it off and smiled at the face he loved most.

The image had been complete for days. Every time he had tried to give it to her, something strange would happen.

He couldn't abandon Father when his heart was aching, or Mother as her belly churned. Little siblings were nuisances at any age.

But now, the atmosphere was still. There was no hint of a storm.

I'd be stupid to lose this chance.

He folded the parchment and tucked it into the cloth. For the first time in many suns, he was forced to lock the door behind him.

***

Now, don't get distracted.

He strolled through the woody entrance to Na-ir. Normally, he would have warned her he was coming, but he knew she'd forgive him for this surprise. Para always forgave him.

Natsir patted the shawl bundle as carts creaked past and dogs barked near his feet. He had to sidestep a crowd of cackling villagers.

He overshot the chieftain's house. *Shatter the stars!*

It unnerved him to be touched by strangers; although, in his frequent bouts of unconscious movement, he often found himself walking into several people who felt the same.

Natsir looked around one more time before stepping back out into the fray, deciding it was best to follow along the shops than to take the most direct route through the square.

As he passed by Etutsa's door, his conscience forced him to stop. Next to the healer's shack, a member of his family was slumbering on the cold autumn ground.

"Father?"

The healer's door was closed fast, but he could hear noises resonating through the wood.

"Sit down, Marl! I've had it with you!"

Natsir gulped. Mother never yelled. Baby brother was in deep trouble, but he deserved it. He shook Father's shoulder. The poor man wouldn't budge. It was understandable; he'd been troubled and sleepless for days.

Three more tries was all Natsir was willing to give. Nothing. His meeting with Para would have to wait.

He shoved the presents into his shirt, leaving a strange bulge, and then pulled on Father's arm. *Mother Sun, give me strength.* Ligaments in his shoulder strained. "I'll take you home. Wake up!"

The commotion in the shack dissipated, although he still heard terse voices.

Natsir huffed and heaved. Marl was quick and lean, but *he* could move boulders. What was this sleeping man but a fleshy, immobile boulder? *I'm the strongest, tallest young man in the village. If I can't move him, no one can.*

He leaned into the great mass by the door and heaved once more. Father toppled over and snorted.

Natsir frowned. *This is ridiculous. I should leave him here.* He felt uncomfortable for thinking it, but there was no use pushing dormant boulders.

The decision was made for him. Several people shrieked, parting the crowd, as a man raced to the healer's door. He was carrying young Pas, the blacksmith's apprentice.

"Help! Please help!" The man moaned and fumbled to bang on the door.

Some of the villagers stopped to stare but did nothing.

Natsir pounded for them. He could smell a metal tinge mixed with dirt and wood—a pool of blood. He stepped back to let them enter the shack.

The door slammed but the shouting continued.

Mother Sun send healing rays to your young servant!

Natsir turned back to his task. To his surprise, Father was sitting up, a hand clutched to his head.

"*That* was what woke you up? That!"

Father crossed his eyes and stared. "What's going on?"

It was no use being angry. Natsir lifted him by the arm, rolling his eyes as he heard the parchment crunch in the space next to his abdomen. "Pas has suffered a nasty accident."

Father stumbled to his feet and winced. "Do they need help?"

"They'll be fine. You need to get home though. You look horrible."

The old man accepted his son's shoulder and the embarrassing hobble back to the cottage. He fell into his bed. Pilgrim settled on a pillow beside him.

"Where are you going?" Father grumbled.

"Don't worry. *I* am coming back." Natsir shut the door and ran.

***

The mangled shirt and creases in the parchment refused to cooperate as he approached G'Nirac's house. The painting had suffered a minor smudge on the horse's flank, but it was barely noticeable.

This time, Natsir approached from the back end, around the woods.

Para? Are you here?

He reached out to his heart's desire in the warmth of the afternoon sun, passing barren fruit trees and rows of squash and herbs. Calico chickens dared not disturb him. He was resolved and not in any mood to hear chitchat from hens.

Her sweet, watery voice floated through the garden leaves. *Nat! Is everything well?*

Para marched out from the house in her bare feet. Her stare made him blush. She wiped her hands on her apron and looked around the house, smirking as if contemplating something unsuitable for a chieftain's daughter. Natsir's heart bounced.

"Wanna go riding? Meet me in the stables." Para winked. She was already wearing her favorite riding dress, a hazel green.

He was soon peering around the entrance to the stables, relieved to find only the horses there. The sweet, equestrian smell filled his sinuses and he took it all in. This was one of the most blessed places in Na-ir, and he planned to frequent it forever.

Natsir ran his fingers through a chestnut-colored mane. He'd been given free access to the chieftain's horse. G'Nirac could no longer ride. It was one of several kind permissions he'd received from the chieftain of late.

"How are you feeling, friend?" He tossed the saddle up. "Where should we go today?"

Anope stamped and the sleek fur of his back twitched. *Let's go to the cliffs. Clouds are rolling in.*

It was good advice, as usual. There was still time to make the northern cliffs before sunset and be back into Na-ir without much fuss. It'd be a perfect place to be alone with Para and profess his feelings.

The Star of Na-ir entered the stables, gliding past in her boots and pressed garments, riding gloves on her small, slender hands. Her father would have been aghast at her lack of a shawl, but Natsir loved the way her red hair danced around her shoulders as she raced ahead of him.

Want to go to the cliffs?

The answer was always yes. Para placed her foot on her horse's stirrup. She didn't need his help, but for some reason he gave her a hand up.

Rinpiels whinnied, twitching her white coat. *You'll brush me well, Gifted One. I've already been ridden twice today!*

Natsir laughed and made a solemn oath to pamper her later.

Para paid no mind to his amusement as she righted herself in the saddle, easy with his abilities to see and hear things she could not. She stroked Rinpiels's mane and flashed her handsome blue eyes. Marl had been right; her affection was obvious.

They took the stream path through the meadow, avoiding the town altogether. Not a thought passed between them, though Para stared, pink brightening her speckled checks. Natsir longed to count every fleck.

She dismounted as they neared the edge of the cliffs.

Below, the rush of water whispered secrets into the stones, a sculptor chipping away with some grand design. The clouds caught golden swatches of light in Para's hair and held onto them, molten steel falling through vaporous hands.

My painting doesn't come close.

This was the stillness he'd been looking for. Only the rustle of an autumn breeze and the call of birds echoed through the woods. The wet earth and debris smelled deep and savory as the horses' hooves pressed into the soil. This was perfection.

While they watched Anope and Rinpiels nuzzle in the cool air, Natsir had an overwhelming urge to press his lips to Para's, to place his hands on her waist. It shocked him, but it was hardly the first time. She came very close, pressing against him as he leaned into a juniper.

"I love this place. It's so beautiful."

He reached into his shirt for the painting. "I've something else beautiful for you too."

She started and turned to face him, blue eyes tinged green as the golden sunset focused on the spot they'd claimed.

"Please close your eyes."

Para pursed her lips and jiggled. When they were young, his surprises were often flowers or interesting stones, treasures. He was relying on the memory of this.

Natsir positioned the opened painting on the blue cloth, hoping to make everything look more attractive, and held tight to the edges so insufferable Wind wouldn't abscond with it.

"Open up."

She blinked but didn't look down. Instead, she giggled at his dumbfounded expression.

Leaves crunched behind her and she turned. "Oh, look! It's your brother."

Natsir tucked the gifts into his shirt with a slight groan. Of all moments! Didn't he have better things to do than plague his family with selfish woes?

As Marl passed by the juniper, he started and looked up. The same thought crossed both brothers' minds. *What are you doing here?*

"Hello." Para nudged closer.

"Hello." Marl rubbed his neck and looked around. "Are you alone?"

"Yes," Natsir snapped, startling everyone but himself.

"Oh. It's a nice sunset. I'll leave you to enjoy it." Marl didn't seem himself. He was as empty and wet as a new clay pot. He turned on his heels and slinked away.

Para bit her lip. "He's sad. You should talk to him, Nat."

Her bumbling suitor crossed his arms and pouted. He was livid with his brother for always being in the way, for always bringing himself to the center of everyone's lives. Marl was the eye of a dangerous storm—one he didn't want to be pulled into.

She laughed and placed a gentle hand to his arm. "Oh come now; he's your brother."

Natsir was unable to say no to those bright, pleasing eyes. She took the reins from the tree and the horses reluctantly pulled away. He knew how they felt; the moment was gone.

"Thank you for the sunset, Natsir Ganwin." She blushed and came to his chest, looking uneasy, guilty. She brushed his skin. "All of them."

Gathered energy spilled out in a rush. Natsir took Para's face in his hands and kissed her. She tasted of blackberries and smelled as sweet. It was the rightest thing he had ever done. Her crystal eyes widened.

"You're welcome." Natsir raced after Marl.

A quick glance at the cliffside revealed the mauve silhouette of a woman leaning against a chalk-white horse. The very image of his joy.

***

"All right, where are you?"

The large shoeprints had vanished from the upturned earth. Natsir glanced high into a pine and shook his head. Marl was dangling from a branch, his lanky legs kicking.

"Come down. Tell me what's wrong."

This wasn't the first time Natsir had found him crying in a tree. The boy was made for mischief and whippings.

"I'd prefer to remain, please." Marl leaned into the trunk and heaved his chest.

"I'm too old to be climbing after you, baby brother." Natsir shook a finger. "*You're* too old to be up there."

Scolding wasn't working today. Embarrassing him might do the trick.

"What would Hereu think if she saw you acting like a child?" No woman wanted a pouting, whining creature for a husband.

Marl grinned and wiped tears from his face. "She'd join me, coward."

Natsir sighed. Hereu was either blinded by love or incredibly tolerant. He tried to keep a patient tone, though he was certain there was a part of him Marl might uncover, a part resembling Father in a righteous rage.

"I'm not afraid of the tree." *Or you.* "I'm just mature enough not to be up in one."

"You know, if you climbed trees more, you wouldn't be so uptight." Baby brother stuck out his tongue and tossed a twig.

"Marl Ganwin! Get down. Now!"

A flash of brown fabric and black feathers descended, an owl in battle with a crow. "Fine! Sheesh, Nat." *Why is everyone yelling?*

If Natsir had to waste precious time meant for Para in order to handle his brother's problems, he was going to make the best use of it. He took his brother by the collar and pushed him south.

"Let's walk, shall we." He was surprised to see fear. "Now, why are you out here? I heard Mother yell in Na-ir. Don't tell me nothing's wrong."

They walked for some moments in unbearable silence.

"I'm confused, Nat. I'm not sure what to do."

"All right. Tell me. Why're you confused?"

Marl wrapped his arms around his shoulders. "What am I, brother?"

It was a sincere question, but Natsir laughed. "You're a pain in the backside."

Marl stiffened. "Am I that bad? I don't mean to be."

Nasir laughed again. It was the most ludicrous thing he'd ever heard. Marl thrived in chaos.

"No, seriously, Nat. I don't want to be a pain in the backside."

"Then you should stop being such a selfish prick."

You sound like Father.

"Yeah, well, I'm starting to understand him. You make everyone crazy. Sometimes I think life would be simpler if we all ignored you." It felt good to say these things aloud. It gave him an affable energy.

Marl collapsed onto a boulder and burst into tears. Natsir felt the seductive warmth leave his cheeks. His baby brother had never looked more alone or more vulnerable.

"What're we going to do with you?"

The youth continued to sob.

"You're not always bad. You try; but you forget to think about others. We have lives too."

"That's not true, brother." Marl wiped at his face and hiccupped. "I love you all. I'd do anything for you… and Para too."

Natsir cringed. It *had* been Para's decision to end their romantic moment, not the crow's.

"I do what Mother and Father ask. I keep their secrets. They pull me in so many directions."

"What secrets? They share everything: home, bed, and mind."

Marl shivered and tapped his foot against the great stone. "Father has a sword, covered in jewels," he spat out quickly. "It's hidden in the side boards of the shed. It's rusted, but you should see it."

"How do you know this?"

"He showed me. He told me about his time as a soldier. Mother thinks he threw it over a cliff. We had to lie." He ran his hand through his hair. "It was fun at first, but I learned about Surnow, and I'm certain he and Mother were there."

Natsir gasped. These revelations were otherworldly, unreal. "What's Sur…? Never mind. If Mother and Father have secrets, it's their business."

Marl jumped up and slapped him on the shoulder. "Exactly! They keep putting me in the middle though. Sometimes I think I know too much."

"Or too little." Natsir crossed his arms and leaned into the stone. "You don't have to reveal their secrets to be obedient."

"I don't?"

"No, just apologize. Even if you think you did nothing wrong. Things will sort themselves out. Like Mother says, be the better man."

Marl smiled. It was pure and innocent and it made Natsir remember why he loved his brother.

Damn it! Make up your mind. Are you a temperamental boy, a playful man, or the other way around?

"You're always so useful, brother. I don't know what I'd do without you." He threw his arms around Natsir and jumped with glee. "You're right. Let's go home."

When they entered the cottage, Father was staring into a fire. Mother hadn't returned and Pilgrim had vanished.

The old man didn't look as they entered. "Hello, sweeties. How's my little family this evening?"

Marl stiffened and turned. Natsir blocked the way. *Ha! And you called me a coward. Move! I've changed my mind. He looks like death itself!*

Not happening, little brother. You've angered the bear. This is his cave.

Father stared, then jumped up with arms open wide. "Where've you been?"

Marl stepped back in fear, pressing into Natsir's stomach and the parchment.

The old man stopped short of grasping him and frowned. "Don't leave again. Let's end this now."

The youngest balled his hands into fists.

"I see." Father stroked his beard and looked around the cottage. He snatched the unused sheets from little brother's bed and waved them. *Baby hold?*

Natsir nodded. This would be effective. They threw the wayward boy into the cloth and wrapped him as quickly as a spider would a fly.

You tricked me! Marl yelped as they bound him in tight knots.

It's for your own good.

Father lifted him like a giant lettuce wrap and slammed him into the floor. Marl gasped. The old man giggled and sat on his legs.

"Get off of me!" Marl kicked and struggled, a particolored bug with a red-faced look of contempt. *I can burn my way free.*

Natsir laughed. *I'm sure you could, hot head, but that wouldn't make you the better man.* He tapped on his brother's chest like a small drum.

Father nudged Natsir with his elbow. "All right, son. We'll play this your way. Spill it!"

"This isn't a fair fight. Let me out!"

The old man chuckled. "Who says this is a fight? I'm just a father having a conversation with his caterpillar son. Are you ready to become a butterfly yet?"

Natsir stopped drumming and chuckled. His brother *was* vain and flighty.

"That's not funny," Marl hissed.

"Ah, you're a snake. I knew it!" Father bounced on his legs to elicit a groan. "You can't be human. You're too dangerous."

Marl stopped struggling and slammed his black head into the floor boards, growling.

"Ready to talk?"

"Yeah, sure." He glared at his brother. *I'll show you a better man, cur.*

Natsir smirked.

"Why did you leave?" Father poked him in the stomach several times until he answered.

"I was tired of fighting. You never listen."

The old man stroked his beard. "I'll give you that. I was pigheaded; I admit it." He gave the caterpillar boy's stomach a gentle pat. "Please accept my apologies. Now, where've you been?"

"In the forest."

"All right. What were you doing out there besides waging war against the elements?" Father rubbed his fingers on his chin and clicked his teeth. *If it's that girl, I'm breaking every bone in his body.*

Natsir stayed stoic, hoping to make a good example. *Don't lie. He's just letting off steam.*

Marl trembled. *If he'll threaten me over Hereu, what'll he do to Mother?*

Mother? You think he'd hurt his wife? Marl that's absurd. He's hot-headed, but he's a village elder for a reason. You owe him an apology.

"Come on, son." Father licked his lips.

I'm fighting another wolf, I think.

It was an odd statement. Natsir knew about Gyr, but that pack was too loyal to the spirits.

Brother, hold my hand.

Natsir felt this was an innocent request, so he did. He instantly regretted submitting. A young man wearing a bright, silver helm materialized in his mind. He held a polished shield with two warriors locked in combat on its face. In his other hand was a jeweled sword. The image was beautiful but eerie. The man had the same eyes as him, the same hair and sharp nose, but it wasn't the same person. The remarkable fierceness in this face didn't match anyone in the room.

The image changed to reveal a forest clearing, searing flames over bodies of black-haired men, women, and children. All around the scene was red—blood and fire. It was hard to tell who was living or dead.

Natsir released Marl's hand and trembled.

That's Surnow.

Father narrowed his eyes, scouting for traitors.

Marl sighed. "I'm sorry. I've been with a woman, but it's not what you think?"

"Son, there are laws in this land; Mlaerian laws, grant you, but they apply." He tweaked Marl's nose and laughed. "You can't claim a woman without her father's consent."

I told you he wouldn't explode.

Marl scrunched his sore nose.

"G'Nirac is forgiving. But those from Selcovi won't be. We need to talk to Vill, I suppose." Father made a childish face and groaned.

"No!" Marl's face went white as he kicked and fought against his confines. "No, you're not listening." The boy's voice was breaking in painful, sharp cords.

Father leaned back again on Marl's legs, stunned.

Natsir sat up. *What're you doing? Stop playing games. The secret is out.*

Yes it is! Marl didn't seem to mean Hereu. *I've seen what he's capable of. I have an idea.* His eyes darted around the cottage. "It's not a real woman."

"Not a real... What?" The old man scratched his head. "I don't understand."

Well, not one of flesh. It's Wind! She's been teaching me things. Remarkable things!

Father's green eyes rolled back into his head. He struggled to stay upright. "What... what things?"

"Let me out and I'll show you." Marl wriggled, ready to leave the cocoon.

"No more fighting. I'm not going to hurt you." Father wiped a hairy hand across his face and groaned. *Such ridiculous lies! When is he going to grow up?*

"I don't want to fight you either, Father. Let me show you. You'll understand."

They stood him back on his feet and unwrapped him. The cloth fell like a king's mantle off his shoulders.

Marl waved his arms at his subjects. "Now, don't be afraid."

Father didn't seem to be adhering to this advice; he looked paler than sleet.

"I've learned a few new skills."

The blaze in the hearth intensified. Father and Natsir shouted and covered their faces. Within seconds, it was gone. The charcoal glowed with molten orange cracks. Marl waved his hand and brought the fire back to its original intensity.

"Handy huh?" He appeared to be looking for approval. He wasn't getting it.

Father trembled. "Is that all?"

Marl, he's more afraid of you than you are of him. Is it your plan to scare him? Natsir was unwilling to admit he was terrified too. The veracity of his brother's abilities was abnormal. He had never seen Mother control fire quite this way. He was certain she could not.

"Nope." Marl strolled over to the old man and touched his arm.

The giant yelped and backed off. His shirt smoked. A hole had burned through the grey cloth, but his skin was unscathed.

"I can make warmth at will. That's why staying out at night can't bother me anymore."

Father sat down and ran his fingers through his hair.

"That's not all though." Marl took Mother's kitchen knife and held it over his arm. "Please forgive me." He sliced through his wrist and gasped. The knife fell with a great clang.

"No!" Father jumped and took hold of him.

Scarlet stains splattered the wood and sizzled on hearth stones. Marl's blue eyes rolled back into his head.

Natsir's chaotic, noisy world stopped; all sound ceased to exist except for the pounding of his heart. *It can't be true. He'd never...* He stood there, dumb and useless. This chaos was new.

184

Marl's eyes fluttered open. "Look. I'm all right."

He pushed out his arm. There was no blood, no scar; the vein ran blue and unbroken. But the bed, wood, stone, and knife glistened. So did Father's hands. It hadn't been a dream.

"I can heal anything. I reknit Pas's severed arm."

Father's mouth fell open.

What are you? You're not a snake, for sure, but you're no longer human. Natsir knew now why his brother had been torn and confused. The problem had never been Hereu.

A giant hand slapped the boy across the face, leaving traces of blood. "What were you thinking?" Father's cheeks and ears were a matching color of red rage. He gathered Marl into his arms and shook him violently. "Don't ever do that again! I love you, boy. I thought you were going to leave us for good." His shoulders shuddered as he tried to breathe.

The Wanderer wheezed under the old man's hold. "I won't, Father. I promise."

"Don't ever talk to Wind again. Hear me!"

The authority in his command was unmistakable. Natsir recognized him then—the man in the shining helm with the fierce hazel eyes. This wasn't the first time Father had seen this much torment.

Marl opened his mouth and looked to the floor. He couldn't make this promise. Wind did as she pleased. "I understand. I'll do as you say."

Father wrapped him in another baby hold, but neglected to use the sheet this time. He rocked him on the edge of the bed and shuddered.

They found a small measure of peace in the silence.

The door opened with a click and they all jumped. Mother entered looking worn and worried. Her blue eyes flashed as she took in the scene. "Marl? What... what's happened?"

He tore away from Father and threw his arms around her. *I'm sorry, Mother. I understand.*

She looked confused, but stroked his hair and kissed his one unbloodied cheek. Her secret outing to Etutsa's wouldn't be revealed. He was wiping blood over the small splotches where her blue dress was already sullied.

It was better this way, but the metallic smells and salty tastes in the warm air were stifling Natsir. No embrace could relieve this ache. He needed the cool of night to wake him. He rushed outside. If they had called after him, he didn't hear; he didn't care.

Wind had finally stolen the boy he had promised to protect.

Natsir's flight ceased when he reached the warbler's tree. The river trickled in whispers as he rested aching limbs against the pine.

The clouds that had made such a brilliant sunset on the horizon when he had kissed Para now floated overhead, grey and looming. In the high reaches of air they parted to reveal the gaze of Father Moon.

He took the practice rods from the pine. They whistled through the air and landed with two satisfying splashes. If the accursed sword had been there, he'd have tossed it too.

Natsir had learned too much today. He no longer wanted to be a part of anything they touched. There was too much blood on their hands.

A small breeze caressed his checks and tickled his neck. It carried with it a tinge of condescending laughter.

Natsir shivered but stood his ground. *Leave my brother alone.*

Oh, my silly boy. She played with his hair and whipped his clothing, tugging at the presents still stuffed in his shirt. *You know I can't.*

Natsir raised a fist and slammed it into the tree. Wind laughed again.

And neither can you. She left him in a flurry, rising high through the trees and into the clouds.

Natsir slid to the ground and fought back hot tears. He pulled out Para's picture and smoothed it against his legs. *Mother Sun, please comfort my ailing heart.*

An ice-cold arm fell on his shoulders and a vaporous breath leaned into his ear.

Don't worry, Gifted One. I'm here.

Natsir sat in the dark with Water, her essence falling from his eyes like drops of his brother's blood.

FOURTEEN

The Star of Na-ir ruffled the skirts of her best blue dress and stood a good soldier in the public square. It was her duty to be the very image of flawlessness, radiant and kind. Nevertheless, she recoiled when the crowd erupted in applause.

Para couldn't hide her discontent. Papa was experiencing more painful stabs in his chest and he wasn't able to keep her in check with his affectionate smiles.

Several old women patted her shoulders; a few men she'd known since birth hugged her. She tried to smile for their sakes, but they all irked her with their ignorance. The entire town believed in a Lufnis she knew didn't exist.

Curled smiles and bows masked a man who'd spent most of his life torturing the only thing he was ever jealous of—so many bruise and tears.

People chatted and exclaimed, reminding her it was supposed to be a happy day. *Is it?*

She watched her brother clasp arms and swear an oath to a woman as contemptuous as him. As they kissed, Para uttered a curse under her breath that Eurgi would be as barren of child as she was in mind.

The nasty Dasha tea her brother preferred might have adverse effects on her womb; it did nothing for Lufnis's disposition. Still, Para had to admit, they were a good match, the monstrous badger and his wife, no matter what they drank.

Soon it wouldn't matter how much he bit and snarled; she'd be gone. She'd leave him and his sour wife to their chiefdom and run to the lush canyon sanctuary that was her second home. The ill-starred letter had already been sent.

It broke her heart to leave Papa, bedridden as he was, but she could not risk being trapped here in this fanciful village prison when he died. The thumb of Rippan, even in the shadow of his overbearing father, was preferable to Lufnis.

But now there was Natsir.

No. Natsir had always been; she was fooling herself to think it wasn't true. She loved him with the same veracity she loved Wind's caress in her face and the smell of cut hay on a spring day. He was as natural to her as thought; such a quiet man to be her wild abandon. Natsir held her playful secrets, her uninhibited desires.

In the twenty suns she'd grown to understand and love him, it had once or twice crossed her mind he shared her affections, but he always remained cool, quiet. She'd resigned herself to think that he must care for her on the same level they both loved Marl.

Para ran for the linden tree as the crowd parted, pressing her back against its supportive trunk. She'd wanted to be a part of the Ganwin family since she'd seen them in the wagon.

Marl and Nojhi were protective and wild. Messa was beautiful and clever—the only mother she'd ever known. And Natsir... Looking into his green eyes was like looking into the judicious face of the Great Father. That kiss in the sunset had been her first indication she was the rightful owner of something as precious as moonlight.

Why had he waited so long? *Damn him.*

Night was falling. Every crunch on the frozen ground made her lurch. She hoped the village would be too happy, too drunk, to notice the red star crying.

A crack in the sheltered branches of the linden tree told her she wasn't alone. Marl and Hereu waved from one of the topmost branches.

Para wiped the tears from her face and pushed into the woods. She hated them both right now, for their freedom, for their bliss. They were never far from each other's embrace, from the light in each other's eyes. Jealousy was overwhelming. Hereu couldn't help she was loved recklessly; Marl had always been more assertive and outspoken. He hadn't meant to ruin that one perfect moment she'd waited for.

I should've known. Nat was always true. I should've said something. She had avoided that sacred recklessness. *Perfect Miss Para*, she mocked herself. But a truth didn't always have to be spoken, did it?

"Para! Para!" A man had found her in the woods. Which man?

She stopped and turned, half hoping to see someone who confounded and pleased her more than any other person could. It was a disappointment, but not a sadness, to see Uncle Etutsa. He was smashing into dormant twig-tangled bushes with deafening cracks, tripping over his feet.

"Marl told me you were in the woods. I didn't believe him. You usually have more sense."

"What do you want, uncle?" The venom in her response was equal to his standard banter, but rare for her usual pretty-smiling countenance. Para's chest was heaving too.

Etutsa stopped and stared. "Lufnis is asking for you. Are you well, sweetheart?"

"I'm fine. I'm always fine, aren't I?" She crossed her arms and shivered. "What's he want with me?"

"He wants to make a toast, to bless your impending marriage."

"He can keep his blessings. They're no better than curses."

The old healer jumped.

Lufnis found them in the closing darkness and approached with the purpose of a man who would not be denied. "There you are, sister."

He tipped his hat at their uncle before placing a forceful arm around her waist. She fell into place instinctively.

"Everyone misses you. Come. Join the celebration."

He knew she'd obey without her black-haired body guard and her tall, blond confidant there to witness his schemes. He might as well have been holding a dagger to her spine.

"Yes, brother." The words fell like stones.

Etutsa's jaw dropped. "Wait for me, my sweeties. Is there something sinister going on here?" he whispered behind his nephew's back. "You know you can confide in me."

Para shook her head. "I'm well, uncle. Things are as they should be."

They entered the orange bonfire light of the square and Lufnis dragged her next to the pillar. People were clapping again. He had returned the pretty maiden to the safety of the village. Now they all could enjoy the warmth of her presence. It was strange how they never noticed he eclipsed her true light.

"I'm overjoyed. But I'm not the only one to find such perfect happiness." Lufnis held his hand out to Eurgi. She bounced to him, looking like some absurd black and brown pastry.

The crow and his love heaved and flapped in the linden tree. Para smiled.

Lufnis cast them a warning glance. "My sweet sister K'Parre shall also soon be married."

Marl dangled while Hereu tickled the line of black hairs on his stomach, not paying attention. Para forgot to listen too; she was used to ignoring her brother. Her blue eyes fell on the seamstress, grinning in the crowd.

"My friend, Rippan Seisyll of the Dasha has claimed her hand."

Para felt empty again, fragile.

Gerna's smile waned. A few villagers clapped; the rest chattered in disbelief.

Marl fell out of the tree with a thud. He held his aching head and looked across the square.

Para followed his gaze. Natsir was standing several yards before her, tall and golden. Messa and Nojhi placed steadying hands on his shoulders. This sight stripped the numbness from Para's mind and her tender soul ripped to shreds. It was an unbearable state of being.

"Oh no! What've you done, child?" Uncle Etutsa's low voice chided.

Para ran. Darkness had come and a star had fallen.

***

Marl was like a hunter tracking a fox. She had no hole. "You're supposed to be *my* sister! How could you do that to him?"

Para whirled around to face the tall crow of a man, choosing to use her claws and teeth. Her heart beat quickly. "It's none of your concern. Leave me alone!"

"Not until you tell me why you chose darkened Rippan over my brother!" His fists were clenched.

She'd seen this stance and this resolve before. It was her fault Marl was always eager to fight. She'd always urged him on. *I've been using them. One as a playmate, the other as a whipping boy.* She tried not to cry. "I don't know why you're surprised. He's never showed any interest."

"Shatter the stars, Para! He follows you around like a foal. The whole town's in shock. Gerna's taking it personally."

He pointed to the lights of the village behind them, daring her to deny it. The distant drumming of a bonfire dance echoed through the trees.

"Don't tell me you never noticed."

"Nat knew about Rippan's request. Why didn't he ask me to marry him if we were anything more than friends?"

Marl's jaw dropped. He was floundering for a perfect explanation, but didn't seem to have one. She couldn't explain it either.

"He should've approached me tonight, if I was that important to him, not send his brutish baby brother."

Marl tore his feathered head. She wanted him to hit her, if only to give her an excuse to hit back. Lufnis hadn't taken the fight out of her after all.

"Oh, come on! We both love him, but you know Nat is a darkened idiot. He takes forever to act, and he gets advice from the damned cat! Besides, he didn't send me. He told me to leave you alone. He's convinced Lufnis did this to trick you. He thinks you're being polite because it's his wedding; in the morning you're going to say he was mistaken."

"He has that much faith in me?" Para unclenched her fists.

"Like I said, he's a darkened idiot." Marl approached her carefully. "I left him in the stables, with Father, Mother, and Etutsa. He's waiting there because he's certain that's where you'll be when you're ready to talk."

She sighed. She was given to Rippan, forced into him like iron into fire, ready to be molded into Dasha nobility. What could she tell Natsir?

"I take it he'll be waiting with the horses a while."

Para fell to the frostbitten soil and sobbed. As always, Marl came to her rescue. He sat down and placed an arm around her shoulder. She didn't pull back. It was hard to be angry when he loved her and Natsir so furiously.

"There's nothing I can do. Lufnis has me trapped."

"Why should his opinion matter?"

"Because he'll be chieftain, because father will soon… leave us." She shivered and he tightened his grip. It felt like the hugs Nojhi had often given her as a girl. *You've your father's strength of purpose. Always the hero.* She was unable to stop the self-loathing. "I'm either to marry Rippan or be forced to serve Lufnis and Eurgi forever. He's told me he won't allow me to marry another. I'm too great a prize."

"Or I could break his head open." White lightning danced in Marl's eyes. "Listen. You're family already. You know we'll do anything for you. The entire town loves you. You're the Star of Na-ir—not because you're beautiful, but because you're kind and selfless. So selfless you'll relinquish your heart's desire to obey your brother and keep peace."

Para looked to the dust. Her remorse came out in small white puffs and her tears sharpened; the night was freezing fast.

Marl tapped her shoulder. "Chieftains can be deposed." His tone was masculine and very serious. "If Lufnis doesn't watch his step, he'll have an uprising on his hands."

"Are you saying you'd challenge him?" She blinked. The prospect was exhilarating and terrifying. She'd no doubt the dark boy could win, though invoking a challenge was archaic. It was still law.

"When have I not challenged him? If he treats his own sister abominably, he's not worth our spit. I'm not following him."

Para embraced Marl and laughed. He was young and bold, but not foolish. "It would be better if Nat kicks his backside, though. He'd make a better chieftain."

"But Nat is too levelheaded to kick someone's backside."

They snickered a while before realizing they'd nothing left to say that wasn't painful.

"So, what's in your shirt?" She had felt something hard.

Marl pulled a bottle from his pocket. "Oh, this? It's whiskey. Etutsa gave it to my brother."

Natsir didn't drink; he already had ways of feeling sick and dizzy and her uncle knew this.

"He says it's medicinal, but Nat pushed it on to me. He thinks I'm a reckless, drunken cur, I suppose." Marl slumped and looked down, sloshing the bottle. "I scared him the other day and I don't think he's happy with me."

"I'm sure whatever you've done this time, he'll forgive you." She smiled remembering the many times Nat had rescued them when they were children. She missed those innocent embraces when she would leap like a bird into his arms. "It's not like him to hold grudges."

"Yeah. He'll forgive you too. Already has. You can still make this right."

How? Belonging to Rippan made her ill, though there were worse men. Incurring Lufnis's wrath frightened her more. *Am I such a child that I'm afraid of retribution from a man three suns my senior? All of Na-ir is on my side. They were cheering for*

Nat too. "You're right, little brother, but I think I need more courage." She snatched the whiskey.

"You weigh next to nothing. This stuff will kill you!"

She laughed and took a giant swig of the spirit, taking on the burn and the tingle in her throat and sinuses. She practiced not screaming, holding the liquid, warm and pungent in her mouth. Tears forced out of her eyes; this time they didn't freeze.

"All right. Stop! You're courageous; I believe you." Marl swiped the bottle.

She coughed. "I'm ready. Take me to Nat, please."

Marl offered her a hand. She didn't take it, choosing to clamber upward and trip over the frilled hem of her dress. The spirit coursed through her, a river of sharp needles. It was going to be a strange and difficult walk back to the square.

***

They were surprised to find Natsir near the linden. Marl faded into the tree like a phantom, his dark form hidden but for his jeweled eyes.

"I've been calling. Why didn't you answer?"

Para blushed. Her pain and guilt must've closed her mind. It was best to get to the point; they'd waited long enough. "I was wrong. I shouldn't have let Lufnis force my hand. He can make love to a goat for all I care."

Natsir raked a hand through his hair. "I was hoping you'd say… something like that." From his pocket he pulled a crumpled blue mass smelling faintly of lavender. "I've been trying to give you this for a while, but certain *things* kept getting in the way." He glanced at his brother again and frowned.

Para unraveled the package.

"You bought the green, remember? I was too nervous to tell you this color made your eyes shine brighter."

An ice-cold breeze danced over her. Instinctively, Para placed the shawl around her shoulders. Parchment fell out. She unfolded it with the trepidation of revealing a prophecy.

Mother Sun radiated from the crumpled backdrop, on fire and bespeckled in golden dust. It was a verdant spring wherever she was.

Para's breath caught in her lungs, mingling with the whiskey fire. "Is this me?"

"That's what you look like to me." Natsir reached out to touch her arm; his grasp was gentle, tentative. *Why do you think I have so much trouble telling you how I feel? You're all I've ever wanted since we first came to Na-ir. I love you.*

I'm no goddess, Nat. I'm a coward. Why would you want such a wife?

He pulled her into him. Her spine ached where his fingers pressed. She kissed him, not feeling she deserved the opportunity, but taking it, nonetheless. She'd worry about Lufnis and Rippan later.

He released her and cocked his head. *Why do you smell like elderberries and whiskey?*

A shout from the square startled them before she could answer.

"I rescued your fair maiden, Marl." Cyan placed a hand on Hereu's back and pushed her forward playfully. "Where've you been? Eurgi got her claws into her. That thing can chatter like a woodpecker!"

Hereu pressed into her love and gave him a passionate kiss.

Marl's countenance brightened. "I was rescuing another fair maiden."

Natsir frowned again. His knuckles pressed into Para's vertebrae.

"Well, sort of," the crow stammered. "She rescued herself."

"Of course she did. She doesn't need a wild phantom to protect her."

Marl slumped into the tree and sighed.

"Ouch!" Cyan tapped on his drum and smiled coyly. "We could all use something to take away the tension. No offense, but Cousin Lufnis's wedding is boring." He shoved his lap drum in front of Natsir. "I'm exhausted; my hands are as red as Para's hair! Wanna play instead? I'm afraid the guy playing the fiddle went home, though."

"No thanks. I'm busy." Natsir's arm wrapped tighter around Para. Now he had her, he wasn't letting her go.

She blushed.

Marl thrust a hand into Hereu's skirt pocket and laughed as she squeaked. He gave her a peck on the cheek. "I can play the fife."

"That'll work!" Cyan exclaimed. "Still, it would be better to have some rhythm."

From over Cyan's shoulder, Para could see her brother staring, red-faced. There was no sign of the other Ganwins. The lack of supervision was invigorating. "Has there been a maidens' dance?"

It was an unspoken tradition for Telmah weddings, the perfect way to show eligible men what girls were still fair game. It was archaic and wild. She knew what it looked like, having always watched from her cage the beautiful women fly.

Cyan shook his head with a lusty smile. Natsir blushed.

Don't worry; I'll be good.

"What's the maidens' dance?" Hereu asked, her doe-brown eyes turned to Marl. She frowned at his expression and smacked him on the shoulder.

"Don't worry. It's an easy dance. You're a maiden right?"

Hereu blushed and picked up a stone. Marl placed his left fist to Cyan's jaw.

"Ha ha! All right. I believe you!" Cyan led the way to the middle of the square. Lufnis made an instant and purposeful approach, but Cyan pushed past him. "We're going to liven things for you, Luf."

Lufnis stammered. Para was bemused by her cousin's bravery; it bolstered hers.

They set up near the great pillar, away from the waning bonfire Retat tended while nursing a large flask of something. Natsir sat in the grass with the drum, looking like a nervous man holding a babe in his lap, while Marl leaned against the sacred stone.

The crowd gathered at Cyan's beckoning. A few Selcovian maidens recognized Hereu and joined with giggles and twirling skirts.

Cyan looked at Nerid and Rej as he shouted. "Only maidens are welcome to participate!"

The newlyweds scowled.

It was normal to play a rolling tune for this dance: *The Miller's Daughter* or *Lambs in the Meadow*. The goal was to start off slowly and then quicken the pace. The dark youth winked and started playing, blowing quickly and furiously into the little flute like he was the master of air and sound itself. It was a very pretty and ruckus melody, though slightly sharp in key.

Natsir slapped his leg. "I can't play to something *that* fast."

"But that's *my* song," Hereu shouted, already playfully swaying. Her oak eyes radiated.

"All right, brother," Marl said, blushing. "I'll slow it down." This time the melody was sensual, listening to wind chimes on a tender breeze. They reverberated obedient to his creative will.

Natsir provided the heartbeat to his brother's lyrical soul.

The girls gasped and turned to Para. She was meant to lead them.

As she took her first step, the chieftain's daughter disappeared and the square glowed with a brilliant red, speckled by starlight.

The sweet shepherdess twirled into a blue-brown blur. The other girls dissolved behind them, though she heard them laughing and teasing.

Para twirled her hips and raised her arms into the air freely, mimicking a street dancer, bejeweled and clad in silks. The shawl around her shoulders slipped.

As she twirled, she met two sets of eyes: one pair green and full of awe for her true beauty, the other brown and so contemptuous they didn't see her light at all. They alternated in her mind and swirled, leaves reflected in a pool. The brown no longer bothered her as long as she knew that with each revolution the green was still there.

The Selcovian girls gave up in fits of laughter and fell into their men or acquaintances without much fuss. One didn't have to be the best dancer to find romance. But Para and Hereu took it to heart. The two of them clasped hands and swung around, unable and unwilling to let go of the exhilaration of doing what they wanted.

The dance ended in a truce as they fell into a massive giggling pile of feminine limbs and blue skirts.

Hereu gasped and clutched her chest; there was so much wild abandon in her. "I think we both won!"

"I think you're right!"

The shepherdess skipped over to Marl and knocked him down with kisses. He was as pleased with her as she was of herself. They slipped off into the crowd.

Para flew to Natsir and jumped in his lap. He submitted to her act of passion. After a tender kiss, she opened her eyes to see Cyan's hazel stare.

His arms were crossed reproachfully, but his mouth was turned in a smirk. "That was clever cousin, beautiful. Could I have my drum back?"

She groaned. She had plopped down on top of his instrument.

Natsir fished it out from under her backside. "Sorry. I'll buy you another."

Cyan nodded. "Not your fault, friend. It was Para's boney butt that smashed it. I can fix it though." He waved the drum in salute before walking away.

Para returned to her bold ways. She was full of energy and happiness and reluctant to let it end.

They were interrupted by footsteps. Natsir looked up, but Para, thinking it was Lufnis, pulled him back into her.

"A-hem!" The cough wasn't her brother's. Nojhi stood beside them, tall and commanding, but kind. "Pardon me. I'm not sure what's going on here. You boys don't tell me anything anymore." He glanced across the square. "So, there's no marriage to Rippan then?"

She shook her head and blushed.

"Good. I was worried. It'll be nice to have you in the family, sweetheart." He said this with genuine warmth and promise. "One question though. Who's that girl you were dancing with? I think I recognize her."

"Oh Hereu, the shepherdess, Vill and Dalis's daughter." She caught Natsir's worried expression too late to shut up. *Oops. Stupid whiskey.*

"I thought so!" Mister Ganwin's great, hairy hands slammed together with the exuberance of a man preparing for hard labor. "You can go back to sucking the life out of my son."

They stiffened as he bounded across the square.

"Well, hello, Miss Wind. I've been dying to meet you. You're smaller than I thought."

Para groaned and slammed her head into Natsir's chest. Her mirth depleted. "I didn't know it was a secret. Marl's going to kill me."

Natsir laughed. *Don't worry. He won't survive the night any way.*

She stuck out her tongue.

"He's not the only one who wants to kill you." Lufnis emerged from behind the pillar and frowned. Eurgi stood next to him, looking tired and rejected.

"Congratulations on your marriage," Natsir said. "However, I think there's been a misunderstanding. We should talk."

"There's no misunderstanding. My sister promised herself to a noble man of the Dasha and is now cavorting in drunken abandon in the lap of a farm boy. You should be ashamed, K'Parre."

"No, brother! You should be ashamed. I would have never written that letter without your constant threats. I regret letting you win. I'm a Telmah woman, not a Dasha slave, and I'll choose to love whomever I want."

"I'm glad to hear you say that, sweetheart. I was beginning to believe you'd lost all ability to think for yourself."

Lufnis whirled around in panic, nearly knocking over his wife in the process. The chieftain and his brother were in the square, one old man propping up the other.

Papa allowed Etutsa to guide him closer. "Is what I hear true?"

"Father… I… You shouldn't be out here in this cold."

"I'm well enough for this. I *am* still chieftain." G'Nirac pointed to Natsir. "I've already given *this* man my blessing. A formality though, I assure you. Rippan Seisyll, however, isn't suited to my daughter. I know he's your friend, and I know how protective you are of your little sister. However, forcing her hand is deplorable! Would you marry her to a man who can't think for himself? It matters not how kind he is when he does only what his temperamental father expects."

Para was sorry the square was empty. She wanted everyone to have a good seat for Lufnis's verbal whipping.

Her brother slumped, but dark eyes flashed defiance.

"Now, I'm sorry this has created a small disturbance in your wedding, but I think we need to make things right as soon as possible." Papa placed a hand on Eurgi's shoulder and she shivered. "Forgive us, my girl, but I must take your husband. We've business. A letter needs writing." He pushed Lufnis forward but chuckled at Para still nestled in Natsir's lap. "I'm sorry I didn't realize what was happening sooner, my girl, but you reclaimed your autonomy tonight. However, please permit me to agree with Lufnis on one thing."

"Yes, Papa," Para answered with a small squeak.

"You're still the chieftain's daughter, sweetheart. Don't forget to handle yourself that way." He bent down with a slight groan. Etutsa maintained a careful grip on his arm. "Except when Lufnis is watching."

His whisper tickled her ears.

FIFTEEN

A black bit of cloth landed on Natsir's head. It smelled of cedar. He peeped out of the few ragged holes, watching Para rummage through a trunk.

Natsir pondered her well-made bed as he smoothed his hair back into a respectable fluff. The past few days had worn him out. If he collapsed into it, would she forgive him?

"You're sure you want to go riding?"

Para looked up, ecstasy in her crystal eyes. He was already loosing this unspoken argument.

She placed a finger to her lips. *They'll hear you.*

Lufnis and G'Nirac were still grumbling in the kitchen, sipping cups of pungent tea, deep in an argument over the best way to tell a certain warlord's son that a ginger woman was never his.

They'd already escorted forlorn Eurgi upstairs. Para had patted her sister-in-law's sloped shoulders and given her assurances that the night's circumstances weren't a bad omen for a marriage. Natsir found it endearing. She had her father's kindness, but she also had a way of being thoughtless—like now.

Para gave him a larger green cloak and took the black one off her bed. She was being practical and impractical at the same time and he had neither the energy nor the patience to deal with it. If she took the thin, ragged cloak that fit her, she'd freeze herself ill. He sighed. Her newer attire hung in the kitchen and there was no way she was permitting them to retrieve it.

No, take the better one. If you're insist on going out, I'm not letting you freeze. There might be frost. She allowed him to drape the heavier cloth over her shoulders.

They tiptoed out of the chieftain's house, though Natsir wasn't sure if secrecy was warranted. G'Nirac knew better than to suspect him of anything devious, though Para had her moments. She was avoiding her brother on principle tonight.

Despite their efforts, they startled the horses in the stables. Natsir apologized as they stamped and whinnied. Para tossed a blanket on Anope's back.

Sorry, old friend. Natsir secured the worn saddle. *The lady is in a tizzy tonight.*

If horses could chuckle, Anope would have.

Natsir reached down and procured the other woolen blanket for Rinpiels.

Para placed a hand on his shoulder. *I was thinking we could give her a break tonight.* She glanced at her horse and blushed. *I've been riding her a lot lately.*

The white creature glowed like fog from the corner of the stables and concurred.

Natsir was a dense, heavy man; this was why he rode the more muscular Anope. The smaller Rinpiels could never handle him. But would the old cart horse be able to take both their weights?

Para's blue eyes were insistent, but he couldn't understand why. If she wanted to be close to him, she could wait until they reached wherever they were going, couldn't she?

He gave in. *If all of our children look like her, they're going to be spoiled.*

The horses agreed.

Anope turned his head around in his stall and gave them both a mischievous look. *Get on, Gifted One. Make sure you hold her tightly.*

Para leaned into her father's horse and gave him a sweet kiss on the muzzle, mumbling thanks.

The creature twitched. *It's a good thing she's not like you. She'd be invincible.*

Natsir chuckled and tossed his love on the saddle, surprised he still had strength in his arms.

Can we go to the lake, Nat?

He was so comfortable nestled into her warm back. He yawned. *The lake? That's a long ride.*

The last time they'd visited Lake Cycei was in the spring. They'd picked flowers and watched baby brother dive for stones. It had been an easy day, but the brief memory made Natsir tense. Marl had his grip on everything, even recollections.

Please? Para snuggled into his chest. She'd a knack for this—subtle ways to make him compliant. Most of the time, he didn't mind.

He groaned and slumped his head on her shoulders. Everyone else was allowed to be in the Blessed Unknowing now! They'd their whole lives to be together; sleep was fleeting. His aching limbs and eyes were unforgiving.

All right. Let's head by the cottage first. Natsir didn't trust his kin anymore and it bothered him to think they were unsupervised. He guided Anope out of the stables.

She didn't protest. It was suitable payment for her antics.

Do you think they're still up?

Marl might be. Little brother had received a public and painful beating from Father, quelled only by Mother's intervention. He hadn't fought back.

The other Ganwins were indeed still awake, standing outside the shed in a triangle, each to their own point, one screaming and scolding with red-hot intensity. Father brandished a hairy fist at Marl.

Para gasped. *I've never seen them so upset!*

Ha! Welcome to the family. Natsir didn't mean it, but the sarcasm was hard to avoid. There was never peace with so many strong-willed, intelligent creatures prowling the farm.

She elbowed him in the stomach. *This isn't normal! Marl looks pitiful. We need to do something.* She wriggled off the horse. Her red-green form bobbed through the trees. *They're my family too.*

He raced after her. A slight unease warned him to be guarded.

Father was shouting at Mother now. "What do you mean this isn't his fault? Everything's his fault! There's not a darkened day goes by where he doesn't cause trouble for someone."

"Love, please! Let's go inside and discuss this. I've been trying to tell you…"

"Stop defending him!"

Marl stood in dutiful shame, staring at the ground and flinching with every syllable. He was an empty vessel again. Father's anger was a death sentence; one half of his soul had been ripped to shreds.

Natsir shivered. *Little brother has the power to destroy him, but he's holding back.*

Para dove bravely into the middle of the triangle. "This isn't the family I know. Please don't fight." She threw her arms around Father's neck and clung tightly, a green vine swinging with a solitary red rose in bloom. "Nothing is worth this much grief!"

The great bear king couldn't resist the simple joy of being loved unconditionally. "Ah, sweet girl."

Natsir's stomach turned. That was *his* flower, wrapped around the man he most resembled but least emulated. *Why is this making me agitated?*

Marl smiled. *Because somewhere inside of him is a ruthless warlord. Para's your greatest joy and you don't want to lose her because of your crazy family.* He paused. *Also, you're darkened exhausted.*

I suppose you're right. Natsir chuckled. Whatever his brother was, he intended his family no harm.

Now you know why I'm holding on to Hereu, Marl added. *There's only so much of this insanity a man can take. She's my moment of peace.*

Mother approached Father as if meeting the guard at the Stars' Passageway. "Nojhi, please let this go. We've already tried to explain. It *is* my fault. I panicked and begged Marl to keep this from you until I'd the courage to tell you myself. Your son has been obedient and I regret he's suffered."

Para slipped from his neck, her feet landing sharply on the dusty ground. There were tears in her eyes and a pout to her lips. She was disappointed, as if her favorite stars hadn't glimmered as brightly tonight. Natsir embraced her. She felt like Marl's fire and something within her shook.

"Is this *still* about Hereu? That's ridiculous. She's a remarkable girl. You're no better than Lufnis. *You* should be ashamed of yourself."

The bear retreated into the darkness of his cave. "Sweetheart, you've no idea what he's put us through. He's a darkened liar. I'm *ashamed* to admit it, but I've spawned the most selfish idiot in Artnaus."

No one touched the priestess's children, not even the bear king. "Oh shut up, husband! You're just as flawed. If he has a talent for lying, it's because he learned it from us."

Father scoffed. "Well, perhaps you, love, but I'd never treat you with such disrespect."

Mother seethed, hot as coals. Her blue eyes darted. "Then where's the *sword*, Nojhi? I know it's here! Marl carries himself too well not to have had some instruction from you."

He fumbled. "Whether I have it or not is none of your business, woman. My past isn't yours to command!" The moment he said it, the intensity of pure hate left his green eyes.

Mother leaned back on her tiny heels. "Neither are we yours to command."

Father took a few steps forward and glared. He made a noise of contempt, stalled, and cleared his throat, and then raised his hands in the air. Natsir recognized the look. He'd seen that temper quell many times before. He was nothing near a general anymore, just a foolish, old man.

"Look, Messa, I'm..."

Marl jumped in front of Mother. "Don't you dare hurt them!"

The bear loosened his scraggly, golden jaw, teeth gleaming in the moonlight, and stared at his cub. He was dumbfounded, but there was a twitch in his mouth from the force of not answering a direct challenge. "I'd never hurt your mother, or Para! I'm angry, but I'm not a complete darkened cur!"

"Or little sister? You sure do like wailing on me." Marl took the same stance he'd taken during their summer swim by the warbler's tree. This time, the only weapons he had were his words, and they were more capable of injury than the missing rods.

Para tugged Natsir's shirt. *Is there something you neglected to tell me?* The way this night was going, he'd be explaining things to her for a long time.

Father wiped his face with his hand and took a deep, steadying breath. It was the same countenance he'd displayed when Marl had feigned suicide. "I give up. Am I that terrifying?"

Mother released Marl and threw her arms around Father's waist. "Yes, Nojhi. You *are* terrifying. There's not a force on this earth that scares me more, save for Wind."

"Or me," Marl whispered.

Para placed a sympathetic hand to his cheek. Natsir envied her heart's blindness. She thought he was overreacting, being a temperamental youth. It didn't matter now though; the battle was over and the survivors were trying to number their losses.

Mother stroked Father's beard. "We all love you; that's why we tiptoe around your great will and your strong arms. Please forgive us." He returned her embrace and snuggled into her hair.

The silence gave Natsir a moment to retreat into his own thoughts. He looked to his love, his brother, and his parents in nervous embrace and tried to reason why this lie had caused so much turmoil.

"You know what I think?"

Three sets of blue eyes and one set of green settled on him.

"This isn't about Marl or Mother being treasonous, or you being a tyrant. Everyone lies. We all fear losing the best things we have."

He gave Para a tight squeeze. He knew he was right; he wouldn't have spoken otherwise, but it worried him he might be evoking the bear's primal rage again.

"You're afraid of losing the person you connected with most: Marl. But you've forgotten Mother. Without her, you're nothing. She allows you to be better than what you think you are. In her quest to keep this family peaceful, she has forgotten you're what gives her purpose."

His mouth was dry. Natsir swallowed and tried to finish his thoughts.

"You both used Marl as a representation of your desires, a way to fill the void you left in each other, but this has nothing to do with him. You need to work this out on your own."

Jaws dropped. Natsir tapped his fingers on the small of Para's back and waited for the bear to roar. He was tackled from behind.

Marl shoved him to the ground, laughing. "You son of a…" He stopped short of his curse and wrapped Natsir in a massive hug again. "That's the most eloquent you've ever been in your life, you idiot!"

Para stood over them, unafraid, with wide, innocent eyes and a clever smile illuminated by Father Moon. They were children again, trying to capture the wild creature with black hair hiding in the dark woods.

Father released Mother and strolled over to the pile that resembled his sons. "Our worst offense is forgetting that you're watching o'er us." He wrapped Natsir in a bear hug and messed with his hair. "You didn't get your intelligence from me, that's certain! And you, little monster, didn't inherit any of it."

Marl's vertebra cracked.

"I love you boys, but Nat's right, only one of you can push me over the edge. You're too much of me, and I'm not sure I like the person *I've* become."

"I don't know." Marl winked and rubbed his spine. "I think you're tolerable. Who doesn't love a potbellied, balding man with a temper?"

Para gasped. Father laughed and gave her a gentle pat on the head. "Don't worry, sweetheart."

"Natsir's right. We never should've lost sight of each other." Mother tapped Father's stomach. "We should go inside where it's warm. We've too much left unsaid."

"We've all got somewhere to be." Marl nodded to Anope waiting in the trees.

Natsir laughed. Little brother was giddy with the weight taken from him. He'd been absolved of his crimes.

Marl jumped like a squirrel in search of a mate and began a determined stride to Na-ir.

"Where are you off to?"

"I'd be in your way in the cottage, and Natsir and Para don't need me on their romantic ride. I've got my own lady to attend to."

"Really, boy? You're going to bother her now? It's nearly dawn! Vill must hate you."

"Hereu's still awake. She's been crying by her hearth, worried sick. I can't ignore that." He raised a slender, black brow. "Could you? I've work in four hours, too. Etutsa will kill me if I'm late."

Natsir wished he had Marl's stamina. In four hours, he'd be no better than a pumpkin in the garden.

Mother beamed with pride. "Tell Hereu not to worry. We're not all as crazy as we look. At least one of us isn't."

***

Para yawned and snuggled into his stomach as they made their way down the sloped grasslands to the lake. She wiggled in the saddle while they discussed the eventful night, her legs and arms wrapped around him for support. Her speech was starting to slur.

A few hours ago, he would've been bitter with her for falling asleep while he was forced to remain alert and attentive, but he didn't mind it now. The confrontation in front of the cottage had ruined his mind for sleep, and all he wanted to do was find the silvery glimmer of Lake Cycei. Mother and Father's plight had reminded him there were more important things than the Blessed Unknowing.

"You'd be a great chieftain," Para mumbled, on the edge of that ethereal place.

Natsir laughed. The very idea was ridiculous to him.

"I'm serious. Marl thinks so too."

"He thinks dancing around with sticks half naked is a great pastime as well."

She hummed before mumbling again. "He loves you, too."

"I know."

Natsir stopped the horse and looked down on Para's peaceful face. Her hair burst in ringlets from her hood. The blue shawl peeked out from the buttons near her freckled, chill-white chest. He watched her breath rise and fall in grey puffs with those delicate breasts.

It was a shame to wake her. But the naughty satisfaction he gained from shaking her shoulders was irresistible. He had to grab her skirts to keep her from slipping.

She angled her spine to lean into him and stare at the landscape. Father Moon sat low in the sky, nestled over the horizon with his cloak draped over one shoulder. Lake Cycei was as still and blue as her eyes.

"Look! How beautiful!"

"Is this what you wanted?"

She shuffled on the saddle. "Well, I *was* hoping to see the sunrise too."

Natsir resisted the urge to smack her; resorting to Father's discipline tactics would have adverse effects on their relationship.

"Para! You kept me up all night to see a sunrise?" He wasn't looking forward to spending more hours with his eyes protruding from his head and his neck resisting all efforts to remain upright.

"Yes. We've had a childhood of sunsets; I'm ready to see the sunrises with you."

She was a creature of symbols and meanings. All things connected. For him, nature was nature, but he was learning women were women and they were something odd within nature. He kissed her cold lips and held tight to her waist.

She wasn't done pestering him. "Also, we haven't had *our* fight yet."

"Excuse me. Our fight?" He ground his teeth and narrowed his eyes. The expression must've reminded her of his father because she looked down and blushed in shame.

"Yes. There are some things we need to discuss if we're going to be married."

He released her waist and crossed his arms. The chance to scold her was tempting.

"I've already fought with your brother, my brother, and your father tonight. I might as well continue." She turned her nose up and tried not to smile. "It's your fault anyway."

This was a trick. He hadn't lied to anyone. No one had been hurt. The worst he'd done in the past few days was curse, and that had never been in Para's presence. "All right. Fine. What did I do?"

Para copied his posture and took one massive breath. "How dare you wait twenty darkened suns to tell me you loved me? I'm worth more than that. I pined after you for so long my mind was boggled and my heart heavy as stone. You've got a lot of nerve!"

Natsir opened his mouth to answer but she pushed him in the stomach, still on fire.

"Marl says you take advice from the cat. If you've been listening to that mangy beast about how to love a woman, I swear I'm going to pluck out his fur, hair by hair and then start on you!"

She took another rasping breath and grasped the saddle horn for support. Her eyes exhibited the telltale signs of exhaustion and regret, but she was smirking in the shadows.

The horse turned its brown muzzle around. *Is this going to be a while? I'd prefer it if you'd stop squirming on my back.*

Natsir's temper quelled. He backed down Anope's flank and took Para by the waist. She looked apprehensive as he scowled and lowered her to the icy ground. It was sometimes helpful to be able to understand situations she didn't; it left her guessing. Right now he was aware she thought he was going to thrash her.

Father Moon and his luminescent children disappeared behind ominous clouds. Icy Wind raked against their skin and Para gasped. She pulled the great green cloak tighter to her chest and squeaked as Natsir pulled her closer.

"It's about to snow. This isn't the best night for this."

He felt guilty seeing the tears in her eyes. She meant no harm; she wanted to start their romantic suns together in a way that defined her excitement and put behind them the uncertainty of their past.

White puffs of moisture puffed from his mouth. They took on the form of an attractive face, with piercing iridescent eyes. They weren't alone.

"To answer your questions, I didn't wait twenty suns. You've only been of age for five. Five suns isn't bad, is it?"

Para shook her head, though he knew she wasn't satisfied.

"And I told you I loved you when I was eleven. Remember?"

She recoiled. "You have to be joking, Nat! We were hanging upside-down from the linden tree and eating elderberries. You expect me to take the word of a boy in a tree and hold on to it for fifteen suns?"

He laughed. "I'm not the sort to lie, or change my mind. You know this." Everyone in Na-ir did. "Have I ever been insincere?"

Para raised a hand to scold him again, but found she could not. "No. You've never been insincere." She sighed and leaned in closer. "I'm not as unshakable as you, Nat. Remember I need reminding."

Anope whinnied.

This turn of events amused Natsir. He hadn't counted on winning this argument, but he was glad he had. He gave her a kiss on the nose. "Point taken."

Her blush was all he needed to know the tactic had worked.

"I never intended for you to wait. I conceded to the fact you deserved better."

She scoffed, although this wasn't false modesty on his part.

"However, I realized my life would be miserable without you. Some sage advice convinced me to consider the possibility, but, you know me, I stewed over it for a while. It wasn't Pilgrim, by the way. He's dying."

Para gasped and threw her arms around his neck, forcing him to stoop. "I'm sorry. I didn't mean it. Poor, old Pilgrim!" He held her close and stroked the green cloak restraining her wild hair. "If he wasn't giving you such *bad* advice, who was?"

A shimmering form, fluid and cool, embodied the moonlight that no longer shone through the clouds. "Why don't you turn around and see?"

Her body tensed. She dropped from his neck and turned. The figure moved forward. Para's blue eyes met Water's and she screamed.

Natsir placed a hand over her mouth and forced her to bow. She gave a muffled but justified whine of terror.

"Greetings, Water. Pleasure to see you."

The pleasure is mine. Water returned the bow, a queen from a magnificent nightmare. *Greetings, K'Parre Sinbel. I'm afraid I'm to blame for your five suns of torment.*

Natsir snickered and removed his hand. Para trembled and pressed against him.

Don't be afraid, child. You're loved by the children of the Sun and Moon. No harm will come to you.

"Who…what are you?" Para whispered.

I'm one of the three sisters. I'm sure you've heard of us… in childhood stories by the firelight. It's my task to watch over all things wet and sustaining, like this lake. She pointed behind her. *Those clouds.* She pointed up. *And innocent humans who happen to need me to survive. That's my most favorite task of all. Your reaction is why I don't present myself to those who aren't gifted. But I think you're able to take this encounter in stride.*

Her praise had a sobering effect on Para. She dropped from Natsir's embrace, a pinecone ready to seed. The beautiful spirit smiled.

Blessings on your upcoming marriage. She spoke with such authority it had to be true. *However, I do bring a warning.* Water placed a hand on Natsir's shoulder, searing her will into him. *Your brother is still restless, as he will ever be. His intentions are noble, but his way isn't clear to those who doubt. You know whom I mean.*

Natsir rolled his eyes. He didn't want to give any more speeches.

I must beg your patience with him. Support him as you did tonight. His life depends on your love and devotion, no matter what creature my sister might turn him into. Do you understand?

He didn't, but he nodded.

Remind him of his humanity and of your love. Do those things and all will be well.

"What mischief is Marl up to now?" Para squeaked, too curious to stay silent.

I think we should be asking what he isn't doing. It would be simpler.

Para laughed nervously. If ancient spirits came to tell you your brother was misbehaving, the crime was most likely not amusing.

I'm yours if you need me, Natsir. Water flew apart in crystal perfection and the remnants fell over them.

All traces of vegetation disappeared, wiped away by the coming of winter. The lake crackled and groaned. Para snuggled into Natsir and hummed.

"So, after all you've seen tonight, do you still want to marry a Ganwin?"

She turned her blue eyes on him. "Well, I'm marrying the best one, I think."

The sky glowed in crimson gold.

"Thank you for *this* sunrise, Nat."

"And all the ones here after?" He kissed her.

They stood in silence, the humans and the horse and the unseen spirits, as Mother Sun rose over the clouds, penetrating their cold, grey exteriors with enough intensity to combat the retreating night ruled by her mate. Everything came into focus.

When the great burning disk had reached the tops of the distant trees, Para peeped like a bird waking to greet the dawn.

Natsir followed her inquisitive stare to eight tiny forms bubbling from the glassy, auburn waters, coming to rest on the shore line. He walked over to them, assuming they were fish or something mammalian with which he could converse.

He found a peculiar sight. Four sets of shoes sat on the shore. A sleek, brown otter waved before disappearing into a pool of light.

Natsir chuckled at the mischief of Water and dwelled on the innocence of his own brother, who was no different from that otter: curious and wild.

***

They fell into a lover's pile in a chair by the hearth, unwilling to leave and so weary they could barely move. They were still wrapped in their cloaks but equally wrapped in each other. Para's warm hair fell in cascades over his shoulder. This was perfection, even with Lufnis staring in contempt.

"I suppose you're happy with yourself."

Natsir opened one eye and smirked. The man before him had the look of a person who'd conquered a rich kingdom and then lost it in a dice game. "I'm happy with a lot of things," he teased, pulling her limp body farther into his lap.

Lufnis spat into fire and turned on his heels. Let the little badger think what he wanted. This wasn't his dominion yet, and he was of no consequence to anyone, least of all the future Mistress Ganwin.

SIXTEEN

Marl held tight to the fife in his pocket. *Hereu? I'm coming.*

There was no answer.

Are you asleep? He peered into the window. She was slumped on the edge of the hearth. He smiled, remembering the passionate way she'd danced in the square.

The door was locked. He tapped on the window. The shepherdess didn't stir, but he hadn't expected her to. If thought couldn't wake her, distant sounds wouldn't either.

Or maybe the type of sound mattered. He sat down on the porch and pulled the fife from his pocket. It was a cheap thing Vill had bought her, ill-made and ill-tuned, but it had given them much pleasure. He placed the mouth to his lips and sighed into it. Wherever they were, she'd know him by this song.

His gentle, off-key call was interrupted by a click and the creak of wood. She fell into his lap.

"Oh thank the stars you're alive!" Hereu scrambled into his neck. Her eyes were red with tears and her cheeks sunken with fatigue. She looked pretty in her disheveled and miserable state, but this was the last time he ever wanted to take in this sight.

Marl placed the fife over his lips in warning. "I'm fine," he assured her, though his backside was still sore. "Sorry I kept you waiting."

She kissed his forehead and looked him over like a mother cat bathing kittens. "Are you sure you're well? How could any man treat his son that way? What's going to happen now?"

Let's go for a walk. Get your cloak.

They could talk freely in the forest and he was too tired to channel for three hours. She nodded and ran back inside. Hereu returned draped in black and pulled the door into place with the perfection of one used to sneaking around.

They headed north to the meadow. Once they'd passed through the first wave of oak and pine, Hereu returned to her previous question. "What's going to happen now? Is our wedding off?"

Marl growled. "I'm not losing you over something that stupid."

"But your father doesn't want us to be together. He was so angry." She clasped his hand. "That man scares me!"

He brought her fingers to his lips. "He doesn't scare me. Besides, Telmah men are allowed to make their own decisions once we're of age." He was barely that, but still within the law; they could call him boy all they wanted. "We aren't controlled by our fathers. I don't need or want his permission." He showed the man respect out of love; it wasn't always earned.

"But you're not Telmah."

Marl grabbed her chin to look into those wood-stained eyes. He never wanted her to think she had to hide from him. They wouldn't be like Mother and Father, withholding glances or thoughts.

"You're right, but I've always lived here and G'Nirac still holds me to the same laws. Sometimes they work in my favor. Besides, you've nothing to fear. He hated I was forced to lie to him, not that I want you. He likes you."

She jumped. Marl knew she was remembering the first time she'd seen Nojhi Ganwin near Retat's shop. She had said he was such a sweet man. She was probably reevaluating that now.

"When he saw you walk passed us in the market with Trouble, he thought you were pretty." Marl took in the musty ash smell of her hair.

"I wish we could marry now. It's silly to wait after all we've been through."

He pulled her close and looked into the night sky. Clouds gathered in the center, threatening and grey. A small division in a wayward cloud revealed the Stars' Passageway. The souls of the righteous passed through that beautiful, shining hilt before finding rest among the other children in the sky. It looked more like the destination than the journey.

A chirp near his ear forced him to look down. Hereu was peeking into the realm of the dead, too. The radiance glistened in her eyes. Traversing that reflection was the closest a person like him would get to those heavens.

"Why not? We can do anything." Sometimes the best roads were strange and perilous, but they led to such perfect destinations.

"Marl! I was wishing aloud. We can't. We promised to wait for spring."

He tried not to giggle. For some reason, past oaths didn't seem so exacting anymore. He felt a childish freedom tingle through his blood. "I know, but that's because no one wants to frolic in the winter. But we don't have any money for such things anyway."

A scolding brewed behind her eyes.

"I don't need the entire village to help me celebrate our love. There's more than one way to marry."

Hereu sighed and shook her curls. "Marl, I'd rather avoid a public display, too, but our fathers would strangle us and our mothers would provide the rope to do it. I don't want to be murdered for our love. Those stupid songs talking about valiant, dying lovers buried together with roses blooming from their graves can darken off." She was serious.

The laugh escaped him before he could control it. He wasn't trying to be condescending, but her fears were amusing. The reason their parents were fierce in their resolve was *because* they loved their children—irresponsibly, but it was love all the same. You couldn't murder one you loved.

"And Nat would wrap me in bed sheets and smack me. So? I don't care."

He concentrated on his abilities, watching the orange flames dance in her apprehensive eyes. The rest of the forest disappeared with the intensity of his glow. The power it displayed made him ecstatic.

"They'd have to touch us first. I'm tired of playing by their rules." Marl looked to the sky and brought the flame to meet it, an offering to the only lights with any real control over their lives. "There's always something beautiful beyond the clouds. Wanna travel with me?"

He waved the flame out of existence. Night's shadow closed in on them again. They watched the smoke rise to the ancient children above.

"I keep forgetting you can do that. I'll travel with you anywhere, Marl Ganwin, strange powers or not. You don't need to impress me. In fact, I'm the last person who's going to fall for that foolishness. The real you is more endearing. You're not the powerful terror you pretend to be." She turned her nose up and tried not to smile. She knew him too well. "I suppose it doesn't matter when we're married. You're my kind of idiot every day."

Her answer made his soul warmer than any fire. He took her by the waist and swung her around until she faced the entrance back to Na-ir. The squeal of glee she gave him was as precious as starlight.

"Good. Let's find another idiot."

***

They knocked for some time before the healer's voice emanated from the weathered oak door of his shack.

"Who's there?" A cough and much shuffling ensued.

"It's Marl. Open up."

They waited for some minutes while the old man fiddled with the lock, grunting and groaning. Etutsa squinted from a crack. He was dressed in a night shirt with a large blanket on his shoulders, a small candle clutched in his shaking fist.

"What do you want in this darkened hour? I've half a mind to…" He slammed the door when he saw Hereu. *You're supposed to warn a man if a lady's come to call!*

There was more shuffling.

Why do people slam doors on us? Hereu hadn't seen Etutsa in his night clothes.

Marl snickered.

The door opened again, this time wide. The old man had found his britches. *Do you want to get fired?*

No, sir. Please forgive us. We couldn't wait. It was a cryptic choice of words.

Etutsa raised an eyebrow and looked to Hereu. A man who'd seen everything could easily jump to conclusions. "Oh, is all well?" He took her by the arm and rounded on Marl. "Do I need to smack the snot out of a certain apprentice?"

Her brown eyes widened and she shuffled, trying to remove his hand.

A voice from the other side of the shack answered for the lovers. "Nah, sir. You don't have to worry." Cyan strolled over, conspicuously missing a cloak. "She's a maiden. She told me so."

Marl pulled Hereu closer and contemplated pushing his friend's chin far into his jaw. The maiden took the nobler route of revenge by sticking out her tongue.

Etutsa ignored the naughty exchange. As the self-proclaimed saint of the village youth, he'd seen such banter many times before. "Did Toren lock you out of the house again, Cyan? It's too cold out here. You can huddle in my place again, though I think you're getting sick of this old man's company."

Marl faltered. "You sleep here?"

"Sometimes. Grandpa won't have me in the house when I'm up to trouble."

Hereu laughed but stopped when she realized he wasn't joking. "What could you have done that he'd let you freeze to death?"

"Well, I did entice pretty maidens to dance." Cyan crossed his arms and looked around before speaking in a mocking old-person voice. "Any man who'd ask ladies to behave in such a fashion doesn't deserve to sleep at my hearth." Cyan shrugged. "Let him think what he wants."

The dance had been Para's fault. The girls could take responsibility for their own actions. But Marl was certain there was much Cyan was also guilty of. His mind was dark.

"If you'd stop hanging out with the likes of Rej, Toren wouldn't think you were a miscreant."

Hereu nodded in agreement.

The blond balled his fists and milled his crooked teeth. "Who says we're friends. I hate the cur!" He backed into the doorway. "I can't... Just shut up!"

They jumped as he stamped into the shack. Cyan settled into the chair and grunted. His behavior was troubling; he wasn't the type for angry outbursts. What hold did Rej have on him?

"All right, Cyan. All right. We'll discuss this with Toren later. I'm getting sick of your company too."

Etutsa shook his head and sighed. A trembling, gnarled hand wiped over his weary face. His arthritis was acting up. Marl felt guilty for waking him to such pain.

"So." The old man rounded back on them. "What problem do I need to solve for you children three hours from sunrise?"

"Marry us, Etutsa!"

The healer cackled and slapped him across the cheek a few times. "Oh no! I'm not getting involved. I value my life, wasted as it is."

"Oh come on! You did it for Yimette and Gan."

Cyan opened one hazel eye.

The healer scrunched his shoulders. "You've no proof. What makes you think I'd allow *children* to do something that stupid?"

"Because you're a dupe for romance, and because there are only three men in town who're allowed to officiate weddings. G'Nirac wouldn't have kept it a secret from Namnor, and the blacksmith wouldn't have married his own daughter to a soldier. That leaves you."

Cyan snorted.

Etutsa coughed and sputtered. "All right. You caught me," he growled. "I'm still not going to bestow you with the honor. You're too young and too smart for that nonsense. Besides, Namnor doesn't scare me half as much as your father, and he claims ownership of several blunt instruments."

Marl set his scrappy, black jaw. "Are you a coward then?"

The old man set his stubbled jaw in equal defiance.

"We're getting married, even if we've to walk to Mirot and see the blacksmith there." Marl took off like a swift with Hereu in hand.

"Wait! You don't have to go that far."

The apprentice suppressed a wicked smile. Etutsa wouldn't want anyone else to be a part of this moment. The healer had too much invested in him to let him walk away. They ambled back to the shack to hear his compromise.

"You could have an Erutani marriage. It wouldn't involve me at all."

Cyan stared. He'd lost all ability to feign disinterest now.

"An Erutani marriage?" Hereu blinked.

Etutsa was grinning from ear to ear now. This had to be a trick. "Yes, sweetie. It's simple, the perfect cure for lovesickness. Ask yourself a few questions. Do you choose this idiot?"

Hereu laughed as Marl's face twisted. She was the only one allowed to call him an idiot. "Of course, sir, I wouldn't be here otherwise."

The old man nodded, waved the candle through the air theatrically, and turned to his apprentice. "Do you agree with her choice?"

Marl groaned. This was indeed a trick. "Yes! You know she's all I've ever wanted."

"I know, boy." He winked. "Your affection for each other is… obvious."

Cyan rolled his eyes. Marl didn't care; there were worse things they could be doing.

"Now run along and do what you will. I've sleep to acquire." Etutsa shooed them off the porch.

"That can't be it! There was no ceremony, no clasping of hands. How can you say we're married?" Hereu placed her hands on her hips. If she'd had a rock, she would've use it.

Etutsa chuckled. "You're not. I said you had to do it all on your own. It's Erutani not Telmah."

He pretended to walk back into his shack. Marl shook his head and laughed. This was a clever ruse. The healer knew the two of them would be too afraid to act on something unsure when it came to solidifying their relationship.

"I don't need an excuse to make love to her."

Hereu slapped him upside the head. Cyan snorted.

"I think you're trying to trick us."

"I'd never trick you, boy. I love you like a son." The healer placed a hand to his chest. "Besides, it was acceptable for your parents."

Marl raised his hand in protest and then stopped. It had never occurred to him Father would've chosen to follow an Erutani custom, or that his perfect, proper mother would've done something reckless.

"Of course, it's illegal according to the laws of Artnaus, so…"

Hereu rounded him. "What kind of woman do you think I am?"

The healer stuttered, attempting an apology. Marl wasn't paying attention. His woman's purity wasn't in question.

"Wait! Are you telling me my parents' marriage isn't legal?"

Cyan cackled; it wouldn't be a secret for long. "I guess that makes you a ba…."

Etutsa slapped a boney hand against his mouth. "Shut up!"

He turned to his apprentice and sighed, his face awash with regret. The game they were playing had gone too far.

Ire rose through Marl's stomach and into his mind. The need for revenge poked and pestered, like a needle sewing stitches. *Is that why you tried to take my Mother from him?*

The old man went white and grasped the shack. He shoved the candle into Cyan. Hereu's sympathetic squeak forced Marl to reevaluate his wrath.

Vill was right. I need to control my temper. His anger and gifts were conflicting forces, two souls in constant opposition. *Mother told me.*

I'm not sure what Messa said, but Marl... I... He stuttered and trembled. "All right! I'll marry you. But you have to promise you won't pull me into the storm when your father loses it."

"You'll be spared any crazed retribution."

The healer tried to smile.

"So, what do we do?" Marl slapped his hands together. He wanted to move forward and be done with this ridiculousness. There was little night left.

Etutsa wiped a tear from his eye and cackled; it was a merciful sound. "Weren't you paying attention during Lufnis's wedding?"

The lovers frowned.

"You'll need someone to officiate—myself." Etutsa pointed to his chest. "And a witness." He glanced at Cyan, who groaned. "It's expected you provide payment though."

Marl shivered. Most of his savings were now resting in G'Nirac's coffers. He'd already bought the land on the meadow.

Etutsa grinned. "What's the matter, boy? I pay you well enough."

Hereu stared. He hadn't told her yet, although he was certain now G'Nirac had told Etutsa. Marl had two silver coins to his name. Did he need them now though? Payment for *his* services would come again soon, and he could eat whatever was in the forest. He fished them from his pocket, handing one to Etutsa.

The old man coughed before he could hand Cyan the other. "That's all you have?" He raised a grey eyebrow and clicked his tongue. "I'm afraid my services are worth more than one silver coin."

Marl slammed the second coin into his hand.

"Well, now you've nothing to pay Cyan."

"That's all right. I don't…"

Etutsa waved off Cyan's gallantry. "Rules are rules. Sorry."

Hereu had endured enough of their war of wits. She groaned and pushed her love in the chest before leaping from the porch. Whatever happened, Marl knew she'd forgive him, but her walking away made him ache worse than any beating.

Wait! "Wait! I do have something." He dove into his shirt and pulled out the bottle of whiskey. It was warm and moist, but still good.

Hereu wagged her head from side to side and stomped back. It would've been a humorous display had the fire in her countenance not made all three men nervous. She waved a hand, daring the healer to try and call off the proceedings now.

Cyan snatched the bottle. "Nice, Marl, but it's half gone."

Etutsa sniffed.

"Nat gave it to me." Marl ran a hand through his hair. "Para drank it though."

The healer chuckled. "That explains the dance. I suppose that passes as payment." He grabbed Hereu and Marl by the arms and made them face each other. Humming, he fiddled with their stances.

Cyan snickered.

"Wrap your arms."

Marl felt the warmth of skin underneath her cloak and relaxed.

"Now, Hereu Misyl, will you take Marl Ganwin as your husband?"

She frowned. "I've already answered that question."

Etutsa returned her expression and pointed a slender, white finger at her nose. Her eyes crossed. "Do you want me to do this right, or not? Answer the question again."

"Yes."

He turned. "Marl Ganwin, do you take Hereu Misyl as your wife?"

"YES!"

"Well, kiss her."

Marl dropped Hereu's arms and took her by the neck. She gasped and pushed back, not expecting such a climax after the ridiculousness of Etutsa's ceremony.

The old man chuckled and smacked Cyan, who looked absurd with sleeplessness and boredom. "Hey! Do you bear witness to this union?"

The blond yawned. "Yeah, sure. I've seen everything. Every darkened thing."

Hereu gave Marl another kiss and blushed. Her eyes widened as she caught Etutsa's knowing smile. "Wait! What was the difference?"

The healer chuckled and counted off his fingers. "Two other people, two silver coins, and a half bottle of whiskey." He gave her a gentle hug. "Does it matter? You're married. Now, get off my porch! Don't you have any compassion, Mistress Ganwin, not letting a poor, old man sleep?" He shooed them into the square and pointed to Marl. "See *you* in two and a half hours!"

He ushered Cyan into the shack and slammed the door.

Marl kissed his bride again. *Let's go!*

They ran west through the darkness. The clouds were now one accumulation, threatening a frost. Hereu shivered and stumbled as she tried to keep up. He was forced to stop so she could breathe.

She fell into his arms. *Goodness, Marl! I can't match you.* They waited in the center of an ash grove while she regained her abilities. *Where are we going?*

This section of the forest should've felt like a second home. That memory of comfortable summer nights in her arms thrilled him. He placed a determined hand to her back. The hollow wasn't far.

Hereu laughed when they neared the oak. "You have to be joking."

He draped her cloak over the entrance, pulling back one corner for her like a door.

"Oh, stars, you *are* an idiot." Hereu settled into a blanket of foliage. "It's dark and cold."

Marl closed the cloak flap behind him and waved a hand. The trunk illuminated instantly and warmed. He moved the fire from his palm down to a pile of leaves and twigs. It sputtered but didn't waver. Grey smoke floated out between the cloak and the tree.

"You've learned to control it!" She blushed when he raised his eyebrows. *All right, I suppose that's impressive.*

There was too much he wanted to do and too little time to satisfy him. He started with a slow, gentle kiss. She settled into his shoulder.

"Hereu Ganwin, I'll always love you."

Her brown eyes blinked in understanding and desire before she pulled him down with her into the golden leaves of their bower.

***

Snow had been falling for several minutes, stacking outside of Oak Hollow. It pushed its way under the cloak and melted with the heat of Marl's abilities and romantic desires.

He poked his wrist with the tip of Hereu's knife. He'd sharpened it with a stone and created a small pile of black ash from some bark. Each time he made a mark in his skin, he'd sprinkle some of the powdered ash into the bloody indentation before willing the wound closed again. The image he was trying to tattoo was almost finished. It just itched and needed more details.

Hereu startled him with a yawn, rolling over in the leaves and snuggling into his crumpled shirt before opening her earthy eyes. *Hello, husband. What're you doing?*

I'm marking myself as yours.

Marking yourself?

A few leaves had attached to the moisture on her thighs. He sighed as she brushed them away. Her naked form slid into him, but it was morning. He hated to leave her.

Doesn't that hurt? She took his wrist, turning the image to get a better look. *Why would you tattoo a rat on your arm?*

The little hollow got hotter, or at least Marl's cheeks did.

"It's not a rat! It's supposed to be a mouse, a field mouse." He snatched his limb back and fussed over the image. What did it need: rounder ears or a longer tail? He started on the scarification again.

Hereu laughed. "Sorry, but it looks like a rat." She kissed him on the neck. "I suppose it doesn't matter. No one will see it with your clothes on anyway. You could've chosen a better symbol. You know I hate my name."

She rested her head in his lap. It was hard to finish his self-appointed task with the brown of her eyes on his face and the softness of her hair falling around his middle.

"I guess I could've made it an apple blossom." It was an endearing idea. He contemplated healing the mouse tattoo and starting over.

Hereu giggled. "On second thought, keep the rat! You may have to roll up your sleeves. Such a manly healer, he has flowers on his body!" She showed her tongue.

Marl laughed and moved the knife to her nose. "You've your mother's ability to emasculate."

She nestled into his stomach and watched him finish, kissing it the moment it was complete. "Well, it looks better. Do me now."

Marl stiffened. Taking a knife to himself was one thing, but putting a mark on her made him sick.

Hereu frowned. "Why not? If you can do it, I can."

"I'm not sure I can manage *your* pain. What if I hurt you?"

"You never know unless you try. Here, prick my finger. I won't scream. Blood doesn't bother me."

He made a delicate cut, concentrating on her well-being and comfort. She flinched, but her bravery was astounding. She trusted him completely.

"I felt pressure, that's all. I should have something for your name. What does Marl mean?"

"I've no idea. Probably something my father made up."

"Oh, well." She tapped his bare leg and hummed her song. "What about the fife?"

Marl frowned. He didn't share Natsir's artistic abilities.

She bit her lip. "All right. No. What do you think then?"

He looked to the snow, whiter than apple blossoms, and thought of the perfume. "I could put little rain drops."

She closed her eyes and thrust out her wrist. Marl pushed it away. He didn't want this symbol easily seen. He was pretty sure this broke his promise to Vill.

"Here, sit up. I've an idea." He smoothed back her auburn curls. "Ready?"

The imperative need to protect her and the coming of dawn forced him to work quickly. Hereu shivered with every touch, but not once did she cry out or sob. He was proud of her. Soon, three black raindrops fell from the brown-red cloud on top of her head.

"All done."

Her smile turned into a pout. She couldn't see it. He leaned forward and took a handful of snow from just outside. Something told him to breathe on it; it refroze into a crystal disc. Marl placed the knife above her neck and maneuvered it until the reflection fell on the makeshift mirror.

"There. You're my little mouse…"

"And you're my rain," Hereu finished. She set the mirror down; it melted into the leaves.

They drank from each other again as the golden light of morning crept in across the snow. He owed it to Etutsa to keep his appointments; they'd made a mockery of the old man's time to be in the Blessed Unknowing. But here was the blessed knowing—knowing every spot, every curve, every sound of the person he loved most. He contemplated staying a while. It was unlikely anyone would be awake this early on such as cold morning. Surely Etutsa was too drowsy to keep track of time.

His mind was made up for him.

Are you finished yet? Covetous Wind had grown tired of being ignored. She'd been teasing him from her invisible hiding spot since they'd entered the tree, making much commentary of his ability to make love. *You humans are so sluggish!*

The cloak door rose from the tree and floated away. The moment was lost, as his vindictive tutor had planned.

Hereu shrieked as a chill entered their shelter. He tried to cover her.

Bring it back. We can't leave the tree like this.

Wind laughed and the branches overhead shook. Oak Hollow groaned. *But you look much better.* She pushed inside and tittered menacingly, raking debris. *She doesn't.*

Marl flattened his muddled hair and ignored the insult to his wife, thankful the spirit hadn't tried to exhibit a visual comparison. *Please, I'll speak with you later. Give us back the cloak!*

As you command, Wanderer. Wind stopped dancing and tossed the cloak back on the tree. It was an odd thing for her to do—obey a commandment.

Hereu sighed as their hideaway warmed again. "What did we do to rile her now?" She reached for her blouse, knowing better than to trust that Wind wouldn't mess with them again.

Their courtship had been rife with strange instances and encounters with air. Hereu often received painful hair pulls, pushes down hillsides, and whispers in her mousy ears. If Marl hadn't been who he was, she might've suffered some strange calamity by now. Yet, if he were normal, his love would've never had the opportunity to become Wind's competitor.

"I think she's jealous," he whispered and pulled his shirt over his head. He fished a few dried leaves from his armpit.

Hereu scoffed. There was no way he'd ever convince her she was more important than some invisible, ancient force.

She should be jealous.

Wind huffed, showering them with tiny ice crystals through the bottom of the cloak flap.

Hereu ignored the attack and pulled her gown over her head. "Could you lace me up?"

He fumbled with the cords. Leaf litter stuck out from her curls. He was tempted to command them away, but part of him thought them too endearing. Besides, it would infuriate Vill.

"I guess we should share our news." She wriggled in her tight dress. There was no time to fix it.

Marl leaned his shoulders into the tree and shifted into his britches. "I'm already late. You have that honor, unless you want to stay with Etutsa and me all day. But Vill might come looking."

"And Mama will be worried. I'll wait for you at home. But *you're* going to tell your family."

Marl was certain one of them already knew, but he agreed.

They trudged through several layers of snow on their way back to Na-ir.

Hereu gave him a warm parting kiss before leaving him at the healer's shack. "Wish me luck."

"You don't need it. You have your mother!" *But call if anything goes wrong.*

She squeezed his hand and crunched off into the snow.

He fought the urge to follow her and knocked on the shack door. There was no answer, but it was unlocked.

The other men were snoring loudly. Cyan's neck was twisted so that his head rested on the edge of the table. He'd have a strange mark on his temple later.

Etutsa had collapsed into his cot, dressed but disheveled. This sight would've made a grandmother coo affectionately, but it made Marl hot. He should've told Wind off; a few minutes wouldn't have troubled anyone but her.

He settled into Etutsa's chair and unfurled a scroll.

The cobbler's son had a rasping cough. Those remedies contained peppermint, elder, and yarrow. The elder would be tricky to prepare for the small dosage required for Laohin, but Marl was confident he could concoct the tea.

Everything was made into teas. In fact, Gerna needed more bee balm tea for her arthritic hands and back. Marl contemplated sneaking in some willow to make her more comfortable.

The rest of the tasks were scrawled through with ink, all completed the day before. It was useless for the common man to fight against the ravages of weather and better to wait it out by the fire. Warmth would always come to those who prepared beforehand and those with patience to see the winter through.

Marl had always taken for granted his fortunes. With Father and Natsir commanding their farm, warmth and security were never an issue.

He spent the rest of the morning listening to snores and sounds he didn't want to investigate. Hereu never contacted him. This was a good sign. Vill had accepted his defeat. Marl tried to formulate his speech to Father and Mother. It went along the lines of a swift apology followed by a "Look! Isn't your new daughter precious?" Mother *might* laugh. It was the closest he could come to being contrite.

He wrapped the finished teas into parchment paper and sealed the edges with wax. Etutsa refused to wake, so he kicked Cyan in the shins instead. Cyan grunted and rolled his head off the table, catching it in midair before he fell off the chair. Marl pushed him back against the wall and smacked his cheeks lightly.

"Cyan. Hey Cyan!" His friend opened one eye and groaned. "I'm delivering these medicines. Tell Etutsa I'll be back if he wakes up. Got it?"

"Yeah, sure, I'll tell him. What time is it?" He yawned.

"Midday." Marl snatched the packages and stepped outside. "Wake up, lazy."

Marl smirked as he closed the door. Something clamored against it. He hoped it wasn't an amber jar.

The deliveries took longer than expected. Gerna fawned over him. She swore he looked older. Was it the beard growing in? Was he taller? He'd never felt so relieved to walk out into snow, but she didn't let him leave easily. They stood in the doorway for some minutes after his supposed farewells so she could interrogate him about his brother and Para.

"It was a misunderstanding," he lied.

Reassured she hadn't caused a row between the lovers, Gerna finally sent him on his way.

The cobbler wasn't interested in family troubles. He demanded to replace the ill-fitting shoes.

"I've worn these for moons, Chaun; they'll be fine."

Marl was shoved into a stool and tossed a new pair. There was no use protesting. The Telmah of Na-ir were willful and helpful. You loved to disagree with them, but you never turned them down.

His wife and father-in-law were at the shack when Marl finally approached.

Cyan opened the door and pointed behind them. Hereu squealed and jumped into Marl's arms. The men covered their ears.

Something shook in her curls. Marl jumped. "I'm always finding things in here, but they usually don't move!"

A black-and-white kitten poked its head out and stretched weaponized paws. It gazed with two intent green eyes.

"That's a dinner invitation," Vill scoffed. "Your brother sent it. What's wrong with your family?"

"Isn't he adorable?" Hereu snatched the kitten from her hair; its claws tangled in her tresses. "He loves to snuggle." She hummed and pulled a note from her pocket.

Cyan groaned and rubbed his neck. "Woman, if you don't stop squealing, I'm going to kick you!"

Marl willed a stone from under the snow into his hand and chucked it. It landed on his friend's yellow crown before bouncing off the side of the shack.

"Ouch! Hey!"

Vill chortled, impressed with the quickness of his son-in-law's vengeance.

The handwriting was Para's. She and Natsir wanted to celebrate, and Mister and Mistress Misyl and Mister and Mistress Ganwin were invited to dinner. *Leave it to Para and Nat to make things formal.*

There was more to this than a celebration though. It was a ploy to get him to confront his parents, and Natsir was providing a less-intimidating environment. His eye caught more ink, crudely rendered and badly spelled. "Talc to the kat."

Marl looked at the creature, struggling in his wife's choking embrace, but purring, nonetheless. *I'm Destroyer of Lizards. I'm here to speak to the Wanderer, not be squished by this annoying woman!*

You don't look too upset, Destroyer. Marl smirked. *What's your message?*

The kitten crawled its way out of Hereu's hands and leapt back into the safety of her hair. She giggled, unaffected by its ability to mutilate other types of mice.

If you don't bring your wife and her family to the cottage tonight, your brother will see to it that you'll need to use all of your healing abilities to sit down. It blinked. *Also Para's sorry. Not sure why.*

Thank you, Destroyer. Marl reached out to his brother. *Nat! You didn't have to threaten me. The kitten was a nice touch though. Hereu's annoying everyone.*

Natsir laughed loudly. He was at G'Nirac's. *Good! I figured I should combat obnoxious with obnoxious. Congratulations, baby brother! See you tonight.*

Marl turned to Vill. He was standing patiently, his arms crossed in defiance, but with a not-too-angry expression on his face as he regarded Hereu and the kitten.

"Well, I suppose we'll be paying a visit to the other half of the family tonight."

The old man's amusement vanished.

"I'll get you all at sunset." Marl stroked the cat and kissed his wife goodbye.

As he approached the doorway, Vill cuffed him. "You were supposed to wait 'til spring!"

Cyan jumped, expecting a fight, but Marl laughed and shrugged. There was nothing the shepherd could do to him now: the blessing had been given and the opportunity had been taken.

"See you this evening, idiot." Vill left a hole in the snow and hobbled off.

Hereu forced the warrior kitten to wave goodbye before following her father home. *See you tonight.*

Marl was delighted to see her contented and unharmed, but he made a mental note to smack the snot out of Natsir later. This unusual devious behavior wouldn't go unpunished.

Destroyer would approve.

SEVENTEEN

His youth had been unfortunate—ambling through hills and valleys as a starveling—angry—scrimping and stealing to survive. Not all of it was painful though. He'd been lonely, just not alone. It had made him strong, a warrior, but at a price.

His deliverance rested in his arms now. Such gentleness should've never been given to an uncouth aggressor; yet she gave it to him freely. He wasn't a man who deserved much, but he knew how to take.

Are you in the hills again, love? Messa sipped her tea and leaned her raven head into him.

How did I hide that darkened sword from you if you can still read me this well?

The weapon now slept on the table, unwrapped, as if waiting to be rested on a warrior for burial. Nojhi glanced at it and shivered.

Should've never let my innocent son touch it.

I wanted to believe the lie. She'd already forgiven him. *Besides, it was the children I concentrated on, not you. The son you told is a skilled manipulator.* Messa kissed the scruff of his chin. *I also don't like confrontation.*

"Ha! You've created a lot of it lately, my priestess." Nojhi should've known better. Erutani weren't flowers growing in forest clearings, but the wild rivers. Sometimes, there had to be a flood.

Messa elbowed him in the stomach.

He kissed the top of her head and pulled her closer, half into his lap. "Is there anything else you haven't told me?"

She stiffened and blinked. A wicked smile blossomed from her clenched jaw. The resemblance to their youngest son was unsettling. "Your bald spot is expanding, but, because you're taller than over half of Na-ir, that's hardly a problem."

He gave her backside a hardy smack. "I already know that!"

Nojhi also knew his calf muscles ached when he walked long distances and that he could no longer go days without sleeping. He made stupid mistakes too, losing grip on tools and causing himself minor injuries. More scars had been obtained as an old farmer than as a general—but not more than as an orphan. There'd been many beatings in an attempt to tame the wild boy. His chest and back still bore faint traces.

"I mean about you and the boys. Marl scares me!"

The memory of his son, bloody and unconscious, still made him want to vomit. The loss would've been a blow to him in every way; yet a scant two days later he'd threatened to harm him for a childish defiance. The fault was his. Marl was only a boy, manipulated by tantalizing and free things.

He hadn't been much different… once.

Messa yawned. Their third child was also demanding. Nojhi moved her closer, sloshing some of the tea. He'd take care of that later; she needed sleep.

She moaned and snuggled into his warmth. "I know, love. I'm apprehensive too. But I've told you everything I know—about the summer harvest celebration and Hereu, what the sisters told me."

He scoffed. Those bitches were playing games—if they existed. But they had to for Messa to be so certain. It troubled him to think his wife was speaking to things less tangible than air.

She took a great, rasping breath and shivered. "About Vill and Surnow."

Nojhi nodded and rubbed her shoulder. It was a subject they both didn't want to explore. He took another glance at the sword and flinched. *I'll annihilate that thing in Namnor's fires.*

Nervous with dread, he looked around the cottage. Every knickknack and cracked pot spoke of happy moments: the overused kettle, the jar of honey, and the two beds by the hearth—one made and the other a mass of sheets with a collection of river stones beneath it. It had been a castle compared to the wagon, but now the place looked as meager as Etutsa's shack. How had four people existed here without killing each other?

"I should've built walls. It would've given us less space, but more privacy. I still should."

Messa rumbled. "Don't bother. There'll be the two of us in the spring. Well, at least just for the spring." Summer would bring something new to their family garden.

Nojhi was terrified. Being a father again was more frightful than riding into battle. He was losing sons, rough and forgiving of his coarse ways. How was he ever going to rear a daughter?

"She'll need her space. I don't think I want something innocent seeing all my vices. I never should've been informal with the boys." *What if the girl is more vulnerable?*

"Husband, look at me. She'll be mine too, and I can tell you no child, male or female, is *that* innocent or fragile." Messa laughed at his scowl. "I'm certain she'll be as stubborn and ridiculous as us."

"Suppose you're right." Nojhi slapped his leg, recalling the one Ganwin with an easy temperament. "Where'd Nat get his brains from? I swear; he changed right before our eyes. A few moons ago, it was hard to tell he had opinions. Now, he has more wisdom than a priest."

"They've both grown into fine men. They'll continue to do so, I think."

"Yes," he agreed, though he was unsure *man* was a fitting label for their youngest son. But what else did you call an accomplished healer? Marl had made something of himself. "I wish I'd the strength of purpose and resolve they have. They're better men."

Messa squished his cheeks and shook her head. He smiled.

"I guess Tilran will be all right too?"

She dropped her hand and cocked her glossy head sideways. "Tilran?"

Nojhi ran his free hand through his hair and hummed. "I want to name this one. You got Natsir, and… Wind got Marl." He coughed into his sleeve. "Means *starlight*; heard it in the orphanage once. I figured it was a gentle enough not to get her in trouble."

Messa's perfect eyes widened. "Water named Natsir. You were too excited to have a son to listen."

He blushed. It had taken him a long time to trust her about the strangeness of nature.

"Moon wisdom, warrior, and starlight—our poor children." She cackled and fell into him. "I like Tilran; it's pretty. Tilran Ganwin. The spirits told me they're content with our sons. We'll name her whatever we want. She's *ours*."

He rubbed her leg and tried to smile. "Well, we know *she's* safe, but where are our rapscallions? One of them should be home by now." He peeped out the window above their bed. Everything was grey and white. "It's snowing too."

"I'll see if I can find them."

Her eyes darted and sparkled. It was still an odd sight, knowing she was no longer in the room, but wandering through a void.

"One boy is at G'Nirac's, asleep in a rocking chair." She laughed. "I'll let you guess which one."

"What about Marl—at Vill's or Etutsa's?"

"Neither. He's in…" The cup clattered. "Well, um… Don't be mad, love, but I think…"

Ire rose. Nojhi looked around for something to release the tension. There was Messa or the sheets. He chose the safer option. "All right. Let me have it. What's he doing?"

She stared at the brown puddle. "I'm going to have to stop checking in on him, now he's..." She stopped again, tears in her eyes. She looked uncomfortable. "Married."

Nojhi pulled the edge of the sheets. Blood rushed away from his knuckles and into his eyes. Every part of him wanted to go after Marl, but he stayed poised. Stillness would come if it killed him; it had to for his family's sake. He released the fabric. "How nice."

Messa reached for a pillow and pretended to hug it. Her eyes were wide and her arms were goose-pimpled. He ignored the fact that this *was* partially her fault.

"Are you well, love?"

He coughed and she jumped. Nojhi sliced his hand down the soft shield and forced it back into her lap. He needed to see her fearful face to control his anger. She took a sharp breath, preparing for his roar.

"I'll live." He took another deep sigh. "Or at least I will, if I manage to get some sleep."

Being passive was taxing. Nojhi slammed his body into the bed and closed his eyes. He would dream of suitable punishments in his delirium, but they would be confined to the Blessed Unknowing. Marl didn't need to know this blow was more painful and debilitating than an accidental thwack to the head.

***

They woke to a shout and a massive thunk against their bed. Under the strain of sleep-cloaked eyes, the cottage looked empty, save for Pilgrim the furry knickknack. Nojhi wondered if the noise had been a dream, or one of those elusive spirits— until the floor spoke.

"That... that was unpleasant."

"Nat?" His son was lying in the puddle. "You all right?"

"I'll live. Sorry for startling you." Natsir groaned and flicked tea off his hands.

"Welcome back. We thought you'd moved into G'Nirac's."

The boy shuffled uncomfortably.

"Don't worry. I already know about your brother. He won. I surrender."

Messa gasped and hugged Nojhi, but his resolve was false. How could he give up on something that mattered so much?

Natsir frowned. "Oh, yes. Marl and Hereu… They'll be very happy." He crossed his arms and looked to the window. "Para's outside. I'll be right back."

He stepped over the puddle and marched to the door.

A brief flow of winter air penetrated the cottage. The girl entered, draped in a dusting of snow, but radiant as always. She was wearing the blue shawl. The boys had been right; the color suited her.

Para skipped with a personal satisfaction that said she was on the edge of something exhilarating.

Nat might not be capable of mischief, but his betrothed is!

Nojhi missed those days where he could chase the children around the woods and tickle them until they couldn't breathe. The sweet chieftain's daughter had never found him terrifying; perhaps Tilran would be the same.

Natsir slammed the door shut against the flurries and guided Para over to the table, well away from the mess on the floor. He found a rag. Messa tried to stop him, but the boy always took care of things.

Para watched with a radiant smile, her arms folded in her lap. Once Natsir was sitting, she began. "Are you *well*, Mister Ganwin?" she asked sweetly.

He almost believed he was on his deathbed. He was still *in* bed! He climbed out of it to join the couple. "I'm fine, love," he lied.

The girl raised an eyebrow and wriggled in her seat.

Nojhi forced a laughed. "I promise. I know about Marl and Hereu. This fool has decided to let things be. There's no use in getting angry." He patted her hand. "I apologize for my temper, sweetheart."

She nodded in acceptance of his penance, but looked to the rusted sword. "Very sensible. I'm glad. We have some news to…"

Natsir raked his hands through his hair and mumbled. "We're married too!"

Nojhi's familiar friends—impatience and ire—knocked on his mind again. They weren't welcome. He unclenched his fist and forced a smile. *By the glowing ancestors! Are both my sons going to abandon me?* He swallowed and steadied himself. "Lovely!" *What are the odds I'd get rid of you two so easily?*

I'm sorry, Father. Natsir looked pained. "It was G'Nirac's idea."

"Papa thought we had suffered enough, and he was worried the town would bombard Nat with questions. It's not fair to put him through all of that. Papa knew you wouldn't mind."

G'Nirac lied; the old man knew Nojhi didn't prescribe to the more permissive Telmah attitude. Young men were no better than children, easily molded. The wrong craftsman had tried to shape his youth and it was something he wanted to avoid for his sons.

"It was also a… well… Rippan can't claim something that belongs to someone else. There were many agreements. Onaryc was using Lufnis's inexperience to force G'Nirac's hand."

The men relaxed. In matters of force and war, this reasoning was… well, reasonable. The women stiffened; war was the last thing they wanted to dwell on.

"I see." Nojhi stroked his beard; it was starting to thin. "It's a dangerous thing to play games with Onaryc. Watch out for that brother-in-law of yours, Nat. If he's got the chieftain of the Dasha whispering in his ear, he may be corrupted." The warning was spoken out of purest love. *And if that's the case, beat the snot out of him and take over yourself. You know you can. There's no man in town better suited.*

Why not? Ril had used the same laws to gain mastery over the tribes. What would it hurt to ensure someone less violent was in control?

Natsir looked at his powerful hands, but didn't answer.

Para sobbed. "I don't know what we'll do when he becomes chieftain."

Her groom took her into his lap and held tight to her waist. It was an odd sight. *My boys show affection like me.* Marl was right. It was creepy.

In a rare show of willfulness, Natsir changed the subject. "Because we're not having a celebration in the spring, we thought we might have a little gathering here. There are too many ears at G'Nirac's home." He stroked Para's curls and sighed. "Tonight. We've already delivered the invitations."

Para rocked in her husband's lap like a naughty girl on a swing.

"Sorry we didn't ask first. I felt it might be easier to do it now since Marl is … unpredictable. We'll be busy building our homes this winter." *We should all gather and celebrate, as family, even if it doesn't make you happy, Father.*

"We'll handle everything," Para offered. "Nat and I aren't afraid of a little work to make this nice."

Nojhi wiped his hands over his face and groaned, unable to contain the contempt within him much longer. Surely they knew what an inconvenience this was. "How many did you invite?"

"There are nine of us."

Nine people in a tiny cottage! Were the young ones out of their minds? He slammed his fist on the table and groaned. The company recoiled. Nojhi tried to smile; it wasn't convincing.

"What a fine idea. Let's get started!"

***

The cottage was loud, but pleasant. Nojhi could hear the crackle of the magnificent fire over the chatter, but its warmth soothed his troubled mind. Laughter echoing through the wooden walls was also a welcome surprise.

Natsir and Para flirted and clamored. It was amusing for them to play house, good practice. He envied their optimism and energy, but not their tasks; Nojhi was very comfortable now.

Etutsa had settled in next to him, as silent and amused by the couple as he was. They drank G'Nirac's traditional gift of wine while Messa cast the bottle contemptuous frowns. She didn't approve of spirits in her house, but Telmah had few vices; this one could be forgiven.

Clean and warm house, stew in the pot, good company, and a tender tingling rushing through his blood. Why had he been angry again?

A knock on the door made him remember.

"You must be Dalis," his wife cooed. "I'm Marl's mother, Messa." She gave Mistress Misyl her hand.

The woman wasn't what Nojhi had expected. Her body was fragile, but her demeanor was as graceful as a queen. She removed a ragged, snow-dusted cloak and passed it to Natsir. "I've no doubt you're his mother! You've the same wise eyes." She waved to the rest of the company and motioned to someone outside. "This is my husband, Vill."

Nojhi frowned as the stocky man entered his home. The shepherd wasn't as dirty as usual; his brown mass of hair was combed. Either he had some self-respect or his wife did for him.

"The children will be along shortly," Dalis trilled.

Etutsa and Nojhi snorted.

"Please sit," Natsir offered. He guided them to the table and put down platters of food.

While the men stared like grumpy children, the women chatted like old friends. Nojhi had never heard his wife talk so much! She had been isolated in this village. It would be nice for her and Tilran to have another woman to look to in times when men were a nuisance. Nojhi would learn to tolerate Vill.

How did he acquire a woman like that?

Messa interrupted his speculations. *Your son is giving his poor wife an inspirational talk in the cold. You scared the girl, love. Please, please be on your best behavior now. I'm growing fond of this woman!*

Nojhi snorted. *Don't worry, love. You and Etutsa have worked your magic.*

She showed her tongue.

Dalis cackled, but quieted into rasping coughs as the door creaked open.

A crow flew into the cottage and turned his deep, magnificent eyes on the party. Marl smiled with the authority of a king and pulled his brown conquest inside.

Nojhi hadn't registered the girl's features at the wedding. He tried to take her in now. *I knew it! The lamb!* Hereu was draped in black wool and clutching a parti-colored kitten. *What's with the cat?*

Natsir popped a slice of roasted squash into his mouth and smirked. *Oh, that's my revenge.*

Hereu was squeezing the fluff ball.

Messa shook her head. *Revenge on the cat or Marl?*

Nojhi tapped the table, considering his next move. It was easy to see why Marl found Hereu endearing. She had her mother's sweetness but also her father's fear. The boy needed someone to protect.

"Hello, everyone. May I introduce my beautiful wife, Hereu?" Marl placed a reassuring hand on the girl's back and kept his pleading blue eyes on his father.

Nojhi shuffled slowly, barely breathing for fear of spooking her. She was a doe expecting the sharp sting of an arrow. He wanted to change that, to mend the torment he'd caused. He stretched out his hand. Marl took it, fearless.

"Well done, son."

Nojhi released his spawn and pounced on the unsuspecting woman. She shrieked. Something hissed as Nojhi placed the dizzy girl back to the floorboards. His quick-thinking son had rescued the forgotten kitten. Marl threw it on the bed next to Pilgrim and smirked.

"Welcome to the family, sweetheart!" Nojhi kissed Hereu's forehead and leaned closer to whisper in her ears, taking in the unseasonable smell of apple blossoms. "But let me give you some advice. Watch out for this one; I hear he's too much like his father."

Eyelashes batting, Hereu whispered back. "I think I can live with that."

***

Two old warriors took a stance on the porch and stared. Nojhi tried not to laugh. It was comical to think this angry, wee man had ever been a soldier in his army; but then again, it was more about strength of purpose than strength of arm.

The storm had already passed. The only moisture in the air came from their wine-warmed breaths now.

Marl joined them. He hadn't been invited; Nojhi wasn't ready to speak with him, but he couldn't ask him to leave. He could, however, command him to close the door.

The warm glow from the cottage vanished and night became more intense, revealing the Stars' Passageway overhead. The old general didn't like looking into the colorful countenance of death, but for some reason his eyes were always drawn to it.

"Why did you call me out into this darkened cold, Vill?" The buzz of the wine was gone and in its place was a headache.

Marl leaned against the house and waved a hand. A small, orange flame sparked into his palm. The porch warmed. "Feel better now?"

They each slapped him across the ears. "I told you to stop!"

The boy pretended the attacks never happened. He blew on his palm and the fire disappeared, conceding back to night's blackness. "All right. If you two want to freeze…"

Neither warrior responded. The flame sputtered back into being. Light danced off Marl's handsome, dark-lined face. If a precious and precocious child resided within those terrible eyes, it was held captive in horror.

The fire boy dropped his creation on the porch. Nothing but air was consumed. The old men coughed, pretending not to be alarmed.

Vill pulled two rolled objects from his pocket and gave one to Nojhi. "I figured you might enjoy this." He winked and passed his through the flame, placing the gnarled stick into his mouth and drawing in a long drag of the warm, white smoke.

Nojhi muttered thanks and did the same.

You smoke spirit root, Father?

Nojhi tried not to look into those eyes. Whether that was a child's curiosity or a grown man's admonishment, he didn't want to know. The smoke left his mouth and entered back through his nose, tingling with a sweet, woody taste as it ravaged his sinuses.

"No offence, but I'm not too keen on your boy," Vill began, puffing.

Nojhi was sure this sentiment included his Erutani wife, but the man had sense enough not to insult his woman.

"There's too much selfishness in him." Vill snarled, but Marl shrugged.

Nojhi resisted the urge to smack the shepherd in his son's defense anyway. The statement was true, but it didn't need to be voiced. Vill didn't remember what it meant to be a boy.

"However, I've the utmost respect for you. You've nothing to fear from me, sir. Nothing." He coughed into his sleeve and rocked. "I knew who you were from the moment we met."

That was troubling. Nojhi's balding head and stomach paunch should've concealed the great man he used to be, transforming him into a simple, tan and callused farmer instead, albeit a tall one.

"Go no further. There are those here who don't know what we know. I'd rather keep it that way."

Vill opened his mouth to speak and then closed it. He took a nervous puff and sighed, staring out into the whiteness enveloping the trees. "Was an honor, nevertheless."

"By the inconstant moon it was!"

The chatter in the cottage stopped.

Nojhi took a long drag of smoke and contemplated the last time he'd ever done so before. He'd been much younger then and more vigorous. The herbs caressed his lungs and seeped into his bloodstream with the alcohol. It was a rush he sometimes missed.

"I know who you are, Father. You're General Hama and you led the slaughter at Surnow."

They threw him off the porch. He landed in the snow with a muffled thud.

"Are you daft?" Vill whispered. "Those are words you never say aloud!"

Marl laughed and slapped snow off his head and shoulders. "Such foolish old men, you're afraid of your own shadows. There's no one here."

Nojhi reached out a hand to pull his son up. He didn't need it, but there was a yearning in him to be polite to the daemon, to pacify it into submission. "He's right, son. It's dangerous to speak those words in the open. Who told you these things?"

"I figured it out on my own, based on what Mother and Vill told me." *Also, I stole one of your memories. Natsir knows too.*

On instinct, he slapped the boy, hard. "The two of you better keep your mouths shut! This is serious."

A glimmer of innocence sparked in Marl's eyes. "We would never betray you."

Nojhi sighed and took him into his arms. "I know, son. It's not my skin I fear for. If anyone ever found out, this family would suffer. G'Nirac and the village might too."

"I understand." Marl choked. "I'm sorry." *I came out here to beg your forgiveness… and Vill's too. I know I can be an idiot sometimes.*

You certainly can! Nojhi grunted. He couldn't muster the resolve to apologize himself, but part of him wanted to. He looked the boy in the eye. "So, we all agree. Never speak of this again. On pain of torture." His gruff declaration didn't mask his pleasure well. *Baby hold style.*

Marl snorted and nodded. This gesture had been apology enough to pacify him.

"Yes, of course. My daughter's safety is also at stake." Vill took Nojhi's hand and shook it, but gave Marl an indignant hiss. "Don't think this changes my opinion. One false move and…"

"You're not allowed to murder my son."

The little man stammered.

"However, if he ever starts anything, let me know and we'll take turns beating the snot out of him. I have ways."

Vill's shoulders relaxed. Marl shook his head and crossed his arms over his chest, tears in his eyes.

"Why don't you head back inside, Vill? We'll catch up."

The shepherd tossed his smoke into the snow. Marl watched him leave.

Nojhi took another drag. "What memory did you steal?"

The boy swallowed. "Nat and I saw you in your armor, looking in your shield."

Nojhi dropped the smoke and stepped on it. Was it possible they were both terrified?

"Then I saw Sur… the battle. All of the bodies and the fire. I don't think any less of you, I suppose. I'm in shock. I couldn't understand why she was afraid, why she wanted to hide." Marl sobbed. "When you showed me that sword, I had this fanciful vision of you bringing vengeance on the wicked. But they weren't wicked. They were just people."

Nojhi leaned into his son. Marl's bravery was as much an act as his patience. "Yes, they were. I'm not proud of what I did. I showed you that sword because I realized suns ago what you said is true; people suffer for the mistakes of others. I don't want anyone to suffer again for what I've done. It's a hard thing to live with, but we still need to protect those we love."

Marl nearly knocked him off the porch. He clung like a coat and took several steadying breaths.

The fatherly desires in Nojhi to comfort his son were overpowering, but a deep nagging to discipline the little beast for all of the trouble he had caused was tempting too. "You don't have to fear me, boy. I just want you to remember one thing."

Marl released his neck. "What?"

Nojhi kicked snow onto the fire. The darkness had some advantages; it shielded him from the full visage of his crying offspring. He used his knee to make his point. There was a muffled gasp.

"I'm your father. And I love you." *But I also expect obedience. I don't care how old you are.*

Marl's silhouette nodded slowly.

Good. Nojhi released the slender, perfect neck and moved toward the cottage. *Feel better now, Father?*

Actually, yes. Nojhi pushed open the door. *You might want to put snow on that though. Wouldn't want to disappoint your wife.*

Marl tossed a ball. The frigid clump slid delightfully down his back.

The view inside lifted Nojhi's spirits more. But, it was getting late, and his old body needed rest.

"So." Nojhi slapped his hands together. "Have we discussed where our little sweeties are living for the time being?" He waved a hand around his tiny, open cottage and smirked.

Vill groaned in the light of his wife's clever smile. There was only one answer to this question.

"Curse the path to eternity! I just got him out of my house!"

EIGHTEEN

Marl woke, as he did every morning, to the blissful, sweet smell of hay tucked into a lumpy mattress and the sight of two russet eyes full of mutual ardor and veneration. There was a simple relief in the curve of his wife's youthful cheeks and the way her shoulders moved ever-so-slightly with the gentle pulse of her breathing. When she yawned, she squeaked and her petite nose scrunched. She had been well-named.

There was nothing better than this, except that they would relive it for every day of their lives hereafter. Her simple sweetness was more precious than the heavens. When she was with him, there was peace.

"Is it spring yet?"

Hereu asked him this every morning, as if he could command the seasons. She was sick of being cloistered—sewing torn garments, listening to her father grumble, and snow.

Marl chuckled. "Not yet, love. I'm sure there's still a frost outside."

Hereu pulled their frayed blanket over her bare shoulders. "I don't know if I can take more."

He smoothed sleep-tossed curls from her eyes; a stray strand fell over her crown in a loop like a mouse's ear. Marl left it there, bemused.

"Can I stay with you and Etutsa today?"

"No, love." They'd already tried that method of appeasing her reckless soul.

"Please? I won't break anything… again. I promise."

"Nope."

He snuggled in next to his sighing wife. She relaxed and accepted his kiss. Under the caress of old blankets, they fondled each other and tried not to make too much noise. Marl would be late again, but Etutsa was getting used to it.

Vill wasn't. He accosted the door and growled each morning. Today, he was running out of clever statements. "Wake up! It's past sunrise!"

Unable to relinquish the hold they had on each other, they finished what they'd started, muttering curses for the interruption, and then quickly dressed. They had one thing on their mind now: to finish that house in the meadow as soon as possible.

"That's what I should do today. I'm sure I could prepare the rest of the foundation on my own." Hereu flexed her slender arms and smirked.

Half of the grounds had been cleared in the previous weeks. Materials were available in the forest, cheap as long as one could do the labor, but it was a real effort for two people—even with his abilities to melt frost and move earth.

Marl gave her backside a mild smack. "I'm ready to get out of here too, but I think you should wait until I'm off. Remember how *she* likes to harass you when you're out alone."

Hereu huffed. Wind's jealous antics were growing more terrible. The most recent being a skull bruising thwack with the arm of an ash tree—who apologized for its use in such torture—and a slip across an icy hill cropping. There seemed to be no way to appease the spirit, though he was still practicing her strange exercises in the evenings. Something had to be done; he would not stand for his wife to be terrorized. The solution had to come before spring, or she'd never be able to take the sheep to graze.

"Come on. Let's get some breakfast."

Hereu needed to eat. He did too, but he had foolishly promised Wind that he wouldn't eat flesh anymore. He forgot the Misyls were Mlaerian, eating more animal substances than any human vein should process. Marl missed his mother's ability to turn vegetables into something satisfying.

Dalis enjoyed cooking and took a renewed interest in it now he had joined the family. He recoiled from the briny smells of boiled eggs and seared pork, but modified his disgust as his mother-in-law gave him a hopeful, fragile smile.

"Hungry?" She tossed bits of gristle to Destroyer and Broom by the hearth. A hot egg was shoved into Marl's hands. "Please sit."

"No, but thank you…"

"Nonsense! You're a skinny man. A little something will be good for you." Dalis was of the opinion men who didn't eat well must be too distracted to take care of themselves. While he was in her house, she was determined to remind him of this notion.

Vill grumbled over a cup of tea and glared.

Unable to tell her no again without sounding impolite, Marl shoved the egg into his pocket and mumbled thanks. Hereu fiddled with a basket on a nearby shelf; from it she pulled out a small heel of bread. He caught it and winked before waving and turning toward the door.

"You can't leave now," Dalis exclaimed. She stood near Vill holding two cups of her hard, black tea and pouted; it was as endearing as her daughter's oft expressions.

Marl sighed and walked back to the table. He wrapped an arm around her fragile shoulders. It made him ache that there was little opportunity to give his own mother an embrace. He cursed himself for the bitter youth he used to be.

"I'm sorry, Dalis. I'm late. I'll see y'all tonight." He gave Vill a mocking salute with the bread and strode quickly to the door.

The shepherd was adept at revenge. "So, you with child yet?"

Hereu shouted. "Shut up!"

Vill shouted back.

Marl looked through the crack in the door; eager to show his father-in-law a few things if he went too far. But the punishment had already been dealt. Vill was moaning over his clothes, covered in black sludge. The animals were helping with the cleanup.

Dalis winked. "I'm sorry, love. You know how much my hands shake."

Hereu burst into fits of childish laughter and fell out of her chair.

Marl longed to cradle her tremulous body and laugh with her, but he shoved the bread in his mouth, closed the door slowly, and walked a few yards to work. They would be fine without him.

Etutsa was more forgiving than Vill. Marl gave him an offering anyway.

"It's time for Mistress Hedar to have her child. Do you think you're up for the task, boy?" The old man snuck the egg off of his desk and cracked it with boney knuckles against the hard wood surface, coughing.

"I suppose. Do you have the herbs for Laohin ready?" Marl was eager to check in on the cobbler's son. His cough was worse; others in the village were experiencing the same disagreeable symptoms.

Etutsa nodded and pointed to a package on the cot.

Marl took the bundle and cradled it. Children would be nice, especially ones as sweet as Laohin. "Is this everything that's ready now?"

The healer choked on the last bits of egg.

Marl put the package on the table and stared into dark-blotched eye sockets. "Are you well, Etutsa?"

The man shivered and pulled the wrap tighter across his shoulders. He concentrated on the honey concoction in front of him. The cot had been slept in again.

Marl pounded the table. "Damn it, old man! You can't live like this."

He grabbed the healer's hands and sent a flume of warmth into the arthritic joints. Etutsa gasped. Tears pushed out of the laugh lines in his eyes.

"You promised you'd stay with your brother. Why're you still trying to eke out an existence in this wooden cave? This is foolish!"

The old man turned away. "Now you're defender of the weak minded, not just the weak."

There had to be a way to make this darkened shack livable. Marl waved his hand and held out a bright orange flame.

"Don't do that here! What if someone saw you?"

Marl dropped the flame to the ground and set his jaw. "I wouldn't have to do this if you would take better care of yourself. There's a sickness. What's this village going to do if you die?"

He noticed the clay pot under the table and scooted Etutsa's chair out of the way. The aloe plants had withered, shrived coils of brown succumbed to the frost and lack of sunshine. Marl tossed the soil and decayed matter outside and set the pot in the center of the room. Some broken willow sticks made convincing fodder. The materials weren't consumed, but Marl allowed smoke to rise and carry through the shack before cracking open the door.

Etutsa shuddered. "I think Na-ir will do well without me. I'm too old, too stubborn. It's time to leave this practice in more able hands." He hugged his chest and rocked on his heels. "I've rendered myself useless, my boy. I give up."

Marl pushed him back to his chair. The healer had a flair for being overdramatic and emotional. This was another ploy for attention. "Shut up! You're sick and you're not thinking clearly. Thaw out."

The old man refused to sit. He dropped the blanket from his shoulders and wrapped boney fingers around Marl's waist. "Thank you for your confidence, but I'm afraid no thaw will change my mind. In fact, the times in my life where I made the worst decisions were those when I was hot." Etutsa shuffled to the bed and wound his sheets into a ball. "I don't have much, do I?"

He stooped to tug up some of the floor boards.

"What're you doing, you senile fool?" Marl hissed.

A single board lifted to reveal a hole lined with plaster. Etutsa removed two bottles of whiskey, tucked them into the sheets, and put the board back into place with a clumsy swipe of his foot.

"There! I'll be seeing you… healer." He waved goodbye and made a stiff stride for the door.

Marl snatched his collar. "Don't think so! I'm not in the mood for games."

"I'm not playing. I give this shack and everything in it to you. I've had enough of this existence and it's had enough of me. You're strong, smart, and feisty; you can handle it. I've faith in you, young man." Etutsa swung open the door and marched out into the snow. "The key is on the wall," he reminded as he trudged.

Muttering curses, Marl grabbed the package for Laohin and the key. The fire in the pot flickered out of existence as he turned the lock. He wasn't ready to lose the healer's advice, and he certainly didn't want to relinquish his company.

By the time they made it to their destination, Marl was in no mood to be polite. "Good morning. Does this belong to you?" he snapped as his sister-in-law opened the door. Marl pushed Etutsa inside, wanting to slap the stupid grin off his white-whiskered face.

Natsir waved from the kitchen, looking bored. *G'Nirac isn't well. He's refusing to see Etutsa though. I think the two of them are quarreling again.*

Para stared with wide-eyed apprehension. "Is there something wrong, uncle?"

Etutsa shoved the mass of sheets into Natsir's arms and winked. "Nothing's wrong, my girl. I've decided to live out the rest of my suns in peace and comfort. I'm retiring." He plopped into the rocking chair and warmed his hands, sniffing savory chestnuts. "I apologize for giving you another mouth to feed, but I know you don't mind, love."

"Oh." Para rolled her eyes. The cult known as family had a strange hold on people. "Congratulations, Marl. You're a fine healer. You'll make our village more comfortable."

"Thanks." It was like being abandoned on someone's doorstep. "When this codger comes to his senses, will you see he makes it back to the shack safely? We've too much work for games."

Natsir gave him a hearty smack on the back and laughed. "Sure, brother. We'll take good care of him." *Our day's wasted anyway. How's your place coming?*

Marl sighed.

Etutsa kicked off his shoes and dangled his stocking feet. "Ah… You certainly will, boy." He melted into the chair. "Could you do one thing for me now, Nat? Go tell *my* big brother we need to make an announcement in the square. I think it would be best if we made a show of it. The more sponsorship the elders can give you, the better you'll be able to keep these simple people happy."

Natsir didn't move; he looked to Marl for support, nodding at the whiskey bottles peeping out of the sheets. No one was sure if Etutsa was serious or drunk.

The old man waved a gnarled hand and laughed. "Shoo! You're wasting time."

"You're wasting time, Etutsa!" Marl groaned. "You're being ridiculous and I'm tired of this." He marched out of the chieftain's house and ran through the square. The key to the shack smacked in his pocket. Little crystals of fear and remorse dangled off his cheeks. *Damn him! I can't do this alone.*

Natsir broke through the heat in his heart, washing the ire like bathing a dirty child. *Don't be upset, brother. He's proud of you, and so am I.*

***

"Sweet heart, are you trying to bore a hole into the hillside?"

Hereu stood near the pine as Marl took out his frustrations on the soil. He had taken a massive chunk of the mud and stones out by force of mind and now he was dumping the carnage like vomit down the side of the hill. It rolled and splattered to the woods in a strange, dirty waterfall.

"I don't understand why you're upset. This was what you wanted, isn't it?"

She'd been at Telm's pillar in the square for the announcement, but she hadn't heard the thoughts of the people as Marl was presented as their new savior. Those who knew him in his youth were bitter to find the Ganwin ruffian was in charge of their health and well-being. This was nothing in comparison to the thoughts of those from Selcovi; the scenes in their minds would make a murderer blush.

That black-hair, that seer, he could be trouble.

It stung and festered. The elders and his father and brother had stood with him, beaming with pride, making much show of his skills and knowledge—too much show.

In that agonizing moment, he was both comforted and disturbed to see Chaun and Pas standing close by and smiling. He'd saved one—without his knowledge; Etutsa was a skilled liar—but the other was very near to losing his son. The Wanderer's gifts had proven ineffective in something that mattered more than producing warmth and mending bones.

Marl cursed his fickle heritage and took a step back to contemplate the clumps of muddy soil. It looked like a larger version of the tantrum he'd thrown on the vegetable garden the day Father had shown him the sword. That darkened thing was now hidden in Vill's house, a strange and uncharacteristic request from his mother who had decided they might need to make use of it someday.

A nagging, breathy whisper was spurring him on, feeding the fears and doubt. The spirit spoke in a language he understood today: remorse and bitterness.

Etutsa had earned this retirement, but Marl wasn't certain he'd yet earned the prestige of filling such a position. He'd been an apprentice for less than a sun, and didn't have the respect of the majority of his people. If only he'd been a more obedient youth.

Hereu wrapped his shirt around her arms and tapped her foot. She was used to his moments of lengthy self-reflection, but sometimes the lack of an answer made her disturbed.

Marl coughed into his arm and straightened to appear more mature. "Who says I'm upset? I decided to make a cellar, that's all."

She laughed into Wind's taunting whispers, hands on supple hips. "That's supposed to be our bedchamber. I'm not sleeping in a mud hole; it looks like a tomb."

"Well, now we've a place to hide when the rabble comes," he scoffed, unwilling to let the anger go.

"Stars and mountains! You're an idiot, not a coward." Hereu tossed his shirt into the air and roared. "Etutsa trusts you. He's been the healer in Na-ir for decades. He knows what he's doing."

Marl jumped into the hole and groaned. Everything had been exactly the way he wanted for this moment in life. Without Etutsa's steadying presence, how was he going to remember not to use his powers? If he lost his head once, everything he'd worked for—his wife and this life—might vanish.

Hereu looked down from the edge of the hole, her beautiful but contemptuous face framed by the grey clouds overhead. "I'm not one to be ignored."

He snickered. They enjoyed a tumultuous relationship, but he knew her limits. When it came to his self-assessments, she would not allow him to be disparaging.

She rolled her tree-bark eyes and leapt on top of him. His chest and legs stung where her elbows and knees landed, but it was a momentary inconvenience; the bruises she'd created were gone within seconds.

Hereu settled her mass of curls into his chest and tapped on his ribcage. Marl was tempted to dive into her neck, to drink of the rain on her skin, but the ache in his soul made him too lazy to be playful.

"Listen. I know I don't give you enough praise, but you have amazing abilities. You can do more than any man in Artnaus." She kissed his sternum and smirked. "Etutsa's a good man and a skilled healer, but he could never match what you do. No one can. Why do you think you're unworthy of this?"

He stroked her hair and wiped mud from her dress. The mess didn't bother him—he liked her wild—but it gave him something to do. "Because all of Na-ir thinks so. I heard them. If they knew the truth about me, they'd go insane." He took a deep breath and tapped on her arm. "I can't use these powers outright; if I do, they'll chase us out of town. My gift's no good anyway. I can't heal Laohin."

Marl tried to hold back sobs, but his trembling chest shook his little bride.

"I can't heal your mother…"

He had tried, oh stars, he had tried. Whenever Dalis slumbered in her chair by the fire, he would concentrate on the sickness within her lungs. It refused to yield for the fervent cries of a son of Erutan.

Hereu sat up, ramming her knee between his legs. She ignored his hiss of displeasure to focus on the ache in his heart. "Is that what this is about?"

He looked to the mud-coated, root-splattered walls and sighed.

"Oh, love, please don't let that affect you. You'd have to be a god to cure everyone." She leaned on his legs and curled her hair. "But you're as powerful as the three sisters. If you can't make someone better, it was never meant to be. My mother is stronger than she looks, and Laohin will feel better once the weather warms. You keep them both very comfortable now."

She gave him a tender kiss that tasted like pork. He hoped Wind didn't count that as insubordination.

A tear streaked down her tan cheek, an amber shard in the sunset. "Once they understand you as I do, there will be no reason to doubt."

She didn't have a gift for healing, but her warmth was inspiring. It was a remedy for him. He slammed his black head into her breasts and cradled her tightly. "I'm sorry. She's your mother and I'm acting like it affects me more." He wiped the wet streak from her face. "I'm such a cur."

Hereu snickered.

He looked deep into her forgiving eyes. "Sometimes I think you've a greater strength of purpose than I do. You see things more clearly."

"No. Mama taught me not to worry. You have to accept fate." She poked him in the chest and moistened her lips, indicating this wasn't always a bad thing.

He took the invitation.

This had to be preordained. What else could explain how easily they fell into each other; how neatly they fit into an embrace? As long as his fate was connected with hers, he should stop worrying about what it meant to live. He was a young man; everything he wanted was in his arms.

His hands moved up her blouse and onto her back. Responsibilities could wait.

"You've married a wise woman, Marl Ganwin."

G'Nirac was a white–black statue against the grey sky, imposing but kind.

"Forgive the intrusion. I felt it best to make my presence known."

Marl laughed and wiped mud from his chest. Hereu's blouse was mangled around her chilled shoulders and she was covered in black smudges.

"Greetings, my chieftain. Well met. What brings you to my humble house?"

G'Nirac chuckled. "You have your father's humor. I'm well. My troubles are more of mind than body. However, please come here. I don't think my old bones or eyes can stand the strain."

It was a miracle the chieftain had made it up the wet hill. Why hadn't he just sent a summons? Marl climbed out of the hole with the expert impulses of a cat.

"How much you've grown! I held you the day you were born, but I knew then you'd…"

G'Nirac stopped short. The mouse was still trying to make it out of the hole.

"Oh. Please forgive us, Hereu."

Marl leaned over the side and smirked. She looked tempestuous with her clothes in disarray and her hair bursting from her head—perfect in his opinion.

Please help me. I'm too short.

Marl stroked his beard. *You're not short; the ground you're standing on is.*

She blew a curl away from her dirty face and clenched her fists. *That's the stupidest thing you've ever said, and you're not known for your wit, love.*

Well, if you're going to be disobedient and not accept my compliments, I'll leave you in there.

Hereu kicked the muddy wall and mumbled filthy curses.

Marl turned to the chieftain. "She'll be fine. What do you want to tell me?"

The old man grinned and coughed into his sleeve again. He hadn't heard their banter, but he could probably tell there was romantic mischief afoot. "I've been remiss, young man, and I must apologize. A part of me said I shouldn't interfere with how you progress. Still, I've taken a great interest in your well-being, Marl, even when I wasn't present.

Tutsa's told me much about your abilities. I know what he's done has upset you, and I'm sorry. While I'm proud of the young man you've become, I can't help but think this is a mistake."

This declaration stung in ways a healer couldn't mend. If the wisest of Telmah didn't have faith in him, he was nothing.

"I don't mean to insult you. I think you're meant for greater things than the life of a country healer. I know you're somewhat familiar with your heritage, but do you understand *what* you are?"

The Wanderer.

Good! I'm glad I'm not the first to tell you. Have you spoken to the sisters then? G'Nirac nodded to Hereu still kicking in the pit and raised an eyebrow.

"She knows everything already. It's safe to speak in front of her."

She stopped and stared, a few tears in her oaky eyes. But he dared not rescue her now. G'Nirac had information on something that'd been plaguing him for moons—no, his whole life—and he was unready to break the spell the old man had on his fate.

Hereu would want instantaneous revenge; he was willing to let her have it, but that would be another distraction. The old man had waited twenty suns to deliver this message; it may not be offered again.

Mother told me almost a sun ago. Wind's never left my side. Water and Earth don't speak with me, though.

"A pity." G'Nirac sighed. *All the same, let's keep this private. There's unrest in Na-ir and some want to stop you from your purpose.*

And what's that?

Marl's heart quickened and bounded like a squirrel in chase of its mate. He was hoping the chieftain knew something his mother and the spirits didn't. It was a poor prospect, but he was willing to risk the wasted time. With all he'd already accomplished on moonlit nights, he knew Wind wasn't preparing him for a gentle future.

"Let me out of here now!" Hereu was going to have a hard time removing the dirt from her nails when this was over. *This isn't funny, you darkened cur!*

G'Nirac made a move with his cane to pull the panicked woman to safety. Marl feared the old man would fall. He guided him from the edge and shook his head in caution. Hereu growled.

Quiet love, the men are still talking.

A sharp sting hit his back. The projectile, a grey river stone, landed in the upturned earth. Marl blushed. Normally, this would've made him laugh, but his wife had shown disrespect in front of the chieftain. It was his fault; he'd provoked her, but he was still tempted to spank her for the interruption.

You're a cur. She sat down and wept. "I don't want to be alone in here. Please, let me out."

G'Nirac hummed. "I think your joke has gone too far, my young friend."

Marl nodded and stared into the chieftain's tea-brown eyes. Hereu was going to make him a very sore man, but he couldn't put this interview behind him so easily. "I know, sir, but I'm too anxious to hear you. Please tell me what you know." He looked down on his wife and sighed, delivering the message he should've declared before. *I'm sorry, love. Give us a minute. I'll make it up to you.*

Hereu didn't acknowledge him.

"I don't know much," G'Nirac hurried, still watching the sobbing woman. *The spirits share little. There are dangerous mysteries to nature.* He scratched his beard. *Your destiny is connected to that power. You're meant to heal, but not just Na-ir. When the time comes, they will know how to guide you. Until then, I want you to be on guard. Be careful how you carry yourself in the open.*

At this point, Marl was aware of his bare chest, proudly displayed in a frozen world that couldn't hurt him. As the village healer, he needed to start practicing what he advised.

My spy tells me there's talk of an uprising. There have been several attempts on my life.

Marl hissed. *I think I know the villain … and your spy.* He turned his blue eyes on the chieftain and hungered for violence. *Say the word and I can make sure this person never bothers you again.* Lightning fizzled out of his eyes and his fingertips. He had learned much in the last few weeks.

G'Nirac jumped. "I admire your loyalty and your resolve, but that won't be necessary. I believe I have a handle on the situation." He nodded toward the weeping woman in the hole. "However, I fear for your safety and for your loved ones." *Much is asked of you, but they'll always be tied to your fate. It'll be a difficult road for them too.* He squeezed the Wanderer's hand. "Be gentle, with them and yourself."

Marl rubbed his neck and bit his lip. Gentleness was difficult for him, but he had to try for his family's sake. "I understand, G'Nirac. I appreciate your advice." *I'm your man if you need me.*

"I know. Thank you." The chieftain gave his shoulder a steady pat. *Remember to be careful.* He stepped back and flourished his hand over the pit, like a performer ending a play. "I leave you to your wife."

Marl jumped back into the hole, pulling his forlorn bride from the mud in an exuberant embrace. She didn't say anything as he kissed her tears, but the contempt in her red-stained eyes was undeniable.

"I'm sorry, sweetheart. Let's get out of here."

Hereu allowed him to push her little body on to the ledge. He smiled sheepishly, expecting to hear a few embarrassing but deserved curse words.

Instead, she administered a salty kiss. It was a clever ruse. She released his lips, wet eyes aglow with fire, and placed a hand against his chest. She pushed. Marl landed with a crack on the cold loam.

"I wouldn't try that again, love," she admonished, kicking the rock back into the pit; it landed on his stomach with a smack. "Wives know how to torture husbands too."

She nodded to G'Nirac before twirling her dirty, blue skirt and striding away.

Marl climbed out of the pit again and sighed as he threw on his shirt.

They watched her float down the shadowed hill, a drop of rain on a dried leaf. There was going to be an interesting battle tonight.

G'Nirac chuckled. "She's a good match for you. You're lucky. Few women are as self-aware." Remorse glimmered behind his kind countenance. "Many aren't afforded that opportunity."

"She a dangerous little thing."

The chieftain shook his head and sighed. "It's part of youth, my boy. She'll calm down with time." He winked and patted Marl's arm. "And so will you."

They laughed and made their way down the hill at an old man's pace, tracking the feisty Mistress Ganwin.

G'Nirac sighed. "You know. Laedi used to throw rocks too."

NINETEEN

Crisp sighs of snowfall, the crackle of an ethereal fire, and the methodic rumble of a creature's purr were overtaken by the determined grinding of stone on stone.

Hereu leaned against the door frame with Destroyer of Lizards in her arms and tempered the silence-that-wasn't-silence with a few hums. The queen of the meadow was in no mood to indulge her king's boredom.

Marl knew better than to break into her thoughts now, either through the craft of an Erutani spy or by asking for admittance into her sacred realm. The loss of her touch made him cantankerous, but he withheld his temper and his longings in contrite respect. This was punishment for the pit incident.

He looked at the uncomfortable mattress and sighed. Was she waiting for him to do something? He'd already apologized, but not for his admonishment of her actions around G'Nirac. Her behavior in the village reflected on him, and he could no longer be perceived as the wild Ganwin boy.

His chastisement had an effect. Hereu greeted visitors to the shack with much warmth and affection, discomfort hidden by youthful smiles.

Marl supposed he should be grateful. Na-ir chattered less now. He could hear as people shuffled past the shack. The new healer was fortunate: a position at such a young age and a sweet-natured wife to cater to his needs.

Ha! Marl groaned for the contrariness of it all and gathered his herbal creations.

There was some reluctance in him as he donned his coat. It felt odd choosing to hide; he'd spent his whole life being obstinate. G'Nirac's decree to be still was having a painful effect on his pride.

"You have to go out now?"

Hereu smelled of flowers and foreign spice. The frequent use of the perfume was an excellent indication her love for him hadn't withered. He still had a few more suns to wear her down with infuriating behavior.

Marl approached and raised a hand to stroke her hair. Her tears made him reconsider; it was safer to touch the cat. Destroyer stretched in bliss, contorting into a furry scepter.

Can you give us a minute, friend?

The feline cocked open one green eye and jumped from the woman's arms to settle on the old cot.

Marl gestured for his wife to move away from the door. She complied, shaking her head against the fog of her mind.

"My deliveries can wait." He closed the door too aggressively; snow fell off the roof in a great thud.

"Is there something wrong?"

Marl tossed the packages back on the table. "You've been ignoring me for days. Don't you think I've been punished enough?"

Hereu looked at his shoes. "Well, I only meant to punish you the first day, but then things got out of hand. I know you didn't mean to be cruel."

Thank the stars! Marl put an arm around her waist. "So, why are you still torturing me?"

She wiggled. "Because that stupid, dark hole made me remember something vile." She wiped tears from the grey patches below her eyes. "Once I thought of that, all sorts of memories came back. It's made me melancholy. I was hoping you'd see I was feeling off, but I know how worried you are."

She leaned her head into his chest and shuffled against a copper button, trying to find the perfect spot to rest a plump cheek.

Marl tightened his grip on her hips. "So, we're avoiding each other out of respect for perceived notions?"

She sniffled, clinging to his coat pocket.

He smoothed back auburn strands. "Don't cry. We've our whole lives to get this right. We just need to talk." Marl gave her nose a gentle tap in mock scolding.

Hereu hiccupped. The kiss he stole was sweeter than wild strawberries.

"Let's start now. Tell me."

She broke away with a snort. "You think you can heal anything don't you."

It was Marl's turn to stifle emotions.

"Oh, I'm sorry, love; I didn't mean to bring that up again. I guess we're both sensitive." Glass jars tinkled as her hips jostled the shelf. "Let's forget it. I don't want to talk about it."

Marl balled a fist on the small of her spine, pulling her back into his center. The muscles in his neck tensed. There was one person who could terrify his love so deeply. "Is this about your father?" He might not be able to heal everything, but he could comprehend suitable methods of justice.

"No!" The shepherdess jerked her curled head, paradoxically knocking a bottle of bruise salve off the shelf.

He caught it.

"No, Marl. Please let this go. I love my father as much as you love yours."

The salve found its way to its proper place on the shelf with a hard clack.

Hereu shrank back into her shoulders. "Papa's not perfect, but it doesn't matter."

"Why shouldn't it matter?" The tension in his heart burst like spirit root smoke. Bloody bodies in the grass merged with the bruised arms of innocent women. It was impossible to be objective about his dislike.

"Because, if I were ever in danger, my father would be the first to come to my aid. And because my mother loves him for what he is. I do too. Love doesn't mean you expect constant kindness." She placed a small hand on his chest. "Temperamental hearts can't always be still. We're proof of that!"

Changing her mind was like reversing the flow of a stream. He took a firm hold of her shoulders and stared into the wet, fertile soils of her eyes. There was still time; there was always time to convince her she was wrong.

He leaned into her mouth and breathed his will into her body. *Vill wouldn't be the first to come to your aid. I'll never leave your side.*

I know. She allowed him to kiss her again.

It was midday, but the energy within him wouldn't be denied. Still clinging to her lips, he fumbled in his pockets for the shack key. It turned in the door with a determined click and rested in its groove.

Hereu broke away from him, laughing. "What are you doing?"

"Something reckless." Marl pushed her to their meager bed. "Like you said, temperamental hearts aren't easily stilled. Mine is beating like Cyan's drum. I want to see you dance."

"What about your work?" Hereu giggled, curls tumbling over the lumps of hay and cloth. "What if someone drops by?"

"The door is locked and right now your troubles are all I want to soothe."

Marl threw his coat on the chair and fell down next to her, pulling her cold body into his unstoppable warmth. He slid his hands across her waist and placed eager lips against her neck.

There's more than one way to speak.

He made good use of his powers in silent communication, and Hereu understood every word, responding in kind.

The familiar tickle of air against his neck jolted him. *By the glowing ancestors!*

Destroyer gave a nervous mew and jumped from the empty cot. *My ailing great-grandfather needs a visit. I take my leave.* He bowed to the spirit and proceeded to squeeze through a crack in the wall. His slender, black tail gave a contemptuous twitch as it disappeared into the white glow of winter.

Marl pulled Hereu closer, unwilling to leave his desires unsaid.

But she opened her eyes. "Oh no!" *Your mistress is here.*

Don't call her that!

The hairs on his neck prickled with the vibrations of the chaotic mass. Wind's cold, wet-clay attempt at skin touched his shirt. The buzz of her breath on his head was terrifying.

Marl swallowed and looked into his love's jealous stare, willing the white reflection to a blur. *Ignore her. I've told her we're done.*

"At least she's clothed today," Hereu snapped.

The tiniest sensation of a breeze hovered on his ear. He shivered, but dared himself not to move. Hereu was sometimes too courageous for her own good, but she could never have the familiarity with the spirit that he had. This wasn't as benign as dancing in the rain barefoot.

Marl stroked his wife's arm, trying to still the hot suspicion. *She's toying with us.* Even in childhood diversions, Wind hadn't been one to be denied. *Calm down, sweetheart. You know she fashions herself that way to rile you. Don't give her the satisfaction. I don't care what she does... or what she looks like.*

Another unfortunate swipe at her lips was denied him.

Go away!

Wind chimed; he wasn't winning this battle today. She'd a talent for making life difficult.

I can't help it, Marl. It's working, Hereu responded to his earlier comment. She took a deep breath and allowed her gaze to break from the whirling, demonic form overhead. The shepherdess's stern resolve was striking. "The only reason I allow her near you is because of the whole Wanderer nonsense. If she were any other woman, I'd rip her heart out!"

Wind hissed in his ear playfully, taunting the shepherdess to try and fulfill this threat. His wife's cheeks flushed and she reached out to strike the spirit. Marl had to grab her hand. There was no way she could ever cause a creature of air pain, but pride was a universal thing, and Wind had more than that at her disposal. Hereu would be the loser of such a ridiculous battle.

Don't be silly. She doesn't have a heart. Besides, her internal storm would shred your hand. An unfortunate stick in one of their mock battles had proven this. There was nothing left but sawdust.

The shepherdess growled. 'Remember that if you stick any part of you inside her too!"

Wind laughed. The shack shook.

Finally frightened, Hereu squeaked and pressed into his chest as the bottles clanked in their coffins. She couldn't see the purple blush of his cheeks or the fact his jaw had dropped open in shock.

That's the most vulgar thing I've ever heard! He shook her shoulders. *Listen! I've already said it; I won't say it again. You matter more to me than that bitch and you always will.*

Then make her leave!

Hereu stood and stumbled backward. Marl extinguished the orange flame before her hand entered the fire pot. The shack fell into darkness save for the white glow of the demonic presence before them.

"Please, Marl. Don't listen to her anymore. I don't like what she is... the things she makes you do. This can't be your destiny."

He sighed and wiped a hand across his face. It *was* possible the spirit was using him to her own devious ends. *I've tried, love; she's being difficult. You can't escape air. She's there whenever I piss!*

Nature had little decorum.

They regarded each other, trying to devise a plan to remove the humming threat in the room.

Hereu squeaked. *Those black eyes are terrifying; they've come to eat my soul.*

Wind made a move toward the hearth-pot and stood erect in her gaze. Normally a hodgepodge of materials and colors, she was now draped in a gentle drift of snowfall, peppered with evergreen needles in an intricate pattern only Gerna's skilled hands could replicate. Hair, or what could be called hair, fell down in a long, black mass of crow feathers.

She pressed closer and sneered. The shepherdess trembled, clutching the side of the pot.

"Leave her alone! You've had your fun." Marl stood to attention.

Wind closed her mouth and nodded in mock respect to the brown woman before rounding on her protégé. *You'll meet me tonight; we've too much left to do and very little time.*

He stared into the white lightning of her black eyes. *Uh, no. G'Nirac told me to be careful.*

Feathers tickled his cheeks but he wasn't amused.

What if someone saw us out there? It's too risky.

Putting this off is risky, Wanderer. She hissed and whirled in a circle. *You're so damn stubborn!*

Several dried, purple plants fell to the floor and crumbled into dust. Marl sighed. He'd have no way to replace those lavender bundles until next summer.

G'Nirac also told you to listen to the spirits. I AM A SPIRIT.

You're also a useless bitch. Go away. She might be something ancient and powerful, but she acted like a spoiled child. *I don't need you to live my life.*

Wind stopped throwing her tantrum and stared. The lightning in her two dark holes was replaced with something crystal blue and beautiful, a reflection from a memory she and time knew. *If I could make you understand.* She looked to the ceiling and heaved her chest in a motion resembling a sigh. *I may not have a physical heart, but I know what heartache is. I've had centuries of it.*

She ruffled his hair. This serene action made him unnerved. He looked away from her pained gaze.

I miss what once was. You look like... If you were mine...

He wasn't one to be possessed. Blue fire sparked from his fingertips and one black feather smoldered in quiet agony on the floorboards. *I'll never belong to you! Get out! Now!*

A knock on the door sent the spirit whirling through the shack. If he wanted to lie low, Wind was going to make it difficult for him.

"Hello. Are you in there?" a timid voice called.

Hereu crashed into his shoulders. Bottles and papers plummeted to the floor in mock suicide, rolling in death throes. Marl threw an arm around his wife's waist and fashioned more blue fire with his free hand.

"Hello!" The woman's worried voice was muffled by scorned spirit moans.

The door rattled again. Wind saw her opportunity for revenge. With a flick of her delicate, white wrist, she forced the key to turn. A significant click followed. The moment the door swung open, she dashed through it. Cold, wet snow and a shower of feathers blasted the unfortunate visitor.

Two women screamed in panic.

When the whirlwind had faded, only the blue glow on Marl's fingertips betrayed that anything mystical had happened.

Hereu came to her senses quickly. She pushed him into his desk and placed a gentle kiss on his forehead. *Calm down, love. You were brave, but the battle is over.* She pointed to his trembling, sparking hands. *I'll take care of everything. Stay out of sight.*

She raced to the door, forcing it closed against her hip. Marl heard a groan from the porch and then a startled exclamation from his love.

"Oh, Nerid!"

Marl closed his eyes and surveyed the scene from within and without. Focusing on anything but his anger and resolve might make it easier for him to return to something more human.

"What on earth was that?" Nerid craned her head to snoop through the doorway. Her golden hair was in a tight bun and her slender body was draped in a long, brown cloak. It gave her a matronly effect. She was hiding from someone.

His fingers illuminated the desk in the corner behind the door in brilliant blue. Hereu glanced and gasped, still trying to formulate a response. For once, *he* was proving to be the distraction.

"A stupid crow." She ran her fingers through her hair and caught a stubborn tangle. "He flew into the shack when I left the door open. I was trying to catch the darkened thing, but now the place is in shambles. Marl's going to kill me."

It was such an expert tale; he wanted to kiss that mischievous mouth! The sparks disappeared as he imagined Hereu chasing around a real crow in the shack.

"Oh. I'm sorry. I take it Marl's out. I was hoping to ask him for more of a… um, remedy." Nerid leaned into Hereu's ear. Marl saw the glint of her startled eyes as they passed over the chaotic shack, but, thankfully, she didn't see him.

"Wait here. I'm sure I can get you what you need." Hereu closed the door, creating a barrier between them and the potential for much village gossip.

What was she asking for?

Wild carrot seeds. What do those do?

Prevent little huntsmen. Marl stifled a snort and gave her a pat on the backside, starting to feel whole and mortal again. *Here, I'll prepare it.*

He retrieved a jar from the floor and portioned out several brown clumps composed of tiny, beetle-like entities. He chopped the false bugs into course clusters and sealed the material in parchment.

Tell her the price has been reduced. She owes a copper.

Why are you being nice? Hereu took the package and headed for the door.

Marl shrugged. *I feel bad Wind accosted her. And… I wouldn't want to have that cur's babies either.*

The shepherdess tried not to giggle. She handed off the package, delivered her husband's message, pocketed the copper, and relocked the shack. Her smile of relief dissipated when she saw the mess in their tiny home.

Darken my light! Now we have to clean.

Marl waved a hand. Snow slipped under the door and out the many cracks in the walls. The black feathers collected in a bouquet and settled on the desk—they would make good quills for his notes. Lavender powder settled on a shelf.

Dangerous broken shards gathered into the center of the room, reforming into the shapes of amber bottles again as they floated above the clay pot. Heat from his hands melted the glass into liquid. He blew on them and they cooled solid. The healed bottles danced back onto their shelves next to their neighbors.

"Stars! If only you'd known you could do that when you had to clean this place for Etutsa."

Marl laughed and slipped on his coat. It upset him how he could do things without prompting, like memories from a life he never lived. Another wave and Hereu's cloak draped across her shoulders.

She hummed and fastened the copper clasp. *I don't think you need Wind. You seem capable of learning this stuff on your own.*

Marl was tired of all of it. "Are you hungry?"

Hereu nodded.

"Good. Me too. Let's get out of here."

He guided his wife outside and locked the door. Marl found a small piece of chalk and wrote on the door in large, sloppy Mlaerian letters, *Healer Without.*

They paraded through the square to the cobbler's shop.

A golden head rounded the corner near Vill and Dalis's house and paused in front of them, mumbling.

"What're you doing, my boy?" Marl queried, deepening his voice to tease.

Cyan snarled.

"You look lost. Something got you flustered?"

Hereu dug her nails into his side. It was a warning to behave, but Marl found the challenge too delicious to renounce. The scrap with Wind had allowed some of his true personality to surface; he no longer wished to close the box over it.

"You're one to talk, Mister Ganwin. You two look like you've been touched by a ghost."

Marl laughed. The bachelor was smarter than he looked. "She went that way," he offered, pointing in the direction of the linden tree. "Not more than fifteen minutes ago."

Cyan narrowed his fair brow. "The ghost? I'm not sure what you mean."

"She has wild carrot seeds. A strange thing for a married woman, don't you think?" Marl nodded toward the great tree and smirked. "You'd better hurry before you lose her again."

"I think your husband's working too hard, Mistress Ganwin. He's not making much sense."

Hereu rolled her eyes.

"Take care of yourself, friend." Cyan flashed a crooked-tooth smile and whispered, "Thanks." He disappeared into the crowd.

Marl beamed. G'Nirac had a handle on things.

***

Sleep refused to come. The more he experimented with fire, wind, and light, the more his body could make do without rest. When it came, it was a delightful relief, but only because the Blessed Unknowing was filled with his most favored desires. Marl leaned on his elbow and stared at one of them. Hereu's breathing was even and pure.

He contemplated getting out of bed and working, but the chance to be peaceful was thrilling. Marl gave her a kiss and settled into her side. She rolled, pulling her shoulder from her night shirt. He placed a warm hand there. It gave him immense satisfaction when she sighed and settled. The little shepherdess was safe with him

276

nearby. Marl touched other tender spots of exposed skin, caressing and kissing to still his heart, while taking every effort necessary not to wake her.

Hereu curled into her center and frowned. Her legs kicked and she gasped as if caught in a swift current, unable to breathe. *Another nightmare!*

He moved his hands to her head and concentrated on the images in her mind. This was an invasion, something he'd sworn he'd never do again without permission, but he pushed past his guilt with the necessity of making her content.

The vision from the void wasn't the horrifying parti-colored visage of Wind, but the face of a gruff and violent man, short and smudged all over. Marl didn't recognize him.

The man pushed and shoved. Where were they? It was difficult to tell; Hereu was in a panic.

Marl jumped when she screamed. Rough hands grasped parts of her body he thought only he had ever touched. When a nasty, yellow-toothed mouth found Hereu's protesting lips, he broke away from the vision and gasped, tears falling from his stunned blue eyes.

Was this an anxiety-induced fantasy or had Hereu gone through this? He willed himself to take another look.

The man was tending to a sore jaw in the corner. *Good girl!*

But she was still screaming, unable to leave her wet prison.

Vill materialized. In his hand was a knife, the same knife Hereu carried with her at all times. A few threats and some well-placed cuts to the perpetrator's shoulder sent him recoiling out of the pit.

Oh stars! No wonder she was upset with me.

In the waning dream, Vill scooped her into a tender embrace. "There, there, darling. Papa has you."

Marl hissed. This couldn't be the same creature who'd bragged about the slaughter of Surnow.

Hereu's breathing quickened and the nightmare replayed, tearing her away from her rescuer. This scene would hang on a shelf in her heart and knock loose whenever something tried to shake her resolve. It must be a tremendous burden to bear alone, this secret terror, this knowledge of the worst of mankind.

How can you be so brave, love? I'd go mad, but you spend every day with such grace.

Marl kissed her forehead. He'd never possess that strength of character. It mattered more than strength of mind or arm.

He willed the fife to leave her cloak pocket. Marl played an old lullaby Para had taught him, an easy piece about babies in fields of flowers. Hereu settled into her pillow. When the lullaby was done, he stole another glimpse into her dreams.

She must've known this tune from childhood; the scene in her mind was a perfect meadow, abloom with lupines and daisies. Her tiny hands clasped her vibrant mother. They danced, giggling around a flock. Vill sat near a tree with a fife between his lips.

The evidence was irrefutable. The shepherd was Hereu's first protector and first source of mirth. He'd taught her to love and to dance, and those things she'd carried with her in her passion for the man lying next to her now. This was the vision she saw of her father, not the sulking, bitter man Marl perceived. Like Nojhi Ganwin, the old shepherd had another side.

All right, love. You win. I'll give him a chance.

Air pressed under the door and settled in beside him. *Your wife has led a rich life.*

Empathy made him less apprehensive to the spirit's presence. Marl stared into the black spaces of her icy face. But Wind had no terrible countenance tonight.

I've come to apologize. I was wrong, playing games with her sanity and your patience.

He raised an eyebrow. She smiled sheepishly, eyes glowing blue again.

My sisters tell me I've many troubles. You've a strange effect on me… and sometimes I let my desires hinder my purpose. I've been told humans are much the same.

Small flurries puffed from her mouth. Marl snorted and shook his head, holding his hand out to catch the intricate snowflakes. They melted into steam. *This is true. I suppose I can forgive you.* He stroked a curl away from Hereu's face. *But we can't keep practicing. If anyone ever saw us, I'd lose everything.*

The spirit frowned and the humanness disappeared, leaving the visage of a corpse.

Hereu means more to me than life. I won't sacrifice her happiness if I can help it.

A chilled hand rested on the mattress near his leg, searing his skin. *Some sacrifices are difficult. I'll change your mind with her help.*

He scoffed; there was slim chance of that. Hereu still believed the spirit had been frightened away. She'd be very angry to see the whirlwind presence by their bed tonight.

Look at Selcovi. Wind gestured to brown curls.

Marl took hold of his wife's temples and concentrated on the city of her birth. He was terrified of what else he might see. *Show me Selcovi.*

Her malleable mind complied. Cobbled streets and tall buildings rose out of the void, leading him through rows of colors and sounds. The capital was a loud, vibrant place full of music and chatter. There were too many extremes, but it wasn't horrifying.

Hereu and her many friends—that sulking Eurgi included—skipped barefoot past stalls filled with gaunt and miserable people. The adults were hollow, but the youths were joyful. It made him happy to know some of her memories were pleasant, if fleeting.

Very fleeting. The bright sunshine in her dreams gave way to a strange brown darkness. The children hid behind a plastered wall, screaming and covering their faces against the choking onslaught of dry topsoil. Marl had never seen the ground shift like that. The soils of Na-ir were wet and stable.

This strange memory made Hereu stir in her sleep. She was on the edge of darkness again. The aggressor from her previous memory stepped out of the dusty shadows and dropped her back into the terrifying confines of the pit.

"No!" *Think of something happy, love. I'm with you.*

Yellow teeth faded into something more pleasant: the smiling face of a young man leaning against a great tree—it wasn't her husband. This boy was shorter, brown-eyed with dusty blond hair, and she was enjoying his attention.

Marl broke away and blushed. *I'm not her first love. I wonder what happened to him.*

The spirit stopped smiling and looked to the pot full of fire. *The boy was a thief. He was caught.*

There was sadness in the corners of her eyes. The boy hadn't suffered an admonishment in the public square or a whipping at home.

Wind tickled his cheek. *I love how innocent you are. It hurts to know you won't be for long. Those experiences aren't unique. Many lights have suffered for the legacy of that tyrant Ril. It's left a deep scar.* The snow-clad maiden sighed. *A gift has been given to you no other may possess. It's special, but you must trust in it. Acknowledge what you are.*

If I have a choice, then... He hesitated. *I don't want to be the Wanderer. Why should I care about Selcovi and its inept rulers? The city will do itself in. We've a good life in Na-ir. We're safe.*

Wind whirred. *No, you're not! This isn't about the capital or the kingdom; this is about balance. If you submit to this task, you'll have unimaginable power.* White lightning sparked in her eyes. *Dalis and Laohin would no longer have to suffer.*

He took a sharp breath. Could there be such an ability lurking inside of him? Was it possible to reverse the will of nature and heal something no one else could heal before?

She caressed his cheek without touching it. Her offer was more tempting than the tantalizing drape of leaf gowns. *Meet me at Oak Hollow tomorrow evening... alone. No distractions. I'll show you what must be done.* She slipped off, leaving one black feather behind.

A knock on the shack door forced down the dream. "Marl, wake up!"

Hereu stirred, pressing her supple hip against his knee as another knock echoed through the wooden box they called home. Hair in violent tangles, she stared as Marl slid into his britches and unlatched the door.

Vill bounded inside and sat down, gasping for breath.

"Are you well, Papa?" Hereu stifled a yawn and pulled the sheet over her indecent form.

"I am darling; just getting old. Can tell you one thing though: I'm not drinking any more of your mother's herbal sludge. I saw fewer nightmares when I drank whiskey! Swear I saw the ghost of a woman leave out of here. She was snow white, but she had dreadful black eyes. Looked straight through me! Merciful stars, it was quiet the hallucination."

My father better be drunk! Hereu twirled the black feather. She was far from witless, and it was going to take some effort to convince her nothing had happened.

Vill chuckled, oblivious to the heaviness in the room. "What do you recommend for something like that—hallucinations of the dead in the dead of winter?"

"Rest. I'd prescribe rest." Marl winked at his wife, hoping his politeness would eliminate all suspicions. She afforded him a half smirk. He was in trouble again; it was better to accept it and move on. "You should be getting some now. Why are you here?"

"What? Oh!" Vill shuffled in the chair, coming to the realization no smoke was emitted by the fire. He cocked his head and stared into the flames, amazed. "Damn chandler came pounding on my door looking for you. Says the baby's giving his wife trouble. Poor man begged me to find you and ran back home."

Marl rolled his eyes and reached for his shirt and doublet on the cot. "Why would he go to your place? I've already told everyone we're here in the shack now."

Hereu gave a startling, merry laugh. "I think I know why. *Healer Without!*" She pointed to the door.

Marl narrowed his eyes and opened the shack to the cold, craning his head around to see white, grainy letters still scrawled on wood. He huffed. There was no use erasing it now.

"We had it open for the rest of the day. I guess Mister Hedar saw the message and panicked." Hereu set the crow feather on the floor and smiled. The healer at his worst was easier to forgive than the Wanderer at his best. "Do you want me to go along with you?"

"No, sweetheart. I think I should be fine." He needed to prove he could do this alone. She wasn't offended; when it came to work, she knew he was a solitary man.

A quick check on the chandler's home told him the little woman was near her time, in much pain.

He snatched a basket from the floor. Marl found willow bark and rose oil to comfort the new mother. He took some golden seal, hoping he wouldn't have to use it to speed labor. Some spirit root might be helpful too. The chandler would have cloth and water for the child, but yarrow might be needed for blood loss later.

Vill snorted at the fuss he was making. Marl smiled. He didn't expect someone used to menial labor to understand. These remedies were like deciphering an ancient scroll.

He set the laden basket on his desk and threw on his coat before giving Hereu a kiss. "I'll return soon. Come on; let's get you back to Dalis."

"No, thank you. I'd rather stay and keep my little mouse company. Birthing can take hours. Dalis spent a day and a half cursing my name with this bit of trouble." Vill pinched Hereu's cheek. "You would think she was in labor again the way she's bleating. Apparently, it's my fault her *babies* left!"

"I wouldn't mind company now I'm awake. Marl can let me know how things are going."

"I'm all right with that." Marl felt it necessary to state that the shepherd was in his house with permission. He could play the game as well as the old man, and with far more civility. "We'll visit Dalis tomorrow." He blew his wife a quick kiss and left the shack.

His long legs and magical warmth made quick work of the snowy way across the square. When he knocked on the chandler's door and was met with the ragged, terrified face of a man not much older than his brother, he knew he was in for an interesting night.

They trudged up narrow stairs to a bedroom over the waxy shop. Mistress Hedar was plastered to a cot in a room smaller than the healer's shack, awash with feverish sweat and eyes glassy from pain.

A normal healer would've had to check her dilation and the pace of her contractions and heartbeats. He'd seen Etutsa do this many times before, but Marl didn't have to invade her privacy; he could tell the babe would come within a few hours. It was too bad he hadn't been present for the rest of her labor; this was one time where his gifts were useful.

He did all he could to make Mister Hedar believe he was knowledgeable. They fetched pillows to make the woman more comfortable and water to wash her. The chandler bit his nails and stared from the edge of the bed.

"Don't worry, sir. Your wife will be fine."

Mistress Hedar let out a startled scream and moaned. Her husband tripped over his own feet, knocking into a carved oak cradle on the floor. "It's all right, Jolenta. The healer's here."

Marl put a small dose of willow bark on her tongue and rubbed some rose oil on her neck. The fragrance was comforting and it worked wonders on the nervous father too. The chandler sat.

Satisfied he'd made good show, Marl took hold of Jolenta's hands and sighed, closing his eyes to concentrate on her pain. He was able to relieve much of it, but he left some sensation there. Etutsa had told him pain was necessary; sometimes it advised humans on what to do with their bodies. Mistress Hedar would need to know what to do soon.

She gasped. "That medicine of yours works quickly. What else were you doing?"

"Oh, I was praying for you."

The absence of intense pain made the chandler's wife pleasant and talkative. "A faithful man! There aren't many of you left."

Marl blushed and ran his fingers through his hair. He was anything but faithful. Father Moon had a record of every swear word and disobedient act written down on some long scroll, ready for admonishment when his time came to travel through the Passageway gates.

"I shouldn't be surprised, you being what you are."

He couldn't help but frown.

"Sorry, that sounded rude." Jolenta took his hand, pressing it in firm friendliness. "When G'Nirac welcomed you into Na-ir, we were skeptical, but after all this time, it's certain you and your family are special."

The chandler and his wife had not been present for his beating in the square a few moons ago or they would have a more popular opinion.

She yawned and snuggled into her pillow. "Always knew you were going to be the next healer—ever since the dog…"

Mister Hedar laughed. "Mister Ganwin won't remember that, love. It was long ago, before I placed a wick in my first candle. A cart hit a dog in the square. You were four suns or so, but you cried over that dog and tried to help it. No one else would. My father wouldn't let me leave the shop to rescue you. I was afraid you'd meet the same fate as the dog. We're a busy little village. But you ran to the healer's shack and begged Etutsa for help. He showed you how to bind its leg and keep the creature happy."

"You watched it by Telm's pillar for hours, such a smart and caring child," Jolenta beamed. *I've never seen such passion for life. Those eyes match your perfect soul.*

Marl blushed. He didn't remember this moment of his life, but he must've been chasing Wind again. There was no other reason he had be alone at such an age. Natsir the baby-watcher had always had a difficult time keeping up with him.

"What happened to the dog?"

"He was the best dog I've ever known. I named him Eru."

Marl pretended to cough so he could wiped at his tears. The chandler's wife laughed; she was no fool and could see through his act with those wise, brown eyes. She'd be a wonderful mother; so would another brown-eyed woman he knew.

He mused over future progeny and starred at Jolenta, willing her to take things easy. After a few minutes, she hummed and succumbed to a blissful rest. For over an hour, the chandler and the healer said nothing to each other, contemplating life's joys and mysteries in their own ways.

When labor intensified, Jolenta moaned. Marl sent another wave of energy through her, hoping she was too far gone to notice the mystical help.

The chandler wrung his hands. "Why do we do this to them? We know where it leads, how much pain it causes." He tapped a foot against the cradle and sighed, tears streaming down his cheeks. "We allow them to risk death so we can create new life. It's absurd."

Marl nodded, sympathetic. The new father hadn't yet met the result of this torment. These efforts were a product of two souls, and worth it.

Jolenta opened her eyes. "Love of the stars, Din! Do you have anything that'll make him shut up?"

Marl snickered. The sleep juice was in the shack and he'd have no more sleepwart tea until spring. He winked and passed the nervous man a roll of spirit root. Din Hedar didn't question this sage authority.

***

It was two hours until sunrise. Marl knew he looked stupid from equal measures of work and joy, but the chandler shop now had another loud, healthy mouth to feed. The child was perfect and whole. The mother was already healing from her trials thanks to him.

He set his basket of goods on his desk, not wishing to startle Hereu or her father. She was wrapped in their blanket and snuggled into Vill's shoulder on the floor, smiling behind her rambunctious curls.

Vill snorted and opened one eye. "Back already? How's the little guy?"

"It's a girl. Very healthy with lots of brown hair. They named her Sinnie." Marl sat in his chair, too contented to be upset the shepherd was still in his home.

"Darken the moon! Certain it was a boy. That poor woman waddled. Must be an active female."

Marl stretched. "Nonsense. Stuff like that doesn't indicate who a child will be."

The shepherd shrugged; he couldn't argue with a keeper of life and death.

Hereu shuffled. "I told you it was a girl, Papa. You owe me black wool come shearing day." She winked.

They'd known for moons the chandler was blessed with a girl—the chandler hadn't. Why had she tricked her father?

Vill scoffed and tweaked her nose. "Fine. You made a lucky guess. Had to be one or the other."

Marl was tempted to point out that was wrong—Etutsa had told him many tales—but that might be too strenuous a topic to traverse in the coming of dawn.

Vill yawned and coaxed Hereu off his arm. He stood, creaking and moaning. "Well, I'll be off now to spread the gossip with Dalis. See you later... *son*." He winked and hobbled outside.

Marl locked the shack. "What did he say? I was getting used to *idiot*!"

Hereu smiled and shook her head. They must've had a talk while he was out.

It had been a productive night indeed. Marl ran his fingers through his hair, feigning shocked. "I think I might need to lie down!"

The pensive chandler cradling a tiny bundle across the square would've given them a stern warning on the possible consequences of what happened next.

***

"Mother Sun shines blessings on the heather as you and I make our way. There's nothing we cannot weather, just to have this blessed day."

Hereu was singing an old-fashioned love song in dulcet tones while washing clothes in a bucket by Marl's head. Her hair was wound high with a woolen scarf, revealing the rain tattoo speckling her neck. Her hands were glimmering and wrinkled raw from the wash water, but still youthful and pink. No sight could've been lovelier.

"Hold me in the light of Father Moon; give to me your warm kiss. Never will I relinquish, my love, such true happiness as this."

The shepherdess drifted into hums as she wrung out his shirt and laid it carefully over the cot to dry. His dripping britches were hanging over the chair. There was little space in this hole.

Hereu heard his restrained huff and leaned over for that kiss from her song. "Welcome back, o' great healer," she teased, tickling his neck with her chilled fingers. "You're the talk of the town today. Everyone's excited about that baby."

Marl shifted to his stomach. "I don't know why they're talking about me. Jolenta Hedar did all of the work!" He glanced around the shack. "I can't believe I slept. What time is it?"

"It's mid-afternoon. After last night, I thought you needed rest."

"Thank you, sweetheart, but I wish you hadn't. Now I'm going to be behind." He dried the clean clothes with his heat, forcing the damp into steam, and dressed.

Hereu sulked.

Marl walked the two steps to his desk and looked twice at his task list. All of the items had been crossed out.

His wife jumped, wringing out her night shirt into the wooden bucket.

"What's this? Everything's marked." His first inclination was to be annoyed. She must've tampered with the list in an effort to distract him from working. She looked guilty.

"I took care of everything this morning."

"You did?" He sat in his wet chair and stared. This was something he hadn't anticipated. She wasn't trained, and she'd never shown an interest in the practice. "Seriously? But how?"

Hereu stood and brushed water off her skirt. "What? You didn't know I was an expert healer too?"

She placed indignant hands on her hips and tossed her head back. The scarf loosened and her voluptuous hair fell around her.

"I read your notes. Laohin's cough is gone. He will still drink the *yucky* tea until the weather warms. Gerna's hands feel better, but she's complaining about her shoulders and back. I advised her to use a chair to embroider rather than a stool— my mother's wisdom."

She sauntered into his lap and pushed the parchment to the table.

"And Sinnie is an adorable, wrinkled bit of sunshine and eating well. In fact, all of the Hedars are well, although Mister Hedar is flustered." She wrinkled her nose and placed a finger to her chin. "Oh, and I removed a thorn from a boy named Tessin. He wasn't too happy though. He only wanted to see you."

Marl groaned but stroked his industrious wife's back with much regard for her intelligence and kindness. "The baker's youngest, pain in the backside—follows me everywhere and talks incessantly."

"Well, now we know who *your* apprentice will be."

That wasn't the Telmah way of things. Their eldest son would have first chance at the profession. Tessin might be a good option if Vill's curse came true, though. He took another glance at the parchment and sighed. "Well, now what am I supposed to do, Mistress Ganwin?"

Hereu smiled and got him a heel of bread. He gobbled it.

"If I didn't know any better, I'd think you weren't grateful for my help."

Marl choked on a crumb, unsure if she was angry or teasing.

She rolled her eyes. "You could make the rounds again if you don't trust me."

He blushed and shook his head, though he was scanning the village for any sign of turmoil—a blessed stillness was over the town. Unwilling to start a fight that might cost him more of her affections, he finished off the bread and shoved the list into a drawer.

His wife's oaky eyes sparkled. "We promised to visit my mother today."

They spent a pleasant afternoon with the Misyls doing odd chores and chatting. It was good to watch women work at the hearth.

They were aflutter about the newest member of Na-ir. Dalis was most excited; she was expecting another Ganwin soon. Vill gave an uncustomary chuckled when Hereu's cheeks turned scarlet.

Marl made faces to make his Dalis laugh. For some reason, the old man took to the game readily, sticking out his tongue or fluffing his beard. Their larking had a good effect on Dalis. Being nearer to her daughter made her whole.

They ate mutton stew, or at least the Misyls did, and talked well into the evening. There were no troubles, no tasks. It was such a strange thing: everyone was happy.

Marl contemplated a bit of mischievous dining. Surely it wouldn't be sinful to consume the small amount of mutton left in the pot. A blast of white flurries through the door was Wind's austere warning she was still monitoring his every breath. One soft, black line twirled in the air and landed on his foot. He picked up the feather and shut the door. There was still a decision he had to make.

Hereu eyed him suspiciously. *Have you been summoned then?*

He placed the feather in the fire and returned to her side, feeling ill. *No. Don't worry, love. I'm ignoring her.*

Hereu rolled her eyes and set her jaw; she'd every reason not to believe him.

I promise. She's not winning this battle. Neither was he. His wife looked more indignant than a wet badger. He kissed her cheek. *Trust me, please.*

Hereu sighed and took hold of his right hand, stroking the length of one of his fingers. *I do trust you. It's that spirit that scares me. I'm afraid she's luring you into a trap.*

Here now. I may be an idiot, but I'm not stupid.

She gave him a blessed smirk.

Dalis lapsed into several painful coughs.

Vill smacked her back. "Don't trouble yourself, son. Dalis needs to rest. Don't you, love?" He escorted his wife to the hall. "G'night, young'uns."

With the night ended, they headed home to their tiny shack. Having already slept most of the day, Marl was allowed to tinker as Hereu drifted off to sleep. He swore that he wouldn't see Wind.

The powers he had were a nuisance, forcing him to keep his true feelings and desires in check. It wasn't as if he was unskilled in regular human matters. The sickness that'd plagued his people for weeks was losing ground; Laohin was a lively little boy again. Still, there were Dalis's wasting lungs to consider.

That cough tonight was the worst I've heard in a while.

Hereu yawned and rolled over on their mattress.

What would I do if she ever got that sick? The chance to take away that torment was more noble and valuable than the act of sneaking out. *No! I'm not going.*

Marl closed his eyes and tried to focus on what he wanted out of life. Freedom: to make his own decisions and to raise a family in a quiet, prosperous village. It's what every normal young man of Na-ir was allowed to possess.

"But I'm not normal. I never was. I've always been the Wanderer."

The vibration of the title on his tongue made him gasp. It was the most painful thing he had ever admitted. But it could not be avoided.

"And my life is already claimed." He wiped tears from his face and reached for the key by the door. Marl kissed his wife's check and didn't bother to put on his coat as he tiptoed outside.

The spirit of all-things air haunted the woods. She smiled, a row of chalk for teeth, as he approached Oak Hollow. *I'm glad I was able to convince you. Are you ready?*

"Let's get on with it."

He was terrified. The spirit was calm now, contented. Hereu was probably right. This was a trap, and, after all these suns, Wind would have what she wanted.

The spirit floated near his ear and whispered. *Don't be frightened. You're capable of anything. Forget all the troubles in your mind now.*

He took several rasping breaths; they didn't work.

Focus on yourself for once, on what you are.

He looked inward. All he could think of was Hereu. Her deep, pleading eyes captured in his mysterious heart, jewels wrapped in velvet. She'd be heartbroken—enough to leave him.

Clear your mind of everything.

The weeping eyes refused to close.

Do you see what's inside of you? There's power there. Seek it. Tell me who you are.

He opened his crystal eyes and stared into the face of something that never should've been real. "I'm Marl Ganwin, healer of Na-ir."

No! Lightning flashed from the spirit's dark holes. The effect on the forest was nothing short of a storm. Trees moaned.

He straightened his back and tried again. "I'm Marl, son of Nojhi and Messa… successor of Erutan."

Wind staggered. *Closer. Concentrate. Look deep inside you.*

He caught sight of his wrist and the mouse tattoo. This exercise wasn't as easy on his heart as battling with sticks and fists. Those were tangible and real. Marl didn't want to relinquish the part of him that was a fleshy animal. This power made that part of him feel insignificant and innocent, and it was painful.

Seeing only truth, he spoke this time to a hidden set of sweet, brown eyes. "I'm a boy in want of love. I'm a human and I don't deserve this torment. I want to live. To sleep with my lover and hear her laugh. To run with my children through the trees and swim with them in the river."

His voice broke in the darkness.

"I just want to live."

Wind dropped like a stone. Her false skin drooped and slid across her compacted whirlwind, melting like a carcass on a pyre.

Please release us from this torment. Two blue jewels looked to Father Moon, full and bright. *I'm sorry, Marl. Boys must grow up; spirits must keep watch. I can't alter that. But I love you. I always have.*

She was a creature with nothing left to comfort her anguished existence. Pity washed over him. "If I do this, will it help you?"

Her dark eyes flooded blue. Tears fell from her sunken cheeks. She nodded.

"All right, I'll try." He concentrated on the white-hot presence within his blood, in his breath. He found the proverbial box within his soul and opened it. *I'm Marl. I'm the Wanderer.*

The part of him that was human dissipated around the pulsating brilliance. It emitted a perfect blue light, as blue as his eyes, as Wind's when she showed love. He knew it then. He knew. The young body called Marl was a casing, an intricate box in itself, a stone hearth.

"I'm fire!"

Brown eyes faded away.

"I'm spirit."

The Wanderer raised his arms into the air and demonstrated what his immortal consciousness was no longer naïve to. Lightning flashed in cerulean hues from his fingertips, seductive and accurate.

Wind raised her hands too; white fire flowed from clay digits and touched his. Two halves of one soul reunited.

He didn't stagger or sway as he watched the whole of the forest pulse and illuminate. Let Na-ir think what it wanted. Let the creatures of air and earth be startled. He was what he was, and it was a brilliant and remarkable thing.

Wind moved closer, still forcing her energy against his. *Learn to speak my language. Focus on Father Moon; see if you can meet His light with me.*

Lightning climbed, white and blue intertwining and leaping off each crack as they raced into the sky to meet the Father of All Things. The presence that touched them back was a pure stillness, a gut-wrenching lightness on his soul. The forest no longer existed; light and air remained.

The spirit touched him. Her voice echoed, spoken with many. *You are our brother now.*

The Wanderer laughed.

Women crying out in the void brought the stubborn human back from the edge of his tumultuous, blinding-bright mind.

"We're too late!"

Another cry in the darkness beyond the spirit glow gave Marl the courage to break away. "No! No! Don't hurt him!"

He looked down into two amber stones. The evergreen scent of the forest was replaced by rain and flowers. Marl lurched against the light of the Wanderer.

His wife! She was in front of him… and then she wasn't.

Wind's white fire dimmed. *Why would she do that? Why do they always do that?*

Marl looked through a blue cloud to the crumpled form. "No! Hereu, no!"

Mother came running from the east, clutching her protruding abdomen. She collapsed in a pile beside him. "It'll be all right, sweetheart," she lied.

Marl was certain there was no way he'd feel whole again.

Wind paced through the air, wild and terrible. Messa Ganwin rounded on her, unafraid. *She thought you were trying to kill him! If I didn't know any better, I'd think so too. He looked consumed!*

I was doing the bidding of my father. It was as it should be. The spirit shrieked, hot rage in her mouth and eyes. *The girl's death is on you for leading her here, priestess! You're constantly in the way.*

Marl clutched his chest and tried to focus. Rage coursed through him. "I should've never trusted… I'm enough of a cur without you."

His fire took hold of her and she panicked, trying to break free. The mask fell from her whirlwind as he pulled her into his punishing gaze. Only a small orb of light was revealed in her nakedness.

"You've destroyed everything!"

Marl pushed his blazing hands into her center and concentrated on everything she was and everything she'd ever convinced him to do. She was nothing, nothing but hate and bad decisions.

He settled on a part of the spirit that resembled his own core and twisted it, bent it to his will. A scream moved the trees, a woman's scream, a spirit's scream, not in the throes of agonizing death, but close. He collapsed into his frightened mother's arms.

Wind moaned and reformed into the woman of autumn past. She clutched her rotten-leaf chest, heaving. Water fell from her eyes. *You're stronger than you should be. What have I created?*

Deep in the shadows, two other feminine figures watched and glowed, but made no move to assist their fallen sister or their subjects.

You can't go against the will of time and nature. But for now, there's a light still in the girl. While it's there, use it to make her whole. I didn't lie to you, Marl. You're now the most powerful being on this earth. If you had any sense, you'd all run.

She disappeared into the canopy, wailing. He never wanted to see her again. The other lights followed, blinking out of existence.

There had to be a way to fix this; this couldn't be the end. But Wind *had* left him an apology. Was it a way to remedy things?

He gathered up the shepherdess, solid and cold as stone, and fanned the golden spark still within her soul, willing it to blaze again. A kiss to her wilted lips and the damaged light complied.

Hereu's legs wiggled. She stroked his purple hair and wiped his tears. "Marl, you're alive!"

He rocked. Terror left him too stunned to speak. *She* was alive; that mattered more.

Mother gasped. "Your… your eyes. Son, they're shining!"

TWENTY

This was the most boring darkened backside of a day in the history of mankind.

All things were lying in wait for warmth. Nojhi had checked and rechecked the thatch, needlessly repatching. The shed had been cleaned of any mud and spoiled foodstuffs, all knotholes were fixed, and tools had been sharpened to the nub. He would be planting grain soon, but now the melted snow was unworkable and there was no purpose to his being.

Messa didn't mind. Tilran was taxing her stomach less. She spent her days singing in Erutani as she cooked and cleaned, stopping only to talk in Mlaerian on every subject under Mother Sun.

"Natsir's new house is nice, don't you think? Marl's doing well in his practice. Have you heard about Sinnie yet?"

Nojhi loved his wife, but this constant need to yammer was taxing him. Day after day she would find some new menial task for him to do so she could hold him captive to her whims—today it was peeling vegetables, more damnable squash to be exact. His rough hands weren't adept at it. Constant failure at something tedious was enough to make a man mad.

Had it been game, he would have had everything trimmed and smoking over a fire in half an hour. There was something comforting in those lessons of his wild youth, though he had no one to teach them to now. But the dark heir to his wildness had been on his mind anyway.

"I should go visit him today?" Nojhi stared at his muddled foodstuffs. Marl would've made a remark. He missed those mock battles. "Did you hear me, love? What do you think about me paying Marl and Hereu a visit?"

She stopped singing and gave her wooden spoon a vigorous clang against the pot. "Marl's a busy man, sweetheart. Why would you want to go bother him?"

"Hey! He's my son. How am I bothering him if I want to chat?"

She placed her hands on her hips. This child made her flustered and unkempt. He had to admit the wild hair did make her look more endearing.

"Because we both know when the two of you get together nothing gets done. In fact, you create more work for others. Hereu's too sweet to have to deal with your antics as well as her husband's."

Messa looked around the cottage and turned back to the stew.

Nojhi scooped up the chopped bits of squash. "I suppose you're right. I miss our little crow and his squawking though. I can get him out of Hereu's nest of hair?"

She snorted as he tossed the crude kill in the pot and leaned into her shoulder.

"There's not much to do around here until the thaw is over."

The priestess shuffled under his weight but offered a brief mischievous gaze. Lately, making silly comments about the boys and their mates was the only amusement left to them.

"Am I not entertaining you enough, you old thing?"

Nojhi grinned and shook his head.

"What's wrong with staying here and talking?"

He took her hand and kissed it gallantly. "Messa Ganwin, beautiful priestess and perfect wife and mother!" He declared this with so much exuberance she rolled her glass eyes. "I adore you more than life, but you know talking isn't my manner."

He leaned into her hair, whispering affectionately. "I need more than chopping vegetables to be at peace, love."

Messa harrumphed as she stirred the stew. "All right, Para will be here soon. You could see Natsir while she keeps me company."

Nojhi winced. He'd already been asked to leave his eldest *alone*.

The old general had an uncanny ability to take charge of situations, even when they weren't his to command. Now Natsir had gained a little gumption, the two men weren't agreeing on much. It was a miracle they'd finished that house in the woods without one of them biting off the other's head.

"How does that sound?"

There was a blessed knock.

"I'm coming, Para!" Messa threw open the door.

The red-haired beauty opened her mouth to speak but was overpowered by a more masculine sound. "Can Nojhi come out to play?"

Para squeaked and turned around brusquely. Etutsa beamed in the glow of daylight, a wild hermit who didn't possess all of his faculties.

"Uncle! Why aren't you with Nat?"

Etutsa entered the cottage, nodding a show of respect as he tracked in mud.

Messa and Para glowered.

"Forgive me, my girl, but your husband's boring me to tears. He's as large as a wolfhound but timid as a sparrow! I told him I needed another blanket. The great-footed one trudged off mumbling some nonsense about age not determining wisdom, and then I followed you here.

I can't stand any more silence, and I'm sure he'd rather do without my noise. I need someone more my persuasion to keep company with. Marl's busy. Perhaps Nojhi would like a diversion."

Messa shook her head and looked to Para, a worried expression furrowing both their feminine brows. "What diversion, Etutsa? I won't have you drinking again.

The last time I allowed it, the two of you ended up cackling like hens in a shed for hours."

They'd been found in Toren's shed—by Toren.

Etutsa crossed his heart. Nojhi suppressed a laugh; he knew the healer was lying, but the chance to do something more amusing made him willing to sidestep Messa's apprehensions. He would also escape the dismal company of his less rambunctious son if he ran off with the healer.

Messa raised a black eyebrow. "What would you be doing then?"

Etutsa rocked on his heels and clapped his hands together. "I haven't decided."

Para slammed the cottage door and tossed her basket onto the hearth stones. "Nat agreed to watch you because of all of the trouble you've caused. Someone has to keep an eye on you, you crazed old man!"

Nojhi snorted. "What've you been doing, you cur?"

Etutsa grinned wickedly. "Petty, little things to entertain myself, nothing harmful."

"Nothing harmful!" The young woman stamped her feet. "You put honey in Eurgi's wash bucket when her back was turned. Lufnis had the audacity to blame me. You also damaged the curtain by pulling it to shreds, thread by thread."

"I was curious. The arts of fiber have always been of interest to me. I also used G'Nirac's old cloak as a shelter in the garden. It already had holes in it; I don't know why everyone was making such a fuss."

This was humorous, but also disturbing.

"Uncle, you have to stop behaving like a child." Para turned to Messa. "The finishing touch was when he tripped me on the stairs." She showed them her bruises.

Etutsa went beet red. "Now, I told you, girl; that was an accident. I'd never hurt you. I'm old and misplaced my shoes." He shuffled his feet on the floor boards, refusing to look the young woman in the eye. "I didn't see or hear you coming. You're a rose petal on Wind... like your mother."

Age or not, this was a serious offense. Nojhi saw the chance for merriment unravel like G'Nirac's curtain. If he didn't speak up, the day would be wasted.

He gripped the healer's slumped shoulder. "You've become a handful, old friend. If he's giving you a hard time, I'll supervise him."

The chieftain's daughter didn't know he was capable of more waywardness than her uncle.

Messa knew better. *You two both behave. Please no drinking and no Marl.* She turned to Para. "I suppose that'll be fine. If there's one thing I know, a good man with nothing to do turns into a babe. Perhaps they can keep each other out of mischief."

Para nodded and opened the door again, satisfied that any consequences for their troublemaking no longer belonged to her.

They swept outside. "It's unlikely the most stubborn men in Na-ir will avoid mischief today," Etutsa whispered.

Nojhi snorted.

As they trudged through mud and puddles, they met Natsir, a green blanket wrapped over his arm. A strange, indignant tree in autumn.

Etutsa gave a shout and took it. "Thank you, my boy. You're relieved of duty."

"Wonderful," Natsir snapped. "If you'll excuse me, I think I need to go paint something." He sprinted past.

The healer waved, looking like a sweet grandpa.

They stopped again in front of a fire-blackened oak. Nojhi remembered this place; it was one of Marl's childhood retreats. He smiled into the nearby branches, half expecting to see a dark, naked boy wink at him through the snow-lined canopy, but that man had better things to do.

"I used to love sitting in this hollowed-out tree as a child." Etutsa draped the blanket over his feeble shoulders. "It's the perfect place to hide from trouble."

"I take it you spent a lot of time here then."

"Are you joking?" He winked and pulled two bottles of whiskey from the lining of his coat. "I make Marl look like an innocent puppy. My exploits are legendary!"

Nojhi accepted one of the bottles with apprehension. There were worse things than an angry wife though.

Etutsa took a long swig. Nojhi did the same. They sat in silence, warmed by the whiskey.

There was a blackened spot a few yards from their shelter. The dust and rotten leaves looked recently charred, but not the surrounding area. It bothered Nojhi for quite a while. What could burn in a perfect formation? Perhaps Marl was still frequenting this area after all. That boy was terrifying with fire.

He choked on his last swallow.

"Are you well, friend?" Etutsa gave him a gracious pat on the back.

Nojhi wiped fleeing tears from his cheeks and laughed. "I'm well, old man. Some people shouldn't think and drink at the same time."

"Thinking about your boy? I miss the little cur's company too." He took another swig. "At least he had a right to call me old."

"Messa would say there's no harm in aging." Nojhi flicked a finger on the blanket. The playful gesture was met with a hiss and a sour expression. "I didn't say I agreed with her!"

"I suppose she's right. However, I'd rather my peers not acknowledge I've aged, if you please. I've beaten my stubborn self into a wrinkled mess, but I'm only two suns older than you."

"Bull dung!" Nojhi shouted.

The healer scowled.

"I mean you seem more mature…"

Etutsa burst into raucous laughter. "Now *that's* bull dung!" He smacked the tree behind him and giggled. "My body ages rapidly. I've never been one to have much sense. Knowledge, yes, but sense is foreign to me."

He beamed suddenly, captivated by something locked in his mind.

"You know, I saw you when you were in Thronren. People were jumping in the streets, eager to get a look: the young general like a god, a great golden beast."

Nojhi blushed. The last person to call him a great golden beast hadn't done so in compliment. His wife had been very angry with him.

He recalled visiting the forested northern splendor of Thronren once, at Ril's bidding that he settle a taxation dispute. He didn't remember crowds, but he did remember having to strong arm the village chieftain into relinquishing a large portion of timber.

"That was over thirty suns ago. What were you doing there?"

"Learning how to be a healer… and hiding from my shame."

"What did you do, kiss the blacksmith's daughter?" Nojhi laughed. It was easier to pretend *shame* meant nothing more than a childish act.

"Close, but worse. I loved a woman and then left because of pride. I returned suns later to find her heartbroken and married to another man."

Nojhi cringed. He had always wondered why the healer hadn't taken a wife.

"She gave him a son." Etutsa shook his head. "I never should've left."

"Don't worry, friend. You did make something grand of yourself. I'm grateful for the man you made *my* son into." Nojhi settled back into the tree and sighed, feeling like a rock. "I slaughtered innocents and ran away. What lesson is that? Take comfort you're still a better man."

Etutsa smacked him. "Don't say that! Do you know how lucky you are?" He fumbled in his britches pocket and retrieved a silver coin. "See this here? This is you, worth much and lying in wait to be used. On one side is the dueling Mlaerian warriors, but on the other…"

He flipped it. Nojhi already knew what was on the other side.

"The Sun Tree, tall, proud, and nurturing."

The imprint of a massive cypress, Ril's living and figurative emblem, rose out of his consciousness. He had once held someone close under those boughs. He had once fought for something that tree never asked to be a symbol for.

"Your boys are those two halves: Natsir the noble tree, sheltering everyone, and Marl the warriors, fighting to keep order. They learned those things from you, forged from your fire." Etutsa tossed the coin into Nojhi's lap. "You're of nobler metal than me; you opened your mind to something pure."

The shimmer of the coin resembled the helm and shield he used to wear in his naïve days. It was too painful. Nojhi fiddled with a worn acorn cap. How did they come to this subject? It was something he'd rather forget existed, buried far beneath the world and lost to time like the other half of the acorn. No amount of praise could erase the haunting torment of that stupid act.

"I left many scars, friend. Look what it did to the kingdom… and Messa."

"Bah! The kingdom was built on stupidity. It was destined to fall. Good came from it too—your boys for one thing. Messa made her own choices; you didn't bully her into loving you." Etutsa shuddered, tapping his bottle. "There's *no* man in this world she could love more than you. That love made you better. See? Your mistake shaped you… into an untroubled farmer with a loving family. You can't dwell on it and pretend it defines your whole life."

"Neither can you dwell on past mistakes, friend." Nojhi returned the coin.

The smaller man wiped a tear from his face and looked away. "I'm afraid you're right. Some good did come from my folly, too. But the torment it causes me is evident wherever I turn." He flipped the spark of silver in his fingers and stopped to stare at the Sun Tree. "Para's mine."

Nojhi stood too quickly and stumbled into the oak. "What! Does G'Nirac know?"

The healer pulled his blanket tighter and shrugged.

"Does Para know?"

Etutsa shook his head.

Nojhi slammed his hands into his eyes. "Darken the moon! Why did you tell me? You know I can't keep a secret to save my life!"

The healer smiled past gathering tears. "Yes you can! You've kept one for a long time now and it *has* saved your life."

"Never speak of this again! And to think I wanted this day to be more exciting. I told Messa I was tired of talking. Why under the ancestors are we flapping our lips now?"

"I'm sorry I shared my torment with you, but I was bound to let it slip. I've no sense, remember." Etutsa picked up his bottle and gestured for Nojhi to hand him the other. "But we *are* getting old if drink makes us spill our secrets like gossipy women. I've told this tree my problems; it's time I paid him back." He poured whiskey into the hollowed oak. "There! Now that's done. We'll listen to the wisdom of your wife and behave ourselves—at least in this."

The bottles were tossed into the forest behind them.

"Hey!"

Marl was gathering a collection of sticks. He kicked the bottles, refusing to look at them directly.

"What's wrong with you two?"

Etutsa regained some of his intelligent vigor. "We can do whatever we please, whelp! What're you doing spying? You're supposed to be taking care of my people, not larking about."

"I'm gathering kindling for Gerna. She's been cold and none of her sons are being very helpful—too busy with their own families and apprenticeships to pay attention, I'm afraid."

The old healer slumped into the oak and looked guilty. "Oh, well, I suppose that's noble."

Nojhi saw a chance to make the day better. "Are you busy, son? We could help you?" He cast his old friend an accusatory stare. "I wouldn't mind a *diversion*."

Marl started a brisk walk in the direction of the village. "No, thank you. I don't trust my practice to drunks. Find something else to do."

They scrambled to their feet. "Listen here, you little cur. Is that any way to talk to your father? I only offered you help. Come back here and explain yourself!"

The boy stopped and stiffened. "I know, Father. I ap..."

What was surely an apology was cut short by a loud crash from the canopy. A slap of cold hit Nojhi's his head and shoulders and then slipped down into his coat. He and Etutsa screamed, jumping away from the oak and their invisible attacker. Two rings of snow and a wet blanket remained.

Marl dropped the sticks and fell to the ground, laughing in hysterical freedom. "That's the best thing I've ever seen! You looked like nervous chickens!"

"Why would you do that?"

"I had no hand in it." Marl rolled, clutching his heaving stomach. "You were the fools sitting under a tree during a thaw." He gathered his wood and stood to attention, staring into their smirks.

Nojhi's jaw dropped. His boy's eyes were glowing, bright as a spark of fire in Namnor's forge. "What's going on with your eyes?"

The crow bounded away.

His father scowled. "I know what we're doing the rest of the day."

Etutsa bit his lip. "It's going to rile Messa more than whiskey, isn't it?"

***

The healer leaned against his ancestor's pillar. "Well, are you going to do it or not?"

Nojhi played with a good-sized stone in his right hand. They had already agreed Marl must've used his powers to get out of trouble back in the woods. There was no doubt they wanted him to pay some consequence, but the glowing eyes were still bothersome.

He coughed into his coat sleeve and stared at the healer's door. It was several yards away and frequently obscured by wandering villagers as they moved to important life occasions. He didn't want to risk hitting anyone, but if he moved closer, Marl would be apprised of their plans.

In his youth, Nojhi had been able to down small deer from this distance. He raised his arm to get a feel for the currents.

A short, blond boy stopped and started. Marl used to play with him—Toren's grandson; the name escaped him.

"Move along, nosy," the healer snapped.

Toren's grandson closed his mouth, frowned indignantly, and disappeared into the crowd.

Etutsa threw his hands into the air and growled. "Well! Are we still in or not?"

Nojhi sighed. He supposed there was no harm in pranking his son. The only thing they were going to hit was a door. Besides, he was too curious about the fire in the boy's eyes to let the matter go.

He took a great breath, watched for a parting in the crowd, and thought of venison. The rock dashed like a grey swift and met with the face of a startled brown woman.

Hereu dropped to the porch, looking dizzy and stunned.

Etutsa yelped. "Shatter the stars!"

Several villagers turned. They did nothing else, as usual.

It was such a stupid thing; doors opened, but the only person Nojhi had expected to come out of that door was the young healer. Marl could've heard the rock coming and caught it midflight. Praise the moon Nojhi hadn't been as vigorous in his throw as in days of old. The girl would be dead otherwise.

What in the stars is wrong with me? I hit my daughter-in-law with a darkened rock!

Yes, you did!

The black-haired daemon he most feared was standing behind him. His eyes were still glowing brightly, but out in the open, it seemed a trick of daylight. The tiny blue sparks glowing from his fingertips were no hoax though.

Nojhi hissed, prepared to be flayed alive.

Don't you have anything better to do than make people miserable? Marl seethed. He pushed past, scorching his father's coat. *Go be insufferable somewhere else, useless old man.*

The new healer came to his wife's rescue and ushered her into the shack, slamming the door.

Nojhi felt his heart wrench free from his chest. His favorite son had called him insufferable, useless, and old, and all of those descriptors had been well-deserved.

The crowd was still staring. He hurried away from the square. Etutsa followed. They didn't stop until they were near the meadow.

At the base of the solitary hill, Nojhi sat down and tried not to sob.

Etutsa settled in next to him and looked into the eastern woods. "I'm glad I left him bruise poultice."

"That's not funny!"

"He doesn't need it anyway, and I wasn't trying to be funny." Etutsa played with a twig. "We're lucky he didn't kill us. Lesser men were beaten to a pulp for smaller infractions. We owe them both an apology. But I doubt Marl will ever talk to us again."

"The boy called me useless." Nojhi sighed, feeling the weight of his loss. "I've never taken his words to heart before. It was always banter. I think he meant it this time." Nojhi pulled a chunk of sod from the wet ground. "He's right though. I've made myself useless."

"The boy said those things in anger. Do I need to get the coin?"

This ridiculous response made Nojhi smile. Etutsa was a cur, but he had a point. Nojhi was a piece of silver, worn from constant use, but still bright and worth something when polished and applied to the right purpose.

"No need, friend. I understand. But what am I waiting to be spent on now? Whose hands should I be traded to so I might be useful again? I was forged a warrior. Farming is more taxing to me than anything I've ever done because it keeps me grounded. Warriors can't be horded."

"That's the beauty of coins; they can be repurposed. You've done well as a farmer, father, lover, and friend. There's no shame in that."

"No, I suppose not, but something's been nagging me." He tossed the soil. "What use is peace if I've to cast off a part of myself? I'm meant to confront this."

"Confront what? How? Don't tell me you still want to approach Onaryc!"

Nojhi nodded. "I think it's my destiny to fix this. I started the process that led to this debacle. Why shouldn't I attempt to remedy it? I'm tired of living a coward in the shadows."

"You're far from a coward, and I've no doubt you would make a persuasive argument. But when did you start believing in destiny, my friend?"

"When my son's hands started making fire that doesn't smoke. When my child started behaving more like a spirit and less like a youth." Pain settled into his chest. "I'm going to speak with G'Nirac about something I know I can change. Will you come with me?" The healer was eloquent and that was a useful weapon against the rational chieftain.

Etutsa shook his head. "No, not today. We've done enough damage. If you still feel strongly in the morning, when we're sober, then I'll consider it."

They shook hands.

"Now, I'm going to saunter off and hide before Para comes clucking at me like an angry hen."

As soon as he was gone, Nojhi stood and looked around. He wasn't often in the meadow and he wondered what the view must look like from Marl's place on the small hill. He trudged up the muddy slope.

The meadow would look lovely in a few weeks, a bright green cloth studded with jewels. He hoped Hereu enjoyed the flowers as much as his Messa did.

Nojhi stopped. There was no house on the property. But some work had been done in preparation for a foundation. Surely the boy would've had more by now. There was nothing!

Messa had told him Marl had moved a few days ago. He hadn't paid attention. Apparently, his child was living in a dilapidated shack with his woman, with no time to make a proper home.

Nojhi turned to the pine guardian of the hill and slapped his hands together. "I've got work to do."

Had he been Erutani, the tree might've replied. Still, he heard a cheerful whisper that seemed to agree.

***

No one was happy the old general was barking orders again. Para and Messa had been content cooking and chatting in the warm cottage when he burst through the door, muddy and determined.

They packed provisions and their sewing and followed him to the new house in the woods to retrieve Natsir. The boy was more indignant about the disruption than the women.

"We're helping your brother," Nojhi snarled. "End of discussion. Let's gather the tools."

They progressed along the stream to Marl's hill. Tools were marched up first and then the women. A dutiful and careful wife only when around her daughters-in-law, Messa allowed herself to be carried up. It was comical, but Nojhi was too busy to laugh.

The men ate stew and set to work clearing the land. Marl had made a definite outline in the soil, but some of the areas didn't make sense—the gaping hole in one of the main rooms, for instance. They worked around it.

Well into the labor, someone shouted. A healthy, brown woman sprinted up the hillside to hug her mother- and sister-in-law. Hereu was no worse for the misdeed and still bonny.

Marl took his time. He gave them a cool, penetrating stare. The eyes were alight but the remarkable hands were tame.

Nojhi held one of his out. "How are you, son?"

The young healer tossed his coat in the grass and grabbed a shovel.

Natsir scratched his head. "Why are you angry? Father dragged us here to help you. I didn't realize you needed help."

The spot he had cleared was being unconsciously backfilled. Quick to remedy this folly, the eldest redistributed the mess elsewhere.

"You don't have to do it all, you know. Family is meant for that."

Marl forced his tool deep into the soil. Tears coated the handle by his chin.

Their father knew what he needed to do. *I'm sorry, son. I'd never try to hurt Hereu.* He wiped the boy's tears. Marl flinched but didn't pull away. *I'm a darkened idiot sometimes.*

Bright sapphires gleamed. *Yes. You're Great Idiot… and I'm Little Cur, son of Great Idiot.*

Nojhi hadn't expected to be forgiven so quickly.

I'm not mad at you anymore and neither is Hereu. I'm angry with Etutsa though. The darkened cur lied to me… Marl glanced over at Para and then looked to Natsir. He weighed the shovel in his hands like a sword. *I'll make a deal with you, old man. I'll forgive the incident with the rock, and keep Etutsa's dirty secret, if you do one thing. Never ask me or anyone else about my eyes… or mention them, ever!*

The old general agreed, though his restless mind would be tormented for suns.

Marl threw down the shovel and jumped into his arms, knocking Natsir aside. Nojhi patted the skinny back and rested his cheek in feathered hair. Etutsa was right. His mistake had given him something worth bragging about.

The reconciliation was interrupted by a squeak. Hereu pulled pastries from a basket. Nojhi and Marl accepted them with mumbled civility but Natsir refused. She placed a finger to her pink lips when Nojhi queried this strange act. The contents of these delicacies were a surprise.

"Try it. Para says she'll teach me how to make them if they appeal to you."

Hereu folded her arms and batted her eyelashes, refusing to leave the men alone until her mission was fulfilled. Shrugging, Marl shoved half of the pastry into his mouth and gagged.

"This is fish!"

"I know." She twirled her skirt. "You don't owe *her* anything."

The healer's face paled. He looked around the hilltop nervously. Nothing happened but the slight caress of a breeze. Hereu rolled her eyes and kissed him before joining the rest of the family by the pine.

"What was that about?"

Marl shot his father a disagreeable glare before shoving the rest of his pastry in his mouth and resuming his work.

Right. Eyes. Sorry.

The blue beams seared into his chest. Nojhi started and picked up a hoe, half sensing these tools may be used for a battle if he wasn't careful.

Natsir stood in between them. This simple gesture worked immediately. The three men stopped casting each other dirty glances and focused on their work.

It was hard and invigorating. Nojhi felt blessed to have found something useful to occupy him and for the chance to stand near his able sons.

When the foundation was level, they hauled several old logs up the hill and stripped them down to make posts.

Natsir laughed over his shoulder, after lopping off a stubborn branch, and pointed with his hatchet to the other side of the hill. "Look at our women."

They did and smirked. The ladies were sitting in a circle, braiding their hair.

"Don't they look like the three sisters?"

Nojhi nodded. It was a favorite subject of those artistic priests and priestesses Ril had eradicated. On his desk in Selcovi, the old king had kept a stolen relic of these fabled women caught in mid-dance. Nojhi always wondered what song it was that made them move so suggestively.

Marl coughed and strolled over to kiss his wife. "Take that out now!"

Messa stopped plaiting the brown curls and glared. Hereu smirked.

"Mother, look at her!" Light from his winking eye danced on and off, a fairytale sprite under the tree. "She looks respectable. I can't have a respectable wife!"

The priestess groaned and surrendered; she'd fallen upon a stubborn knot anyway. The two young women ignored the hidden insult and giggled. The boy was rough around the edges, but he'd a certain charismatic way of getting what he wanted.

They worked on until dark, stopping only for water. Marl wanted to end it there, but his father laughed. The little house was starting to take shape and darkness was nothing to a man who could control fire.

Though Nojhi was scolded by his wife, the healer took no slight. Blue flame was placed on the grass beside the women. There was nothing that needed to be said. They went back to pounding posts.

An hour later, aching muscles forced Nojhi to reconsider his earlier exuberance. "I need to learn to act my age."

Marl snorted. "If you did that, old man, you'd never get out of bed."

He gave his youngest a playful push and the boy disappeared with a shout. They'd forgotten about the darkened hole in the hill.

Hereu rushed to the spot. Two blue beacons lit the pit. He was sprawled at the muddy bottom with an indignant look on his face. But her sudden mirth was infectious. Marl climbed out and whirled her in the air. Her legs swung so high she shrieked.

Nojhi nestled close and placed a dirty, aching hand to Messa's belly. He hummed into her braid. "You know what? We make wonderful children."

She turned her beautiful, wizened face to meet his. "Of course we do, love. This family is more precious than gold."

A flutter tickled his palm. He smiled, determined now to be present for the moments when another girl would squeal with glee. After all, how would she manage mischief without him?

***

Etutsa grumbled at his brother's hearth, swathed in an old, green housecoat, a cup of herbal tea in his fists. White stockings were propped on a stool. "Why'd you wake me if you've changed your mind?"

"I haven't changed my mind," Nojhi whispered. "I want to write two letters instead. They don't have to know who the author is and we can deliver them with much secrecy if we're careful. They'll never know they're from Na-ir."

"So you won't stand tall and proud before your enemies then, warrior? You won't speak for your cause and rally their hearts?" Etutsa placed his cup on the table and leaned forward. "Here I was thinking I was friends with a man of much prowess and resolve. My mistake."

"Please. It was your words yesterday that made me see reason. I can't charge into a battle any more. I can't led men with a look and force them to do my bidding. I'm old and settled and I've come to terms with that. My family is more important." Nojhi tapped on the hearth stones and closed his eyes. "But my conscience won't let me rest until I've tried to end this darkened coup of Onaryc's. Rayr and Eni may not be the best rulers, but I'd trust them to care for the people. They inherited this mess; I can help them."

"What would you say in this letter?"

"I'd remind them of the unity of the tribes." Marl's declaration that dogs were placated with kindness gnawed at his heart. "I'd tell Rayr to ignore Onaryc's portion of water and lay claim to an area upstream, in Pryt where we used to fish. It's nowhere near Dasha territory, but if water could be redirected from there, it may save the city."

"Ah, my friend. It's a noble gesture, and I'll help you, but it isn't wise, I think. It takes much work to redirect a river, and, if you do that, you're still taking water destined for Onaryc's people. The boar of the canyon doesn't need an excuse for war. He'll find one with or without this issue." He raised a white eyebrow and shrugged. "I'm certain Rayr has already considered this option."

"You're right. But I built that city as a child in the streets, Etutsa. I defended it and I lauded it as a soldier. If no one else comes to its defense, why shouldn't I?"

"Because it's someone else's destiny to make this right." G'Nirac entered the kitchen, fully dressed and bright-eyed. "Don't look at me like that," he scolded, tapping his cane. Nojhi half expected to be spanked, the chieftain was so somber. "I told you the day we met who was meant for this task, didn't I?"

"I refuse to believe that nonsense. It's not right. Why should my son suffer for my sins?"

The chieftain sat between them, his back to the heat of the hearth. "No one said Marl would suffer, and you weren't the only sinner. Your wife and I share something in common. The spirits visit with me; they've done so since before our first encounter."

Etutsa grumbled. "Do I need to reduce your medication?"

G'Nirac rounded on his brother. "That man *is* the Wanderer!"

"My boy's eyes glow now," Nojhi admitted. "Is that the spirits' doing?"

"Possibly. But I do know it isn't for us to meddle. We must keep still."

It was an impossible task for one full of fire and life. "Then, I should go to Onaryc and make my stance as Etutsa suggests. I don't like the idea of my son being forced. The spirits have never visited me; I never gave them permission to touch my boy."

The chieftain's cheeks turned scarlet.

"I can keep Marl from this destiny. He's happy and I can't allow that to change."

G'Nirac relaxed and rubbed his sore back. "My friend, my friend, I know you love your son. How can any man stand by and watch his greatest joy enter into unknown realms and responsibilities without wishing to take on the task himself? I do understand you, but you must listen. Trying to redirect things will bring your death. Don't forget, Onaryc swore vengeance."

Nojhi tapped his feet against the floor boards. "You think I should be frightened of the fat monster. My actions have helped him. He owes me thanks!"

"You killed his brother! Hacked him to pieces with your sword, and paraded his head!"

Nojhi was ready for a fight again; he flashed an unintended smirk.

"You find that funny?"

"Oh, don't lecture me! It was an honorable fight. Eloh lost and refused to yield after I granted him mercy. The death was fitting for one who doesn't show respect to his better in combat."

The murderous act also had the desired effect on the canyon people. The Dasha never troubled Ril over taxes and other nonsense after that. Just one stupid man had died. Nojhi was proud of this.

G'Nirac threw his hands up and stood. "To a Mlaerian, he may have seemed disrespectful, but to the Dasha, you shamed Eloh's name before your sword ever sawed through his neck. Dasha leaders either win a duel or die. This is what they believe. When Eloh lost and you tried to spare him, you took from him his honor. Then, you ensured his unconventional death would be remembered."

"He got what he wanted. Death and infamy. Onaryc got the chiefdom. I owe them nothing. It was an honorable fight. Any man that says otherwise is a fool."

Etutsa stood now and placed a reassuring hand on his shoulder. It was unwise to label a chieftain a fool, even one so kind and forgiving.

"Nojhi!" G'Nirac tore his hair. "You stubborn man! It doesn't matter if you're right! Onaryc *will* kill you." He pushed the general's chest with his cane, directing him to the kitchen door. "As for Rayr—the greatest rebel will have to be executed to ensure no other rebellions occur!"

Footfalls interrupted this strange battle. Lufnis and Eurgi watched from the stairwell, eyes weary with sleeplessness but wide enough to show apprehension. The chieftain used the distraction to his advantage and struck a fateful blow.

"If you carry through with this plan, I'll disown the both of you! You'll never be welcome in my home or my village." G'Nirac pushed them to the front door. "I've had enough! I'm shamed by your pride and stubbornness, Nojhi Ganwin. You know better than to meddle in greater things."

They stumbled off the porch into a crowd of suspicious gawkers. The village was awake, ready to experience a new scandal.

"Don't think I'm uninformed. I love you both, but your actions don't become men. Stop behaving like spoiled children and forget this. Now!"

"I stand by my words, G'Nirac Sinbel!" Nojhi was shouting—a man ready to fight another duel—but he couldn't stop. "You think I'm stubborn, but you're the fool. Your folly will come creeping out of those shadows you refuse to acknowledge."

G'Nirac slammed the door.

"Let's get out of here." Nojhi wanted to go home and sulk by his own fire for a while.

His old friend trembled and sobbed. "Brother, please let me in. Please forgive us. We were only talking." Etutsa shrank to the porch, rocking in self-pity. "I can't bear it when you're angry with me. At least let me have my shoes!"

His sorrow was painful to witness. The crowd dispersed.

After a moment, the shoes plopped onto the porch. Eurgi blinked before closing the door.

"I could use the counsel of another woman. Maybe Messa will give us a pat on the head and a treat."

Nojhi sighed as he watched his friend plod through the square to his cottage, looking like an absurd walking asparagus in a green dressing gown.

TWENTY ONE

Para smoothed back long, golden strands and hummed over the head they protected. She was itching to cut them, but her scissors were in the trunk across the room. It was the only thing in their home not recently constructed.

She was proud of her industrious, snoring husband. When a task was to be done, he saw it through, and he had a good eye for craftsmanship.

Their bed, assembled from fallen trees gathered in the misty forest, was carved with vines and animals. She fondled the ears of an alert rabbit near her shoulder and mused. His soul was a brilliant light. She was determined to let him shine.

Natsir enjoyed the chance. He was decorating their walls too, giving the place the illusion of a magnificent and ancient temple fresco. He had already started on their den, using pigments donated by her father.

It shouldn't have surprised her that G'Nirac had illuminated manuscripts in his youth. In matters of the past, the chieftain was secretive with everyone, including his children. Still, he was being loving and open with the new couple now, even from a distance.

They had been in the cottage for three days, but, with all of this encouragement, bustle, and inspiration, it felt like home. They found it therapeutic to be away from the buzz of Na-ir and nearer to the evergreen aroma of the woods. The forest chill was a sharp, pleasant reminder there were still things to do.

"Wake up, love. It's almost morning."

Natsir groaned and pulled the blanket up, an ineffective barrier against the cold and the determined red head that peeked underneath it. He was already coming out of the Blessed Unknowing, a smirk plastered on his hairy, handsome face.

"Nat, you promised."

Eyelashes fluttered but the large man didn't move. Para sighed and settled in beside him. She didn't enjoy the morning husband who tried to avoid exertion; the evening husband was more attractive.

"My love! Wake up!"

He opened his eyes and met her exasperation with a light chuckle.

"What's funny?"

"You, sweetheart. It's hard to take you seriously with that grumpy look on your face." Natsir snorted and stretched. His yawn turned into a bear's growl. "After the work we did last night, you're still going to force me to see the sunrise?"

He already knew the answer to that absurd question. Para wouldn't make exceptions. If she did, the beautiful moments would become fewer and less valuable, until they slipped away forever. They had too many suns left together to become lazy in love and wonderment now.

"All right, I don't know why this is important to you, but I'm getting up!" He waved one large hand in the air and rested it against her back, flicking her braid. "Come here."

He pulled her into a tender kiss. Para accepted it gladly, content to know he was awake. But Natsir didn't break free from her lips in the manner of a man ready to leave his bed.

That won't work. She was frustrated by his trick and yet delighted he'd tried.

Conceding his loss, he shrugged, groaned loudly, and rolled out of bed.

"Thank you, thank you, thank you."

Natsir mumbled underneath his shirt. A dandelion top popped out with a sarcastic smile, and green eyes fixed on the thatch overhead; he was trying not to lose his temper. This didn't bother her; he was never angry for long, and dwelling on it now would mean they might miss the journey of Mother Sun as she flitted through the boughs.

Excited, she jumped from the bed and pulled his great arm. He didn't budge.

"I can't advance into the presence of the Great Goddess without my britches."

For some reason, they were behind the trunk and covered in saw dust. He spent precious seconds sitting on their straw mattress trying to rid his clothing of the fragrant remains of tree.

"Please hurry! We'll miss Her."

A delinquent smile split his face. He slid one stubbly leg inside of the garment, noticed more sawdust on the seam, and took the britches off again.

Para threw her hands into the air and whimpered. "Why did you promise if you're just going to make me crazy every morning?"

"That's the fun of it, sweetheart." He chuckled and slapped the britches in the air. "I said we'd see every sunrise and sunset until the day we die. I never said I wouldn't amuse myself." He finished dressing and retreated from her lightning stare. "Hurry up, you turtle!"

When she caught up to his long-legged strides, he was on the porch tucking in his shirt. Father Moon had already stripped the sky of night.

"See, we haven't missed Her yet. There's still time to reach the river."

Para groaned. Natsir's concept of time and distance was different from hers. On a horse, she was swift; on two slender, short legs, she was useless in a gamble.

In a gallant show of respect, he bowed, leapt off the porch, and presented her with a soft, calloused hand. Her acceptance of the gesture made him ecstatic, and this made her feel guilty for her mild tantrum over the issue; he lived to please her.

She fell into his arms and pressed her head to his shoulder. The woods formed into a grey-green haze. When they reached the stream, he put her to the muddy ground with a kiss.

Para looked across the plains at a tiny smudge of orange light. "So radiant!"

She settled into Natsir's chest; he took hold of her waist. There was nothing she wanted more than this, to greet the Great Mother each day with the one she loved and offer thanks. This evening, they would seek the Great Father. Without those Lights, there would be no love and no life; in short, there'd be no Natsir.

The brilliance climbed past the scraggled horizon, casting ethereal arms over them and the forest beyond. Baubled rainbows danced on Water and floated away.

"Why doesn't everyone wake each day for this? It restores my soul."

Natsir kissed her plaited curls. "Most don't have your heart. They don't see beauty and precious life."

This was a dour way to think. There was something exhilarating in acknowledging the mysterious and superior, a great comfort in knowing they were safeguarded. Surely there were others who weren't impervious to the sparkling allure of the creators.

Her metaphysical musings were interrupted by a substantial whirlwind of grass, leaves, and twigs. Para turned her face into Natsir's pine-scented shirt to avoid the debris and trembled as a terrifying, inhuman buzz crept inside her ear.

Our brother is angry, so angry with me, it cried. *I can't still his troubled heart.*

Loose twigs showered them, knives thrown by an inept street performer.

Natsir frowned. "I forgot we have visitors today. Come." He dwarfed her hand with his warm palm. "There's no rush. They're not quite ready."

Para was confused. Since when did the elemental sisters have a brother? Was he the guard at the Passageway—death himself?

By the time they'd returned to the cottage, she was clutching her husband's skin, hoping the strange, angry noises echoing through their corner of the woods weren't some terrifying daemons from the skies.

"It's all right. Marl and Hereu are just being themselves."

He wasn't joking. The youths were standing beside the cottage with fists raised and eyes narrowed. Hereu's curls were in typical disarray, charged with a crackle of energy.

"Listen," Marl bellowed. "You're staying here and that's the end of it. It's too dangerous!"

"No!" Her blue dress undulated as she stamped. "I won't leave you!"

Genuine tears covered her face and Para felt a twinge of pity. The night before, her brother- and sister-in-law had been dancing on the hilltop. What had happened in the last few hours? She released her husband's hand and ran to them.

"Sister Para, talk some sense into him please!"

Marl turned. "There you are. Good morning, brother. I have to go now. Please make sure my Hereu is safe. It's better if she stays here."

"Why?" Para saw no reason for this fight. Hereu was a healthy, intelligent girl.

Sparks flickered near Marl's thigh. "I'll be back this afternoon. Thank you."

Natsir groaned. "I didn't realize Hereu was adverse to this visit, brother. What do you want me to do, hold her prisoner?" He crossed his muscled arms. "Is this about your eyes?"

Apparently, it was. Marl flinched and set off for Na-ir.

Hereu raced after him. "You can't leave me like this!"

Marl stiffened and stopped.

"You can't leave me. After all we've been through, I won't watch you go!"

A flurry of black and blue rounded on the shepherdess. When the blur subsided, the healer and his wife were tangled, kissing away any animosity.

Para blushed and giggled. *These two are chattering birds in spring. One minute they're chirping, the next they're talons and wings!*

Natsir shook his head. *They're crazy! So reckless with each other.*

She shrugged as he placed a protective arm around her shoulders. *There's nothing wrong with being reckless. Some passion is nice.*

A golden eyebrow pushed up his bangs.

Para blushed again. *I'm not saying we should fight, but I wouldn't mind such a kiss.*

Marl released Hereu and stroked her moist cheeks. They didn't have to hear that channeled conversation to know the winner of that argument.

Hereu nodded remorsefully, gave her husband one more zealous kiss, and sobbed as she watched him leave.

The chieftain's daughter knew what she had to do. "Come here, love. Don't fret. You'll see your silly man soon."

Natsir held open the door. Hereu stood there, shuddering.

"Surely you don't hate my company that much," Para teased.

The healer's wife giggle-hiccupped and shook her head. Kindness wasn't a perfect remedy for everything, but it worked well when applied liberally.

Inside, Hereu plopped into a chair by the hearth. "There you are, Destroyer!" The creature cuddled into her neck and purred into the curls. "I've been looking for you, sweet kitten."

"He's visiting Pilgrim."

Para nodded to the smudge of ash on her hearth. It was another uncomfortable conversation, but not as foreboding as marital discontent.

"Our friend's ill and may not make it to spring. Nat and I took him so we can be near when he must go to the Passageway."

"Poor thing." Hereu stroked the kitten and stared.

Pilgrim afforded her a meek but wise glimpse of his radiant golden eyes, suns rising and then setting into night.

"And yet he seems to pity me."

Natsir offered them some cheese, barely hiding his remorse under that beard.

"Thank you for being so kind. I'm sorry we made such a ruckus."

"No need to apologize." He settled into another chair, running a hand through his hair in the way that made him more attractive. "I know my brother better than anyone. You should've seen the fights he and Father had. They can be unpredictable. So can you, I've heard."

She bit her lower lip and looked to her feet.

"I'm surprised he was able to make you come all this way. How did he win that argument?"

Hereu's tanned skinned flashed bright red. Natsir stared, wide-eyed and curious. Para tried not to giggle. It was quaint both brothers had tried similar tactics this morning to get their way. Marl apparently had a talent for it.

"I'd appreciate it if you'd provide me with some information, sister."

The shepherdess jumped and shoved the cheese into her mouth, looking sick and green.

Natsir wasn't one to be ignored. "Please tell me why my brother's eyes now glow, why he's fearful for your life, and what Wind did to anger him."

Hereu choked and shook her head. Para patted the girl's back.

"I don't ask you this to upset you." Nat's reassuring tone was tinged with authority. "My brother has incredible, terrifying abilities. My purpose is to watch over him. But I can't help unless I know."

The purpose was self-inflicted, but Para couldn't scold him for it. There were many times she had also kept a close, unsolicited watch on her *little brother*.

She remembered the smokeless, blue flame from the night before. Natsir had shown her the capabilities of Erutani, but she'd never seen such skills from Marl.

"I promised I wouldn't say anything."

Destroyer mewed, tail twitching. Natsir freed him. His gesture reminded Para of the many times Papa had admonished her as a child. She was delighted to be able to make him a father soon.

"Sweet sister, I'll bear the responsibility for your disobedience."

Hereu stared at her empty lap and sniffled. "Marl loves you so much. He trusts you. I need to tell someone else. Your mother already knows."

He leaned back in his chair, but waved a hand for her to continue.

"The reason he's angry is…" Hereu paused. "I almost died."

Chills shot up Para's neck. No such news had been on the wagging tongues of Na-ir, and Messa hadn't said anything yesterday.

"Did you hear the scream two nights ago in the forest?"

323

Natsir jumped from his chair. "Was that you?" He paced the floor and tore his ragged hair. Usually, only the din of Na-ir could make him this apprehensive. "I'd hoped it was a nightmare!" He stopped and rounded on the girl. "What happened?"

Hereu fidgeted. "No, no, that wasn't me; that was Wind. She tried to kill us; Marl challenged her."

Para shivered. *Wind is capable of murder? How could Marl ever win such a battle?*

"She lured him to the forest promising power to heal anything. I realized something was wrong when I woke and he was gone. By the time your mother and I found them, he was engulfed in fire." Hereu's voice broke as she sobbed. "I couldn't bear to see him burn. I'm such an idiot; I jumped in between them. I didn't feel anything, and I couldn't hear or see what happened, but Messa said there was a fight. Marl won. I was nearly dead, but he kissed me and... and I moved." She took a moment to catch her breath. "That's why his eyes glow. That's why Wind is afraid of him. And that's why Marl's afraid of Wind."

Natsir's silence was as troubling as Hereu's tale. He was breathing heavily. "I see. Thank you, sister. Marl's right to be nervous, but I don't think Wind would do either of you much harm. She's after my brother for other reasons, I'm afraid."

Para stiffened and leaned forward in her chair. "What's going on? First he can make fire from his hands, and now Wind's trying to possess him and he can raise the dead."

"I'm sorry. It's strange. Do you remember the story about the boy born in exile?"

Para remembered an uninteresting children's tale that mentioned such a boy; it varied from tribe to tribe. Many people were born away from their homelands. It had no bearing on how special a person was.

"Well, there's more to it than that." Natsir combed his long hair slowly. "It begins with a bloody, tyrant king, and I'm sorry to say, it's supposed to end with Marl."

***

Para didn't agree with her husband. Sitting in the cottage and doing nothing was ridiculous in the face of such strange events. She wanted to go down to the healer's shack and give Marl a piece of her mind instead of sewing new green curtains.

The way she saw it, he was responsible for the bizarre happenings in the Ganwin family. The fright he'd given Nojhi by feigning suicide was unfathomable, but it explained the sweet-natured man's outburst a few moons before. Hereu's near-death encounter was also his fault.

What idiot makes a promise and then traipses off to do what he wants anyway? Ouch! It was difficult to sew angry. She sucked her finger and grimaced at the metallic taste. *Marl should be treating Hereu like a queen. Not screaming and breaking her heart.*

The last thing that selfish boy could be called was a great warrior or savior. One description rested on her heart.

Coward!

Para tried not to cry. That coward was a better man than most. Hadn't she longed for him to take control of these lands? Hadn't she hoped he'd be her deliverer from Lufnis? Marl was both her baby and her defender—her brother too—and there'd been so many times she had made excuses for him only to rejoice in his playful smile.

Marl loves deeper than anyone. This Wanderer business must be destroying him. It broke her heart. The little crow in the lush trees of her mind flew away. "We're losing him," she whispered.

"I beg your pardon." Hereu laid down her end of the curtain, eyes wide.

Natsir stopped painting and waited for his wife to explain.

I'm well, love. The issue with Marl still has me flustered.

He smiled and placed tiny blood-red dots on the wall.

I like those poppies. She turned back to Hereu. "Forgive me. I keep losing my grip." Para shifted over to the table but couldn't stand; her legs tingled. She hissed and rubbed them.

Hereu fidgeted. "I hate when that happens. Marl might have something for it."

Natsir place another fleck of flowers on his wooden canvas and turned. He didn't frown, but his eyebrows were raised. "Nice try, but *no*." He turned back to his image.

The shepherdess groaned. "I'm in more danger of being bored to death."

Para gathered her bone needles and placed the fabric in a basket by the table. There was no use in trying to be productive when everyone was irritable and worried.

Hereu went over to Natsir, hands on the prominent curve of her body. "This is delightful!" She moved closer to examine every ornate detail. "It looks like the meadow near Selcovi. Blue bells and daisies. I miss that place. Have you been?"

"No. This is my representation of spring." Nat pointed to the wall near the hearth. "That'll be summer, and the other two walls will be autumn and winter."

"It all looks like a dream." She turned back to the spring wall. "Oh! You put in a lamb."

Natsir laughed. There was now a white fleck with an oblong black face nestled among the grasses—so much detail in a few strokes. He was efficient in his ability to create splendor.

"Are you going to paint the whole house?"

He nodded, but Para answered. His humility and his quiet devotion to the project wouldn't keep the girl interested for long. His wife needed to maintain the chatter.

"Yes. The whole house will be painted. I hope we don't run out of the nicer pigments, but Nat can make more from plants. We haven't decided what will be in our bedroom, but the children's room will be woodland animals."

She could already imagine the little ones staring at the indications of their father's masterful mind.

"Actually, sweetheart. I just decided today what I'm going to paint in there."

"Really? What?"

"A sunrise and a sunset." He winked.

Para stopped bouncing and felt warmth flash into her cheeks.

"A man has to sleep you know," he added bluntly.

Hereu laughed as he stuck his tongue out. The shepherdess had no idea how insufferable quiet men could be.

Natsir wasn't offended by Para's ill humor; he was enjoying it. "Your cheeks aren't quiet red enough, sweetheart. Here!"

He applied two blotches of pigment to her face. She groaned and wiped the paint with her fingers. She was tempted to apply the mess to the wall, but Natsir's britches made a more suitable act of revenge. Three red streaks ran down his leg, and she didn't care if they never came out in the wash.

He kissed her forehead before cleaning his brush on an old cloth and dipping it into a jar with a smattering of green. "I'm teasing. We'll still see the real ones. I'll need lots of inspiration."

Para relaxed but poked him in the arm for being tricky.

"That's such a romantic thing to do," Hereu gushed. "Marl and I have the stars; we could look forever." Those radiant pinpoints of light were in the brown expanse of her eyes. She wrapped her arms around her shoulders and blushed.

Natsir didn't notice the tear alongside her nose. He stopped creating a pine and looked to the ceiling. "Too bad I can't color the thatch! Stars would be a marvelous thing to paint."

"It certainly would, but then when would you sleep?" Para twirled her skirt and rocked on her heels. She hoped the silliness would cheer Hereu.

He stared at the pigment. The same smile he'd displayed when putting on his britches snuck back across his cheeks. "You know, *this* is your favorite color. You should wear it more."

Para shrieked as he advanced. Red marks would fade into her already blushing skin, but green would make her look ill. She dove behind Hereu, who shrieked in kind. Finding no escape from the massive paint monster, they retreated to the bedroom.

The shepherdess crashed and rolled on the floor in a fit of giggles. "The Ganwin men share a sense of humor. I'm glad that brush didn't touch me."

"Me too."

In case he followed, Para pressed against the door. He wasn't usually aggressive, but it never hurt to be prepared. Nothing moved, so she ran to the bed and sat.

Natsir's trick had an underlying meaning. He didn't want to be watched, preferring silence in moments of concentration. They would have to find something else to preoccupy them.

It was a difficult undertaking. Both women were distracted and anxious within minutes, wanting to be somewhere else with two very different people. Hereu slammed into Natsir's side of the bed and snickered, twiddling with her dress, her mind on other fanciful, boyish tricks. Seeing nothing better to do, Para laid her braided head down next to the girl and stared at the thatch.

Even with the overpowering mix of patchouli and cut pine, all she could think of was Natsir's vision of golden lights rising and falling, captured in that perfect moment for all their lives. She wished she could capture his smile in the same way.

Her dappled skin goose-pimpled. Out of curiosity, she turned. The shepherdess was also starry-eyed. The girls chuckled and blushed; they'd found something to do. For some time they whispered and giggled, sharing their secrets.

The creak of the door interrupted them. Natsir grinned from the crack holding a plate of bread and milk. He left it on the bed and exited with the intuitive look of a man who knew he was interrupting something in which he didn't want to be involved.

Milk glistened on Hereu's lips when she spoke next. "You're lucky to have spent a childhood with both brothers. What were they like? Marl always looks embarrassed when I ask."

"Ha!" Para laughed and tore the rosemary loaf. "His misdeeds would make an old woman faint. You should ask Cyan, though. Those two were always being whipped for nonsense." She let the bread dissolve into mush on her tongue before swallowing. "I spent more time with Marl when he was a babe. He's always been deviant. Natsir hasn't changed either. He's just bigger now."

A memory of the young Ganwins playing in her father's house made her choke on her milk.

"Oh, how funny! Now that I think about it, I used to bathe your husband in a tub in our kitchen." Messa had often relied on Para to watch the boy when he was a handful, and it had been such fun to play mother with the lanky, black-haired toddler.

Hereu snorted and took another larger helping of the bread. "When did you realize there was something special about him?" She licked her fingers.

"Last night. He never did any of that around me until I saw the fire on the hill." She roamed the forests of her mind in search of a spark of that strange, blue light. It had never been there. "He's always been strong and intelligent, but those traits aren't unique." Para shrugged, feeling detached. "I've always seen him as more like his father, frankly."

"I see. I suppose he was telling the truth then about being surprised by his talents and the prophecy. It's difficult for him to face such rapid change. I haven't been supportive. I want him to succeed, but that spirit terrifies me." Hereu twirled her ringlets and sighed. "I knew when I saw him he was the Wanderer, though."

Para dropped her cup. "How? I've been around Erutani most of my life and I know little."

Auburn curls bounced as the shepherdess jumped off the bed. "My mother told me. My grandfather was the last scholar in Thronren. He knew a lot about that prophecy." She wiped crumbs from the bed. "Papa has differing views, but there's something exhilarating about a baby growing into a person who can affect such change."

The whole affair was still too unreal. "It doesn't bother you that your husband might have to bring down a kingdom?" *Or build it up.* The spirits were vague.

Hereu's resolve in the matter of destiny was striking. She straightened, a revolutionary on the brink of war. "Not in the slightest, the kingdom had it coming!"

Para recoiled. The shepherdess blushed and stretched out her hand.

"Why don't we stop gossiping behind our husbands' backs and finish that stupid curtain? I've done nothing to earn my keep today."

"Nonsense, you're family. But you're right about that damn curtain. Let me find my scissors." Para's red braid fell into the trunk—the only two things she had left of her mother. She rustled through clothing and knickknacks. "Drat! They aren't here. I must've left them at Papa's."

Hereu flew to the shutters and opened them. She nodded to the fragrant midday scene. "Let's go get them, then." She lifted her skirts and jumped outside. "I'm dying to feel the sunshine on my face. Your father's house can't be less safe than here."

Para fidgeted. "Let's have Natsir fetch them for us. We can sit on the porch for fresh air."

Hereu took off like a stone skipping on water. "Come catch me then!"

Marl's going to kill me! Para stamped her foot and slammed the shutters.

Natsir was by the hearth, holding Pilgrim in his lap and stroking Destroyer behind the ears.

"Is it time?"

He nodded.

"I'm sorry, love. We've another problem. Hereu jumped out of the window and ran off." It was like losing a horse for not stabling it properly.

Nat shuffled to a stand, placing the ragged, furry body on the hearth stones. "I know I promised, my friend, but I need to go after her. Para and Destroyer are here for you though."

The sudden realization that death was indeed visiting their home today made Para weep. "No. Stay. I'll find her. It's my fault for letting my guard down. She's as bad as your brother!"

He kissed her forehead. He was more than willing to break his promise if it meant providing her assistance. She didn't want to give him the option; it was too cruel.

"I'll be fine." She gathered the cloaks. "I'll get her and then I'll whip her."

Natsir smirked.

Para said a final goodbye with a kiss on a black brow, leaving a bejeweled dot on his fur as a token of her affection. She left her husband with a quick embrace and the intention to hold him in his grief soon.

Hereu was waiting by an ash grove some distance from the cottage.

"That was a mean trick. I'm tempted to tell Marl and see what he does to you."

Color drained from Hereu's cheeks.

"Let's head back. Pilgrim's dying, and Natsir's in no mood to deal with this right now." Para was the one who wanted to smack her, but evoking the wrath of someone larger usually had the desired effect.

The shepherdess's eyes watered with genuine empathy. "I'm sorry. We should give Nat and his cat some privacy." Her small foot pressed deep grooves into the mud. "Now that we're out here, what would it hurt to go retrieve your scissors and then come right back?"

"Hereu Ganwin, really! Between Marl's temper and your manipulative nature, I'm afraid to meet my nieces or nephews."

"Oh, you don't mean that."

She didn't, but this was ridiculous; there was no reason she should be in charge of a grown woman. It was as ludicrous as minding her uncle.

"Please, let's go. Marl wouldn't have to know. I can't bear to be restrained."

Para sighed and reached out through the air. *Nat? Hereu insists on visiting Papa's house. I don't think I'll get her to relent without dragging her back by her curls.*

She could sense his amusement… and apprehension. *Please be careful.*

We'll be back soon. I don't think she'll be trouble if we let her have her way in this.

He agreed to let them go as long as they were back before Marl returned in the afternoon. If not, he gave a mild threat to come down there and place Hereu in a baby hold that would embarrass her for decades. Para remembered those. They were fun! But she had enough maturity to know now wasn't the time for games.

Hereu watched her cautiously, eyes darting. Para took a stick from the ground and swatted her backside. "Move it, trickster." The switch pointed to Na-ir.

The girl gave a squeal and skipped through mud.

***

They paused by a dormant apricot in the garden. No voices were coming from the house, so they crept through the back door and stole into Para's old room. There was nothing in there but a tiny cot and a dirty green blanket. Uncle Etutsa was no longer sleeping in the chair by the hearth. This was good, but it bothered her to think he was unsupervised.

Retirement is another word for "lost one's mind."

Hereu looked under the bed in an ill-advised attempt to be helpful and shrugged.

"I guess the scissors were taken when my uncle moved in. Perhaps they're in the kitchen."

The hearth was oppressive from the heat of boiled chicken in the great pot. Cups of tea sat on the table, but Eurgi and Lufnis weren't there.

Another cautious search proved unfruitful. This was frustrating. She was certain her uncle would've left the scissors here; he left everything in the kitchen, from notations on a certain villager's bowel movements to trimmings from his whiskers. She shuddered to think her tool might've already been absconded for that purpose.

She was ready to leave when Hereu opened the large cupboard—a strange place to leave scissors, but it never hurt to look. They gazed at a full store of food stuffs:

jars of oils and honey, grains, nuts, and cheeses. Both girls took in a deep breath to enjoy the bounty. It looked lavish, but it was stocked for guests and the needy. Para had spent many hours preparing delicacies from these.

The aromatic moment was interrupted by something on the stairs. Para stiffened and placed a hand over Hereu's mouth. The shepherdess rolled her eyes and gave a miniscule squeak as she was shoved into the cupboard. Para closed the doors and peered through the crack.

Lufnis and Eurgi entered the kitchen, dressed in somber grey, but smiling with hands clasped amiably. They stopped in front of the fire and whispered in each other's ears. He embraced her from behind and rocked in a simple dance, his head resting on her round shoulders.

"They look sweet together," Hereu whispered. "I'm glad she's happy."

Para snorted. "At least he treats his wife well. Let's hope they take this affection somewhere else."

The lovers stared into the fire for some minutes before Lufnis decided they should sit. Eurgi plopped into her brother's lap and he shouted. He pulled scissors out of her dress pocket.

His sister groaned.

"I bet you don't want those back now, do you?" Hereu teased.

"Don't be childish."

"I'm being childish? You have us hiding in a cupboard. Let's get out of here."

Para shushed her, leaning closer to the crack to hear. She had a strange feeling. The couple was easy, but there was heaviness to their tone.

"I'm sorry." Eurgi wrinkled her nose. "They were in our bed again. I forgot they were in my pocket."

Lufnis made a pleasant noise. "Uncle Etutsa again, I suspect. We need to find something to entertain that scoundrel."

For once, Para agreed with her brother.

"When the task is done, we'll see if we can't make him better preoccupied."

"Are you sure this is the only way, love?" Eurgi took the scissors back. "I don't feel right."

"Neither do I, but he's given us this task. We must see it through… or the village will suffer." Lufnis sighed. "Don't worry. I'll handle it. There's no reason for you to be involved."

Para stiffened. What was her brother planning?

Eurgi shook her head. "No, you're my husband. I stand by you."

Their tender kiss was interrupted by a slam of the back door. Lufnis jumped, knocking his wife to the floor. Para tried not to laugh. Usually only Papa made him this flustered. But Papa didn't slam doors.

A fearful presence entered the kitchen and moved near their hiding spot.

Hereu gasped.

"Good day, Mister Corraidhin." Eurgi scowled into the fire.

"Did anyone see you?"

Rej swaggered to the hearth and brushed against Eurgi. He tossed his bow and quiver on the table. The women in the cupboard shivered.

"Darken the village, no; I went around the back as ordered, my liege." He flashed a toothy, yellow smile.

"Don't call me that! And I won't have you being vulgar around my wife."

"I don't much care for having women here. They're trouble, the lot of them. You sure she's not going to spoil our plans?" He looked at Eurgi like she was a delicate bowstring, only useful bound and in his hands. "I don't trust my woman as far as I can throw her."

"Things will go to plan as long as you keep your mouth shut and listen."

"Good! The fat man's riled. His messenger said he thinks you're stalling, letting your feelings weaken your resolve."

Para cursed her vantage point. She couldn't see her brother's face from this angle, but she did see his shoulders droop.

"Ha! You *are* a coward. The man's a damnable idiot and you're still acting like an obedient child." Rej shoved Lufnis backward. "We're ending this now, even if I have to be the one to do it."

Eurgi clutched the scissors, but Lufnis moved her away. Para was disappointed. Those scissors would've been put to good use inside Rej's neck. Lufnis apparently wanted something more definite. He snatched a carving knife from the wall and pointed it at the huntsman.

"Shut up! Don't question me again."

Rej chuckled; the only thing that frightened him was Marl.

The cupboard spies held each other. There was so much fear and anger in the kitchen, someone was bound to be hurt.

The shepherdess's body was a clammy blanket draped against Para's arm. "I'm calling Marl, but he won't answer. What are we going to do?"

"Hush. They might hear us." Para tried her husband too. *Nat, please answer me.*

Nothing. But… it was impossible for him to ignore her!

Hereu sobbed, clutching her hands to her mouth. The poor girl was adventurous, but she had seen too much violence in her young life to be brave now among the spices.

The argument stopped abruptly. There was a shuffle of footsteps and then the door flew open with a crack.

The shepherdess shrieked at the sight of Rej's insipid face. She ran and then collapsed. Scissors stuck out of her neck, a raised nail in wood.

Eurgi wailed, large tears falling from her eyes. Blood trickled from the carpet of brown curls and dribbled beside her feet.

Lufnis dropped the carving knife. Para stared and didn't fight when Rej wrapped eager arms around her waist and pulled her from the cupboard.

"What should we do?" Eurgi fell on her knees, cradling Hereu in her lap.

"Quick, woman! Take those damn scissors out!"

She obeyed. More blood poured from Hereu's tattooed neck. Eurgi shrieked and tried to close the gash with her hands. Lufnis rounded on Rej.

"Look. I told you involving the women would be trouble," the huntsman snapped. "What's your plan now, oh great master?"

A voice like a whisper from the creator moon fell on the scene. "What plan? Why is Eurgi crying?" G'Nirac entered the kitchen. "Rej, release Para! You're not allowed in my home. I made that clear when..."

The huntsman pulled her tighter and moved aside. The old man gasped. It was fortunate he had his cane for support. "Stars on high! Hereu! What's happened?"

"I didn't mean to," Eurgi choked. "I was startled and... I had the scissors..."

Lufnis cradled his wife. Blood painted her skirt and the side of his britches. "It was a horrible accident, Father. The girls were hiding in the cupboard."

"This grieves me considerably. We must call for Marl."

Papa's brown eyes darted in his head and then settled into further shock. He had learned what the girls had already discovered. No message could leave the Sinbel household to find the mind of any Ganwin helper.

"Para, fetch him! There may still be time to save the poor woman."

There was more blood on the floor than there ever was on Retat's apron, but she struggled to break free. The huntsman laughed and held fast to her abdomen, infuriating the Sinbel men with a lick of his lips.

"No, Father. The girl is gone. There's no need for the healer now." Lufnis pulled a large rock from his pocket and handed it to his accomplice.

"What is that?" G'Nirac shouted. "My son! No matter how you feel, I can't allow the girl to bleed to death. This is his wife, damn it! He should know!"

"I'm afraid we can't, Father." Lufnis guided his woman to the hearth. "I feel sorry for Marl's loss; he's made quite the young man of himself. But, as I stated, this was an accident and nothing more can be done."

"The elders won't see it that way." G'Nirac tried to hobble out of the kitchen.

Lufnis came to his side and shut the door. He shook blood from the knife.

A dirty, metallic-scented hand press against Para's mouth.

"The elders will never know. I'm afraid Hereu got in the way, but this." Lufnis brandished the weapon and swallowed. "This is murder." His voice cracked and the knife sliced through G'Nirac's heart.

The old man made no more than a groan, fell to his knees, and collapsed. The cane fell with a clatter.

"I'm sorry, Father. Forgive me."

The sound of his apology was more horrible than a daemon's kiss. Para kicked and twisted.

Eurgi didn't move, vigor drained from her face.

Lufnis looked deep into his sister's eyes, tears streaming from his. "It's a terrible thing. I wanted you to be safely in the canyon. Why aren't you with your man?" He formed a scowl again for the huntsman. "Put her out. Take her to the stables and keep her from running."

Rej grunted.

Before she blacked out, she saw two bloodstained bodies with shocked, brown eyes staring into nothingness. The Blessed Unknowing couldn't wipe that memory from her.

***

Para twisted and struggled in the hay, a nasty gag in her mouth like a horse's bit. A low chuckle came from the shadows. "You're a strong one, little lady."

Rej produced a small bottle from his pocket and poured some drops on his handkerchief, another dirty thing. Para shuddered. She kicked and tried to scream as he moved the cloth near her speckled nose.

"Now, now, my pretty. Be a good girl and sleep, or your brother's going to make me do something mean. Such a shame too." He paused to run his other hand through her hair. The braid had either fallen out in her struggle, or, more disturbingly, had been loosened by her captor.

Three horses kicked and struggled in their stalls.

"Shut up you crazed beasts. I'm not hurting her... yet. Am I, love?"

They continued to thrash.

Para braced herself for assault. If that rag touched her nose, she would be a more compliant victim. It was possible she had already been.

A knock on the stable doors gave her reprieve. Rej tiptoed over and peeped through a crack.

"Who's in there? Open up!" Natsir's tone was strong and commanding, but not brutish. "Para, are you in there?"

She couldn't reply. A fleeting thought made her wonder about the strange dark rock her brother had given Rej. Was there a type of magic being used here?

The huntsman removed the bar. "What do you want, Mister Ganwin?"

"I'm looking for my wife and my sister-in-law. Have you seen them?"

Para kicked and screamed, desperate to be heard.

"I see them all the time—lovely girls." The monster giggled.

Someone's feet shuffled.

"Nah, I haven't seen them today."

"Are you sure?" Gravel crunched again. "I know she's here. She told me she'd be here. Lufnis is behaving oddly and now you're guarding the stables. If I didn't know any better, I'd think the two of you were up to something."

Rej snorted. "Don't blame me if your wife runs off."

The large shadow moved away from the stable door. Dread returned. Now she was at the mercy of a man who enjoyed his abilities as a butcher.

My love, you could've throttled him. You could've saved me.

She sobbed as the huntsman reentered the stables, a self-satisfied smirk on his face. He mumbled and spat, pulling the handkerchief from his pocket. "There, there, sweet one, time to sleep. Bastard's going to have to take care of himself from now on."

Para flinched and squealed, closing her eyes against the horror to come.

She felt cool air. There was a loud thud. She opened her eyes to see Natsir looking bewildered and shocked. He was standing over Rej with a shovel.

"Para! What's happened?" He removed the bindings around her sore limbs and teeth and pulled her up.

"Lufnis has killed Papa." Para clutched his coat and trembled, sobbing in his protective arms. "Eurgi stabbed Hereu before that. They were going to kill me too."

Natsir cradled her tightly. "No," was all he could manage to say.

The horses shifted in their stalls. He turned and spoke in his subtle way to silence them.

Anope says we should get out of here. He's worried.

Natsir tossed her on the creature's bare back and climbed up behind her. They heard a shout as he spurred the horse on through the open door. Rej rushed them and the horse took off like a falcon.

The forest shifted in a grey blur.

No, Anope, we need to go back. We need Marl. Natsir stiffened. *Oh! Na-ir isn't safe. Rej is after us.*

Para turned to see the man in pursuit on her brother's horse. An arrow darted near her arm and she shrieked. Rej was a huntsman for a reason, the best shot in town.

I don't know how to lose him, Natsir admitted.

They rode on at the mercy of Anope's animal insight. The trees thinned into patches of juniper. They were nearing the cliffs!

Para, listen. Hold tight and don't let go. Promise you won't let go.

She consented, sobbing with the weight of his words. *What are we going to do?*

"Something reckless." Another arrow spun over his head. *Mother Sun, protect us.*

Anope stopped sideways at the edge of the cliffs.

Para flailed and screeched in Natsir's tight embrace, a tumbling red hawk. They splashed into the cold expanse of churning river.

Roaring waters in Para's ears and the crush of liquid in her lungs forced her back into blackness, but not before she caught the brief glimpse of something gold in the sunlight.

TWENTY TWO

Messa's ample belly heaved and her short legs thrashed as she did her best not to fall out of her chair. "I can't believe that little man scared you off the porch! I wish I could've seen that! Husband, did your thick head hit first or your backside?"

Opening his mouth now was inadvisable; Nojhi didn't want to be kicked out of two houses today. Also, she might tend to his wounds later if he let her have her laugh.

Nojhi was ruminating on how she could make up for her insubordination when their companion gave the table an angry slap. "Messa, please! As the wife of a prominent man in the community, you should be embarrassed and shocked."

The priestess snorted into her tea. "My friend, if I was going to be embarrassed, I would have been long ago. You forget; I'm Marl's mother." There was no hiding her crow-like smirk. "You two knew better than to breech the issue again. It would've been funnier if he had beaten your backsides with his cane."

"Some priestess you are!" Nojhi sputtered. "We're trying to prevent war."

Her black lashes fluttered. *Sweetheart, you're too old to pout.* The playful seduction dissolved into a smoldering warning. *Besides, you're getting everything you deserve. How could you make a decision without consulting me?*

He shivered; wallowing in her affections was no longer an option today.

She moved on to the healer. "I'm sure G'Nirac appreciates your concern. However, if I remember correctly, the last time you proposed this, the elders dismissed it as too risky."

Both men twiddled their fingers like reprimanded children.

"Why don't you go home and change out of that ragged coat, Tutsa? I'll keep you company when you return wearing something more decent."

This time Nojhi laughed.

"I'm not going back!" The healer pushed his mustache up his nose. "My brother isn't much of a fighter, but when he's angry, it's safer to stay away." He closed the coat tighter around his hairy, thin legs. "Besides, I'm perfectly decent."

"Of course you are," Nojhi snorted, eager to bring the discussion around to someone else's folly. He poked at a hole in the side of the garment. "As long as you don't move."

"Oh, don't you start with me. I'm suffering now for being your faithful man." Etutsa harrumphed and turned to the hearth. "The least you could do is not emasculate me."

"Too late." Messa shifted out of her chair and tottered on her heels, a hand on her stomach. "Come now. Don't sulk. The boys must have something here they've outgrown."

"I think swaddling clothes are out of the question," Etutsa snarled.

She searched under Natsir's cot. One ragged, patchy shirt flew across the room and landed on the healer's sputtering head. A pair of work-stained britches followed, tumbling on the floor.

They left their friend inside, mumbling to his own devices, and rested against the door frame, casting each other glances too youthful for their ages. Nojhi stole a few kisses.

A short while later, they were shocked to hear an exclamation. "Stars and mountains! Messa, this isn't going to work."

Nojhi cracked open the door. Etutsa was standing by the hearth looking like a child wrapped in a blanket. The shirt was large, but the britches were monstrous. He blushed, gathering everything to his middle.

"I'm sorry, my friend. The boy took after me."

Messa peeped inside too. "Oh! Nojhi's wearing the only belt. I'll fetch some twine. That might help."

Her journey to the shed was excruciating for Etutsa. He tapped his feet and looked around the room while Nojhi grinned. When she popped her silk-black head into the house again, he jumped, almost losing his grip on the britches.

"Here you are."

Messa bound the garments to his waist. The healer blushed again.

Nojhi should've found this charming, but this moment of awkward glances left him with a sudden, nagging dread. The bumbling person before him was once a wife stealer.

Etutsa was younger, he told himself. *And Messa isn't foolish or unfaithful.* But this made her more desirable.

"I could gather it," she offered. "I already have your measure with the twine."

The old healer's eyes watered. "Don't trouble yourself. Rac's hissy fit must be over by now."

Messa insisted and reached for her sewing basket on the mantle.

The thought of her hands all over that man again made Nojhi burn. He yanked the basket away. She blinked and stepped backward, looking meek and confused.

"I won't have you straining yourself over this old man's inability to dress himself. It might take all day to make those clothes fit, and I can fix the problem."

He pulled her into him and gave her a long, domineering kiss. Shocked, Messa blushed and leaned into his chest. This was what he needed. The little priestess wasn't the sort to break a bond.

"I'll go back and ask for your clothes. I owe G'Nirac an apology and I'll speak on your behalf. You were only trying to help me."

Etutsa relaxed, brown eyes bright.

What are you doing, husband? Please don't torment G'Nirac again.

I'm not planning on it, love. I'm apologizing and getting Etutsa's clothes.

She nodded and turned to their friend. His brown eyes were firmly fixed on Messa's blue.

Were they having a private conversation? The apprehension snuck back into Nojhi's heart. "Why don't you wait here?" He shuffled over to the healer and pushed him onto Marl's bed. "Don't let this trickster lead you into trouble."

He kissed his wife goodbye and took his coat.

Her smile softened. "Don't worry, love. The only trouble I follow is you."

***

He ran to the village, eager to escape the dismal thoughts in his mind and to hold the only thing that mattered in his arms again.

They'll be fine. Messa doesn't suffer nonsense.

A few folk tipped their hats and a few more turned up their noses. He ignored both slight and respect as he made his way to the chieftain's home. A hand on his arm forced him to stop.

"Ho, my friend!" Retat wore respectable garments, free of blood and animal carcass. It must've been some Telmah spiritual day. "In a hurry on this Renewal Day are we?"

Nojhi took his hand and gave it a hearty shake. "Forgive me, I'm distracted."

The butcher winked and gestured toward the great house. "G'Nirac's rant? Don't let it worry you too much. He's been under a lot of strain." Retat squeezed Nojhi's shoulder.

"I know. I'm off to apologize now. I don't have the sense to be quiet when I get an idea."

Retat laughed and shook a stubby finger. "Oh, I know you, Mister Ganwin. You care so much you forget to tend to yourself. Like father like son, I'm afraid." He placed his hands on his hips. "You're fortunate to have a woman like Messa who doesn't allow you to forget your purpose. Marl and Hereu are too young yet to be that responsible, I suppose."

"What do you mean?"

"Your boy takes his position seriously! Smart man he is—a good man. The townsfolk tell me." He frowned. "But your boy's going to starve if he doesn't start accepting payment for services." He pointed over to the shack. The door was wide open to the village—like Marl.

"Thanks. I may need to have a talk with my son before I see G'Nirac."

"My pleasure. It's good for a son to hear the wisdom of his father."

Nojhi cringed.

"Must get back to my spits or *my* father is going to rise from his grave and skin me like a goat." Retat winked as if this was amusing and shuffled across the square.

There was no reason to knock as Nojhi bounded into the tiny room. "You're a fool," he barked, forgoing formalities and leaning against the desk.

Marl flashed a polite smile. "Good afternoon, Father. Didn't get enough of my company last night?"

Nojhi faltered, feeling out of place in this clean, respectable world of secret healing knowledge. "You heard me. Where do you get off being so stupid? How are you going to take care of yourself and Hereu if you can't afford to eat?"

"Oh, yes." Marl shuffled his papers and shook his head. "Some of the villagers can't afford to pay. The harvest was leaner this sun; you know." He turned in his chair and folded his hands over his knees, emitting self-importance. "I'm not going to let someone suffer if they don't have coin. I accept some wares when they offer." He pointed to a black blanket draped over the mattress on the floor; it was Gerna's craftsmanship. "Sometimes it's food. I give it to Hereu or Dalis."

"Fine," Nojhi huffed. "But you've a duty to that girl. You'll understand when children come. Sell the wares to someone who can afford them. That'll help until the spring harvest."

Marl nodded, caressing his unsubstantial beard. "That's good advice. Thanks."

345

"Damn right it is! Now, as soon as you're finished for the day, you get your backside and your wife and…" He stopped. Someone was missing. "Where's Hereu?"

"She's visiting Nat and Para today."

"Oh." Nojhi shuffled, unconvinced the girl wasn't hiding somewhere by the strange tone of his son's voice. "Well, at any rate, you both come to dinner tonight. I'll drag you to the cottage if you resist."

Marl stood and offered his hand. Nojhi took it, bewildered by the formality.

"Sounds pleasant. Hereu and I will come by after sunset." Marl sat back down, his movements restrained, meek.

Nojhi shrugged. Small spats between lovers wasn't something he could fix. He moved.

"Father?" His son trembled, large tears magnifying the strength of his blue-beam eyes. "Have you ever felt a strange sense of dread, one you couldn't explain, one that drove you mad with fear?"

Pity washed over the old general. He closed the shack door with a quiet resolve and embraced his boy. "All the darkened time, son. All the time."

Marl's back bones cracked. He loosened his grip.

"It was worse after I married your mother. And worse still when you boys were born. But honestly, I've never shaken that foreboding. Don't let it worry you too much. It's the curse of deep love. Realize you've no control over what happens. Give her some credit for her intelligence and let things be what they are."

Nojhi stored that wisdom into a place in his mind normally meant for ways to please his wife.

Marl wasn't comforted. "This is more than being protective and cautious. I can sense things now. I can feel the change float through the trees and settle into the soil. Something's going to happen today, but the sensation can't offer me any answers and the spirits refuse to acknowledge me."

"You sound like your mother. Remember, she tends to overreact. She sees things, but sometimes they make her panic for all the wrong reasons." Nojhi flicked a finger upside the boy's head. "You're half of me too. We're strong, rational men and we're not afraid of anything."

There was some truth to the power of gumption. The healer smiled.

"We shape things. Maybe the spirits aren't talking to you because it's not worth their time."

"I suppose." Marl shrugged. "I can't shake it. I've watched Hereu all morning, worrying myself ill, but she's fine. My love is safe—and bored. Now I'm monitoring the village. Nothing's happening though. They're all just laughing about the fight this morning."

Nojhi growled. "Sometimes I think those people need their tongues ripped out. Or their eyes so they've nothing to gossip about. Oh well." He used one dirty palm to pat his son on the head. "Things are what they are. Don't let it worry you." Nojhi shuffled over to the door and opened it, hoping he was leaving the boy with something useful to ruminate on. "See you tonight."

"Sure, Father. Be careful. Love you, old man."

"Love you too, son." He gave a quick wave before stepping out into the sunlight, ready to face his own feelings of dread.

***

No one answered the chieftain's door. Odd until he remembered he'd come unexpected and there was a new lady of the house.

Things are sure different now the children are married.

He knocked again, hoping Eurgi wouldn't be too shy to let him in. The girl's kind actions this morning told him she was a good match for the sulking future chieftain.

His polite tap became a frantic pounding. If the young woman was downstairs, she wasn't acknowledging the guest.

I'll go the back way. It's rude, but we're family now.

He was shocked to find the garden door cracked and a roaring heat pulsating from within the house. Nojhi pressed his face into the intolerable heaviness.

"Hello! G'Nirac? Eurgi? Lufnis?" No answer came.

Marl's unexplainable dread crept up his spine. Had someone been in an accident? He pushed passed the door frame and fought against the debilitating pressure in his skull.

The kitchen, though shut tight, was the source of the heat. Saying an unfaithful man's prayer to Mother Sun, he pushed the knob.

Waves of steam accosted him, smelling of Retat's slaughtered wares and burnt hair. Someone had left the pot unattended. Coughing, he fumbled around the foggy room for a pitcher of water he knew must be on the mantle and sloshed the contents. The fire hissed.

The chicken and vegetables had been cooked to a tan crisp, all of the broth boiled away. Nojhi tried not to laugh. It was such a waste, but in his younger, hungrier days he would've still struggled to eat the damn thing. He was certain G'Nirac's old teeth and stomach wouldn't find this meal favorable. Etutsa would be a darkened cur about it.

"Poor Eurgi. I guess she's not much of a cook." He stamped at the ashes. There was no point in leaving it smoldering. "Girl's lucky she didn't burn down the house!"

He bent over to examine something stuck to his shoe. The blackened thing crumbled in his hands, but he could see it once was fabric. It was curious, but not enough to explain why the kitchen had been subjected to such strange behavior.

He dusted ash off his hands and stood. A turn to survey the rest of the room made his knees buckle.

Two human-formed heaps drowned in a deep, brown-red coating of liquid around the table. He stepped back and trembled, forcing the heels of his hands into his eyes.

Something terrible has happened. Messa, do you hear me?

The only person who could pull him out of this torment, both past and present, didn't acknowledge his pleas. He called for his sons. Nothing. There was silence so perverse it burned.

Many cycles of the sun surviving wastelands and warlords helped him muster strength. He edged over to the first body and moaned, tears plummeting from his eyes onto silver hair.

G'Nirac would never be able to accept his apology. The man was laid across the floor, a carving knife in his chest, with a face as white and barren as the tops of the great mountains to the north.

Nojhi pulled the utensil from his friend and examined it. The knife was lightly covered with blood; most of it was on the floor with his large footprints.

He leaned over the body of his daughter-in-law and choked on his pain, stroking the cold cheek with his other hand. Marl's premonition had been correct. Why wasn't the girl with Para and Nat?

Where's my eldest son? Oh stars on high, please tell me my children are safe!

There were no other bodies in the room, but the murderer might still be nearby.

Footsteps approached, echoing into his ears and leaving scorch marks on his courage. The old soldier raised the knife to his middle and prepared for a fight.

The chieftain's son fell back into the cupboard and fled.

"Lufnis! Wait! You don't understand!"

Too bewildered to recognize the absurdity of his own actions, Nojhi followed the boy outside.

A crowd of villagers gathered. A few men fell on him, wrenching the knife from his hand. Nojhi was thrown to the ground and kicked. He felt small, a skinny, remorseful child being punished for theft.

"I didn't do it," he moaned. "I didn't. Not this time."

He was still declaring his innocence when they dragged him to Telm's pillar and bound him with rope. The bindings cut into his wrist and pressed his ankles together.

"Why'd you do it?" A ruddy Mlaerian spat. "How could anyone kill G'Nirac?" Women and children screamed.

"How could anyone kill little Hereu?" Nojhi wondered.

No one listened to his mutterings; they never mattered. All of the faces spread into a strange white-brown blur and the cries repeated like the call of river birds.

The old general was unconscious of time as he focused on the terrible pain in his chest. The heartache of days long past had come back to visit him; he was once again nothing more than a figurehead in some madman's game.

"Nojhi!"

The cry of his name was a sharp one, dancing off the stalls and carts and scattering the crowd as easily as a man wielding a knife. Messa was running to him.

Wearing clothes adjusted through careful manipulation, Etutsa was at her heels.

The priestess crashed into the pillar and fell. *What's happened? Why didn't you call?*

He was unable to answer.

She clung to his neck and trembled. "Why is he tied up? What's wrong with all of you?"

The elders didn't have to explain. A few villagers had taken it upon themselves to offer proof of the murders. Hereu and G'Nirac's blood-crusted bodies were laid before the pillar.

Etutsa crumpled, the color drained from his face. "No! It's not possible!"

The priestess wailed and looked to the men charged with her husband's protection and secrets. "Tell me you don't believe Nojhi guilty of this."

"No, he's not capable." The blacksmith spoke softly, strong but trembling hands hidden beneath his black-smudged apron. "Don't fret, Messa. No harm will come to your man."

It was a lie, but she didn't know that. If ever Nojhi were in trouble, they were supposed to deny everything and smuggle Messa and the boys from Na-ir. None could save a traitor.

Lortews shook his head. "G'Nirac and Mistress Ganwin can't tell us who the monster is, but we'll find him, I assure you all. Did anyone witness anything? Can anyone provide us with information?"

The villagers whispered.

The baker frowned. "Who saw him near the bodies first?"

Telm's pillar spoke, cracking and unsteady. Lufnis emerged from the safety of his ancestor's stone. "I did. I… I went to the stables for a while. When I returned to the house, I found Mister Ganwin standing over Hereu, our carving knife in his hands. My father was…" He looked to his feet. "I don't think Mister Ga…"

"There! You see," interrupted a young man from the throng. "We can't allow him to live, knowing what he is. Dispense justice, Lufnis. You're chieftain now."

Retat caught Lufnis before he fainted. "Leave the poor man alone. *Our* tribe doesn't behave irrationally. Once we have the evidence, the remaining elders will determine what to do next!" He nodded to Etutsa, tears pushing from his kind, heat-withered eyes. "I'm sorry for your loss, my friend. Can you tell us what you think of all of this?"

The healer leaned over his brother and trembled, stroking the clammy, worn skin of an aged cheek. "They've been dead for hours. Nojhi couldn't have done this. He was with Messa and me all that time. Hereu's wound is too small to be from a carving knife." He stood and dusted off his ill-fitting britches. "Quite frankly, I'm terrified. The real murderer is still free."

The death demander spoke again from his safe place of anonymity. "Don't trust him! We all saw what happened this morning. The giant threatened G'Nirac and he forced you both from his home."

The elders fidgeted.

"What about the black-haired boy?" another new resident offered. "Remember what he did at the wedding? All because of that sweet girl."

Someone whispered about a rock.

"Yes, the young healer," a woman concurred. "Poor boy. This man is a monster!"

Neighbor chided neighbor.

"My father isn't a murderer!"

Marl stood near Lufnis, his fists clenched and his striking, tear-soaked eyes on every naysayer. Vill was behind him.

"Release him! Now!"

Namnor cut Nojhi free.

Marl trod over to the corpses and fell to his knees, stroking Hereu's curls.

"Can you save her?" Vill wrung his hands. "Can you bring her back, boy?"

"I'm sorry." Marl's voice cracked. He gave the little body back to her father. "She has no light left. I'm useless to her."

The shepherd crumpled into a pile and moaned. Nojhi and Messa rushed to their son, cradling his long, wilting body in their arms. He was sobbing.

Hush, love. She kissed his cheeks. *Where's your brother?*

Marl shook his head.

Lights help us! My baby may be gone too!

"If the giant farmer isn't the culprit, who is?"

The clap of hooves on cobblestones preceded a cry that chilled Nojhi to his spine. "Clear the way! In the name of King Rayr, clear the way."

That voice gripped the old general like a bird being strangled for supper. He held his wife tighter.

A figure appeared from the eastern edge of the crowd, tall and exacting on a black horse. Blacker eyes commanded a respect bordering on madness. Tyrc hadn't changed much in thirty suns.

"I'm Captain Tyrc Fiochag of the King's Guard. Where's Chieftain G'Nirac Sinbel?"

The crowd pointed to the bodies near the pillar. Etutsa backed into Marl, drawing attention to the boy. The captain gave the bodies and the mournful, young healer momentary glances, but Nojhi could see the eager spark in Tyrc's eyes.

Their time of peace was over.

"Most unfortunate. Has the murderer been apprehended?"

The little tailor spoke. "I'm afraid not. One was accused, but we've ruled out his involvement."

The captain followed Daerth's eyes to Nojhi and a wicked smile crept across his face. He waved for his men to approach.

Nojhi took hold of his son's shoulder and readied to run.

Lufnis centered himself between the guards and the villagers. "Why have you come here? Na-ir has already declared she doesn't need protection from the kingdom. We're all farmers and ranchers. We've nothing to offer you."

Tyrc sat back on his horse. "Ah, the new little chieftain. I'm here to enforce the law."

"This is a tribal matter, sir. It doesn't concern the king." Lufnis balled his fists and took a step closer. His villagers took one step back.

The captain dismounted. He took Marl's stubbled chin and examined him like a fish in the market. His other hand clutched a rock pendant at his neck.

"An old law has been reinstated. It's a crime to harbor Erutani. They're dangerous." Tyrc didn't notice the small sparks of blue fire near his ribs. "If we don't eradicate them, we leave ourselves open to attack."

The women of Na-ir gasped for love of their sweet healer. His mother trembled.

Lufnis seethed. "Marl is one of us. I've known him his whole life. I'd trust him with mine."

Such strange things to hear. Marl faltered, blue sparks dissolving into air.

"Get out, captain! Get out of my village!"

Tyrc pushed Lufnis out of the way. "Arrest the black-haired boy and the woman with child."

Nojhi's heart panicked but his head did not. *Run, boy. Take your mother and run. I need you to do this.*

What about you?

He didn't answer, but turned, ready to meet the challenge in those black eyes. "Touch my family and I'll rip you apart, Tyrc!"

The captain smiled. "Ah, yes. How have you been, Hama? It appears this tribe harbors traitors. You're lucky, Mister Sinbel. I could also arrest you, but I'll not rob this village of two chieftains today. You aren't much of a threat, anyway. Such a pity; your *father* was a man of much resolve."

Tyrc mounted his horse and watched in gleeful anticipation for an impending scuffle. There'd been one thirty suns ago, when Nojhi had been leaner and stronger and Messa had been a slight–figured girl. They'd narrowly escaped with their lives.

Marl clutched the blade of the sword brandished in his face. The guard at the other end gasped as blood trickled down his arm. Steel glowed blue soon after. The soldier yelped and bolted.

Ready for the next challenge, the healer gave a childish laugh and brandished a flame in his gory palm. Villagers who'd cooed over him as a mischievous toddler shrieked in surprise and scattered into the stalls.

Nojhi didn't need powers to get his point across. His brawny fist worked well. "Boy, get out of here!"

"I'm not leaving you!"

Marl became a great pyre. Blue flames spread and stretched into a circle around the center of the square. The startled faces of the villagers of Na-ir and the retreating king's guard disappeared behind a massive wall of light.

"How are you doing that?"

The boy smiled and pointed to his eyes. He turned to the shepherd huddled with the remains of his daughter. "I'm sorry we must leave. I wish these terrible things hadn't happened."

Lufnis placed a hand on Marl's arm and blinked back tears. "I'm sorry for your loss as well as mine."

"Thank you." Marl took his other hand and shook. "You're brave. I've misjudged you."

"And I you!" the new chieftain declared. "If I'd only known you possessed such abilities…" He trailed off and turned to his father's most trusted allies. "Where will they go?"

Etutsa had the answer. "Thronren, Thronren is the best place. I've friends there and they don't dally in kingdom matters like the Dasha. I'll lead them there." The old healer embraced his nephew. "I love you, boy, but there's nothing here to keep me, and I doubt Captain Tyrc will be forgiving of my assistance with the scuffle. Bury your father." His voice cracked. "Say a prayer for him. Remind him of my love."

"What about Natsir and Para?" Messa moaned, compressing her hands and rocking on her heels. "I won't leave without all of my children."

The new chieftain fell off his uncle. Tears gathered in his eyes again "You're not safe here. If I find Natsir and my sister before the guards do, I'll send them to Thronren. Anyone associated with your family will be suspect. If you linger, it'll cost you."

"We can only hope your son and his wife have already escaped from the village," Retat concurred. "Tyrc won't waste time here when Selcovi needs him. We'll ensure their safety."

An arrow flew over the wall, catching fire as it whizzed in search of a victim. Marl caught the blazing stick and blew out the sparks like a candle. "We need to move. They're trying to get in. My fire will hold them indefinitely, but we can't stay here forever. We're endangering the village." He tossed the charred weapon to the ground and sighed. "I've a plan. I can control this fire. I'll spread it to the linden tree and then open a doorway. We'll head into the forest. When I extinguish the fire, none of us will remain. They won't know what to do."

They gathered the bodies and readied for flight while he took in a great breath and waved his hands over the southwest edge of the fire. It crept along the ground and sparkled as it curved around the great tree of Na-ir. He gave his once-wife a kiss and took a dagger from her cloak.

"I loved her more than life. Take care of yourself and Dalis."

A split the size of a tall man opened in the fire wall. Vill left with his burden into the shadow of the forest, heading for the river. The elders shuffled through quickly, carrying the previous chieftain.

Lufnis turned to the healer before stepping through the fire. "Don't worry, Marl. I see what you are now. Do what you have to do. Na-ir will always welcome you."

Flame rejoined flame.

"All right, we'll wait in case the movement behind the wall was noticed. They can't hear us in here, but Tyrc doesn't strike me as someone who likes to fail."

Nojhi couldn't help but smile. "Right. He's a darkened cur with the bite of a wolf. The only way to escape him is to be sneaky and agile."

"Tyrc was at Surnow." Messa shivered and clutched her stomach. "I was holding a baby then too. This is hopeless, Nojhi. That man is relentless. We thought he was dead!"

Etutsa gave her a loving pat. "Don't worry. Marl and I know these woods like we know our own fingernails. We can survive and thrive as long as we keep moving and keep thinking."

Nojhi handed him a downed soldier's sword. "Protect Messa."

The flame path opened. She looked back once, tears streaming down her beautiful face, as they faded into specks of dust.

Nojhi was both heartbroken and impressed. This power was beyond anything he'd ever seen before. "Lufnis is right, son. You're a marvel. I don't know why I was afraid."

Marl gave him a shy smile and bounced Hereu's dagger in his hand.

"We'll mourn them properly when we're safe. Let's get out of here."

The healer nodded and brandished a hand. Nojhi ran through the new gap quickly, eager to reunite with his frightened lover. It took him some time to realize someone wasn't following him along the blue glowing path.

He turned. The main wall was several yards behind him, solid and domineering. Swearing under his breath, he jogged back to the linden tree to rescue his son.

Marl. Where are you?

I'm still in the circle. Keep going.

The boy's thoughts were controlled, but the feelings behind them were despondent, fatalistic. A thought pierced Nojhi's mental armor. The young man with sad blue eyes still held the dagger.

Darken the moon! Nojhi placed a hand against the flames and hissed. *Get out of there now!*

I've seen the murder in his eyes. He'll not rest until he tracks us all down. I'm strongest and fastest. I'll lead him off. Don't worry, Father. I'll find you later.

Ice in summer! This is stupid. You're powerful, not immortal.

He slammed a fist into the linden and looked back. Etutsa and Messa were still out of sight. Good. He was going to have to keep them waiting.

Tyrc loves recklessness. He feeds off it. Don't do this.

I love you. Run, idiot.

Nojhi took a running leap through the wall instead. His skin and hair sizzled and his clothes smoldered. The wall dissolved. He heard shouts from the guards. Marl had set other fires. The black crow was teasing his assailants well.

A feathered head flew away.

Sun's tits! I'll never catch him.

Nojhi dove behind some pines and inched his way along the back of the village, treading through the chieftain's garden. He quickened his pace when he reached the stream. It was a gross error. His brawny body cracked through fallen twigs and shoved against brambles.

Not everyone had followed Marl.

A stag bounding through his domain in autumn, he turned in time to see the dark of the hunter's eyes. A sharp sting broke his canter. Nojhi crashed into an ash.

"You're a fool, Hama," Tyrc chided, motioning for his guards. The hound dogs swarmed, their arrows bared. "It's remarkable you've evaded capture for so long."

Nojhi groaned and pushed his body up the tree. It was useless for him to fight. His days of errant showmanship and might were long gone. "My son, my son." He clutched the arrow. "Please. He's a boy. He means no harm."

"That *boy* used a magic more powerful than any in Artnaus have ever seen. How fortunate he's still young… and as foolish as his sire. Don't worry, Hama. You'll see your family again. I'm certain if you plead, the guard to the Passageway will let you in. Then again, everything you've ever done has been a disgrace."

Nojhi spat on the captain's neck. "There's nothing, nothing disgraceful about my life or those I love. I tried to be a good man. I lived a good life while I had it. Do what you will with me, but leave them alone."

Tyrc wiped away the saliva. "Hama, let me be very clear. No good can come from traitors. I'll hack them apart and use their blood to feed pigs. Nothing will be left of you. Nothing!"

He dragged the old general back to the center of the village. Eyes peeped out from stall windows and homes. They blinked as he was bound to an old hay cart.

Tyrc pushed against the arrow. Nojhi shrieked. His death in Selcovi would be anything but peaceful.

Forgive me, love.

Her anguished cries carried him into nothingness.

TWENTY THREE

He could no longer feel the sting of cold metal on his wrist. Everything righted itself despite his best intentions, but the ritual was soothing; one more slice, one more swatch of red to slide down his arm into the soil before the gash disappeared. His desire to be free of pain and remorse was against whatever plans were left for the Wanderer. The spirits needed him to suffer, but he refused to let them have their sacrifice. All he wanted now was to be at those gates, to see *her* amber perfection shimmering among the stars and take her hand through eternity.

He would keep his promise. He would spend forever at this sordid game to have her back. The dagger swiped once more below the mouse tattoo. Scarlet liquid bubbled like an artesian spring in which the creature was likely to drown.

Marl wept.

"Let me go!" He wasn't speaking to the mouse… or to the ghostly face across the hill.

I'm sorry. Wind peeped out of the shadows, white and delicate as an apple blossom. *Marl please! You can't keep doing this!*

He sliced through skin again, pressing so hard his wrist nearly severed. The wound tingled, itched, and then reknit.

Stop now! I won't watch you do this.

"Then leave."

You know that's impossible. We're forever intertwined, and your existence is more precious to me than my own.

She moved to his chest and peered into his face with startling gentleness, light looking into light.

Marl, I made you. I love you. We share a power, but your human form is still transient. You can die.

He met her gaze and smiled. If he could die, he could be free. *They* could be free. He reached out a hand to grasp her inner-light. "How? Tell me how!"

She backed away. *The last thing I want is for you to suffer. But I'm not foolish enough to provide you with that information. You still have a purpose. We need to leave.*

"My purpose was her! I'm not leaving the soils of Na-ir!"

As all confrontations seemed to do, the brief argument with the spirit opened his mind to other ways in which to achieve his goal. He jammed the dagger into his chest—such excruciating pain, but only for a moment.

Marl blacked out to howls like a thunderstorm and fire like a lightning strike on a tree.

***

He was unhappy to wake to the smell of dusty fur mixed with old blood and the feel of a moist tongue on his cheek. Instead of heaven, a hay-colored dog stood inches from his face.

Wake Wanderer. You've much life to live.

The dog was apparently an agent of Wind. But she had vanished. There were others on the hill.

"What're we going to do?"

Marl recognized Dalis's sweet sing-song voice. She was wringing her delicate hands and shuddering into her husband's shoulder.

"I don't want to tell that poor woman she may have lost another loved one today. It's no good to have both our hearts broken."

Vill rubbed her back and wiped away tears. "There, there, love. I'll tell Messa the horrible news. Have to. Can't let her worry forever."

Dalis sobbed and nodded.

"I know, love. I had hoped for them too."

Marl's heart could take no more of this. It pained him worse than the dagger to think his death was causing so much grief. He wouldn't rob his mother-in-law or his mother of a child now. That promise to Hereu would have to wait; she had eternity after all.

He stroked the sheep dog. *Speak for me, my friend. Let them know I live.*

It was a coward's way of bringing peace, but the dog didn't seem to mind. Broom wagged his tail and shot off the ground with one determined bark. The healer gave his furry companion a weak scratch behind the ears. There was nothing else he could offer.

The cool touch of Dalis's hands fell on him and the wet kisses of her tear-soaked lips pressed on his forehead. "Thank the Mother!" she shrieked and wrapped her arms around his neck. "You're not dead!"

She leaned back on her heels and her hands found the dagger. Dalis clutched the hilt and stared.

"Boy… you don't know how happy I am… I can't believe… I have to thank you for what you did in the village. I've never been so scared." The little shepherd fell to his knees and sobbed into the dog. "You've got something. The women knew, but I was too stubborn to admit it. I owe you…"

"Please don't. It doesn't matter now." Marl stood. The meadow and his mind came back into focus. "Why is Mother in Na-ir? Have the plans changed?"

"Oh, you poor child!" Dalis clutched his torn, red-pasted doublet and shook her head. "You don't know. You were distracted…"

"What's happened?"

The shepherd shuddered. "You father was captured. He's on his way to the gallows I expect."

Marl lost the use of his legs. It wasn't possible! He had trapped the guards in Na-ir, including Tyrc. After nearly thirty suns on the run, the great general had been captured. But the man was a beast, still a marvel of strength and intelligence.

"The elders and I were near the river waiting for nightfall. Lufnis slipped back to check on his wife and the state of things. He returned to tell us Hama had been captured—an arrow through the thigh." Vill winced. "We think he was looking for you and got distracted. They carted him off to Selcovi before we could make it back to the square."

Marl slammed a blue-lit fist into the pine and moaned with it. He couldn't locate his father. "Stars, old man! I told him to go with Mother and Etutsa! I need to find them."

The shepherd shoved a pack into his hands. The healer opened it to see sleep juice, poultice, bandage cloth, and food.

"Where'd you get these herbs?"

"Lufnis."

Dalis placed a hand on Marl's shoulder and squeezed. "People do strange things when they grieve: sometimes good, sometimes bad." She dropped the dagger into the pack.

It would be difficult to attempt another journey to the Passageway without thinking of those perfect, brown eyes full of tears. This woman had suffered, and yet, there she was, standing proud and selfless before him. There had to be a way to leave her with something not as terrible as her loss.

He kissed her quickly, willing the sacred light within him to touch her fragile body and heal her tender lungs. She clutched her chest, feeling the power surge.

"I love you, Dalis. Thank you for everything."

The little woman burst into tears and tackled him, squishing the contents of the sack against his empty stomach.

Vill spoke for her. "Love you too, li'l crow. Come. I'll take you to your mother. I need to see if Etutsa has any more plans for us while we remain in Na-ir."

Dalis leaned against the cobbled remains of the unfinished home and waved goodbye, her faithful sheep dog pressing against her red-stained heels. Marl struggled to turn away from the unbearable, pure sight before the cover of trees forced her visage into shadow.

Vill put a hand to his shoulder. "I need you to promise me that you'll not waste this opportunity."

"What opportunity? I've lost everything." Marl shuffled the pack on his back.

"Not everything. Remember she's happy now; she's safe and free, and my baby won't hold it against us if we take our time getting to her. My daughter was something to behold, strong, beautiful, and intelligent. It was the greatest joy of my life to raise her. I should have told her, but I'm a bitter fool. But you're still here, and now I see what Hereu saw. You're a burning, expressive force… for good." Vill's brown eyes were day-hidden stars. "Don't give up."

Marl cringed. If lives had reasons, Hereu would still be with them. What had she accomplished in such a short time but to unintentionally break hearts that had come to love her?

"All right," he sighed, willing his countenance to seem obedient and calm. "I'll keep your words close and think on them."

The shepherd flashed a crooked smile. "Good. Good. Now, if you ever find another woman as patient as my girl, you had better treat her right."

He felt the sting of the dagger in his heart again. There was no denying he'd treated Hereu causally, and it was too painful to think he could've loved her better in their brief moment together.

They tramped past the Ganwin cottage, pretending it wasn't there.

Vill grimaced. "Another thing, there's no need whatsoever to tattoo a respectable girl's body. None. Looks like drops o' blood. Scared the snot out of her mother. Did the two of you have any sense?"

Marl was shocked. Tattooing Hereu's neck had been the least of his crimes. It hardly mattered now. "It was supposed to be rain drops. She asked me to do it."

He thrust his wrist out to show off the mouse. It no longer bothered him to see it still scurrying there; it was a piece of his lover he would never relinquish—as faithful as she was.

Memories of Oak Hollow made him smile rakishly. There *were* some things Hereu had left behind too beautiful for words.

Vill smacked him. "Stupid is what it was! You need to learn to be smarter. Altering your body is a powerful thing. It invokes magics that should not be taken likely." He tripped over a few roots.

Marl groaned as he sidestepped the hazard. "Sure. Any moment I'm going to turn into a mouse. I can see it now. I've already got the black whiskers."

The shepherd snorted. "Mouse! Damn, boy. I thought it was a rat." He poked Marl in the ribs, stumbling over a gopher hole. "Do the world a favor and don't ever take up illumination."

***

Messa Ganwin was cradled next to Oak Hollow in all-embracing misery, eyelids red and puffed out from constant tears, more haunting, beautiful, and fierce than Wind could ever make herself. Below her sizeable, fertile belly was her lover's sword. Delicate hands clutched the jeweled hilt.

Marl thought of the dagger and hoped his mother wasn't coming to similar conclusions. If there was one person meant to live life and make the world better, it was the priestess who had borne him.

I almost left her like this... forever. His knees tightened and his chest strained. *I abandoned her when she needed me most. What sort of son am I?*

Etutsa trembled with his back against the oak, wringing his hands. He looked to his apprentice. *I've been trying for hours, but I'm not worthy to comfort her.* He crumpled and sobbed. *She needs her Nojhi. Messa can't survive without him.*

Marl moved forward.

"Nojhi?" Mother squinted into the shadowed woods, hope lighting the beautiful features of her face. "Marl?"

The priestess stood and the sword fell from her lap. The definite thud was a reminder of his father's horrible fate.

"My baby! My boy! Where were you?" She wrestled him into an embrace and covered him in kisses. "Why wouldn't you answer me? I've been calling you boys for hours!"

He clutched his mother and tried to still his body, willing it to be strong and resilient because he'd been so weak before. *My brother! Natsir! How could I've forgotten my brother?*

The good woman saw the slash in his doublet and the crusted blood painted over his chest and britches. She bawled, her blue eyes reflecting a relentless nightmare.

"I'm well, Mother," he lied and clasped her hands. "Has *anyone* seen Natsir and Para?"

She shook her head.

"I went to their cottage," Vill answered. "Nothing there but a dead black cat on the porch. I've looked all over town, as have the elders. If they're here and safe, they don't want to be found."

My poor brother. "They were supposed to be with Hereu, and... Something terrible must've happened to them too." Marl took a deep breath. "Thanks for trying."

The shepherd grunted. "Stars and mountains! We're family. I can't leave you stranded." He looked around the trees. "We should split up. There has to be some trace of them."

This was an impossible task. They didn't have much time if Father's fate was considered.

Remembering what he was, the Wanderer focused his light through the forest air. "There *is* a trace. I know where they are!"

He threw the pack at Vill and bounded off in the direction of the warbler's tree, holding on to the vision of his brother's golden head.

Natsir's light was faint. Marl splashed headlong into the water, and swam for the other shore. The river slapped against his face, blurring his vision.

I'm coming, Nat. Hold on!

A calloused hand surfaced near the boulder. Natsir's skin was sharper than snow. Marl kicked against the current and pulled, trying to dislodge the great body from a potential wet tomb. A small red form peeped from behind the stone—two hands clutched earnestly.

Thank the stars!

The combined weight was too much. He leaned into Natsir's pallid face.

You have to let go of her, Nat. Trust me. Trust me, please. I won't let either of you die.

The light within the great man sobbed and their hands separated. Para slipped back under, but only for a moment.

Marl dragged them to the beach. They were fading into the Passageway. He planted his wet mouth on Para's colorless lips first, breathing into her body.

Chests heaving and eyes wide with dread, the others crashed into the warbler's tree. "What're you doing?" Etutsa screamed. "Have you lost your mind?"

Mother gasped. "Stay back! My son knows what he's doing!"

A tiny cough broke the tension. The company fell on the gasping girl, holding her while water trickled from her lungs. She shivered in her wet clothes and looked on the body of her husband.

The priestess cradled her. "It will be well, sweetheart. Thank the Mother and Father he found you!"

Marl didn't hesitate with the other kiss.

Natsir's green eyes flashed in the sunshine. "Brother?" He clutched his shoulder and shivered. "Where... where's Para?"

Relieved to hear that tenor, Marl pointed to the frazzled red head. Natsir smiled, but didn't move. Something else hadn't been remedied. There was a broken arrow shaft in his shoulder.

The eldest cried out as his brother examined him. It came out cleanly and the wound closed.

"Thank you, baby brother," he whispered and pulled him close.

Marl sobbed.

Something mewed and sneezed. Natsir lifted a soaked ball of black-and-white fur from his pocket. The tiny creature unfurled in the great hand and sneezed again.

"Forgive me, little friend."

Destroyer of Lizards stretched out to full form, as unimposing as a pebble, and flicked his long black tail. Droplets spread like freckles over Marl's nose.

Yes. Well. Next time you leap over a cliff, Gifted One, please remember there might be a cat in your pocket!

TWENTY FOUR

Too much of her life had been shared with that man to not feel his absence, and the impending dread of his certain demise was pressing on her, threatening to suffocate with its terrible, horrible prophecies. The spirits had said her boys would be happy, but they hadn't said for how long.

Esimor and Hereu never had a chance in this world. Women like them never did.

Messa struggled to function as she cradled her distraught daughter-in-law. Para hadn't spoken a word since her rescue. Her eyes remained glassy and distant, fixed on her husband.

Natsir paced around blue fire, tearing his hair and mumbling with each new bend in the manly discussion.

Marl sat on a stone next to Vill and Etutsa and stroked Nojhi's sword, listening to his brother's tale of adventure. "So Destroyer wasn't exaggerating. You jumped over a darkened cliff! *You*, the mighty prince of caution, jumped over a cliff... and you took Para and an innocent creature with you. How?"

The eldest shook his head.

The ability to survive such a fall was unexplainable to a man with little faith. Etutsa avoided the subject altogether. "I still can't believe Lufnis is behind all of this. You've had your differences, but that boy couldn't have killed his father. He idolizes him, always has."

Natsir stopped pacing and stared. He was patient, forgiving, but never gullible.

Vill nodded. "I don't know about this Rej fellow, but I've never been weary of Lufnis. Why did he help us then? None of it makes sense."

The freckles on Para's arm goose-pimpled. Messa smoothed it away.

To think, Nojhi might've been executed here in Na-ir for that darkened cur!

Now, the old general would face a worse ending among his own people. She shivered and placed a hand on the kitten by her thigh. It gave her more response than Para; it purred. The rumble against her palm was soothing.

"I *saw* murder in Tyrc's eyes." Marl pushed the tip of the rusted blade into the soil. "And I'm certain he wasn't surprised by G'Nirac's death or Lufnis's anger. Is it possible the two of them had planned this? Perhaps it was a trap for Father. With all of my abilities, I couldn't read them, either of them."

A tiny voice came from red curls. "Did this man have a rock?"

Natsir scooped Para into his arms and carried her over to a pine.

Marl stared, blue eyes flashing something akin to supreme knowledge. "A rock, sister? Tyrc was wearing a stone."

"Yes. Black stone. Lufnis had two large ones. I couldn't call you for help as long as I was near them."

The young healer passed the sword to Vill. "Show me!"

Para gasped as he approached.

Messa stood too, jostling the cat. *Be gentle.*

I know Mother, but we're running out of time. "Please show me. It may be helpful."

Para hiccupped and nodded.

"I monitored you and Hereu this morning. Last I saw, you were giggling in the bedroom. What happened next? Think and I'll do the rest." Marl placed his hands on her fiery head. His blue eyes darted for a moment and then he guffawed.

"I don't care for that, boy!" Vill seethed, pressing the gilded hilt to his thigh. "What about the day of my daughter's death strikes you as funny?"

Marl removed his hands and stiffened. "Nothing like that. The girls were being playful; I was surprised to see it." He winked at Para who looked more like a dollop of clotted cream sprinkled with spice than an innocent girl. Repositioning his hands, he spoke to his mother. *I'd spank her if she was still alive.*

Messa tried not to smile for Vill's sake. Hereu had been a spunky thing and the priestess didn't doubt the young woman had been mischievous before her death.

Suddenly, Marl stepped backward, pride and admiration for his headstrong wife wiped from his handsome features. "It's all true. Lufnis killed G'Nirac, and the girls got in the way."

Para sobbed. Natsir stroked her curls until her cries subsided.

Vill handed back the sword. "Well, that settles it. We go back to town and lop off Lufnis's head. I'll not rest until he's the one tied to that damn pillar."

"No!" Natsir stood frantically, pulling his fragile wife with him; she hung from his neck like a chain. "I don't think vengeance is advisable."

There were several shouts of protest.

"Look at the evidence. Artnaus is on the brink of war, G'Nirac refuses to get involved, and now the Selcovian guards are here. We also have to wonder what else these strange stones can do. Lufnis wasn't working alone, and he may have more support than we realize." Natsir placed a reassuring hand on Vill's shoulder. "Something must have prompted him to do what he did. Killing him now might bring destruction on us and the village from whomever is behind this. Our friends are safer if we don't meddle."

Marl stared at the emblem of his father's past. Messa wished she could tell him to ram it through Lufnis's heart, but she knew what vengeance could do to a person.

The young healer sighed. "I hate to admit it, but I think you're right, brother. Rej mentioned a fat man. Do we know him?"

Etutsa frowned. His heart was also in a terrible state. It didn't matter how disagreeable his nephew had been; the healer loved him. Killing him could never be an option. "Only fat man I know outside of Na-ir is Onaryc."

"Is it possible he's controlling Lufnis? The two did try to arrange a marriage."

Vill snorted. "Impossible! If Lufnis is working with Tyrc, he's *not* working with Onaryc. The issue is between the Dasha and the capital. Tyrc controls the capital! If they're working together, we're in trouble."

Everyone with a beard grunted.

Natsir hummed and approached his mother. Messa stiffened. It was difficult to look into those green eyes and not feel regret, though she loved him as much as the man he resembled.

Mother, we've wasted much time. I concede to your wisdom.

She had none left to give. He could lead this group. He was practical and, right now, that was what they needed most. She shook her head.

All right then. He turned back to the rest of their party. 'It's either Father or Lufnis, and, right now, the best course of action is to help Father. I'm proposing Marl and I go to Selcovi. The plan to seek aid in Thronren is a good one, though. Mother, Para, and Etutsa will go there and seek counsel."

"Are you crazy?" Vill snapped. "You can't dance into Selcovi and rescue General Hama!"

Natsir narrowed his eyes and smiled his father's stubborn smile.

Vill faltered. "Well, what am I going to do while your gallivanting through Artnaus?"

"Keep an eye on Lufnis and Rej. See what more you can discover while we're gone. But don't tell the other elders. We want to preserve their ignorance until we have something we can use."

Marl jumped, swinging the sword. "Find Cyan Vercinget. He may be able to help you."

Messa snorted. Toren's grandson was an excellent candidate for espionage. The little troublemaker had taught Marl many naughty pastimes, among them how to be sneaky and adept at petty thievery.

"Who in the darkened sun is he?" Vill hissed. He blushed when he remembered he was in the presence of ladies.

Messa had already forgiven him the vulgarities. Today was a day where cursing was appropriate.

"Um... I mean I don't know this lad."

"Cyan's my good friend. You met him once. Remember?" He placed a hand on his chest to mark a level of height. "He's this tall with green eyes and blond hair like my brother but not as good looking. G'Nirac used him as a spy. He may know more than he realizes. Find Cyan and the two of you can keep an eye on Lufnis, Rej, and those guards."

Vill accepted his fate. Marl checked the area before he sent the old man home to bury his daughter.

"I've scanned for Father too," he said once the little man was out of sight.

Messa felt her insides drop around the being within her.

"He's holding on, but unconscious. They've stopped for some reason. If we leave now, we might catch up."

He took the pack and removed some bandages, pausing to stare at a blue bottle and fife. These mementos he placed into his doublet pocket opposite the obvious rip. The bandages he tied around his waist, securing his father's sword in a haphazard belt.

Para shivered. "We're going to travel through the dark? Should we get the horses?"

Natsir kissed her. "It's for the best. We risk Lufnis seeing us if we sneak into his stables. Mother, Etutsa, what do you say?"

"I think it's the only choice we have." Messa folded her hands over her belly and yearned for her love. *Don't worry, little one. We'll get him back.* She'd argue with her sons over the particulars of this adventure later. "Let's go."

The comforting blue flame flickered out and Marl led the way. They followed the river along the ridge.

The spirits watched, six bright points of light. Messa didn't dare contact them for fear they would make modifications to the plan. Saving Nojhi was all that mattered to her now.

They reached the cliffs at sunset. Marl halted the party for a brief rest.

Natsir and Para relaxed into the side of a juniper as Mother Sun settled beyond the horizon in a sea of brilliant orange. All but Etutsa bowed.

"We're at the edge of Na-ir. Never thought I'd have to leave it." Marl took a clump of soil and put it in a breast pocket.

Para pointed to the southeast. "What's that blue glow? Did you do that?"

"Oh, yes. I should fix it." Marl waved a hand and the fires disappeared. "There! That should confuse those stupid guards for a while."

The new leader of this sad little band motioned to his astonished family. They followed.

***

Wind hung over the tree tops and watched her little crow leave the nest. It was time for the Wanderer to wander.

And this time his mother cannot protest.

CAST OF CHARACTERS

People of Na-ir (the Telmah)

G'Nirac Sinbel	Chieftain of the Telmah, kind and devout, if a bit naïve
Laedi Sinbel	G'Nirac's dead wife, Etutsa's secret lover
Lufnis Sinbel	Son of G'Nirac and Laedi, scheming and cruel, working with Onaryc
K'Parre/Para Ganwin nee Sinbel	Natsir's wife, secret daughter of Etutsa and Laedi, raised by G'Nirac
Etutsa/Tutsa Sinbel	Brother of G'Nirac, the village healer
Hereu Ganwin nee Misyl	Marl's wife, headstrong shepherdess, refugee from Selcovi
Vill Misyl	Hereu's gruff father
Dalis Misyl	Hereu's sickly but kind mother
Cyan Vercinget	Marl's oldest friend, Toren's grandson, spy for G'Nirac
Toren Vercinget	A farmer, grandfather of Cyan
Pas Piler	Gerna's youngest son, apprenticed to the blacksmith, suffers an accident
Mercen	Refugee from Selcovi, another apprentice to the blacksmith
Gerna Piler	Village seamstress, town gossip, Pas's mother
Fane	Gerna's oldest son from a previous marriage, father of Gan
Eurgi Sinbel	Hereu's friend from Selcovi, Lufnis's wife
Retat	The village butcher, another gossip, but he means well
Namnor	The village blacksmith, father of Yimette and Lyrig
Lyrig	The blacksmith's youngest daughter, Marl's old girlfriend
Chaun	The village cobbler, father of Laohin
Laohin	The cobbler's sickly son
Nerid Corraidhin	Rej's wife, hates him
Bolar	Nerid's forester father, mean reputation
Rej Corraidhin	Nerid's husband, a cruel letch, in league with Lufnis and Onaryc
Yimette	Namnor's oldest daughter, wife of Gan, runs off to Mirot
Gan	Fane's son, husband to Yimette, runs away to Mirot to be a soldier
Lortews	The village baker, husband of Posgi, father of Tessin
Posgi	Lortews's wife, mother of Tessin
Tessin	Lortews and Posgi's youngest son, wants to be a healer
Daerth	The village tailor, childless
Jolenta Hedar	Wife of Din, mother of Sinnie
Din Hedar	The chandler, husband of Jolenta, father of Sinnie
Sinnie Hedar	The newest member of the village, daughter of Din and Jolenta

People of Lafret (the Dasha)

Onaryc Seisyll	Chieftain of the Dasha, the fat man, contemplating war with capitol
Rippan Seisyll	Onaryc's son, Para promised to him

People of Selcovi (the Mlaerians)

General Hamnojhina/Hama	Nojhi's past self, a celebrated warlord
King Ril Ithern	The man who combined the tribes into a kingdom and shaped Hama's future, father of Rayr and Enisnus
King Rayr Ithern	Son of Ril, brother of Enisnus, a kind but ineffective king
Princess Enisnus Ithern	Sister of Rayr, daughter of Ril, warrior, aggravating Onaryc over water rights
Captain Tyrc Fiochag	One of Hama's oldest friends and enemies

People of Surnow (the Erutani)

Erutan	The ancestor of all Erutani
Esimor	Erutan's first wife, died young

The Ganwins

Marl Ganwin	The Wanderer, son of Messa and Nojhi, brother of Natsir, husband of Hereu, village healer, favorite of Wind
Nojhi Ganwin	Farmer with a past, husband of Messa, father of Natsir and Marl
Messa Ganwin	Priestess, wife of Nojhi, mother of Natsir and Marl, favorite of Earth
Natsir Ganwin	The Gifted One, son of Messa and Nojhi, brother of Marl, husband of Para, favorite of Water

Creatures

Pilgrim	Natsir and Marl's friend the black cat
Destroyer of Lizards	Great-grandson of Pilgrim, a feisty messenger
Broom	Hereu's sheep dog, a very good boy
Arnab	Chief rabbit
Fluffer	Also known as Kerna, a moody ewe in Hereu's flock
Trouble	Hereu's favorite of the flock, a black lamb
Gyr	Head of the local wolf pack, starving and desperate
Rinpiels	Para's white horse
Anope	G'Nirac's sturdy, brown horse, loaned to Natsir
Veem	A yellow warbler, gives Natsir a warning
Eru	Jolenta's dog that Marl saved as a child

Elementals

Mother Sun	Creator goddess, mother of the three sisters
Father Moon	Creator god, father of the three sisters
Wind	One of the three sisters, molds Marl into the Wanderer, true name unknown
Water	One of the three sisters, molds Natsir into the Gifted One, true name unknown
Earth	One of the three sisters, true name unknown

ABOUT THE AUTHOR

Melissa Widmaier is an editor with a heart for wide, open spaces. When not manipulating words, she can be found camping with a camera in hand, getting lost among things green and growing. She lives in Arizona with her husband, three boys, a barrelful of cats, and a rambunctious corgi.

melissawidmaier.com
Instagram: mwidmaier_author

OUR TALE CONTINUES IN

A Crow in the Canyon

www.ingramcontent.com/pod-product-compliance
Lightning Source LLC
Chambersburg PA
CBHW021130260626
47169CB00005B/1537